Atonement to a Greater God

Dan Martin

Atonement to a Greater God

Copyright @2019 Dan Martin

All rights reserved. No part of this book may be used or reproduced by any means, graphic, electronic, or mechanical, including photocopying recording taping or by any information storage retrieval system without the written permission of the author except in the case of brief quotations embodied in critical articles and reviews.

Certain characters in this work are historical figures. Some of the events described really happened and some of the setting in this novel depict real historical locations. However, this is a work of fiction. All of the other characters, names and events as well as all places incidents, organizations and dialogue are either the products of the author's imagination or are used fictitiously.

Published by Indie Publishing

Because of the dynamic nature of the internet, and any web addresses or links contained in this book may have changed or no longer be valid.

Cover design by istvandesign.com

This book and other books by this author can be ordered through www.danmartinbooks.com

PROLOGUE

Louis Packett was an old timer who lived through the battles of 1812 and had the wounds to show for it. A straight-line scar carved out skin and bone at the corner of his eye before moving across his skull and taking off the top of his ear. One thing left little doubt: the scar traced a thin line between Louis living or dying on the battlefield.

That wasn't all that Louis had to contend with. The war also took his right foot just above his ankle. He kept his stump wrapped in a gray linen cloth fit onto a thick woolen insole that often seeped pinkish. The amputation prompted Louis to swing one arm for balance when he walked, like a wounded bird trying to fly. And if you got close you could smell his infection.

My generation called him 'Looney Louie' and I was as guilty as anyone else. But still, something about him fascinated me. After I was older and got to know him a little bit, I couldn't say he was all that crazy, just a little unsettled at times from what he had been through. Once I got past his unfocussed eyes and the head spins he used to focus his vision, I discovered a rational man who generally preferred to be left alone.

Once, I had been hunting a few miles from home and it was freezing cold when I encountered Louie's shack in the bush so I stopped in to get warm. He met me at the door, checked me over for a long moment, cocking his head back and forth, then he grunted, swung the door open wider and motioned me inside.

I suppose he could tell I wasn't dressed right for the winter day and I was half frozen. I thanked him before moving quickly inside and hovered over a blazing fire he already had going in his hearth. I waved my hands through the flames and rubbed them together to get some feeling back. He stood and watched me for a moment, then pushed a chair towards me. Louie put an iron kettle over the fire and retrieved two enamel coated steel cups from his cluttered table and set them by the fire for a few minutes. Then he moved the kettle off the flames, opened the lid and tossed a handful of tea in the boiling water. He watched until the leaves sank to the bottom and then poured two cups. "Tea?" he asked.

I clasped the hot cup, still trying to get heat into my frozen fingers.

"It'll start some warmth inside of you too," he said.

Suddenly I began apologizing to Louie. "Sorry," I said, "I guess I shouldn't be out hunting when it's this cold. Or I should have dressed."

Louis looked down at my hands. "With cold hands you'll never hit anything anyway. When your fingers are numb you don't get a feel for the trigger."

Then Louie looked away, like he said something out of place, or maybe he was testing me to see how I would answer. I realized that if anybody knew something about shooting and killing, it was Louis Packett.

"I guess you did some shooting in your day, Louie," I responded, not knowing if I should have said anything. Some old timers wouldn't talk about the war. But Louie glanced at me and I knew something I said was okay with him.

"I hear people talking war stories and war heroes and I listen, but unless you been there you don't know a damn thing." Louie was no longer looking at me but past me. I think his mind was on the battlefield.

"Must have been hell," I said without much real feeling in my voice. The tea was warm in my gut and the heat of his fire started seeping through to my skin. I was feeling better and something was resonating with Louie.

"I remember fighting on a day like this one," he said. "That's how I know that when your fingers are numb on the trigger you can't hit shit. But I came through that one," he added. "Yankees had been hovering around for a week when they came across the Niagara to take Upper Canada. I guess they had no appetite for the cold either, and turned back," he said.

Louie kept talking about the war and I sat with him long into the night until his pot of tea was drunk and I just listened so I could warm up. I had never heard Louis talk so much. I think back now and it was probably a relief for him. He told me what it was like to be the last man standing on a battlefield, all his friends dead or dying.

"It happened at an outpost on the little Lacolle," he said, "and there wasn't an ounce of glory in any of it. I just stood there numb, feeling the blood run down my face and my foot spouting a thin geyser. It was like watching from outside your own body and the world suddenly gone quiet except for screams and moans of men dying. And I envied the already dead," he added.

I sipped on my last cup of tea. He stared at me. Then his head began a long series of circles that sent his eyes rolling around until they re-focussed. Pretty soon he was talking again and he stared straight at me, like before.

"And it's a strange thing waiting the last while to die. Things flow back to you like everything moving in slow motion. I knew a girl once. And I remember word for word our whole last conversation, the smell of lavender in her hair and the way her lips went when she said my name. I recalled it all in just seconds when I thought the end had come down on me, and more."

I sipped the tea. Louis could brew a great cup.

"My barrel was jammed and me standing defenseless – just waiting. I watched my dad hugging me, a big man, his blue shirt smelling like sweat and my mom wiping her eyes on a dish towel. I took the squirrel gun over my shoulder and left. I never saw them again. All that came back in those few seconds."

"Oh yeah," I said. "A farm family left behind with no squirrel gun." I smiled and sipped, then realized I probably said the wrong thing.

Louis looked at me a long time. "Maybe someday you'll feel it," he said quietly. "Things you locked away coming back fresh and vivid when you wait the end." Then he added, "Facing a certain death and surviving will change you in ways you never thought possible, and the flashes you have while waiting never stop coming back either."

Louis died in November of 70' after I started my education at Trinity. I showed up for his burial more out of curiosity than anything else, along with a few others. Looking back, nobody acknowledged the passing of a great war hero. There was no mourning. More than anything else people were just curious. What will they do with old Looney Louie's bones? Maybe a few wanted to catch a morbid last glimpse of his gimpy body dead. Anything useful about Louis's life had ended with the battles of 1812.

CHAPTER 1

I lit the last candle on a swaying chandelier above a dining table set with linen and silverware. My mother was planning a dinner party that evening, always driven to secure her place in the social hierarchy and I was at that awkward age, not quite old enough to join the stoic, worldly conversations of the men and becoming unhappier assigned to help out my mother with her dinner party scheduled for the evening.

There was still plenty of daylight when my father walked through the door, closing it quietly behind him with the restraint of a pastor entering a chapel. But I knew full well the paradox of my father. I realized at once that it was the typical restraint that saddled his fury. I glanced quickly at my mother. Her eyes widened and she stared at him for a long moment, then turned abruptly, ascending a winding staircase, stopping briefly to assess the situation once more before climbing higher and out of sight. It was a predictable reaction whenever she suspected trouble between her husband and her son.

I dropped from the chair and faced my father. He was more imposing than ever in his high top-hat and elevated riding boots.

"We'll talk in the courtyard," he said, his movements still methodical and restrained but his puffed-up red neck betraying any pretense of composure.

I followed him through the door. I reassured myself, at least now I was a grown man, too old to receive a caning for whatever displeased my father.

"Sit down," he said, motioning me towards a garden bench. I sat down keeping my eyes locked on his dark gaze, trying to pretend I wasn't intimidated.

"Professor Trelawney has contacted me with disconcerting news this afternoon," he began, standing over me, the redness becoming brighter and spreading into his face. He stood there for what seemed an eternity staring down at me, his eyes growing darker and more intense. "Cheating is what he tells me! cheating on examinations." said my father. Then he turned abruptly and began pacing back and forth in front of the bench, his arms stiff and his voice growing in pitch.

"And there you were, constantly reassuring me following all the long nights of drinking and *tom catting*, for lack of a better word. Telling your father that all was well. Bringing home straight honors on every academic report. I am sure you were feeling quite smug watching your father beam with pride, and then countless dinner parties suffering with a pasted smile through all my bragging. 'Yes, yes,' I told everyone, 'my son topping his class in second year of medical school,' as I shelled out thousands. It was a small price to pay, indeed, for the pride and honor of the family."

He stopped pacing for a moment, his jowls quivering, as he banged his open hand on the top rail of the bench. "Now this. Practically the lowest of all! is what I'm sure many will say, cheating on examinations!"

He stared beyond me at nothing I could determine, as his expression slowly became more contemplative. "Somehow you found the exam key, Professor Trelawney tells me. Even he doesn't know how you did that. It remains a mystery to faculty and college security alike. But the worst of it, the most disappointing for me is getting caught!"

"Cheating?" I responded quietly, sensing his fury might be abating somewhat. "And just how would he know that? What proof did he offer for such a transgression?" I said, my voice filling with indignation.

My father began pacing again, but more composed, maybe even more thoughtful. "The professor said it was like laying a trap for a sleuth. He had suspected cheating for some time, so he altered the examination key, changing one or two answers to make them so erroneous that anyone with an ounce of knowledge regarding the lecture material would know better. And that was when it came out, on *your* examination and that of your so-called friend, Stephen. Practically verbatim, barely even a change in punctuation, he told me, the evidence overwhelming. I dare say he caught you red handed. How could you be so gullible? But no matter now." The old man sat down on the bench beside me letting out a long audible sigh.

"The professor is still correcting papers," he continued. "Maybe there are others involved too, he doesn't know yet. But as *you* should know by now, there is zero tolerance for cheating at Trinity. Trelawney had the courtesy and good graces to warn me so I don't attend the board meeting Thursday night to suffer shame in front of everyone."

He stood up and locked onto my gaze. "Also, perhaps the good professor is providing an opportunity to salvage the reputation of this family," he responded pensively. "A son cheating on exams and expelled from Trinity. What will the decent people of my riding think of that? And Sir John A.

who trusted me to a post in his cabinet. And now McKenzie, definitely less tolerant. Perhaps if you just withdraw quietly."

I bounded from the bench. "You're away ahead of yourself, sir!" I exclaimed. "I demand to see the proof, to see these, so called, examination answers and compare them to the key myself. And you should await the evidence as well."

***

I wandered down to the stables. The farm hands had put the horses inside for the night. I enjoyed the college life immensely: polo, the rifle competitions, the rowing and wrestling teams to say nothing about the night life. But the program was becoming more and more difficult, compromising everything, and especially father's willingness to open his pocket book for me. I dare say I was having the time of my life at Trinity and I thought that should account for something.

The guests had arrived. My parents were preoccupied now, making sure everyone was enjoying the hospitality. I put a harness on Diamond, my favorite mount and the fastest horse in the stable. I hooked him to a light buggy. It was getting late. My parents would be entertaining guests until well after midnight. Stephen lived two miles away.

It was a twisting trail through the trees and around the edge of the lake to Stephen's family estate. I rehearsed what to say, to draw Stephen away for a while. He would secure a can of lamp oil and I could see no other way to get out of the mess than to burn all the evidence. Trelawney always marked papers at his vacation cottage on the lake a few miles down from Stephen's place.

I tied Diamond to a hitching post just outside the property and attempted to walk as buoyant and unconcerned as I could to the front door, which Stephen answered.

"Would you like a stroll outside on such a warm evening?" I asked Stephen. "Maybe a ride somewhere quiet. We can plan this week's chemistry presentation." He would know full well something was awry.

"Yes, yes, of course," responded Stephen as he took in Diamond's sweat covered body. He called to someone in the parlor that he expected to be gone a while.

"Okay, what's up?" he asked as he guided me around a carriage in the front yard and through a metal latch gate to a trail leading into the pasture meadows. I told him everything about my father's conversation with Trelawney.

"Do you have a can of lamp oil?" I enquired.

"Of course. Do you want it in the buggy? You want to burn the exam key if we can get back in?"

"No, I'm thinking of something else. It takes too long figuring out those locks. My guess, he changed them anyway, as a precaution."

"Yes, certainly he would change the locks."

I pushed Diamond hard to make the professor's cottage before dark. "I don't see any other way," I told Stephen. "If the cottage goes, we get everything. Remember last time it was all there. Our old papers, recent papers, all our old examinations, the key. It's where he keeps his stuff. It will most certainly all be in there, and we want it *all* gone, no evidence left at all."

I pulled Diamond in close to the cottage for a fast exit.

"Isn't there a better way to do this?" inquired Stephen.

"Not with the time we have and who knows when he might show up. There were storm clouds and lightening earlier. They'll think it was a strike."

"I'll spread the fuel and you do the match," I said.

Stephen stared at me a long time. Finally, he said, "How about I spread the fuel and you torch it. Your arms are longer."

"Alright," I answered. "What are you waiting for?"

Stephen hauled a metal kerosene can out of the buggy and screwed in a long tin spout. He gave a splash of fuel up the side of the cottage and another splash beside it. "Fuck it, that's enough."

I dug out matches, scratched one across the striker plate and tossed it towards the fuel. The match fizzled in midair. "It's too fucking wet - all the humidity." I pulled out several matches, squeezed them between forefinger and thumb, lit them on the striker plate and tossed them all into the kerosene. A blue flame moved along the path of the fuel and finally fizzled. "We need way more kerosene," I said. "Give it a real shot, soak down the vines all around the door and give a big shot up the door, it's inset and dryer, as is the window pane. Soak them both."

Stephen unscrewed the nozzle for a larger opening, soaked down the side of the cottage, the wood pile, the door, and window pane. I tossed a match and the fire started with a *poof* and climbed the side of the house, becoming a roar in no time. The dry siding beneath the eaves became an inferno of circling flames as we jumped into the buggy. I whipped Diamond into a gallop and we fled along a dirt trail toward the lake and circled back to Stephen's estate.

I dropped him off and made it home in the dark. I past the reins to Jesse, a stable hand who slept in a cubby beside the barn. He would take care of Diamond. I came in through a back way and upstairs to my room, a discreet route that I used frequently. Guests were singing and having a merry time as my mother played gay tunes on the piano. A slight aroma of fine wine and cigar smoke was in the air when I fell asleep on top of my covers.

***

I spent the day at Trinity and Trelawney didn't show up for classes. Nobody said anything about a fire; however, it wasn't unusual in any circumstance for a professor to have something more important. The informal class rule was to give him fifteen minutes and then the remaining time was our own. I continued to feel pretty relieved, maybe a bit cocky. I thought we were off the hook for cheating, I was becoming more certain of it. I caught the second half of a polo match, relieving a friend of mine who had to run. He left me a bay gelding that knew the precision of the game better than most players.

After the match, I retrieved my own mount from a stable near the college and got home just in time. The smell of a great dinner was roasting in the oven. Father entered the house just after I was settled with the day's newspaper and the intermural sport scores.

He entered with hat in hand, his expression glum. "What is the trouble, Milton," my mother asked. She seemed able to gauge everyone's mood before a word was spoken.

"Very bad news," he replied, after a quick glance toward me. "Professor Trelawney has passed."

I'm sure I telegraphed something to my father as I straightened quickly in my chair. I didn't know if I should be relieved or apprehensive at such harsh news.

My father continued a cold look towards me, not trying to hide his dark mood. "Some say murdered. His cottage burnt down with him inside."

"How dreadful!" mother responded.

"Whatever happened?" I replied, my voice weaker than I would have liked.

"Some believe that lightening started the fire. But others think it was deliberate." He continued his dark stare at me and finally he said, "James, I need a word with you outside."

I sat on the bench in the courtyard. My father sighed a long audible sigh and sat down beside me. "James," he began, "what do you know of this terrible tragedy."

"Why nothing sir. It is the first I heard."

"James, once again you are not being truthful to your father. When you returned the buckboard late last evening, you neglected to remove a can of lamp oil in the back. Rather careless of you, don't you think? The stable hand requested that I examine Diamond this morning. His mane was badly singed." He stared deep into my eyes and I stared back. I had prepared nothing. I didn't expect Trelawney to burn up inside the cottage.

He remained quiet a long moment, just looking me over and finally he started again.

"A man is dead, James, and even I can't stop the police inquiry and the charges that could well be murder once a motive is uncovered."

That scared the hell out of me. And I have no doubt he sensed I was scared. And I knew my father, he would expect the sheer gravity of his discourse to break me: that I would begin spouting the truth of the whole matter. But I remained as poker faced as I was able to. I could barely articulate my own stupidity, but still I knew a confession was unlikely to do me any good. I kept my mouth shut and listened.

"Furthermore," he continued, "there was an eye-witness description of a buggy, two passengers and a pacing horse that looked similar to Diamond speeding along the lake last evening about the time the fire was reported. But, of course there are many black pacers with a gait similar to Diamond if someone chose to inventory all the horses in Ontario, don't you agree, James?"

That gave me a glimmer of hope. He knew perfectly well I had been lying but still I think he was looking at a way out of this mess too.

"Yes sir, I'd say there are many black pacers similar to Diamond in Ontario." Then I clammed up again.

He stared at me for several more moments with a more or less knowing expression on his face. I'm sure he had long since dispelled any doubts about my innocence.

"I spoke to the Prime Minister this morning," he said, "and fortunately Mackenzie continues to support MacDonald's mustering of young men for a force that we are calling the Northwest Mounted Police, to bring Canadian law and order onto our frontier. American whisky traders seem bound and determined to take things over. We must assert our sovereignty.

"Of course, there is normally a long screening of young men chomping at the bit to undertake such an adventure in the West. But I spoke to McKenzie and I underscored all your assets. I told him you were prime for the adventure, a bright, physically fit young man who could endure great hardship when necessary. He said he would be delighted to inform the commissioner that he has personally selected such a dedicated young man to join the force."

"I believe Stephen would be up for such an adventure as well, sir," I said, "even if it means giving up the good life at Trinity."

"Oh yes," my father replied. "I put in a word for him too. I suggest you prepare quickly though, as the training force assembles at New Fort in Toronto for orientation just two days from now. That will give you time to get your things together. After drills, you will be off to North Dakota and finally our great Northwest.

"Just one more thing, James. Do try to make this work. The penalty for murder is still execution, even in the new confederacy: sometimes firing squad, sometimes hanging. But I doubt they will find you for a very long time if you remain on the frontier. Justice unwinds slowly here most of the time and the government does not stay on top of these files forever. Since it is only a matter of days before the end of the term, I shall simply tell people you left early in preparation for a summer's adventure on the frontier." He sighed. "And not exactly a lie either," he added as he walked away without looking back or bidding me good bye.

CHAPTER 2

It was barely daylight when Stephen and I with a small bag of personal belongings secured an omnibus to transport us to New Fort so we could report for duty with the Northwest Mounted Police. Stephen knew more about the mission than I. He had, no doubt, followed the newspapers regarding formation of a frontier police service.

He babbled the whole way, jumping from topic to topic. "We are the second wave set to join with the first wave in Fort Garry," he said. "A wide net was cast for recruits, the only prerequisites: able-bodied, of sound character, able to read and write, and ride. The mandate: preserve peace and apprehend criminals throughout the Northwest territories."

I had never seen him quite so out of sorts. He was pale and his mind seemed to dissociate at times. "All I really wanted was to be a doctor and help the sick," he murmured.

"Is Trelawney really dead now?" he kept repeating, talking more to himself than to me. He appeared in a daze about the whole thing and that worried me. It seemed not to have sunk in for him that the good life at Trinity Medical was over. A few times he mumbled about how sorry he was. I assumed he meant the fact of Trelawney being inside when the cottage went up. All I felt was an urgency in the pit of my stomach to get as far away from Toronto as I could.

Finally, I intervened, "Stephen, pull yourself together, man. It will be us dead next," I reminded him, "unless we can catch this police train out of here. We'll stick together as much as we can until this blows over. Should be a piece of cake." Stephen seemed to settle a bit.

New Fort was built beside Old Fort York in the heart of Toronto. Two eighteen-pound guns still projected through the east wall of the old fort, an infrastructure that probably hadn't changed since guys like Louis Packett would have trained here back in 1812. Maybe Louie was even among the Canadian militia that shot down American invaders here at Old Fort York. It wouldn't surprise me. But prior to now, I had no particular interest whatsoever in the place.

Old Fort York was a contrast to the new fort which was less than thirty years old. Old Fort was a conglomeration of log constructed buildings with notched ends and mud chinking. New Fort was modern with long stone buildings for barracks, mess halls, stables and out buildings. An expansive parade and training grounds of turf, dirt and dust covered most of the areas beyond the barracks.

We arrived right at six o'clock, as ordered. The area had already filled up with over a hundred men stretching into two lineups. We were ordered to "line up!" and directed to the closest line. The long string of men terminated in a booth behind which sat an officer in a red tunic, Sergeant Major Sam Steele. He passed us a single sheet of paper, a document that I quickly read and signed as follows:

> *I, <u>James McGinn</u>, solemnly swear that I will faithfully, diligently and impartially execute and perform the duties and offices of the Police Force of the North-West Territories, and will well and truly obey and perform all lawful orders or instructions which*

I shall receive as such, without fear, favor, or affection of or towards any person whomsoever. So help me God.

Stephen likewise signed his document, *Stephen John Woodward,* and we were now both constables in the force of the Northwest Mounted Police, earning $.75 per day. Obviously, we weren't particularly enthralled, but neither did we have time to mull over what had just happened, and I was glad to see Stephen's mind have to focus on what lay immediately ahead.

We were now under the charge of a bellowing Inspector William Jarvis who assembled us into three groups that marched forth into what became D, E and F Divisions. Stephen and I were in D Division. Foot drills began immediately, followed by marches and parades that continued unrelenting under the hot sun of early June, punctuated with the booming and scolding voices of officers. The air was filled with the smell of men's sweat, horse manure still fresh in the dirt, flies, dust, and the guttural sounds of men straining to keep pace.

Drills continued until dark with a short break for mess at noon sharp. The goal of the force was obviously to pump as much training into us as possible in a short time before the long trek to the distant Northwest was to begin.

During mess, former militia men found each other, introduced their comrades and stuck together. An obvious leader among them was a recruit called, Spider Marks, and I had actually heard of him; he was a well-known local militia fighter. Marks didn't try very hard to suppress his contempt when the rest of us struggled to master the drills.

The farm boys were a well-muscled, tanned and determined group, filled with a strong work ethic and they could spot each other across the mess hall like sorting mavericks out of a herd. They sat together. Likewise, some of the clerks knew each other, pulled in other clerks, and hastily formed their own cliques. Stephen and I sat alone over a hurried lunch.

In the stifling heat we drilled. Often, we were under the watchful eye of the highest command, Commissioner George French, who frequently showed up without notice overlooking the drill site, appearing particularly gallant and imposing on his mount, Silver Blaze.

After the first day of drills, we were given full uniform dress and advised to be on the field at five thirty the following morning. Each uniform package included: a red tunic, black breeches with two white strips, forage cap, helmet, high black leather boots, heavy overcoat with cape. We received a belt with revolver and cartridge pouch, and a Snider carbine. During each drill, we were to be in full dress exempting the helmet, overcoat and cape, revolver, cartridge pouch and Snider carbine. The rest we were told to get used to.

At the end of the day, Stephen and I were exhausted and I was glad that we were assigned to the same barracks with adjacent bunks. We compared notes, everything we observed during the day, overheard or were told.

"French's reputation has obviously preceded him," Stephen said, pulling his boots off and falling back on his bunk. His face was drawn with dark rings already forming under his eyes. "They say he's completely ruthless in his command, showing favoritism to officers or recruits that he thinks are up to the challenge. And he has no problem berating subordinates and degrading recruits he doesn't like. He thinks the Force will stand or fall on the quality of its recruits and he apparently conducts his command accordingly."

Stephen was quiet for a long moment, then he added. "The militia boys have been through these drills before," he said, "and they don't mind showing their disgust for the rest of us trying to learning the drills."

It seemed to me that Stephen's state of mind was plummeting again, seeing only the negatives. "I've been impressed with the farm boys, though," I responded, "they look like a lean and hungry group itching for adventure, even though they probably stumble more than anybody else during drills."

"Pretty obvious what motivates the farm guys," said Stephen. "It's the promise of free land in the northwest after they've completed three years of service."

"I expected the clerks to have the most trouble," I said, "but they step lively out there and they're definitely the biggest group."

Stephan was already asleep. I rolled over and tried to relax my aching muscles and finally I fell into a restless sleep.

***

The second day of drills was more torturous than the first; we struggled in the summer heat and were denied sufficient drink to sustain us. Each man was provided a small ladle of water in midafternoon. Three men succumbed to exhaustion or dehydration and were lifted off the field. It was our worst day of training drills and Jarvis kept us long after the sun had set.

Then French himself, mounted on his steed, paraded before the troops in front of the barracks and commenced to lecture all three divisions.

"Men, the hardships we shall encounter on our march and service in the Northwest are hardships beyond what many of you have ever anticipated." He swung his prancing mount to settle him down and continued. "We shall proceed alone into deep unchartered wilderness of the dominion. There will be long marches and long periods of thirst before finding water and places to overnight. We will rely on finding game to feed us as we go along. Game can often be scarce, hidden from sight, or simply unavailable for days on end in the frontier. There will be periods of hunger. And we shall encounter hostile forces, and there will be fighting."

French looked over the recruits for several moments. Then, he began again: "any of you who feel you are not up to the challenge, or have a change of heart, step forth and I will accept all resignations without question or consequence." French continued to ride back and forth on his lively mount looking intensely across the enlisted men. None stepped forth. "At ease men, take your break," he finally commanded and headed off the parade grounds.

That night I lay awake in my bunk, exactly two feet from Stephen's. He was quiet and I knew perfectly well what was churning inside his head. Finally, he spoke to me across the small space that separated us.

"Maybe I'll take up French's offer," he told me, and then looked away.

"Stephen, do you know what our fate would be if we stayed in Toronto?" I asked, and waited for his response but he was silent. "We could be hung or face firing squad. We didn't intend to kill Trelawney but nobody knows that. Motive is easy for a prosecutor once he knows we faced expulsion from Trinity."

Stephen rolled over to face the wall. The next morning he was gone. I showered and dressed in the crisp new uniform and took my place on the field.

Then Stephen showed up and fell in line near me. He avoided eye contact but I was immensely relieved to see him. However, almost thirty men did not show up and were never seen again. It became known as 'French leave,' and none were pursued for desertion.

Dust devils swirled across the training field and it was hot, but at least the training schedule was altered from the endless drills. Jarvis called it equitation: rider training. A long line of horses was led from the stables by volunteer recruits and stable hands who tethered them to lengthy hitching rails along the edge of the parade grounds.

Jarvis had chosen equestrian trainers from the ranks of the recruits to assist him. He informed the men that the volunteers were in charge of today's training and they would give the orders and every man was expected to obey. He sat back on his own mount and observed, providing occasional direction. The volunteers were themselves great horsemen with extensive experience in equestrian training drills. Spider Marks quickly became the leader.

The first drill was referred to as a *ménage*; an exercise without reins or stirrups designed to improve balance of the rider. One thing became apparent within the first minutes: many recruits had lied. Scores of men from different backgrounds were unused to horses and were not competent riders. 'Riding skills' was specified as a prime prerequisite for applying to the Mounted Police.

The volunteer instructors didn't bother to cover their contempt, becoming increasingly punitive in their demands on the inept riders. Their apparent reasoning being that recruits had lied and therefore were deserving of humiliation. The training field became a melee of flying dust, unseated riders, spooked mounts and recruits trying to re-mount or running to avoid the romping horses. Instructors went after the free mounts and red-faced recruits walked back to their comrades on the sidelines. Many who could not master the exercise simply wrapped their arms around their horse's neck or tangled their fingers into the animal's mane and hung on as their horses fled for the stables.

There was a clamoring of staff from the fort to witness the fiasco. Cooks, laundresses, stable hands, carpenters, maids and mule skinners gathered outside to witness the spectacle: police and civilian workers alike roared with laughter at the inept recruits.

The timing of Commissioner French was always uncanny. He appeared on the parade grounds mounted on his flashy horse taking in the chaotic demonstrations of horsemanship before him. I expected him to become furious and commence berating recruits and instructors alike. To my amazement, the normally dour and demanding commissioner seemed unable to contain his own levity and his handlebar moustache spread wider across his face witnessing the antics before him.

Spider Marks revelled in the clumsiness of the recruits more than anyone. Furthermore, he and the instructors appeared delighted to see French so humoured by their stringent drills, which gave them license. They strutted, bellowed, waved hats and became increasingly punitive in their demands on the riders and the complexity of the drills. Stephen and I were among a minority of recruits that managed to stay seated throughout the challenging drill.

Most of the animals were sleek, well-proportioned thoroughbreds. The force had recently acquired a small herd of untrained mustangs that, once they were broke, were expected to be sure-footed and sturdy animals able to navigate the steepest and roughest terrain of the Northwest. Spider had tethered a few of them among the thoroughbreds.

After *ménage*, three sets of closely intertwined wooden barrels were set out on the training field. Three at a time, the recruits were called forth, given a mount and instructed to canter their mount around the barrels, and then complete a second circuit at full gallop through the maze.

Stephen was a competent rider and if left alone he would have navigated the circuitry of the barrels marvellously well, but near the end of his ride Spider Marks waved his hat suddenly before the horse's muzzle, sending the mount into a rapid shift of direction, spinning, plunging back on his hind legs and un-seating Stephen to a thunderous roar of laughter from the crowd.

I was angry. I could not dismiss that Spider had reserved the hat waving stunt for Stephen, humiliating him. It was pretty obvious by now that Stephen and I were both loners, not militia, farm boys, or clerks but Trinity college men, and Marks' attitude said as much. I was next. I approached Marks to take the reins of the mount assigned to me and looked into his face. "Did the militia turn you into an asshole, Marks, or are you a natural?"

The humor disappeared from his face, and his eyes, red rimmed and dust filled, turned cold as steel and locked on mine. "I'm instructor here," he spat the words at me, "and you're insubordinate. Jarvis will hear about this."

"I couldn't care less what an asshole tells Jarvis," I responded and turned to take possession of my mount and begin my ride.

"You'll wait," he said, ripping the reins out of my hands. He took a dozen strides or so to the hitching rails, tethered the thoroughbred and came back with an unbroken mustang, stomping, rearing and fighting the bit.

Other volunteers began holding back their riders, watching us, obviously sensing something extra-ordinary was about to happen. The jubilant crowd was grinning at Marks and me expecting some real sport. I looked towards French. He was staring back at me and he wasn't smiling anymore. Marks passed me the reins with a vicious smirk. "This is your mount. You'll do two circuits."

I took the reins and swung up onto the mustang. I had ridden horses since I was a kid including the darting, twisting and racing polo ponies, and an occasional mount gone berserk on the polo field. I would take my chances. But I had never known a fighter like this one. No sooner was I seated than Spider Marks laid his quirt hard across the flanks of the mustang. The horse took off, his head between his pounding front hooves, kicking, twisting, bucking and bounding across the grounds. For a moment, I thought the saddle would give way under me and I would take a terrible fall but it held fast, and so did I.

I gut-booted that mount with everything I had. He kicked, twisted, reared, and sun-fished to unseat me. But I stuck. Suddenly I was having the time of my life and I had no mercy whatsoever on that mustang. I drove my boots into his ribs with every jarred landing he made on his stiff front legs and with every bounding leap from his hind quarters. Now he was foaming at the mouth and a guttural heaving sound was coming out of him. I slapped his hind quarters with my open hand and pounded his ribs with my heels and soon I knew he was tiring faster than I was.

Then I slipped my feet out of the stirrups and raked him stem to stern with my heavy riding boots, and just for fun I waved one arm in the air. The mustang stopped bucking, blew like a trumpet through his nostrils and raced full speed across the field toward the stables until I cranked his head in a pull-rein effort, heel-kicking his ribs on the same side with my heavy boots until him and I were spinning around the barrels at full steam to the howls and shrieks of delight from recruits and staffers alike. I caught a glimpse of French, his handle bar was stretched from ear to ear.

I hauled the mustang back in beside Marks, dismounted and passed him the reins. He was grim faced and steel–eyed, "you have to do the circuit at a canter now."

"You show us how, militia boy," I said, "you tried to give me a dirt bath out there, didn't you? And make a fool of me. Well guess what, you're the fool."

Marks stepped into me, chest to chest, and the whole place was suddenly quiet. "You cocky little son of a bitch," he said. "you'll cool off under guard, college boy," he added, with all the contempt he could muster.

"Do what you need to do," I said, "but it looked to me like the commissioner was pretty pleased with my ride." I turned and walked away. One thing I knew for sure: I had just made an enemy for life, or as long as we were both serving at the pleasure of the Northwest Mounted Police.

CHAPTER 3

The riding drills went on all day, but with a lot more civility. Marks disappeared for a while, no doubt making his case to Jarvis who would consult with French. I heard nothing further. At sundown, we were dismissed to barracks and ordered to show up the next day with our revolvers, cartridge pouches, and carbines. It would be firearm training.

Stephen and I talked across our bunks in the dark.

"Spider's out to get you," he said, "and that means the whole militia with him."

"I know," I said trying to get comfortable on my straw tick. "I'm watching him."

"I followed a group of them into the barracks tonight," said Stephen. "They didn't see me. One of them said, 'there's gonna be a lot of lead flying tomorrow. College boy better keep his head low.' Marks said, 'yup, friendly fire eh, it weeds out the undesirables.' They all laughed."

I didn't sleep well. But I had a side arm and carbine too. Somehow that made me feel better.

We were up at first light and onto the field. Until well past mid-afternoon we marched through drill after drill with our firearms, like calisthenics with a rifle above our heads, sometimes cradled in our arms like a babe, or across our shoulders. Then we received instruction on both our carbines and side arms in mock drills, loading, aiming, sighting and firing until every man could complete the drill rapidly and with skill and finesse. Finally, we marched back and forth across the parade grounds, simulating acts of combat, thrusting and withdrawing bayonets, mock hand to hand fighting.

Two nine-pound muzzle loading guns, mounted on carriages and pulled by teams of four horses were brought onto the field and we performed endless drills: maneuvering the cannons, sighting, loading and mock discharging. We were thrown into rapidly revolving random groups of four for repetition of drills with the heavy guns, and the recruits of the northwest police were robust, competent men, even if the equitation training didn't reveal as much. For those few hours of intense training we forgot our differences; we were becoming a force to be reckoned with by any adversary, anywhere.

Then our training schedule changed. Rows upon rows of wooden tripods were set up across the field and Jarvis passed out stacks of paper targets to volunteers. We were split in pairs and allowed to pick our partners. Each recruit was given a number.

Stephen and I were a team, not least because no one else wanted us. But that suited me fine. Since equitation, I made no particular overtures to befriend anyone especially the former militia men. The farm men were friendly enough but preoccupied with their own, as were recruits drawn from the clerks. We were now lined up with our carbines, ordered into prone positions on the ground as volunteers placed targets 100 yards distance from each of us. We were issued live ammunition.

Marks was paired with Tom Leslie about fifty feet away. I caught Mark's eye. "Friendly fire, eh?" I called over to him without humour.

He stared at me a long moment and I could see the cogs spinning in his head, putting together what Stephen had overheard last night. Then his eyes shot daggers at me. Finally, he responded, "When the time comes it won't be friendly either, college boy."

"Don't forget I have my own carbine," I responded.

He looked away, then back at me. "That a threat?" he asked.

"No, just a reminder," I said.

"Show us what you got then, smart aleck," he answered, "and remember, right now it's only target practice."

Stephen and I took turns loading each other's rifle. Jarvis assumed command again.

"It's a bit of competition right now, men, to see how you fair with your comrades," he told us. Then we were ordered to position, aim and fire. The paper targets were retrieved and given to Jarvis. The targets were a series of increasingly smaller concentric circles to an inner bullseye of half an inch diameter. Jarvis called out the numbers of those with all three shots within the four inner circles. Half the group were now eliminated, Stephen and I remained. Most of the militia men were still in, including Marks.

After the next round, recruits that had all three of their bullets within the three inner circles were in. I stayed in with four other militia recruits. Marks was in and Stephen was out. After the next round, Jarvis waved one target.

"Nobody going to beat this," he said, holding up a target for all to see. Three bullet holes crowded into the very center. "I believe this target is the property of Spider Marks," he reported to a howl of approval from the militia boys. The rest gave a polite round of applause. Stephen and I gave up nothing.

Marks took up his target from Jarvis and walked past me, the tip of his forefinger near the bullseye with three bullet holes.

"About the size of a college boy's asshole, wouldn't you agree." He howled with laughter at his own joke, then sent a savage grimace at me and strutted away.

Then he turned back, "Oh and in case you forget," he said, "this is still just target practice."

***

It was June 5th, the final evening before the next wave of the Northwest Mounted Police, Divisions D, E, and F would pull out for service on the remote Canadian frontier. Prime Minister McDonald was back in power again and he had received permission from the American government for troops, horses, wagons, oxen and supplies to travel on the Great Pacific Railway line through Chicago and St. Paul to Fargo, North Dakota where we would disembark. From there we would commence northwest deep onto the Canadian frontier.

French knew well that many would be eyeing up the Toronto taverns on the final day of training prior to departure. He most likely wanted to give a message about our future role in policing the Northwest where illegal liquor trade to indigenous people was a major problem and to warn against drunkenness on this night before embarking.

He stood before us on the parade ground: "Men, I am proud of you. I have been in charge of many training operations and few have shown the stamina, endurance and skill that this group has demonstrated. Equitation skills aside, and all of you will be able riders before you reach the frontiers of our country; but I have not seen a group with as many skilled marksmen and complete mastery of so many complex drills in so short time. I congratulate you.

"Now you are a Canadian police force. Many of you have had careers in the military but I remind you that you are no longer military men but police officers. Our job in the Northwest will be to stamp out and bring justice to the frontiers of our great dominion, no matter how entrenched criminals have become in an illegal liquor trade. I expect every man to set his own example. And that starts tonight."

The message was clear: French expected the men to abstain.

Stephen was the first to leave the ranks and neither French nor anyone else was going to stop me from joining him for a celebratory glass of whisky.

I followed Stephen to the first tavern available, to drink a toast with him; it was the end of the beginning of our endeavors as Northwest Mounted policemen.

I pulled up a stool beside him and ordered bourbon on ice. Stephen had already ordered whisky, straight up.

"Well, so far," I said, "nobody has come after us, and I mean the business with Trelawney. But I'm glad we're shipping out tomorrow and as far from here as we can get."

Stephen didn't respond, just downed his whisky and ordered more.

He tossed back three drinks and then he turned to face me. "You never felt a God damn thing, did you? A man is dead, and all you worry about is finding a way to save your own ass."

"What?" I responded with incredulity. Stephen still didn't get it. We were finally getting ourselves out of a terrible mess and Stephen was becoming self-righteous.

"Jesus, shape up, man!" I hissed. "You know we could be facing murder charges here, don't you? Do you know what that would be like? Ever watch a man hang?" I asked. "They say his neck snaps and he doesn't feel anything. But that's a God damn lie. I knew somebody who watched a hanging once and he said that was bullshit. The man kicked and the most hideous muffled sounds came out of him along with slobber and snot and he pissed himself swinging back and forth on a goddam five-foot length of hemp until he strangled with a whole crowd watching."

I was nose to nose with Stephen. He needed to get the point.

"They cut him down eventually and then he started coming around again, kicking on the ground and his face screwing up and grimacing and slobbering and trying to say something. My friend said the doctor finally injected something into the son of a bitch and he finally died."

Stephen was silent. But he wasn't satisfied by three more whisky. Maybe he wouldn't be satisfied with three more bottles.

Finally he said, "Trelawney was still in his forties. He had a wife and kids."

I had no more appetite for liquor. I got up and walked back to the barracks. I woke up at midnight and Stephen wasn't in his bunk. I fell asleep again and woke before dawn. I went out and found him across from the tavern in a ditch. I hoisted him across my back and got him into his bunk with a few men sitting up to watch. But nobody said anything. Fortunately, he had already puked his guts out.

The next morning, I was able to rouse him and get him onto the parade grounds. Under the command of Commissioner French, Divisions C, D and E formed three lines and commenced to march, 150 men altogether, along with five officers and 170 horses. We proceeded to the train at Union Station.

Stephen puked all down the front of his uniform and half a dozen militia men could not keep the smirks off their faces. I broke the line, shoved a handkerchief at him, barely missing a beat. At least he managed to stay in line and keep marching. Next time I noticed the puke was off.

The occasion was apparently historic. A military band joined our march and pounded out lively tunes to the beat of drums and bugling trumpets as crowds gathered along the streets to cheer us on. At the station, hundreds of families, friends and acquaintances gathered to exchange hugs, kisses and handshakes. Nobody was there to send off Stephen or me. I was just as glad.

Stephen was starting to sober up. "What I wouldn't give for water right now," he said. Then he added, somewhat grudgingly, "Thanks for the hand."

"Don't mention it," I said. We boarded the train. Stephen and I managed to get a passenger seat, many of the men had to ride the boxcars. In a cloud of smoke and steam the train cleared the station. The crowd cheered as the band played *Auld Lang Syne*.

***

Our American neighbors had apparently not forgotten the war of 1812. Before we crossed the border, we had to change out of our police uniforms which we wore for show on the last day. We could only cross the border as civilians. Our firearms, ammunition, horses, supplies and anything resembling a military force were to be kept under lock and key in another section of the train until we unloaded in Fargo, North Dakota for our northward trek back into Canada.

We were three days on the train, travelling through Chicago and St. Paul to Fargo, stopping occasionally as the train took on coal and water and we caught a few meals in local restaurants. Stephen and I stayed by ourselves. Some of the militia men could not resist a couple of cheap shots at Stephen. A group of them passed us on our way to purchase food at a stop in Chicago. One turned to Stephen, "Great display on parade," he scoffed. "Nice puke," someone added, and the others howled.

"He left it for you to slip in and fall on your ass." It was the best I could come up with on the spur of the moment, but I couldn't leave it out there like that. Stephen just nudged me. "Ignore it," he said. They glared at us and walked on.

I had a seat by the window as the train left the station.

Stephen was already asleep. The tracks wound around the end of Lake Michigan through short stands of evergreens and low-lying shrubs. The locomotive whistled picking up steam until trees were flying past my window in a mesmerizing blur of foliage. I thought about growing up along Lake Ontario, and about my parents.

My mother would be worried about me right now. She was always a good mother to me, affectionate and caring. And she was always on my side whenever she could be, given the *spare the rod* mentality of my father. My first caning came when I was six, after a fight at school and the master spoke to my parents.

"James was in a fight today," he told them. "He beat another boy long after the boy was down and utterly defenseless. Your son is an evil little boy."

I remember how much I hated that kid, always trying to beat me at everything. Nobody asked how I felt except my mother. She tried to teach me to be nice to people. But I didn't really see it. I was more like my father. The caning I got from him was far worse than the beating I gave that kid. Right now, my father is probably more worried about his status in parliament than about my future, or lack thereof. But I shall never be ungrateful for him. The realization came to me frequently throughout my growing up years. The position he gained in parliament came through sheer determination and hard work, which elevated me as well.

My grandfather was a struggling Irishman. He had a business head and was well connected with the Irish immigrants. Hundreds of thousands of acres of land in upper Canada were awarded by the English king to elite officers, mainly Englishmen, following a victory in the 1812 war. A few officers, like the grandfather of Stephen, kept an estate along Lake Ontario. But most high-ranking officers were not farmers and didn't know what to do with the land. My grandfather brokered deals creating thousands of small acre farms for scores of Irish farmers and he made a fortune in the process. My father expanded the fortune through land deals and, like his father, was admired and respected in the Irish community. As a result, he had little trouble getting elected as MP under the ostentatious, John A. MacDonald.

So, I held no grudge for his harsh punishments. The work of my Irish forbearers brought me a lifestyle I relished. And having some notoriety and wealth didn't hurt me any in my pursuit of Elizabeth Barrett, positively the most charming maiden in all of Toronto. Every young man drooled over her. Her uncle was an English baron and Elizabeth came from a long line of old English money. Her father was a highly respected physician.

I once coyly asked her after a few weeks of dating what she saw in me, an Irish boy of humble ancestry.

"Why because you are handsome!" she responded, and I knew she was as full of the devil as I was.

"And James, I love the way your dark hair swoops across your forehead," she responded with twinkling eyes as she stood on her tip-toes running her slim fingers through my hair and caressing my temples. "And who else breaks into such dimples of the cheek when I humour them? No James, you are indeed charming, and a slight roll of the Irish tongue brings out a wee bit of the beastie in you that I love so much."

And I thought I could lay it on thick. I laughed at her antics. But she had a way of getting to the core of me.

My last night before going to New Fort, I had ridden over to see her. She met me at the door and quickly ushered me inside.

"So how did you know that I was all alone tonight, James, you devil. My parents are out for the evening. I shall make sure the servants are busy elsewhere," then she led me upstairs to her room.

"I'll be back in a flash," she said, returning several minutes later.

"I had to send someone to the cellar for the very best sherry in the house." She poured us both a glass full. "And this wasn't even date night. I am so immensely pleased. To what do I owe such a gratuitous visit."

"Well I don't have good news," I said.

She looked suddenly worried. "Oh no, I pray that nothing will ever take you away from me."

I tried to be nonchalant. "No, nothing that serious," I responded, "but Stephen and I have gotten ourselves into a bit of trouble. It's nothing, and I don't want you to worry your pretty head over it, but I could, by necessity, be gone for a while."

"Oh James, I'm devastated. How long will you be away? Surely you can tell me where you are going. I shall never breath a word."

"It's some trouble at Trinity. Stephen and I are travelling with a group to the northwest to spend the summer on the Canadian frontier. I plan to be back home the moment I can."

"Well, I hope you are back in time to continue your education," she said. "You know my father would love to have you join him as a junior partner in his practice."

"Yes, that is still the plan," I lied.

She poured another glass of sherry for each of us. "Okay then, let's drink to your safe return. And since I won't see you, we need to celebrate our last time together for a while."

We touched glasses and drank down the sherry and she lay back on the bed. I lay beside her and kissed her pretty mouth and a little sigh came from deep inside of her.

"Oh James," she said, "sherry always gives me such a time keeping my skirt from climbing."

She rolled against me and her kiss was warm and tender and sweeter than wine. The sherry and I worked in tandem. Her dress inched gradually higher until it was no longer an obstacle for either of us. She met my rising ardor with the deepest passion and affection of her very own; I had never known anyone more loving and blissfully creative. She had a special place in my heart. It was a worthy send-off. And I was not likely to forget it any time soon.

CHAPTER 4

The train rolled into the small city of St. Paul, Minnesota leaving a long trail of black smoke in her wake. Hissing clouds of steam burst through the brakes of the locomotive, sending a churning mist around the cars as she slowed to a gradual stop in front of the station.

I roused Stephen and we got off the train to a beautiful day. Stephen seemed in a somewhat better mood.

"Aw, St. Paul," he said as if the place offered him some particular comfort or familiarity. He stretched and yawned and seemed to have a new lease on life.

"Did you know that whisky had a lot to do with building this great city," he said.

Lately, whisky seemed to have a lot to do with how Stephen was functioning in general, or not functioning. But ever the historian, he gave me the lowdown on St. Paul and it was good to finally get some conversation out of him.

"Did you know that a French Canadian, Pierre *Pigs Eye Parrant*, got this whole city started?"

"I didn't know," I told him. "But I'm sure you'll enlighten me."

He looked around at the shops and the busy street. "In the beginning a flourishing whisky trade was taking root downstream from here at Fort Snelling," Stephen said, "when military officers chased out the distillers. *Pigs Eye* turned bootlegger and moved here." Stephen looked like he was pretty pleased with the exploits of old Pigs Eye.

"The whole area became known in French as *L'ceil de Cochon,"* Stephen said, "English translation, *Pigs Eye*, and French settlers began pouring in and right here, downtown St. Paul, became a major stop over for travellers and eventually a major trading center."

We began our walk into the heart of the city.

Stephen continued, "It was renamed St. Paul by the Reverend Father Lucien Galtier. The place is now state capital," he said, then he grinned, "and the whole thing built on whisky."

I decided the place had come a long way. We walked along a busy street that ended on a bluff overlooking the mighty Mississippi River where an expansive bridge, supported on high wooden pilings elevated this end of the bridge and traversed the watercourse to a much lower exit beside a river port on the opposite end. It was my first view of the Mississippi, and a mighty watercourse she was. Countless sternwheel steamers, carrying both passengers and cargo moved up and down the wide, slow moving river.

We turned back towards city center. It was a lively place indeed. All the intersecting streets were bustling with horses and buggies, many of a fashionable sort, making their way around and between the street cars that travelled up and down all the main ways. But what seemed to capture Stephen's attention more than anything were the many lager beer saloons with frolicking patrons, singing, cheering and toasting each other with much clinking of beer glasses. And there were the retail whisky outlets that drew Stephen like a hungry dog to a bone. That was his first stop. I tagged along.

"Don't you think you should leave that stuff alone?" I queried.

"I can't," he said, and for the first time I heard a note of desperation in his voice. "It's all I live for now." He bought what he could afford, filled his pockets with flasks of liquor, mostly whisky, and we returned to the train platform.

Gossip around the station was that the James gang was on a tear throughout Minnesota, Kansas and Missouri, holding up banks and trains alike. Reward posters were everywhere and the local chatter was that no passenger was safe. I had my doubts that even the notorious James gang would mess with over a hundred Canadian police officers, with or without firearms. They might be bold but I doubted they were stupid.

We pulled out soon after. Stephen offered me a drink which I declined and he drank by himself, alternating between sleeping, drinking, slumbering, yelling out, at which times I elbowed him in the ribs to quieten him down, and occasionally he took a piss break onto the railway tracks.

I watched outside as the day passed into night. I could not sleep and when I did doze off, the drunken slumbers of Stephen would arouse me. It was the first I realized that he had completely given in to alcohol. We had our drinking times in the past but it was mainly college fun.

Stephen and I went back a long way, so far back I barely remember the first time I met him. His parent's estate and my parent's estate were close together and I remember going to a birthday party for him when he was probably four or five years old and his parents had given him a Shetland pony. We both liked to ride and that was probably what cemented our boyhood friendship: riding back and forth to each other's estate to play.

But as time went on, I had more appetite for excitement than Stephen did and much of the challenge for me was to bring him along into the vices of teenage and young adulthood. That was when I first learned that with liquor, Stephen was as daring as I. His personality seemed to transform under its influence in a most amazing way. I don't like to think I exploited Stephen's propensity for alcohol but he did win me a fist full of dollars with my friends in a bet during my first year of college.

Stephen was very shy about meeting girls on campus and often didn't have a date, although I'm sure many girls would have dated him had he only asked. So, he caught a lot of flak from the guys.

"Stephen will be a virgin until he marries – in later life," they tormented him, even though most of them were virgins themselves but just wouldn't admit it.

So, one day I challenged them when Stephen wasn't around.

"I say, around women Stephen has more fortitude and gall than any of you." I proclaimed to howls of dissent from the whole pack.

"Well, how many of you would bring a hooker to campus and cock-slam her in the locker room?" I challenged to howls of the most indignant censure.

"Stephen wouldn't cock-slam his sister in six months of solitary confinement with her!" one howled.

"I'm saying nothing about his sister," I interjected. "I'm talking about a hooker in this very locker room, slamming her right here with at least one witness."

"I have a hundred bucks says that would never happen," said Bruce, a jock from the rowing team, and dozens of others wanted in on the wagers.

What I knew and they didn't, was Stephen's personality changed considerably under the influence. I had experimented with hookers since the ripe old age of seventeen and I got especially familiar with one of the more voyeuristic among them, Betsie Lee-from-Purgatory, was the moniker her hooker friends gave her. I told Betsie Lee about my bet and promised her half if she could seduce Stephen in the locker room. She had no problem with that. I just had to prep Stephen.

I arranged to meet Stephen mid-morning the next day and told him about a good stash I had put away for us to make the afternoon classes go by faster. He was never more agreeable. I picked him up in my finest carriage pulled by Diamond, my most flashy harness racing standardbred. By noon I had Stephen sailing high and we raced Diamond throughout downtown Toronto, with Stephen waving a bottle of brandy in the air and wolf-whistling every female form we passed. Betsie Lee-from-Purgatory was set to go and warmed up Stephen all the way to the men's locker room, and to make a long story shorter, I pulled in fists full of rich boy's cash that day from every jock at Trinity College, and Stephen was rapidly becoming the big man on campus.

CHAPTER 5

I awoke to the first sign of dawn and a vast rolling prairie that opened up before me somewhere between St. Paul and Fargo, North Dakota. It was countryside I had never encountered before. I noticed sporadic herds of pronghorn antelope that seemed to still be unaccustomed to the passing locomotive; they would bolt away when we approached, then they jumped high in the air, magnificent, bounding leaps, sometimes clearing a height of ten feet or more.

I was fascinated with them. It was the first time I had seen the flighty small ungulates. I was still hoping to witness the vast herds of buffalo that were apparently encountered quite regularly by the train but there was nothing before me except a never-ending sea of rolling prairie until a distant scattering of buildings came into view and we chugged to a stop in Fargo, North Dakota, our destination.

We disembarked and peeled off our sweaty and stinking civilian clothes in a few boxcars set aside for changing. We were allowed to don our police uniforms in preparation for the march north into Canada. But there were unexpected problems. Instead of our seventy-three wagons and Red River carts neatly stored in boxcars, they had been dismantled into thousands of pieces stored throughout the train. We systematically dug them out until wagon parts were spread along the railway tracks and adjacent vacant land and it appeared an impossible task to assemble them.

But French was undaunted. Ever the consummate organizer, he put together a schedule of rotating four-hours shifts of men assembling parts into wagons.

The locals were gathered in raucous groups to watch the performance. "I heard this is the brand new Canadian po-lice force," somebody in the crowd drawled out in a loud voice.

"That what this is?" somebody else responded. "I thought the goddam circus had come to town." The locals roared with mirth, milled, watched, and continued to have sport with the boys in red.

It was too much for the former militia men standing closest to the crowd. Marks lead the way, a wrench in hand, bounding toward the offenders.

"Halt there!" Steele hollered out a command. He stepped in front of the militia men. "Back to work. This is not our country, boys, and these men have the right to say whatever they like on their own soil. We will get on with the business at hand."

"What the hell was that," I asked Stephen.

"Steele just prevented an international incident," he chuckled. "But this could still get ugly."

Stephen was the first to figure out a lot of things. What he hadn't read about, he could connect the dots with an intellect as keen as any I knew. He continued to study the groups for a long time, still grinning. The bystanders were becoming more vocal with their insults to the men in red. Most hecklers had closed in beside a group of the militia boys and were getting increasingly charged up by the Canadian reactions to their chirping.

Marks and company seemed to be tying themselves into knots, one minute trying to stare down the rancorous crowd and the next trying to fit pieces of wagons together. Stephen and I were further away from the heckling crowd and like most of the police force, we were scratching our heads with the wagon dilemma: trying to figure out the huge mechanical puzzle before us.

Stephen turned back to me. "I can see why they think this is funny," he grinned.

"How so?" I asked. "Nothing better to do on a hot day?"

"For two countries from the same roots, living side by side, we couldn't be more different. So, I guess we humor them."

"Well, I find this bunch annoying," I said. "You'd think their own police would be down here by now to break this up."

"Oh, they don't have a police force. Especially not the kind they see here: dandies in red jackets doing a giant mechanical puzzle," he laughed.

"What the hell. No law in Fargo?" I asked, "a pretty big town for no law."

Stephen looked over the gathering crowd of curiosity seekers and hecklers. He grinned. "A lot of towns down here don't like lawmen and I guess that includes Canadian lawmen. Laws here are a lot different. A man with a gun threatens you, you can kill him and it's self defense. In Canada, you need a lot better reason than that to kill a man."

Stephen and I turned our attention to sizing up parts and fitting them together. We ignored the hecklers as best we could and kept our own conversation going.

"I read their billboards inside the station," said Stephen, as he hauled an axle from the pile and set it down in front of us. "Poster said: 'Fill a vacancy, run for sheriff.' The towns people elect their own. Apparently, two men are running right now, *Haggart* and *Pashley,* and their pictures are plastered all over. But there's no election until April. So, that means there's no law in Fargo."

Stephen rolled a pair of high wooden wheels out of the mess and laid them down by the axle. "Whoever wins sheriff gets to appoint local tough guys for deputies," he continued, "somebody handy with a gun, and they dress like civilians. Not like us. And they keep their jail houses full."

We kept our heads down fitting parts together. The thing before us was starting to resemble a Red River cart, all wooden parts, no steel, held together with greased down leather strips.

"They have a horse cavalry," Stephen continued, "but they're more army than police and bent on beating hell out of the Indians."

Slowly the cart was coming together. An odd-looking piece of machinery to say the least.

"They're blue coats," Stephen said, "so we're red coats. And we're just that different."

Stephen stood up to stretch the kinks out of his back and look over our project. He began again, "like French says, our job is to apply the law equally whether white or Indian. But that's going to be a tough sell down here. Indians are used to cavalry men on horseback charging into their camps with guns blazing and everybody goes down. Pretty different concepts when you think about it."

The crowds broke up for a while, then came back with fresh tobacco in their pipes and a few more bottles of grog to pass around. They came for a little more sport. Harassing the Canadian lawmen was apparently beyond temptation.

But the budding Canadian police came through. We ignored the hecklers and eventually most of them started to get bored. With the organizational talents of French, a few evolving from the ranks, like Stephen, with exceptional mechanical acumen, and a contingent of quick, hard-working men, we accomplished what we started. By nightfall rows of brand-new carts and wagons stood on grounds that had been covered under a half mile of parts.

We stood back and admired our handiwork. But the next day we discovered that our troubles weren't over and the circus we put on for the locals had barely began. Most of our horses were handsome thoroughbreds, fast, with considerable long-running endurance but they were not naturally bred to be harnessed.

A few were harness broke but most were not; and once hooked up to carts or wagons a stampede was underway. Wild-eyed thoroughbreds with carts and buggies hooked behind their fetlocks turned the prairie town of Fargo into a rodeo ground with hooves kicking, dust flying, cart wheels squealing and spooked horses racing in all directions with drivers hanging on and their pillbox hats flying. It was a second round of roars and hilarity from the locals.

At Steele's command, Stephen, myself and several others raced off across the prairie on our mounts to intercept the run-away horses; we managed to catch hold of their reins or halters, subdued their charges and eventually brought them back into Fargo.

Finally, the dilemma was resolved by Steele; many of the horses would require a rider to take charge of the reins until the animals, somewhere in the hinterlands of Canada, became properly adjusted to pulling a wagon or cart. Stephen and I were appointed such duties, riding on the backs of harnessed thoroughbreds immediately behind French and Jarvis. All together, we were a convoy of carts, wagons, two mounted guns, oxen, horses, mules and men, a line that stretched for over a mile. A novice Northwest Mounted Police force headed out of Fargo, North Dakota to bring the law to a vast Canadian Northwest.

***

It was a three-day trek across North Dakota. Commissioner French and Inspector Jarvis led the way with French holding his sword high in the air shouting commands to march or halt as he saw fit. Next in the convoy were the constables of all divisions. At the end were the Metis who were hired independently to drive the wagons and Red River carts filled with supplies and drawn by oxen. They were not under the same disciplined command as the police and appeared to be a constant annoyance to Jarvis. They were paid a wage and often arrived late at camp and were not overly anxious to respond to Jarvis commands or be particularly amenable to officer orders and instruction. Frankly, I rather admired their pluck. The oxen were an unruly bunch, frequently defying the drivers and moving off the convoy route to stop and forage. The Metis drivers had their hands full.

The convoy paralleled a small river for several miles while a prairie fire raged on the other side leaving a blackened stretch of ground with a long ribbon of dancing flames carried by the wind and strung out across the prairie far into the distance. By the second day we realized that many of our troubles had just began.

The hearty mustangs were managing well, foraging on the short brown prairie grass. But plans for our thoroughbreds to forage on local vegetation were sheer folly. The animals were bred and raised on oats and alfalfa but unable to thrive on the dry prairie grass. They were slowly starving to death. The journey was likewise creating a morale problem with the men; there was a serious lack of fresh meat and each day was a diet of hardtack, tea and rationed cans of sardines.

Such a massive endeavor to move men, horses and equipment across the Canadian northwest had never been tried before. The expectation was that game would be plentiful on the frontier, supplying the ranks with fresh meat. Such was not the case. Buffalo were found in countless numbers but they moved in unison lost in the vastness of the prairie and we encountered none. Antelope were flighty and often gone before a shot could be fired.

Included in the list of intangibles were the skills of our guides. Most of them seemed to have little knowledge of the terrain. Obviously, they needed the money when they hired on and probably were very reckless describing their familiarity with the plains, water sources, or their experiences as guides. I listened to their stories at night and many of them were affable and friendly men but they were also able to fabricate fascinating stories which I often doubted had much relationship to the truth.

The second night the guides brought us to camp on a windy side hill with barely a pond of water for our needs or the needs of our horses.

Steel lost his temper. "You men are paid to guide this convoy," he bellowed. "This puddle of water is supposed to water our animals and provide camp for over a hundred men?" He ordered them to scout the terrain ahead and not to come back until they found water and a suitable place to camp.

It was well after dark before they returned and led us to a place beside a shallow lake of saline water. But it was the best they could come up with and the next morning we found our first casualties: six of our best thoroughbreds had died, likely a combination of starvation and bad water.

By noon the following day we encountered fresh mounds of the survey commission, marking out the south boundary of our dominion. We followed the line until we encountered a survey crew. The first man we met was standing beside a tripod with a mounted transit level. Jarvis asked him who was in charge and was directed to speak with a Mr. Dawson about a mile further along the line.

As we progressed into the wind I began to sense a most profoundly disagreeable odor that intensified in waves as we travelled west past the survey monuments; it was the smell of death and decay. We sighted a group of men in the distance and rode up to them. A large man in a checkered woolen shirt came over to us and identified himself as Dawson. "This is what scares the hell out of all of us," he said, pointing before him to the scene of a battle.

"This wasn't long ago either," he said, "and right on the boundary line. We're looking at over twenty dead warriors of the Crow tribe. They're riddled with bullets, most have been scalped and mutilated."

It was the most gruesome scene I had ever witnessed. Bloated bodies were decaying in the hot sun, decomposing with skin stretched across their faces and their clothing in tatters. The stench of rotting flesh was overwhelming. Our bugler was the first to get off his mount and retch his guts out while trying to conceal himself behind his horse. Maybe it was a combination of bad food and the reek of decay that set him off but he was not the only one. Gags and purging of vomit was heard further down the convoy.

"You're in Sioux country," said Dawson, holding a scarf across his nose. "We've heard about massacres like this one but this is the first we've seen." He pointed down to a portion of a bright colored sash around his waist. That's why we wear these," he said, "and ribbons on our equipment. The Sioux have agreed to leave us alone to survey the line as long as we display these colors.

"None of the men on our commission are carrying guns, just survey equipment and shovels. So far, we've had no trouble." Dawson said. He turned to peer behind him across the prairie and back to Jarvis. "And they have been watching us too, almost every day. We see them along the hilltops and we're pretty vulnerable."

Dawson looked down our long contingent of constables, horses and equipment lined up for over a mile and shook his head. "I don't know what they will do with a cavalry of police carrying guns. My concern, they might not be as hospitable."

"We sent a respected priest ahead, Father John MacDougall," said Jarvis, "to advise the northern Cree and Blackfoot tribes we were coming through to bring the law. We hope the good father didn't suffer this same fate, that would be bad news for all of us," he added.

The entire convoy filed past the surveyors of the boundary commission and through the middle of the grisly battle scene and decaying corpses of scores of Crow warriors. It was the first hard evidence of what the police force might have in store and the topic of much conversation as we headed north across a desolate prairie. Stephen spent much time with a farm boy recruit, Freddy Baker, and it became apparent that they had an abundant stash that provided them with courage to continue the march, and which they seemed able to hide from the officers. They offered to share with me but I had no particular interest.

Over the next couple of days, I became acquainted with Henri Julien, a sketch artist among the Metis whose work I found quite fascinating. Through him I met a number of the Metis whom I started to enjoy immensely. They invited me to their fire at night in spite of being quite an independent bunch. After supper they sat together smoking their clay pipes, storytelling and singing. I found them open and friendly and enjoyed their stories. I occasionally sang along with them when I recognized the words of the song. They laughed with me at my efforts to master the lyrics and I was quickly accepted into their circle.

A Metis named Pierre was part Cree and very proud of his ancestry. One evening he told me a story over hardtack and sardines:

"In the early days the Cree were at war with the Mandan tribe of Missouri," he began. "One day a Cree warrior spotted a Mandan in a lookout on Butte Marquee. The warrior snuck up on him and killed him."

Pierre let a couple sardines slip down his throat and started again," The Cree warrior carved out the outline of the Mandan in the dry clay all around the dead body. Then he carved out his footsteps up the butte. Huge footsteps. The Mandan was a giant."

"A giant, Pierre?" I asked. "What do you call a giant?"

"Well," he said, crunching down a mouthful of hardtack and taking a swill of brackish water, "we passed Butte Marquee just a short walk from here. It is still day light. I'll show you."

Four other Metis came with us. Sure enough, an outline of rock partially buried, outlined the body of a huge warrior, maybe ten feet tall. "And besides," Pierre said, "here are his tracks." He showed us the rocky outline of giant footsteps up the Butte. Then he pointed to the ground all around the body. "And the huge puddle of blood from the giant is still here after all these years."

I examined the large red pool around the outline of the Mandan. "This is just red lichen growth," I pointed out.

"Unhuh!" Pierre responded. "White men never see the work of the great *Kisemanito* even when I show it to them."

I decided that the truth came in an assortment of forms and colors, especially in the creative minds of the Metis.

The following morning Pierre was late getting started and away behind the convoy. The ox pulling his cart was not so fondly referred to as *Shit-For-Brains* by the Metis drivers. The ox had his own mind and wandered away from the convoy in spite of all the lashing, poking and shouts of *gee* or *haw* from Pierre. The ox stopped wherever he wanted to and consumed the grass in spite of Pierre's sharp demands and pokes with a long stick.

I broke rank and rode over to the ox and dragged him back in line with my mount. Jarvis came storming back to chastise Pierre for being an inept driver and he berated me for leaving rank.

I was at the end of my rope after all the lost wanderings, the sardines, hardtack and poor camping sites.

"Maybe you should try driving this ox and let Pierre ride in front waving his sword around and getting us all lost on the prairie and taking us to camps with no water, like you."

I knew I should have kept my mouth shut but I was angry and never cared much for being berated in front of anyone.

Jarvis came down off his horse and ordered me to dismount and stood face to face with me. "I do not tolerate insubordination from my constables and you will do your time in the guard house," he bellowed.

"Might be a challenge to put together an adobe out here on the prairie," I answered with a smirk.

"You're the new driver of this ox team," he said. He turned to Pierre. "You will take up the back of the line on this mount until I order different."

"The men are out of meat," I said. "The best use of this ox would be in the larder."

He commanded me to take over the cart. I took the reins, bull whip, poke stick and commenced the *gee* and *haw* commands to *Shit-For-Brains*.

A full afternoon of listening to the squealing wheels of the Red River cart and poking an ox in the ass with a stick came to an end when Fort Dufferin came into view, a line of gray buildings behind a low fortress wall on the opposite bank of the Red River.

French followed a beaten trail down to a crossing below the fortress. We stopped on the edge of the river allowing our badly emaciated animals an opportunity to drink.

Then we waded across belly deep with water flowing over the floor boards of my cart. The oxen moved through river reeds and mud on the opposite shore for my first real look at Dufferin.

This was the meeting place of the entire force, with over a hundred men, equipment and horses having just arrived from Upper Fort Garry. They constituted divisions A, B and C. The Dominion Northwest Mounted Police Force was now complete and assembled.

Dufferin was no metropolis. Mud and a row of unpainted buildings provided a rather untidy and bleak setting. The fort was already the main accommodation for two hundred boundary commission surveyors and helpers. Their winter accommodations included a two-story frame building for officers, three one story buildings for general accommodations, a lengthy stable, store house, cook house, bakery and work-shops. There was a large government warehouse, a Hudson's Bay Company store and two whisky saloons. A few slab-sided shanties scattered past the main buildings inhabited by a few locals, mainly Metis.

We pulled onto an expansive field in front of the fortress and Stephen rode past me, his eyes shining at the sight of the saloons. But there was work to be done.

We pulled our wagons and carts into a circle to contain the animals. The existing corrals were full with horses from the Upper Fort Garry divisions. We set up troughs for our horses and provided what oats we had. The survey commission had a small amount of excess feed which Steele quickly purchased. He had expected more. Dufferin was a supply post and not well prepared for the arrival of so many police, animals and equipment.

We erected our tents, set up our bedding and the rest of the evening was our own. I went with Stephen for a drink which included Freddy Baker whom he had befriended and seemed to have an affinity for alcohol similar to Stephen. I had not formally met Freddy and Stephen introduced him to me and we shook hands.

Freddy grinned, "Stephen and I met on the Grand Drunk Railroad." He and Stephen laughed together, slapped backs and downed a glass of whisky from a bottle set before them. They poured another.

Stephen took a swill from his glass. "Here's to our mission," he said, holding up his glass, "to interrupt the flow of whisky into the dominion and dry up the supply." They both roared with laughter.

"Wolves commissioned to guard the hen house," responded Freddy and they poured another drink.

I couldn't get into the mood. I left to walk around the fortress grounds and I passed Spider Marks and Tom Leslie headed for the saloon. "Enjoying the smell of ox shit back there, McGinn?" He and Leslie howled with mirth and moved on. I couldn't come up with an answer and kept walking.

Steele and Jarvis sat on chairs in front of their tent going over maps. It was pretty apparent they had lost trust in our guides to find the way. I walked past the circle of wagons and our horses, all in pretty grim condition with ribs and hip bones extended. The shaggy coats of the mustangs were falling out in chunks but they had more meat on their bones than the thoroughbreds. I nodded a greeting to Richard Nevitt, the assistant surgeon, who was also out for a walk and was checking over the horses.

I continued down to the river, cupped my hands, filled them with water and splashed the cool liquid over my tired face. I sat on the edge of the bank and watched the current flow by. How quickly life had changed from the joys of Trinity College. I thought about Trelawney and wondered if there was an investigation.

I ignored the shouting, cheering and bravado from the saloon until a policeman, a former farm boy, Willie Savine, came over to me.

"I think your side kick, Stephen, has gotten himself in a mess of trouble in the saloon and could use some help," he said and walked away.

CHAPTER 6

I walked back to the whisky saloon. The place was crowded and in an uproar. Something was going on with Stephen and Freddy. I pushed in as close as I could get until a group of former militia men formed a half-circle shoulder to shoulder near the bar, holding every one back.

"That what they teach you in college, boy? To march drunk and make a disgrace of the force?" Spider Marks was taunting Stephen then began slapping him back and forth across his face as Stephen attempted to push him away. Marks kept at him until Stephen swung, missed, and Marks pulled him down on his knees to the floor.

Stephen was no fighter and very drunk. He tried to pull himself up on Marks' trousers while Spider cut loose with both fists on the sides and back of Stephen's head until he collapsed on the floor. I tried to get through to help him but the militia men held me back and Marks eventually let him go. Freddy Baker was flat on the floor, blood streaming from his nose and mouth with Tom Leslie still wailing on him, pounding him senseless without letting up until his own militia friends had to pull him off.

Finally, I got through to Stephen. He was out cold and needed a doctor. I called for someone to get Nevitt, the police physician whom I saw walking near the horses.

Nevitt examined both Freddy and Stephen. Freddy had gotten back on his feet gripping the edge of a table and looking around with a blank stare, like he was still out cold on his feet. Stephen remained unconscious on the floor. The young assistant surgeon collected cold compresses from saloon staff, held them on Stephen's head and face until he finally came around.

"I think he will be okay," Nevitt told me, "he'll probably have a very bad headache for a few days and he needs to continue with cold rags on his head to keep the swelling down." Then he went over to check on Freddy.

The saloon quickly cleared out with much of the crowd going back to their tent or to the other saloon which was already spilling over with patrons. I helped Stephen back to our tent and onto his bunk.

No one spoke of the incident and we didn't hear from any of the officers. Fortunately for Stephen, during the night a thunderstorm came up that scared the hell out of our horses. Many of them jumped through the circle of wagons and scattered across the plains. It took two extra days to round them up while Stephen discreetly recovered in the tent until he was able to get up and walk around, but badly bruised. With the mingling of the left and right wings of the force and many new faces, nobody noticed that Stephen stayed in the tent.

Then there was a further delay as we waited for supplies that were supposed to have arrived at Dufferin including flour for us and oats for the horses. The carts arrived the next day. A ton of flour had gotten wet and spoiled during the long haul. Much of the preserving brine in several barrels of pork had leaked out and the meat became rancid. Oats for the horses was far less than expected.

The next morning Jarvis seemed in a particular hurry to move the men out. No more supplies were forth coming and the saloons and nearby shanties had several women willing to take money, and the men were more than willing to shell it out to them. Jarvis prompted us to prepare to move out.

There had been much talk about the gruesome massacre we had encountered on the boundary line. Many feared we would be next. Our numbers were small compared to thousands of plains warriors. The terror of marauding Sioux had a sobering effect on the second wave of police who had crossed over the remains of the mutilated Crow warriors.

Before leaving Dufferin, French again spoke to the assembled troops. "Many of you have witnessed the kind of trouble that we could encounter in our duties as police officers of the Dominion. And there will be much hardship ahead. This is a final opportunity for any with second thoughts about the job before us to turn back with no questions asked. This is not a mission for the faint hearted and I welcome only those who intend to endure," French said.

A few hours later two dozen men had cleared out. The news rippled through the ranks like a cold wind. I picked up on some of the contemptuous mutterings like, "shameful," "cowards" and "I knew they'd cut and run." I had a hunch those with the most to say would rather disappear themselves than stay. I feared for Stephen but when I worked beside him to take down camp the glass flasks were tinkling in his pockets. As long as Stephen had the solace of whisky I knew he would continue. Jarvis gave back my mount and Pierre was given charge of *Shit-For-Brains.*

The combined force of 275 officers and men, along with horses, wagons, equipment and ox drawn carts prepared to move out of Fort Dufferin on July 8. At bugle call, we assembled into our divisions in full uniform of scarlet tunics and riding breeches.

With the shrill orders of French and the cracking of bull whips, the Northwest Mounted Police began their westward movement in a convoy that now stretched over two miles. Stephen and I continued our assignment behind Jarvis and French.

We moved across a seemingly endless prairie under a hot July sun. Miles from Dufferin, we caught our first glimpse of the Sioux. For a few miles, they paralleled our journey keeping to higher land. Jarvis halted the contingent and passed the word along the line to be prepared for attack but meanwhile we were to keep our carbines out of sight and offer no outward threat.

I was fascinated and could not keep my eyes off them. They alternated between stationary, watchful observation of us, then individual warriors would race their spirited ponies across the plains keeping us in sight. They rode erect and proud, holding their spears high above them with colored eagle feathers catching the wind. But they stayed just out of rifle range and none came close enough to threaten us. Nevertheless, we remained vigilant until they disappeared out of sight into a shallow creek bed on the prairie.

The first night out our guides led us to one of the best camps I had seen since leaving Fargo. We were able to water our horses and indulge ourselves in a clean, running stream fringed with trees that seemed to keep the water cool. Grass along the stream was greener and offered a reprieve for our mounts from the dry brown prairie grass we had traversed throughout the day.

We kept up a two-hour guard rotation throughout the night. My turn came at two o'clock in the morning. A Mountie I didn't know nudged me awake for my shift. The fires had burnt down leaving long glowing circles of embers between the outline of white canvas tents where there were only the sounds of officers sleeping.

I took my carbine and walked far away from the encampment through the fringe of trees until I sat on the edge of open prairie. A full moon sat high above a bleached-white plain and a billion stars in the Milky Way stretched across the sky above me. The prairie was silent with an occasional puff of wind that stirred the grass and then dissipated into silence. I watched the horizon for the silhouette of Sioux warriors that might approach our camp.

Then I realized that scalp hunters stalking our encampment were more likely to move in single file hidden below the embankment of the stream bed. I turned my back on the prairie to watch through the fringe of trees.

A magnificent stag appeared below me, his slender form moving proudly through the cottonwoods. I raised my carbine and took a bead on him, then hesitated. The force was in desperate need of fresh meat to sustain our numbers. But the instruction from French was unequivocal: a shot from the sentry was a signal for every man to come forth prepared to engage an attack by the Sioux. Did I want hundreds of men charging forth with arms? I hesitated too long. The stag had dropped into the stream bed and out of my sight. My shift was up and I returned to my tent for a few hours of sleep.

We travelled all the next day through a prairie that became slightly undulating with grassy hills like waves on an open sea. We saw no more sign of the Sioux but I had a feeling we were not out of their sight. That evening the guides led us far into the night without sign of any water for encampment. Finally, we came across a shallow lake. The water was of questionable quality but our horses were weary and unable to continue, walking with heads down and stumbling. We stopped. We had to use the water sparingly. By morning five more thoroughbreds had died.

The extra scanty feed we had acquired for the horses at Dufferin was slowly being used up. There was much complaining among men and officers alike. We were pulling two mounted guns that took the extra resources of four horses that could have pulled a full wagon of feed for the animals and extra staples for the men. Dufferin was a supply center that drastically underestimated our needs. Jarvis was not in a good mood and neither was I. Many constables including myself had lost all appetite for the hardtack and sardines.

Back along the trail, *Shit-For Brains* had wandered off the convoy despite the desperate *gees* and *haws*, howls, pokes and whipping from Pierre. Far out on the prairie, the ox began grazing oblivious to the animated prodding of Pierre. I rode back to him, dismounted, extracted my service revolver and shot *Shit-For-brains* between the eyes. He splayed out across the ground, harness and all.

At the discharge of my firearm, the entire contingent turned to stare and Jarvis charged back down the convoy waving his hat and bellowing as he approached us. Before he could say anything further, I told him, "this ox has meat on his bones for the men. A ton of flour and supplies didn't show up so we don't need this useless ox pulling a cart."

Jarvis unloaded on me. "I make these decisions. You have a choice: walk with the convoy or make your way back to Dufferin on foot with a discharge." I chose to walk with the convoy.

Sam Steele joined the conference with Jarvis and urged him to have the cooks butcher and salvage the meat from *Shit-For-Brains*. The meat was given a day to cool off and a massive barbecue was enjoyed by all, but it was consumed in three days by the ravenous troops. Then we became a most degraded force again, still lacking fresh meat and the critical protein it could provide. Once again, we were sustaining on a diet of mostly hard tack and a few cans of rationed sardines.

Jarvis continued his malice towards me and I remained without a mount. Frequently, the Metis drivers offered me a ride on the back of their carts or wagons which I generally accepted and I alternated between riding and walking to relieve the weight on the oxen.

The next afternoon we crossed the Marias River which provided an intake of badly needed water but French kept our guides pressing onwards into the late evening for a place to camp. The guides were unable to find palatable water. French made the decision to return to the Marias. We followed the river for a short distance looking for a suitable place to set up when we ran into three canvas wagons of some previous traveller, ripped apart, looted and the remains of two horses, their carcasses partly butchered and left to rot on the ground. The perpetrators of the damage were not readily recognizable but prompted French to assign extra guard duty throughout the night.

I walked most of the following day as the rolling elevations of the Pembina mountains came into view and we were struck with clouds of mosquitoes. It was apparent that we were nearing water as mosquito larvae could not exist on the dried-out prairie. We passed a small pond of reeds and mud where a half-dozen ducks nested in the weeds. No order was given and it was purely an impulsive act by our young bugler, Fred Bagley who, followed by Stephen, Freddy Baker and four or five more farm boys, plunged into the pond with pounding sticks to bring down the ducks. They emerged grinning from the muck with a few mud hens.

Their actions were met with fury from Jarvis and a vicious reprimand for leaving their ranks and conduct unbecoming of the Northwest Mounted Police. I was expecting some company on the long walk but the men seemed to have been quickly forgiven.

Four mud hens were unlikely to make any difference to two hundred and seventy-five under-nourished men but such was our desperation for solid food and a reprieve from hardtack and tea. That night we arrived at a small, wooded lake at the foot of the Pembina mountains and a storm of mosquitoes. Smudges were lit and the camping area existed under a cloud of smoke but offered little reprieve from the blood sucking insects.

During camp preparations, I joked with Pierre about expecting watered down duck soup at the evening meal but no such thing was offered up and it was unknown what happened to the four ducks; however, the chuckwagon cooks seemed in a much better mood, joking and laughing as they went about their duties.

The next morning, we crossed the Pembina River and French struck a northwesterly direction back across a barren, dry prairie with barely a cloud in a stifling hot sky. French was leading the march when he suddenly raised his sword bringing the whole contingent to a stop. "I want the following four marksmen," he shouted out. "Marks, Leslie, Lynch and McGinn." The word was sent down for me to come forth with my carbine and participate. French pointed ahead. Two hundred yards distant was a group of three antelope visible in a notch of the prairie between two small rolling hills.

"We'll have one crack at this, men," he said, pointing his outstretched arm towards the game. He gave his instruction. "Fire only when I give the order." He commenced with the usual three-point instruction. "Get ready men, take aim, and fire."

A split second before the final instruction, Marks fired. He wanted the glory, but he missed. I knew after watching herds from the train what they would do. At the first sign of danger they bolted, then they leaped high in the air to see what was around.

I trained my firearm above the line of the hill until the head and neck of an antelope bounded into view and slowed at the apex of his jump. I squeezed off a shot and the animal crumbled in mid-air. I levered another cartridge into my carbine as a second animal emerged above the hill and I squeezed off a second round. We all knew I hit the mark.

"Utterly amazing!" French spouted. "I believe you potted them!" His eyes glowed. He waved the police convoy onward and I walked with them until we traversed the knoll.

Any remaining herd that might have accompanied the three antelope had disappeared into the prairie, with the exception of two dead animals on the ground.

"Take a man and collect your prizes, McGinn," French commanded with a wide grin as a cheer went up from the contingency of police, except the militia group. Stephen and I sprinted over. We hefted the animals across our shoulders, carried them back and dumped them into a wagon for cooking staff to eviscerate and prepare.

Marks and his cronies, Billy Lillico, Tom Leslie, Gerome Carlisle and Jake Lynch were behind the wagon when we came by. Spider's eyes were smouldering and his face was twisted into a fierce grimace.

"Got a sack of clovers up your Irish ass, McGinn?" he responded. "A thousand tries and you won't do that again."

"You think so Spider? Too bad you're only a marksman on paper," I chided. "Give you a live target and you choke. Oh," I added, "and you're a bit slow, Marks, better work on your fast draw." I laughed at him.

"I need this man mounted and up front here on the convoy," French told a disgruntled Jarvis. What I had lost with Jarvis I gained from French.

The militia boys continued their cold stares as I walked over and took the new horse assigned to me near the front of the line. I smirked at Marks as I took the reins of my mount. I remembered all too well Spider's needling when he won accolades at target competitions in training and his malicious attack on Stephen.

As I swung into the saddle I could not resist giving Jarvis a subtle, mock salute. I expected a storm of wrath from him but French bellowed out his command and the convoy moved forth. It felt good to be back in the saddle. I didn't miss walking in the clouds of dust or riding a cart behind the shit smeared flanks of an oxen.

An unrelenting wave of heat remained across the plains and the fresh meat of the antelope needed to cool before we could safely eat it. The horses were in worse shape than us, now receiving the smallest ration of oats and the dried-out grass that could not sustain them. Another animal collapsed on the trail and Jarvis needed to put the creature out of its misery.

One of the oxen was now down to skin and bones, diseased and too weak to pull a cart. The animal was unbound from its harness and released onto the prairie to survive or perish as it may. Unburdened from the load provided a chance for it to rest and pick through the grass for nourishment and seek its own water. The convoy could not wait.

The guides seemed to have little sense of where we were or where we might find water. We simply marched onwards. French was becoming more concerned for the survival of the horses and each rider was now required to walk a stretch equal to every stretch that we rode. Travel had slowed to mere plodding and it became a question of how long before the bones of a whole convoy might stretch across the plains. Every man became silent in his own plight and we pitched our tents with little conversation and slept.

By noon the following day we arrived at the Souris river. The river valley was below a steep embankment and we barely anticipated finding the watercourse until we were upon it. Below the banks a broad valley unfolded with a thick growth of cottonwoods and succulent grass between the trees. The river itself came into our view: a wide silver ribbon stretching far into the distance.

Our animals were barely surviving, but the smell of water and forage seemed to give them the strength they needed to navigate the precipitous banks to access the water. We allowed them to drink until they were done. Then we turned them loose to graze with no fear of them running off.

Finally, we cut loose with our own celebration. To a man, we stripped off and charged the river. There was howling, splashing, water fights and gulping down the cool liquid until our guts rolled. It was the reprieve that man and beast needed. That day we feasted on the fresh meat of the antelope. To add to our fortune, a boundary commission camp was located a few miles further on the plains. They had a small surplus of supplies and provided a few sacks of oats for our animals along with a ration for each man of bread, pork and real duck soup. It was the first relief for the men and horses since leaving Fort Dufferin.

After two days of rest at the Souris the force proceeded their march west. But even before the last bend of the river faded behind us we were reminded of the enormous challenges. We had barely proceeded a dozen miles when we encountered clouds of locusts that turned us and our mounts into marching silhouettes of green. We used what we could to keep the chitin covered bodies from pounding into our flesh, mostly handkerchiefs, high collars and pillbox hats that we fashioned over our faces and strapped behind our heads.

Worse than pounding our faces, the infestation was slowly destroying any forage left in the brown grass that previously allowed the animals a meager supplement to their dwindling, rationed oats.

The following day we camped at what our guides expected to be a spring, but it had dried out. We dug through the dry dirt until water began to seep into the hole. We baled for hours, providing what we could to our horses and a ration for each man. Far into the night, men took turns laying on the ground over the hole cupping water into their mouths. It was never enough and we remained without game or sufficient nourishment for man or beast.

Upon leaving camp four more of our horses had died. Two very sick mustangs and four additional oxen, all of them too sick or emaciated for our own larder, were turned loose. Boxes of civilian clothing and extra weight from pots, pans, utensils and cooking wear from the chuckwagons were cleaned out to lighten the burden on remaining oxen.

A days plodding brought us to a landmark that was well known throughout the west as a rendezvous point for plainsmen and indigenous people alike. La Roche Percée was a truly magnificent high outcropping of sandstone that rose in an arch, fifty feet above the flat prairie, with a wide yawning hole through the center. Trailing for a stretch of over one hundred fifty feet from the main arch were high columns of rocky outcrops of diminishing height.

As we approached the rock we realized that we were not alone. Two men of metis origin sat on their mounts in the shade of the rock, each holding the tether of a pack horse. The men were messengers from Fort Dufferin.

French spoke briefly with the two men who then led us to a camp location on a tributary of the Souris known as Short Creek, a few miles journey from the famous rock, where the water was fresh and sweet. We attended our animals as best we could, set up camp and accepted a ration of hardtack and tea. French, Jarvis, Steele and the two Metis messengers sat up and talked over firelight far into the night.

CHAPTER 7

Commissioner French was up before sunrise pacing in front of his tent. He had barely slept, feeling the weight of the mission on his shoulders, a mission that was drastically short of resources for accomplishing. He had stayed awake much of the night with Steele, Jarvis and the Metis messengers pondering all options until French made his decision.

He summoned sub-constable Fred Bagley for trumpet call to assemble the men along an open stretch of meadow beside Short Creek. A brisk breeze was blowing in from the west when French rode his mount slowly back and forth in front of the assembled constabulary and Metis.

"Men, we have a most challenging mission in bringing law to the Northwest. And we have not been given the resources necessary as all of you know by now. Messengers from Fort Dufferin have arrived with instructions directly from the Minister of the Interior in Ottawa. We have been informed of even greater burdens placed upon us. There is much trouble in Fort Edmonton which is under the jurisdiction of the new dominion and our responsibility." He stopped pacing his mount and looked across the four rows of constables standing at attention before him awaiting word of their fate.

"We have had to make difficult decisions," French continued. "And we will need to split the force and realign the divisions." French rode back down the row of men. "Twenty-two constables will be assigned to a new Division A, including a contingent of Metis drivers and guides. This group will take a bearing to the north in the hope of finding Fort Ellice and eventually intersecting the Carlton trail to Fort Edmonton. This Division will take many of the weaker animals as grazing is better north of the tree line."

Commissioner French looked out across the force of constables. Already the news appeared to be weighing on the faces of the men. There had been little to celebrate on the march west: poor luck in finding game to sustain them and little reprieve from the punishing challenges of a raw frontier. Would the force now become burdened beyond what the men could bear? With separation of divisions, morale could be compromised. He would ask Steele and Walsh to keep men with friendships together whenever it was possible to do so.

French started again. "The remaining troops will continue west through to Fort Whoop Up somewhere near the intersection of the Belly and Bow Rivers. Our latest intelligence is that the fort has been taken over by American whisky traders. We must gain back our control and bring the criminals to justice."

The commissioner knew he had to convince the men of the wisdom in his strategy if he was to maintain their loyalty and resolve. He settled down his fidgeting mount, rode into the center of the assembled men and commenced his instruction.

"Daunting as the new challenge appears, there will be advantages in splitting the force. These messengers sent to us are familiar with the west and have provided helpful advice. The feed we currently have for our horses might well sustain us on the western arm of the expedition. Established posts like Fort Benton on the Missouri will have supplies. Also, we are told that a Metis guide there, Jerry Potts, is well known to our survey commission. We expect he will help us locate Whoop Up somewhere on the Belly River. We are told he knows the practices and precise travel routes of the whisky traders. He is highly regarded as a skillful guide and once we are able to make contact, he will be invaluable to us moving forward."

French was quiet a long moment and guided his horse in front of the assembled men. "The Edmonton route will present dire challenges but there is more rainfall and the grass more palatable once we clear the locust infested dry lands of the plains. And there is ample game once we pass the tree line. Both commands will encounter difficult circumstances and the force must be prepared to improvise as we go along.

"Division A will proceed under the command of Inspector Jarvis and Major Sam Steele on the Fort Edmonton mission. Our best intelligence is that there is also an active whisky trade at the fort with smugglers coming in from the east along the Carlton Trial and a significant flow of traders from south of the border that are getting through. The remaining divisions will proceed under the direction of sub-inspector Walsh and myself to Fort Whoop Up.

"Now I will turn the matter over to Inspector Jarvis to brief all of you on the challenges we face at the northern fortress."

Jarvis came forth on his mount. "Men, news from Fort Edmonton is a long time in getting here, first being relayed east via the Carlton trail and then back to us by mounted messengers from Dufferin who arrived yesterday.

"But I want none of you harboring false notions that bringing law to the north will be any easier than elsewhere in the Dominion. In fact, I expect it to be more challenging in many ways. Fort Edmonton has for years brought diverse Indian tribes in for trade. And they are tribes with much historical trouble. Often the fort was a center for tribal dissention, warfare and murder. All this has now been brought to our attention."

Jarvis straightened his horse to face the assembled constabulary. "Historically, the Factor at Fort Edmonton has tried to keep the peace but with limited success. Warfare and murder in the area of the fort is a concern to the Canadian government and now the responsibility of the Northwest Mounted Police."

He walked his horse down the middle row to the center of the assembled men, placed his wrists across the horn of the saddle, cleared his throat and commenced talking.

In the last few years there are reports of open warfare between Stony and Cree on one side and Blackfoot on the other. Such battles have raged at the northern fortress for decades, maybe centuries. Recently, we have news of two Sarcee murdered by Cree warriors and the report of a mixed blood killing his wife, all within view of Christian women and children at the fort. This is the kind of trouble we can expect at the northern fort."

He reached the end of the row of constables, turned his mount and continued back through the line-up.

"Men, these lands were, until a few years ago, the domain of the Hudson's Bay Company but these crimes are now our responsibility. Our job is to render justice firmly and fairly to Indian and whites alike. But our first challenge will be carving our own way through vast wooded terrain and eventually to the Edmonton fortress."

CHAPTER 8

Jarvis assigned Stephen and I to Division A for the mission to Edmonton. I cared little about which contingency we would be assigned to but I was relieved that Stephen and I would remain together and ever more distant from Toronto and the trouble with Trelawney. I hoped to see the last of many of the militia men, especially Spider Marks but without luck. Marks, Leslie, Lynch, Carlisle and a few more were assigned to A Division along with Pierre, Julien and half the Metis workers. Freddy Baker was also part of the contingency which seemed to please Stephen.

Nor was I particularly pleased that French was leaving our contingency and Jarvis would be in charge; however, I had the greatest respect for Sam Steele whom all of us knew was not a man to mess with. But he was always fair to me and I could respect his leadership.

We spent a day organizing the new commands and allowing our animals to rest and replenish with clean water. Julien knew the Metis dispatchers from Fort Dufferin. After a hard day spent reorganizing the divisions, Julien turned to me. "The men that came yesterday are old friends of mine" he said. "I've invited them to join us. Come over later and I'll introduce you."

It was getting dark when I made my way over to the Metis camp. The two messengers were well settled and obviously supplied some of their own food rations to the group of

Metis. Julien was stirring a pot of beans over a fire and one of the dispatchers was passing out jerky.

"Leo and Tom," Julien said, "I want you to meet Constable James McGinn." I shook hands with each and I was immediately impressed with both of them: lithe, hardened men, probably in their late thirties and I expected that neither one weighed much more than a hundred and twenty pounds. I had no doubt they commanded the saddle and rode like the wind delivering messages to outposts across the frontier. And like most of the Metis, I found them to be likeable, talkative men.

"So, do you know which direction they are sending you, James?" Tom asked me once I settled down beside their fire and accepted a chunk of jerky.

"Fort Edmonton," I responded, after yanking off a bite, "and I really have little idea what to expect."

"Well, it will be a great adventure you can be sure of that," laughed Leo. "But there has been hell raging up there for a long time," he added with a more serious nod of his head, "and Jarvis didn't tell you the half of it." Leo stopped to take a chunk of meat out of his bag and Tom entered the conversation.

"Let me tell you what happened once, James, maybe three years ago by now," Tom said. "I had just arrived with a sack of mail from Fort Dufferin and was settling in at the fort, enjoying a cup of coffee on a bench outside the walls. Maybe fifty Blackfoot were camped on the river flats below me. It was a quiet morning, nothing unusual about the day at all."

Julien passed Tom a bowl of steaming beans that he set between his feet on the ground until he finished his story. "Then, from the south, the whole hilltop started moving."

A wild look came into Tom's eyes and he continued. "A hundred Stony and Cree stormed over the hilltop with the most blood curdling cries of war onto the unsuspecting Blackfoot. It even scared hell out of me and I ran inside the fort to watch from the tower.

"By now, I could barely see through the clouds of whirling dust and billows of burnt gunpowder from the rifles. A terrible battle was raging below me. Women were screaming and men shouting over the pop, pop, pop of gunfire. I could make out men, women and even children going down. Then the Cree and Stony began leaping off their horses with knives in hand going after scalps. They chased down whoever was still standing, brought them down and lifted their hair. Then they used their knives on the scalps of those already down. In minutes mutilated corpses were all over, some still jerking and convulsing in the throes of dying. Three women and a one child were also murdered.

"Seventeen unarmed Blackfoot had made a run for the fort and got inside. Six were massacred just below me. It was a blood bath! To this day when I lay back and close my eyes I hear the screaming and I see it all like it was yesterday."

Leo put away the sack of jerky that was being passed around. "Let me tell you what else happened at the Edmonton fort, that was more recent," Leo said. "Two Sarcee came in from their camp on the river a few miles out. They were interested in two Cree women camped near the fort and began hanging around. Some Cree men managed to get the Sarcee cross the river from the fort where they shot them both point blank, an execution."

Leo opened the jerky bag again, took a piece and passed the bag to me. "That was just the start of it," he said. "Traders went down the next day and buried the bodies, but they were dug up by the Cree, stripped and scalped. Two Cree women were forced to participate in a scalp dance with tom-toms pounding and long hair of the scalloped Sarcee still dripping blood. Someone I knew watched the whole thing. He said that's just their justice, both sides do it. It was brutal."

"Then, the most recent," Tom said. "just before we were sent here, another murder. A mixed blood, *Kisawasis,* killed his wife. She too was running for the fortress, screaming and begging for her life when he brought her down, ripped much of her clothes off and stabbed her over and over again, some say a hundred times. It happened just outside the walls of the fort with many witnesses. The last I heard he was on the run."

***

On July 29, Jarvis assembled the convoy, consulted the notoriously inaccurate Palliser map, took a compass bearing to the north and proceeded across a shallow ford on Short Creek. It was the beginning of our march to the Edmonton fort. By nightfall we were far out on the prairie and camped at a running stream that suited our purpose. We expected a few more days travel before encountering Fort Pitt with tree cover, more moisture, better grass and water from the North Saskatchewan River.

Jarvis remained vigilant; we were venturing into country inhabited by both Sioux warriors and the notoriously warlike northern Blackfoot confederacy. The two warring tribes were neither friendly with each other nor, we suspected, with white travellers.

Sentries were posted. Both Stephen and I had done our duty and were not selected; however, when morning came the last man on duty, Tom Leslie, was nowhere to be found. Sam Steele sent off the three-shot signal to bring in the lost man. Then he randomly assigned men in pairs to the four compass points in a search for Leslie. Freddy Baker and I happened to be standing together and he sent us south.

We moved away from the convoy on our mounts and travelled parallel to each other a quarter mile apart, keeping an eye to the horizon for silhouette of the missing constable, and also to the ground for horse tracks. A quarter mile out, Freddy signalled me. He had picked up tracks of a single mount moving southeast with the steel shoe imprints of the Northwest Mounted Police.

We followed the tracks and read the sign. About a mile out the rider had suddenly stopped, swung his mount around and moved back and forth as if undecided about something. Then he headed out at a canter. We followed until the horse tracks became superimposed on the tracks of a small herd of antelope.

Freddy grinned. "Leslie is hot on the game trail," he said, "and the glory of dropping a fresh supply of meat at Jarvis' feet."

"And leaving the rest of us sleeping at the mercy of scalp hunters," I smirked.

We followed the tracks far out onto the prairie, miles from camp; it was pretty obvious that Leslie could not resist the temptation of bagging fresh game. We stopped where the horse began throwing up clods of turf and obviously charging forth at breakneck speed. Leslie likely spotted the game and was anxious to fire off a volley of shots and drop a few animals before the flighty herd disappeared into the prairie. Except something had gone wrong.

In the distance were two dark shadows. When we got close it was obvious that the galloping horse had collapsed. We found no sign of injury and likely the beast had suffered a heart attack charging the antelope. A few yards distance was Tom Leslie, dead or unconscious. His legs splayed at a precarious angle and obviously he was busted up and quite possibly the horse had rolled across him.

It appeared he hadn't moved since the accident. I knew that Freddy, like me, had no love for Leslie since the fist fight in Dufferin.

"He isn't going to last long out here," I said. "If the fall didn't kill him, the rotting flesh of a dead horse will bring in wolves to finish him off. Looks like a good place to leave him."

Freddy felt across the body of Tom Leslie, rolled him over, listened for breathing and took a pulse. "Even Tom Leslie doesn't deserve to die out here."

"What you want to do with him?" I asked.

"He's still alive. I think his legs are broken." Freddy hauled him up and threw him across his saddle, strapping him down with rope. Freddy walked the several miles back to camp leading his horse with Leslie beginning to moan like a baby across the saddle. I could easily have left him, a feast for the wolves.

We intercepted the convoy and Leslie was placed in a wagon and attended to by Kitson, the police surgeon. Tom had several broken bones, but he was expected to pull through.

Jarvis questioned the now conscious Tom Leslie who said the camp was already awake and stirring when he decided to pursue the antelope to acquire fresh meat. He believed his guard duty was over. Jarvis was not happy, but Leslie was in bad shape and left in the wagon to recover. Jarvis and Steele studied over the Palliser map and eventually took a compass bearing to the northeast until we intersected the Assiniboine River.

Jarvis followed the southern ridge of the river valley heading northwest until we sighted Fort Ellice on the north side. The fort stood on a high plateau overlooking the Assiniboine River. The river valley was more than a mile wide and we descended to the bottom and followed beside the current until we encountered a crossing shallow enough to ford the watercourse. The valley was a mosaic of grassy meadows interspersed with stretches of aspen and poplar bluffs. The landscape was changing. We followed a crisscrossing trail that climbed higher until we encountered the fort.

Fort Ellice was an older Hudson's Bay fortress with a high log palisade enclosing numerous log dwellings including a few stores. Stephen looked pleased. No doubt there was liquor to be purchased somewhere at the scattering of buildings outside the fortress walls.

As we approached, the main gates were opened to us and a gracious Chief Factor, Archie MacDonald, came out to greet us. The officers were invited inside to be assigned rooms and the rest of us were directed to a grassy area just outside the palisade walls to erect our tents overlooking the grand Assiniboine River valley. We prepared camp in the usual way, except that Fort Ellice was able to supply some provisions to our chuckwagons. The fresh vegetables and a quantity of buffalo meat would be quite tasty and most welcomed.

Since rescuing Tom Leslie, Freddy had become a hit with Marks, Lynch, Lillico, Carlisle and some of the former militia men who seemed to show their gratitude for rescuing Leslie;

or maybe they just wanted his version of events. Freddy was invited to sit with them around their fire. They no doubt had a bottle of liquor they discreetly fed to Freddy and started a game of cards. But I didn't see much change in their attitude towards me and that was mutual. I doubt if Freddy intentionally wanted to make trouble for me as I don't believe that was in his nature. However, what was in Freddy's nature was that his lips flapped more and more indiscreetly as he continued to drink and the militia men seemed to have a ready supply for Freddy.

Stephen and I sat with Pierre and Julien and a few of the Metis around their fire, listening to their stories and occasionally joining in to their songs when we recognized the lyrics. I caught occasional side long glares from the former militia men as Freddy continued his incessant chatter. It was pretty apparent to me that he was having a great time and spilling his guts in the process. I had no doubt that Freddy was expounding on how he alone had rescued Tom Leslie; that I had wanted to leave Leslie out on the prairie for the wolves, but Freddy brought him in alive.

Marks and Lynch occasionally talked discreetly with each other, glancing at me while Freddy was chattering to the rest of the group. Finally, Jake Lynch came over.

"Would you like to join Freddy and the rest of us in our tent for a friendly game of cards, James?" He ignored Stephen, Pierre and Julien. Something about his invitation didn't seem all that friendly.

"No thanks," I responded. "Quite enjoying my own company," I knew my tone was as cold as his. I had no idea what they were up to but I had a hunch that a friendly game of Black Jack was not foremost on their minds.

Lynch walked back, drew a long draft from a flask and stared back at me with something in his eyes that alternated between humor and hatred. I didn't know what they had in mind but I was a lot bigger than Stephen whom Marks decided to pound senseless and I wasn't prepared to be bullied. Eventually, Freddy's chatter slowed down and everyone wandered back to their own tents. There was no congregation in any tent for a 'friendly game' that I could see.

We spent three days at Fort Ellice to allow our horses to gain some strength with good grazing on the meadows and clean water from the Assiniboine. On the third morning, we moved out with additional supplies for our horses, and pemmican to last a few days but Ellice could not part with enough provisions to last us any length of time and we were still reliant on finding game for our own sustenance.

To our good fortune, Fort Ellice was located on the old Carlton trial, a supply route for Red River carts from Fort Gary that would eventually reach Fort Edmonton. We picked up on the trail just north of the fort and followed it across a landscape more and more punctuated with groves of aspen and cottonwood trees along the shallow streams.

By the time we crossed the South Saskatchewan river we were again critically low on supplies for the men. As the trail continued north the landscape constantly changed, with thick wooded areas now and increasingly numerous bogs and shallow, mosquito infested sloughs.

It had been a summer with much rainfall in the north and our progress was once again slow and treacherous. We had to rip-rap with wood and brush to get through the sloughs. Frequently we had to clear new trails to accommodate our large wagons. By the third day, the strenuous work was telling on the men and we were out of any decent food supplies to sustain us. The wooded terrain was now frequented with sign of moose, caribou and elk. Clearly, we were moving into big game country.

At bugle call Jarvis addressed the men. "We are perilously low on supplies," he began, "and much of our equipment, especially the Red River carts, are in bad repair. Today we will retain this camp and attend to repairing equipment and hunt for fresh game. Major Steele will organize the hunt."

Steele sent his top marksmen to do the hunting. He chose four of us and directed us to spread out in different directions: the four points of the compass. I was sent north and Marks west. Two other former militia men, Darren Wells and Ervin Milner were sent south and east.

I wished to avoid Marks as I had no doubts concerning his hatred for me and any fate the militia men may have concocted over their campfires at night. I didn't care to encounter Marks in the wilderness with no one else around and both of us carrying carbines, revolvers and live ammunition. Spider looked over at me with a hard stare that turned slowly into a grin. I didn't trust him. I was hunting but had a niggling fear that I might become the hunted.

At first, I was vigilant and kept a close watch behind me for Marks, but I saw nothing of him and hoped that he stayed, as he was directed, to hunt west of our camp. Thoughts of bagging fresh game became a tantalizing idea and a pleasant alternative to the hardtack and the small quantity of pemmican from Fort Ellice that had kept us going. I re-focussed on the moose hunt. I had hunted moose in Ontario with some luck and I knew the large ungulate's habits quite well. They prefer to browse among the sparse stands of poplar or willow swales where they feed on the tender ends of the lower branches.

Occasionally, especially in summer, they move into low lying marsh areas where they have a particular affinity for the succulent stems of aquatic plants. Now and then they go into spruce cover, mostly for protection where they seem to know their dark coats camouflage well under the dark boughs.

The terrain I found myself in was light aspen poplar, a good place to run into moose. This time of day they are typically in their beds, laying where they are least likely disturbed, often a creek bed with willow or poplar stands nearby for evening and night time browsing. I came onto a shallow creek valley with a small stream still flowing and I followed it. I encountered fresh beds where a cow and yearling calf moose had been lying together beside the stream compressing the grass beneath them.

Their scat was still warm. Something had disturbed them. They could not be far away. Their tracks in the soft dirt of the stream bed indicated they were moving north. The breeze was from the northwest, so they were unlikely to capture my scent as I set forth to follow them. Then I found another track: the fresh imprint of heal marks in the soft mud of the streambed.

Suddenly I had an eerie feeling of being watched. I had to make a decision: follow a fresh game trail or leave and return to camp in order to avoid Marks. By now I was several miles from the camp and it was only mid-afternoon. I decided to pursue the game but I ensured my carbine was loaded and my safety latch off.

I followed the edge of the stream valley and kept a bearing to the north, the direction the moose were moving.

I occasionally found their tracks in soft dirt, still moving into the wind. There were tufts of waxy moose hair caught on low branches and I suspected I was on the right track to encounter them. I reached the top of the stream valley where I came face to face with Marks.

"Well, college boy," he exclaimed, "fancy meeting you way out here in the middle of nowhere out of earshot for any friendly fire, or even not so friendly fire," he said, laughing.

His left hand held the breech of his rifle, the stock already hefted to his shoulder and his right finger stuck through the trigger guard.

"I thought Steele assigned you to hunt west of camp." I said. I elevated the barrel of my carbine towards him but he had me covered and I knew the instant I raised the stock of my rifle towards my shoulder to aim he would shoot me.

"I guess we just happen to come upon the same tracks of the same critter," he laughed. "What a coincidence."

"You been sneaking along behind me all this way, Marks? Like some mangy cur? Guess you knew you couldn't find game on your own."

"Now college boy, you're just way to full of yourself," he smirked. "How else were we going to have a hunting accident without both of us trying to bring down the same animal, you know, like what Tom was doing when he got all busted up trying to bring fresh meat back to camp." Marks was moving slowly toward me, his stare fixed on me and his rifle barrel inching gradually higher.

"I heard you wanted to leave Tom on the prairie all busted up like that for the wolves to finish him."

Marks was crouching now, moving his torso ever so slightly side to side, trying to make a more elusive target for me, fixing his hard stare on me, his carbine now well settled against his shoulder. "How ironic, Tom recovering, and you the one left to feed the wolves."

At least I had taken the safety latch off my rifle and I wasn't going down without a parting shot.

"Well, one thing I know about both you and Leslie: neither one of you can hit shit!"

His eyes flashed contempt. "We'll see," he said, as he suddenly swung the barrel up for a bead on me and I knew his incredible marksmanship. I took the only option I had time for; I crouched and moved quickly sideways discharging my carbine from the waist. His rifle exploded at the same time as mine. His bullet splintered a tree branch inches from my head. He spun half way around and went down.

My heart was pounding. I raised my rifle to my shoulder, trained my sights on him and walked cautiously forward. It might be an old militia trick. I expected him to turn at any moment and attempt to fire into me point blank. Then I caught the sound of his labored breathing followed by torrents of the most severe coughing. I lowered my rifle and walked up to him. He lay on his back now, one hand holding his throat as blood flowed between his fingers, his other hand still gripping his carbine on the ground.

Color was quickly leaving his face. I sat down on a deadfall and watched him die. A calm came over me. Spider stared up at me, struggling to get a breath, the hatred in his eyes gradually turning to fear then slowly becoming vacuous and staring beyond me as a last wheezing breath left his chest.

I stood over his dead body. In death, he seemed smaller. Likely in his thirties, his stubble of beard was soft as peach fuzz in spite of his age. His fingers were long and slim and his palms were calloused and hardened from work. His wrists, knuckles and backs of his hands a mess of scars. He had always driven himself.

I looked into his vacant eyes searching for something, maybe for him to tell me what I should feel. Or what kind of man I was. Maybe what kind of men we were. He was like me: driven, unable to accept defeat, always ready with a cutting remark, a challenge, putting his own needs first. Impulsive.

Somewhere he had family, maybe a wife, or parents, or maybe kids. Should I render some religious thing over his corpse? He wore a blood-soaked crucifix around his neck. Finally, I decided I really could care less about Spider Marks or who might mourn him. He was out of my life now and that was all I cared about. I killed him in self defense and I felt nothing else for him.

What should I do with his corpse? Could I convince a police court that it was self-defence or that he was hunting for me? I could call it an accident, bring back help and a pack horse to carry him in, but clearly an accident would not stand up to close scrutiny by the police, no matter what Marks had thought. I could drag him north until I hit the river, fill his scabbards and pockets with gravel and sink him. But that could take days and leave a suspicious trail. He might wash up somewhere. Nothing seemed like the right idea.

I looked around. On the stream behind me a bear's den had been dug into the bank. Not an uncommon sight along any watercourse in the Northwest. I examined the den. The animal had likely hibernated there last winter for the first time as the soil dug out was not grown over. It would likely return, as bears do. This winter the beast would have company.

It was a large bear that wintered here; maybe a mother expecting cubs before spring. I used a section of a deadfall branch to expand the entrance until I could crawl inside and feel around. The bottom was a much larger area, large enough for a bear and her cubs to sleep out the winter.

I hauled Marks over on his back and pushed him in, head first to his waist. Then I hooked the point of my rifle into his belt buckle, straddled him, and reeled him down deep until I felt his malleable corpse contact the expansive bottom of the den where he slid easily inside. Spider Marks' eternal resting place.

I needed to dispose of the puddle of blood on the ground in case a rescue team should stumble upon it. By now it had congealed. I scraped it all together with the same branch I used to modify the den until I could scoop the blood up with my hands and dispose of it inside the den. I raked over the site until there was no apparent sign of an encounter.

I walked down to the stream, washed my hands and took my uniform off. There were blood smears on my pants and tunic so I soaked my handkerchief and cleaned off as much as I could. I hooked the blood-soaked cloth onto the branch and pushed it all deep into the den alongside Marks. I pulled one end of the adjacent dead fall tree so it hung down over the entrance of the den. It appeared quite natural and concealed the opening.

Dusk was setting in. My uniform would dry before I got back to camp. By dark, I had intersected the trail we had created coming in and I followed it into camp. Ervin Milner had bagged a bull moose. Darren Wells returned empty handed. Steele intercepted me and inquired if I had seen Marks. I explained that the last I saw of him he was heading southwest in the opposite direction of me just as he had been instructed. He was likely hunting along the stream where we camped, far to the west, I reported.

The next day the entire contingent stayed in camp. We had fired off shots in groups of three all throughout the night, a signal for the lost constable. A vigilant group of militia men stayed up all night firing off more signal shots and listening for a return signal of three shots. Just before dawn, Steele fired a rocket above our location to guide him in. The men searched relentlessly for two days, mainly combing the area to the west. At Steele's instruction I went with a search party to the north keeping everyone but me from entering the area where I had killed Marks.

Eventually, Jarvis made a decision: winter would be upon us soon and many would be lost if we didn't move quickly into the wooded terrain to find Fort Edmonton and shelter. But there was much speculation. Had Marks taken the opportunity to desert when least expected and therefore avoid suspicion of desertion and criticism? Had he fallen and inflicted a fatal wound? The whispers were rampant among the militia men. I knew from their looks that many suspected I had something to do with his disappearance. Only Doug Lynch had the audacity to mention it. "See anybody hunting yesterday, McGinn?" he said quietly in passing, staring deep into my eyes without wincing.

I ignored him and walked away. To formally accuse a fellow police officer of homicide? Well, I guessed none of them were quite ready for that.

Stephen ignored me for the rest of the evening. First thing in the morning we were side by side packing up for another day's travel. He lifted a bundle of canvas tent onto his shoulder and turned to me shielding his mouth from bystanders with the tent. "Did you run into Marks yesterday?"

I turned towards him and winked, a slow deliberate wink. I didn't know if he would become self-righteous on me or not but at least I was sure he wouldn't rat. He stared at me a long time like he was catching up to the sheer gravity of my response. Finally he turned away. But there was a slight smile of satisfaction on his face. I felt better. Stephen had always been on my side no matter how much he disagreed with me.

***

Throughout the month of September and beyond, we slogged through the rain on a quest to reach the northern fortress. Our saving grace was that there was palatable grass now for our thoroughbreds and we were able to find occasional game, a moose or elk for our own sustenance. But the terrain was becoming slowly impassible. We were now encountering long sections where we were knee deep in mud and our horses were frequently falling and often too weak to get out of the mud holes. The nights were becoming freezing cold and the horses too stiff to get onto their feet. Often now Steele called for some of us to get up during the night to rub down the horse's legs so they could stand. The men were also becoming sleep deprived and physically exhausted.

All of us began to admire even more the leadership, determination and incredible strength of Sam Steele. More than once we watched him, single handed, wrestle exhausted horses out of knee-deep mud holes. Frequently, we had to stop and build a marquee and rest the animals out of the rain for a full day. We were in a critical race to reach shelter before winter closed in around us. It seemed at times the convoy was barely moving. Every few hundred yards we had to unload, carry everything across the bogs and then pull the wagons through by hand. In the mornings now, we were encountering layers of ice forming across the sloughs.

One cold but sunny morning at the end of October we broached a rise of land to look down on a broad plateau of grasslands populated with teepees and log cabins. Upon a rise above the meadows and over-looking the North Saskatchewan River was a magnificent fortress, far larger than anything we had yet encountered, the beginning of trading tentacles that commenced to the north and west. It was Fort Edmonton, our destination and the center of continental trade for the Dominion.

There had rarely been a word of conversation among the men for weeks as we struggled to survive and keep our focus on moving ahead under the harshest conditions. Suddenly there was something akin to a cheer that rose up and even our animals seemed able to draw on some inner reserve of strength that kept them moving ahead.

A bustling industry of boat building was the center of much attention and activity just below us on the banks of the North Saskatchewan with men sawing, pounding and fitting together lumber and iron, sealing the joints with smoking pots of pitch. The men stopped their labors and turned to watch us file past. We were, no doubt, a ragged lot still dressed in our scarlet serges. A few of them waved and we responded, overjoyed to finally reach a destination we had almost given up hope of finding.

The workers below us had created an impressive assembly of high bowed York boats in various stages of construction along the river bank; boats that would become the vehicles for transporting large quantities of trade goods on the rivers and lakes between Edmonton and eastern destinations on the Hudson Bay and eventually on ships to Europe.

The North Saskatchewan River with its fast-moving current was also the widest we had seen anywhere in the northwest, over a quarter mile of water flanked by meadows of gardens and cereal crops stretching for a mile to the east and west of the fortress.

The fort was enclosed within a palisade of twenty-foot high vertical pine with flanking towers at the corners. In front of the main gates, the land fell away in a precipitous drop to the water's edge. Steele fired off a volley of shots as was customary when approaching most fortresses especially those as remote and isolated as Edmonton with no other way of alerting the occupants of our arrival. Our horses sensed it was the end of the line as their ears perked up and they began a weak trot towards the entrance.

The front gates were opened wide to us and a burly, stern looking man with medium length blond beard and pale blue eyes stood before the whole troop and introduced himself as Chief Factor Richard Hardisty. We soon discovered Hardisty was anything but stern; he turned out to be a gracious and accommodating host. There was ample stable for our horses. We fed, watered and brushed them down. We were invited to return to the fortress.

Sam Steele gathered the men together just outside the fortress walls and spoke to us before we went inside.

"Men," he began, "this is our post for the next several months. It's my opportunity to inform you that no officer has ever been prouder of the men under his command than I am of you and the enormous endurance you have shown. You have given me confidence that I can rely on each and every one of you to do your duty, and together, as a Canadian police force, we will meet the challenges before us." Steele was quiet for a long moment, walking back and forth and looking into the faces of the men.

"I again remind you that the Northwest Mounted Police will be a just police force, punishing only those that break the laws of the Dominion regardless of race or cultural beliefs." He stopped pacing and stood before us. "Always remember," he said, "the people we serve here live in a world much different than anything we've ever experienced or even understood. So, render Canadian justice with strength and resolve but also with fairness and compassion." He studied us for several moments letting his words settle in.

Finally, he responded, "now, we will go inside where Mr. Hardisty will direct us to our new accommodations."

CHAPTER 9

Sky Woman lay back on a buffalo robe. She had lost much blood and felt the exhaustion growing inside her body. But nothing was greater than the tenderness she felt for her newborn daughter who laid on Sky Woman's stomach and suckled her.

She had brought many babies into the world but this child was special because it was her own. Still, the baby was unusually bright, raising her trembling head to look at Sky Woman with shining eyes that could already focus. The baby looked around inside the teepee and then closed her eyes, lay back on Sky Woman's chest and slept.

Sky Woman laid her baby into a cradle lined with moss, the softest she could find and meticulously picked through to remove rough strands that might chafe the tender skin of her infant. Soon there would be a feast. A few from the summer encampment would be invited, those who had a supernatural power for knowing the nature of the infant and possessing a gift from the spirits for finding the right name for the child.

But Sky Woman already knew from her own vision what she would call her baby; she would be *Paniya, one who will be gifted, praised and revered.* She had been resting with the newborn baby on her chest and abdomen when her vision came. Sky Woman was awake, watching the vision unfold before her: a delicate young doe stepped gingerly forth from a dark wilderness, her white tail flicking back and forth, capturing and reflecting the sunlight. Wolves came next, a pack of six, their muzzles bloody from the hunt, crouching, following the young doe who approached the teepee of Sky Woman and her baby. Now the creatures numbered seven in all, casting their shadows as one, walking before the rays of the eastern sun, approaching the red and white decorated flap of Sky Woman's teepee.

The doe walked proudly without fear. The wolves surrounded her as all moved steadily forth, the tails and fur of the carnivores sweeping over the sides of the young doe and all were of one spirit. The deer lowered her head to enter and the wolves followed her inside. They lay down before mother and infant as if in a swoon and they slept. They awoke when the baby woke, but the baby was now a young girl who walked past them as if they were invisible to her as she moved out into the morning sun. They followed her outside where the young doe grazed on flowers of the meadow and the wolves dissipated into a dark forest, hungry and searching.

People brought gifts to hang over the baby's cradle. A medicine woman brought a small cane to hang over the crib in hopes that the baby might live to be old. An old shaman, Red Hawk, had much spiritual power and was greatly feared and revered. He came forth huddled in his worn buffalo robe to welcome the baby. He was old and would die soon and so was filled more than ever with great powers of the spirit world.

Everyone watched as Red Hawk hobbled to the cradle. He studied the baby a long time, squinted down through his old eyes, hovered back and forth over the infant. He grunted, then he brought his palms together and moved them ever so slowly apart until bright light, like a bolt of lightning crossed between. The baby blinked at the flash of light and was momentarily startled before looking away from the face above her.

Red Hawk continued watching her a long time and finally he responded. "She must beware the lightening because whether the white fork will be her friend or foe is too early to know." He hesitated, moving away from the child as if shielding a secret from her. "She won't know the black clouds of summer will always be watching her. The spirits have shown me that. The twins of thunder and lightning can be good or evil upon a whim and they jealously watch her. It is best if this power is never spoken of, and now forgotten."

He pulled together the edges of his robe, turned and bent through the flap of the teepee and was gone.

Sky Woman slept after the feast was over, and when she felt stronger she put her baby in a deer skin pouch filled with soft moss. Her father had made the frame of the pouch from willow, and Sky Woman had weaved the basket together with sinew. She strapped the pouch over her shoulders and across her back. She walked the shore of a river where two pieces of driftwood called out to her when she passed. She searched through the mounds of wooden debris laid down by spring floods from many seasons ago until she found the pieces that summoned her.

She pulled the driftwood from the pile and ran her hands across the wood, wiping away the dust of summer winds to reveal the grain of the wood crafted by the sun, the wind and the fast-flowing water and left just for Sky Woman to find for her baby.

First, the image of a wolf in the grain, his muzzle high, capturing scent in a curving sky. In the other, a doe, her oblique body prancing proudly into the rays of a rising sun. Sky Woman took the ancient wood to her teepee and hung the totems with sinew above the crib of her infant child. It was the first of her baby's learning, to begin to know herself.

CHAPTER 10

Paniya ran her finger tips over the beads of her new moccasins, jiggling each one back and forth, feeling how firmly they were stitched into the light doeskin hide. It was springtime of her fourth year and she knew the colors of each bead, yellow, red and orange in three languages: Cree, English and Gaelic. Most of all, she wanted to hold the new moccasins close to her nose and inhale the scent of smoke in the leather. And she could put them on by herself, wrapping the thongs firmly around her ankles and tying the ends together so they would not fall off. Soon she would be racing through the long grass and around the teepees with her friends.

The sun stayed out longer, warming the earth and the last slivers of snow had disappeared from their hiding places among the pine thickets beside the fortress. The clouds were deep and puffy now and took on shapes that grew, then smudged away like drifting smoke. Sometimes the clouds were faces, or wild geese flying in a formation. Sometimes she saw dogs without tails or ponies with three legs. But gone now were the wispy winter clouds like fraying strands of drying sinew. Already the brown tips of the polar trees were beginning to crack open, soon to push out their sticky leaves with the sweet fragrance of fresh spring days.

It was also a sad season, a season of much regret for Paniya because she knew her father would soon be paddling away with other voyageur in long boats piled high with furs from the winter trading. During the winter he had told her stories about his travels every summer down the river to the ocean where he helped load the fur bundles onto sailing ships bound for countries far away across the sea.

He described the many hardships the voyageurs had encountered on the river, times when they almost lost their fur to the rapids; or times when men came close to drowning in spring squalls. He told her about wind storms on the lakes or ocean bays that pushed them far off course. Always, they feared losing everything they had worked for all winter. He kept Paniya on the edge of her chair with his accounts of danger, but there was always a happy ending.

And in the evenings at the fortress during cold winter nights by a warm fireplace he amused her with tales from his boyhood. "I grew up on the far-away islands of Scotland," he told her. He would sometimes bounce her on his knee and would put a blanket around her if it was becoming too chilly when he told her about his homeland.

"Scotland has some dark woods," he said, "there the elves and gnomes make their homes that are so blended into the trees and the forest that people can rarely ever see them. Sometimes they choose the rocky coves of the sea for their hideouts. And some of the braver ones, or the ones most filled with mischief, build their hiding places in the very neighborhoods where the people lived."

From her father's many stories, Paniya saw the gnomes as small men with big noses who lived secret lives and filled their days with laughter, jokes, fun, and playing tricks on people who seldom saw them. Her father told her tales of how the little men would hide the people's belongings or scare them with loud noises on dark nights. They delighted in leaving the people in heated arguments, blaming each other for the elves' misdeeds as the elves laughed at their own pranks until their sides ached and they rolled on the ground in sheer delight at their clever antics. Sometimes, the gnomes would include children in their mischief, a clever way to gain some petty revenge on an unsuspecting adult.

But one thing puzzled Paniya; she wondered if the people there, or the little men with big noses, knew about the spirits that would come into people's lives. Were they able to see them in visions or talk to them like the people of her camp often told stories about? Her father never talked about the spirit world. When she mentioned it he just seemed confused with what she was talking about. Maybe he didn't know. Only her mother's people knew about the spirits that lived in everything. And Paniya knew.

***

Paniya held the hand of her grandfather, Eagle Hunter, as they walked together through the tall grass of the new summer camp, grass that was not yet trampled down from with the games of children, ponies grazing, the beds of sleeping dogs, or adults going about their chores. Since early morning Paniya had held back tears. Her grandmother, White Raven, had been hot with fever for two days and was now in a deep sleep. Sky Woman could not awaken her. Paniya went with her grandfather to the dwelling of Red Hawk. They called out to him and then opened the flap to his teepee. Red Hawk had been sleeping.

"White Raven is very ill," Eagle Hunter told him. "We fear she will die without the right help."

Quietly, Red Hawk rose from his blankets. He raised the flap around the base of his teepee, allowed a summer breeze to move through. Then he opened the east facing flap and looked towards the early morning sun.

"I will prepare the sweat lodge now," he said, "and then summon the help I need to know what is wrong and how to help her."

Eagle Hunter nodded. "We will wait until you are ready," he said. Paniya sat with Eagle Hunter outside their tent. They watched Red Hawk move into the sweat lodge where he prepared a fire and brought in rocks to be heated. He carried water inside for a cleansing steam. He closed the entrance and remained inside alone for a long time before appearing again and moving directly into the teepee with White Raven while Paniya waited outside with Eagle Hunter and they were joined by Sky Woman who had been inside with her mother.

"He will bring power from the spirit world to help White Raven," Eagle Hunter told Paniya. "Spirits that will know the evil that is trapped inside her." Then he looked down at Paniya as she held tight to his hand. "You must watch closely," he said, "and listen well, and you too can feel and hear the power that comes to the great man as he summons spirits to help him." She stood beside her grandfather watching the teepee of White Raven until Paniya felt a great energy moving forth all around them. Then the teepee began shaking amidst the sounds of a spirit world that Paniya had heard before but only from the darkness of the night forest.

Finally, Red Hawk came out of the teepee. He told Eagle Hunter that soon he would be given the healing chants that would restore her and soon she will awaken. He instructed Eagle Hunter and Sky Woman on what to gather from the forest to sustain her healing when she awakened from the sleep. The next morning White Raven was awake and soon she was moving around and feeling well again.

Since witnessing the healing of her grandmother, Paniya saw firsthand the power of the supernatural. She listened more intently now to the stories of her people who told how spirits could intervene to save them from accidents or animal attacks or at other times inflict evil. She learned that those with the most powerful medicine, the shamans or medicine men, or sometimes medicine women, could do many good things but could also render great damage and misfortune to anyone that lost favor with them. When she came to the fort to spend the winters, the spirits were gone, the magic was lost, and the magnificent, invisible world of the Cree disappeared from her life. Maybe because spirits were not welcome at the fort, or maybe they only existed when people believed in them or understood the special ways to summon them.

But life in the fortress had wonders of its own. Here she learned to read and write and capture the power in numbers and their magical reflections of the real world. Since she could remember, she and her mother worked in the Big House of the chief Factor during the winter. Sky Woman helped Mrs. Hardisty and Paniya was allowed to attend when the Factor's wife taught her children to read and write. Mrs. Hardisty was a kind woman who would read them stories and Paniya would listen in, paying attention to the words that Mrs. Hardisty read until, at age four, Paniya could recognize most of the words by herself. Some days Mrs. Hardisty would allow Paniya to take the books by herself and study the pictures.

Mrs. Hardisty was reading, *Little Red Riding Hood,* to her children as Paniya looked on. Mrs. Hardisty stopped for a moment from reading and reached for a glass of water. Paniya took up where she left off and continued to read the words.

"How did you know those words?" Mrs. Hardisty inquired with incredulity.

"I don't know," said Paniya.

"Has someone been teaching you to read."

"No," said Paniya.

Mrs. Hardisty picked up, *Jack and the Beanstalk,* which she knew she had never read when Paniya was present. She flipped to the beginning. "Can you read these words," she asked.

Paniya began, halting, but covering each word, *"Every day Jack would help his mother chopping wood and milking the cow."*

Mrs. Hardisty called her husband in from his study. "Listen to Paniya," she said, as Paniya began to read.

"Quite amazing," Hardisty responded after listening to her. "Now teach her how to cipher numbers. I spend half my working hours counting inventory, adding and subtracting trade items, prices, purchases, losses and profits and all that. I could use somebody to help me." He laughed.

Mrs. Hardisty took him seriously. By age eight Paniya was able to skim long columns of numbers providing the right answers to Hardisty. He brought her in for an hour each day to check his numbers. Soon he trusted her to provide the bottom line totals on his spread sheets all by herself. Over time, Paniya began working inside the trade rooms, counting inventory, adding and subtracting sales. She quietly listened to the clerks speaking French, English or Gaelic to interpreters who negotiated back and forth with the Blackfoot hunters.

Paniya discovered that all their talk, at first gibberish, began making sense to her.

One day the clerk and interpreter were stuck. A Blackfoot warrior was asking for something that no one could decipher. The man was becoming increasingly agitated and began threatening when the Factor was brought over. He could not understand the man either until Paniya told him.

"He says his wife is sick after having a baby and he thinks she is dying with terrible pains in her stomach that will not go away, that she is screaming with pain all night long and there is no medicine man in his winter hunting camp. He wants a white doctor to see her before it is too late."

Dr. Kitson went with him to his winter camp and was able to expel an infected placenta that saved the woman's life. But word was passed at the fort that Paniya had learned all the languages, just by listening to people talk as she counted inventory and ciphered numbers in the trading rooms.

***

Every spring she sadly watched her father paddle away and Paniya would not see him again until the leaves were turning orange and there would be a chill in the air. Still, there was much to look forward to. After her father departed and summer came, Paniya went with her mother to the Cree camps where all the families came together after a long winter of being apart, split into small hunting parties, seeking enough food to survive the winter.

But Life in the camp was always as different as day and night from life in the fortress. She had been nine when she first asked her mother why their lives were different, why most of her friends either lived in the Cree teepee all year around or some lived in the fortress all year around. Only a few, like Paniya and her mother, spent the winter in the fortress and summer in the camps. She was dying quills with her mother when she decided to ask.

"Spotted Wren and Blue Feather stay in the camps all winter," Paniya told her, "but we stay in the fort during fall and winter. I am glad to live in the fort and then enjoy the camps all summer. But we are different than most."

Sky Woman looked up from a pot over the fire. She seemed surprised for a moment that Paniya asked, then she moved the iron pot onto a bed of coals on the edge of the fire and responded.

"When I was young I married your father and that is why," said Sky Woman. "He worked at the fort building York boats and doing some trapping. Then he was a voyageur during the summer. A few of the women from my village married men at the fort."

"Was it what you wanted?" asked Paniya.

"Yes, back then, it was what I wanted. I loved your father very much. I used to come to the fort in the spring to help my father, your grandfather, bring his store of winter furs in for trade."

Paniya's mother stoked the fire below the simmering pot of water. She placed a handful of quills from the carcass of a porcupine into the pot. The animal was old and the quills were oily and would need much time to boil. She turned back to Paniya.

"There was always work to do on the several-day journey to the fort, so I helped my father load and unload fur bundles onto travois behind our horses. I would cook meals for him and build our shelters at night until we got to the fort where he traded his catch of winter fur for goods and supplies.

"I knew your father always watched for me to come to the fort and that was when he took a break from whatever he was doing, to come over to the trading rooms. I knew he came on purpose just to see me and I liked the idea."

Sky Woman added mashed chokecherries to the simmering water along with handfuls of a slurry she had prepared from the wet inner bark of alder and the outer stripping's of red dogwood. Soon the quills were simmering on the surface, taking in the red dye.

"What did father say to you?" Paniya asked. "Could you understand him?"

"He could speak Gaelic and English but not Cree and I could only speak Cree but for some reason Morris was always the interpreter when your grandfather and I came to the fort. Morris was your father's friend and he would interpret for us. Soon the haggling over prices was finished and your grandfather was quietly looking over trade supplies and I could talk to your father and Morris.

"Your father's eyes were always twinkling when he began speaking to me and Morris interpreted. "He would smile and say, 'I was supposed to be working when I saw you coming on the brown and white pinto, and I told the others, 'somebody is coming to see me.'"

"I knew he was joking and I could be just as coy. I said, 'Oh, the brown and white pinto? That is my father's horse. Did you want to flirt with him instead?'" He blushed, but it didn't stop him. He got Morris to tell me: 'No, I mean the small brown and white horse and the girl in a bright doeskin dress decorated so beautiful with red quills and yellow beads.'

"I just laughed. But I think he knew I liked him."

"Was that all you said?" asked Paniya.

"That was all for then. It was not easy talking through an interpreter and I think we were both shy."

Paniya's mother began retrieving quills from the boiling water. She cooled them briefly and showed Paniya how to flatten them under her thumb nail. Then they were placed back in the boiling dye to take on more color.

From inside the teepee, Paniya's mother fetched a doeskin dress she had recently cut out for decorating and returned to the fire.

"When I got home," Sky Woman continued, "I told your grandmother all about the man from the fort. I think she could tell I was taken with him. To my surprise your grandmother actually seemed quite pleased."

"She wasn't afraid of losing you to a stranger?" Paniya asked.

"It was not an uncommon custom, your grandmother had told me, if you want a different life then you better encourage him. Many women live better lives with men of the fort."

Sky Woman smoothed out the doeskin dress on the grass beside them. She continued, "Your grandmother said, 'life is not easy for our people but women of the fort do not have the hard work that weaken our backs, moving all the time to find new hunting. And we must carry back game the men kill. All that is easier at the fort; women never leave the fortress and the men bring in their own game. Our people often worry about starvation. But women of the fort have plenty to eat all year around.'"

Sky Woman removed the last of the quills from the iron pot and spread them on the grass to dry. Then she set the iron pot aside to cool.

"Your grandmother told me much more about being a Cree wife at the fort. She said the men call them their *country wives* and take great pride in how well their women dress. They bring in broadcloth from the distant markets for dresses and shawls. Jewellery of silver, copper and even gold is common for country wives to wear and often they adorn their wives with long necklaces of colorful stones and beads."

Paniya and Sky Woman knelt down in the grass on either side of the doeskin dress and worked together, laying out the quills in vertical patterns on the dress. Then each end of the quill was passed over and then under with a thin thread of sinew.

"So, how did you and father finally get together?" Paniya asked.

Sky Woman was quiet a long time, her nimble fingers moving the sinew threads more slowly around the quills now, as if deciding what to say. Finally, she stopped her work and responded.

"Well, after your grandmother told me about *country wives*, I was even more taken than ever with the thoughts of marrying your father. I used every opportunity to go to the fort and both your grandparents knew the reason, so they let me go often. Your father seemed to know when I would arrive. I think he had been practicing some Cree words with Morris and we could talk somewhat by ourselves with gestures, sign language and a few words we both knew in each other's language."

Paniya's mother smiled to herself, remaining silent for several moments, as if recalling some long-forgotten exchanges. Then she continued.

"He asked if he could come to the camp to see me. I said I would like that very much. I told my parents he was coming and they didn't mind, and besides, I was old enough to make up my own mind what I wanted to do. He stayed with me several days and we took long walks and we slept through the dawn together. My people accepted us as man and wife. I moved to the fort with him and there were other Cree women and a few white women there too, and life was as my mother had told me: in many ways much easier than in the camps."

"So, it has been good ever since?" asked Paniya. "You and father seem to get along well."

Sky Woman stopped her work and looked across at Paniya for a long moment. "There is always a problem for country wives. And you must know too. Your father was honest with me from the very beginning. He told me that if I became his wife I needed to know that he was the oldest son in his family in Scotland. He said there would come a time when his father would die or become too old to work and he would need to go back to take over the farm and all the livestock. He said if I married him, I could come back with him to Scotland if I wanted. I said I didn't think I could ever leave my mother or the life I knew so well but I said nobody knew the future except the great spirit, and I wanted to be his country wife and let the future be as it might because I never challenged fate."

"Does he still talk of going back to his country? I would miss him terribly," said Paniya.

"I love your father more than anything. We still talk about it, and he is still honest with me. Someday he might not come back from the eastern seaport where he unloads fur. If he gets mail from Scotland telling him his father has died or cannot work the farm, he promised his mother that he would go back, He would need to go on board the first returning ship as the farm cannot go without a caretaker for another year.

"Every fall now when he returns in the long canoes I am immensely relieved to see him and we celebrate. But I know the day will come when he will not return and he knows I will not leave my people either. So, we live our lives a day at a time, happy to be man and wife until the York boats leave in the spring and I don't know if we will ever see him again.

CHAPTER 11

It was her twelfth summer, and this year's encampment was one of the best Paniya remembered, spread out on a long grassy river flat with clumps of saskatoon, pin cherry and chokecherry that tapered at each of the far ends of the flats back toward the river. The wild berries grew mostly along the north slope facing into the summer sun and were already breaking into white fragrant blossoms. The season was earlier than most.

The camp smelled fresh and clean, unlike some of the staleness of the fortress where too many people dumped their winter wastes in the courtyard which didn't smell too great under the warming sun of spring. Here the air was fresh with a breeze off the river and groves of pine higher up the slopes that ushered in a clean scent of the forest. The fresh smells brought back many other memories of summer camps with her mother's people.

Men of the camp had selected this location for its promising signs of game and the abundance of berries and plants for medicine and food needed to sustain the whole tribe together through a long season. Paniya and her mother were among the first to arrive. She would be sharing her teepee with her mother, her mother's brother, Walks Tall, and her grandparents, Eagle Hunter and White Raven.

Paniya helped her mother put together the poles of their teepee. Her uncle and grandparents had brought the long slender pine poles in from their winter hunting camp. White Raven was too old for much of the labor involved in erecting the tent but she watched and often threw out suggestions or commands if they forgot something or their work was getting sloppy.

Sky Woman laid out a tripod of poles and fastened them at the top with hemp. White Raven and Eagle Hunter stood on the bottom of two poles while Paniya and her mother erected the tripod into the air, secured the bottoms and began placing additional poles.

The encampment began to fill. Families came in from every direction, many on horseback, some on foot and most with dogs saddled down with supplies. Paniya and her mother set aside their labors. It was a time to greet old friends they had not seen since the previous summer.

Soon the new camping grounds were filled with the sounds of children playing and laughing. Dogs were barking and many of the women embraced each other while groups of men congregated with much laughter, joking and conversation. They shared stories of their winter experiences and close encounters with trouble: bad weather, frost bite, losing direction in unfamiliar wilderness, scarcity of game, attacks from wounded or diseased animals, illness, injuries, periods of starvation and encounters with good or evil spirits. There were many stories for them to tell and Paniya often listened nearby. These were stories that she knew her own father would not really understand but Eagle Hunter often told fascinating stories of his own.

"Happy to see you made it back," Sky Woman chimed out as a new group followed along the river embankment and broke into the campsite. Paniya soon discovered that two of her favorite friends, Spotted Wren and Blue Feather were helping to prepare their camp. She set down the rocks she had gathered from the river to hold down the bottom of the teepee and she walked shyly over to see them. They compared bead work on their moccasins and the quill work on their dresses. They spoke to each other in Cree.

"Are you ready for double ball this summer, or the races," asked Spotted Wren.

"Yes, I'm ready," said Paniya. "But you have grown, your legs are way longer. You will be hard to beat."

The girls laughed together. "I think Paniya still beats us both," said Blue Feather, "but barely, we both grew more than her."

"This year she will feel our breath on the back of her neck in a race," added Spotted Wren with a giggle.

But there was not a lot of time to socialize. There was much work to do in preparing a new camp. White Raven was kept busy minding a cooking fire nearby and was able to gather firewood with Eagle Hunter who was also very old and quite crippled. Paniya went to help her mother gather the tips of spruce boughs for bedding under the sleeping robes.

Once all the work of preparing camp was complete, summer was a time of much feasting and celebration with fires, storytelling, ceremony and dancing. And there were games and races on foot or on ponies. Sometimes the men would have leg wrestling matches or competition with bow or spear to see who could hit a target best. Always, there was much gambling: who would emerge the victor, or who could win at guessing games or games of chance? Paniya liked the Cree games and specially she liked to watch the women play double ball, her mother's favorite. And by age twelve, Paniya and her friends Blue Feather and Spotted Wren were hoping to join in the game.

***

Sky Woman watched a messenger running towards her camp. It was the cool of morning, the best time to run and the usual way of messaging between friendly camps of the Cree who were separated into encampments by kinship ties, social ties, or just convenience of sharing wider hunting or fishing resources. As the woman drew nearer, Sky Woman recognized Crow Claw, well known among the tribes as a woman whom many revered for her physical prowess and skill in the most robust games that the women loved to play during the summer months.

"I am here to extend a welcome and invite you to enjoy a game with us," Crow Claw said, breathing heavily from running. Then she took a moment, bent from her waist and drew a few long breaths in and out, before beginning again.

"This year our camp is on a grassy flat by the river with a long easy run for double ball, and stakes are already set up for goals, about a mile apart. This is our challenge to you."

Sky Woman thanked her. "We will bring a team," she said, "maybe twenty-five women."

"Then we will have a similar number," said Crow Claw. "Arrive early. We will play until dark. Bring much to wager. We will match what you bring."

Paniya came to her mother. "This year I would like to play too."

"You should have been to the moon house before now," said Sky Woman after a long look at Paniya, "and you are so small. But I think you are a late comer," she said, "and many say it's because the spirits favor you that the blood stays away. Maybe you are ready for the game. You are strong but still small. The game gets rough and you could be injured. It is your decision." Sky Woman sent out word among the teepees of the encampment–those who wanted to participate must come to her. She had no difficulty finding twenty-five women ready to compete.

The women walked in single file towards the neighboring encampment. Some women carried goods on their backs for betting on the game. Others strapped their possessions for wagering on the backs and sides of pack-dogs that were trained to follow quietly through the bush, stifling any urge to bark or growl at prey they might encounter as they progressed through the wilderness.

Sky Woman lead the way and Paniya took up the very end behind twenty-four other women. They moved stealthily forward as was the way of a people used to sustaining themselves by moving quietly so as not to scare off any game they might come across during their sojourns into the forest. This time they were on a mission and they moved at a more or less rapid pace. There was always time later for much talk and gossiping.

The women passed through patches of thick dogwood and clumps of red alder before finding relief in more open spaces under the canopies of pine and fir. Frequently, they encountered fast-flowing streams where they took off their moccasins, leggings or any other clothing that could get wet; they waded through and dressed again. They travelled across long barren slopes that paralleled the river towards the neighboring camp and often followed game trails for easier going.

Sky Woman stopped and listened, her ear cocked into the wind until she heard the distant sound of tom-toms, barking dogs and excited children. She smiled and moved on; she knew they were on the right path. The promise of fierce competition with a neighboring encampment awaited and her heart beat faster in anticipation.

They broke through the bush and onto the open river flats with a line of more than fifty teepees spread along the river's edge. Here they were met with much merriment as women and children rushed to greet them. Old friends embraced while the men gathered in front of the teepees and watched with interest the arrival of a competing camp and the prospect of a lively match between the women of both encampments.

The women set out the goods they brought to be wagered, making sure that the value of the possessions was close to equal from each side. The objects to be won included robes, metal pots, bead work, fur caps, beautiful bracelets, tobacco and much more. It was an age-old game with some rules to be decided beforehand. Both agreed there could be unlimited running once a person had the ball on their stick. Some years they had decided to limit the steps to be taken with the ball, maybe three steps, maybe ten, but this year there was obvious confidence on both sides in the ability of their fast runners.

They agreed that whomever was leading in goals when it was too dark to see would be the winner. No one offered a rule concerning how rough the game might become. But competitive spirits were running high. Paniya knew the games were friendly only in the beginning with Crow Claw's team. She had watched them play before. She had witnessed how tensions grew as the games progressed: tempers would flare, sticks would rise in anger and blood spilt long before darkness closed out the competition. There was great passion for sport with men or women and none liked to lose.

Paniya stood with her own group near the middle of the field. Men watched from the sidelines and she noticed a large magnificent man that seemed to be watching her. He stood head and shoulders taller than all the rest and she had heard the others calling him Two Bears. He was a handsome man.

Soon the game began and the double ball, affectionately called the *buffalo's scrotum* by the women, was cast high in the air and there was a clashing of sticks to capture the object between the two small hanging sacks of sand sewn into the leather pouch. Crow Claw was the first to come up with the double ball and raced forward towards Sky Woman's goal. As she went by, Paniya sprang high into the air knocking the double ball off Crow Claw's stick and onto her own.

Paniya turned to run but was roughly brought down by Crow Claw who seemed more intent on physically charging her than simply recapturing the ball and running with it, or flinging it down the field for a teammate.

The game progressed all afternoon before Sky Woman scored. Paniya and Spotted Wren both captured the ball several times and Paniya demonstrated her speed down the field where she was each time brought down roughly by Crow Claw. And each time Paniya sped across the field she would look over the crowd gathered and catch a glimpse of Two Bears, who was always watching her, his white teeth glowing in a thinly-veiled approval of her game. He seemed to be pulling for her instead of the team from his own encampment.

Darkness was closing in on the players. The only goal had been scored by Sky Woman. Her team, Sky Woman declared, was the winner. It was too dark to see. Crow Claw was furious. "There is still enough light to play. You only want to stop now because you are ahead!" she exclaimed.

"But the ball is lost in the darkness with every toss," Sky Woman countered. "Our agreement was to stop when it was too dark to see."

"It is only too dark for your side. Not our side. We can still see trees against the sky where the sun sinks below the earth. That was once a rule, and shall be again!" Crow Claw charged up to Sky Woman, her stick raised threateningly.

Sky Woman raised her stick with both hands at shoulder level to match the aggression of Crow Claw. Neither would relent.

Crow Claw spoke. "We are a single toss from your goal posts. That is why you want to quit. You have seen the great value of our possessions for wager. You are trying to end the game when we are only one toss from your goal line."

"But no one can see the ball. If you get a toss across our line, how is that fair when no one can see to stop it! That was the rule we agreed upon: we stop at dark."

"Well, you quit then," said Crow Claw, "our side will continue until dark, when there is no light, and we will even the score."

"By your own rule," countered Sky Woman, "we stop when the trees on the horizon are no longer lit by the dying sun. As you can see, the trees are dark now."

"That is because you argued for so long that the sun has set. Now I have a challenge for you. You know full well it would be a tie. We will leave all the goods that both camps brought for the winner. Tomorrow morning each side will chose one woman to run a foot race, the full length of the field. The winner will collect all the goods wagered from both camps.

Sky Woman looked around at her group. It was obvious the women wished to be honorable and fair minded. After some discussion amongst themselves, they reluctantly agree: the outcome was best determined with a foot race.

"Very well, we will settle the matter tomorrow, with each camp selecting one woman to race," conceded Sky Woman.

"It is decided then," said Crow Claw. "And you are invited to stay the night with us. It is a clear night, no rain. We will make you comfortable outside with robes and pillows of down and any that want to are welcome to come into a teepee with any one of us. But now we will feast, there will be plenty of buffalo and moose meat for all to share."

The women soon forgot their differences as a great fire was built, meat was roasted and the women talked and laughed far into the night. Tom-toms played and the men had their own gatherings to gossip, tell their hunting and war stories, leg wrestle, and practice spear throwing by the light of their fires.

At day light, Sky Woman called her group together. "The stakes are high," she said. "We must decide who will run for our camp."

"Sky Woman is the fastest and the only one to score a goal in double ball. She should run for us," said Touches A Cloud. There was a shout-out of consensus for Sky Woman.

"I know I was once very fast on the playing field," Sky Woman began. "But I am getting older. Yesterday we watched Paniya race across the field and only Crow Claw could get the ball from her, but it was never a fair race." Sky Woman turned to face the rest of her team. "It was just

Crow Claw waiting to ambush Paniya, to cut her off at every chance, bringing her down and being far rougher than any other player. Maybe she needs to feel the sting of Paniya getting even with her."

Sky Woman looked down at Paniya and spoke softer with a knowing smile. "And I know from our own fun romps together along the river that Paniya can now outrun me. She has grown much in one year."

Crow Claw called all the players together. "I am selected from my team to run this race and bring home all the prize money. Who is running for you?"

Paniya stepped forth. "I guess I have been selected," she responded timidly, looking down at her moccasins.

Crow Claw could not conceal a wide grin. "A mere girl," she responded. "Are you serious?" she continued, still unable to conceal her gratified smile. "Very well then, a line is drawn between the goal posts where the runners will start. Sky Woman can be the starter and we will begin when she shouts out, 'run' and the winner is the first to race between the goal posts at the far end." Both teams can have spotters at the end if they want to, to determine the outcome, but I doubt it will be close," said Crow Claw.

Paniya stood beside Crow Claw on a starting line drawn in the dirt between goal posts. Her heart was pounding and her head was spinning. She did not remember ever feeling more nervous. A great gathering of men appeared along the edge of the field. The string of bystanders stretched to the distant finish line. Paniya could not even see the posts yet, but they would become visible as she approached the end. Near the middle was a small aspen grove on the edge of the vast meadow. Paniya looked towards the sideline nearest where she stood. Two Bears was watching her.

When Sky Woman shouted 'run,' Paniya burst ahead as fast as her legs would take her, running on pure fear and excitement leaving Crow Claw far behind. Then the realization hit her that the distance was far and she would never be able to keep up such a pace. She looked back. Crow Claw was striding easily on her long muscular legs. She was a messenger, a long-distance runner used to pacing herself for such great distances.

Paniya had covered twice the distance from the starting line that Crow Claw had. But already Paniya was tiring. She slowed her pace to a slow jog and tried to calm her breathing, to catch her breath, to slow her pounding heart. She could already hear the steady pounding of Crow Claw's feet coming up behind her.

Paniya reached the bluff of trees which was half way to the finish line. Suddenly, Crow Claw breezed past her, glancing over her shoulder with an amused smile. Paniya thought of all the goods the women of her camp had brought to wager on this very event. Many had been confident of bringing home precious items to decorate their teepee because they knew the skill of Sky Woman in double ball.

In the beginning Paniya had heard much cheering and excitement from the women of her camp. Now she felt only their disappointment. There were no familiar voices or the sound of her name rising above the roaring crowd. All she heard now were the women and men from the other camp chanting "Crow Claw," as Paniya's adversary was shrinking in the distance ahead of her.

It was barely half way and she was exhausted. She slowed to a mere trotting, panting and gasping for every new breath as she watched the long strides of Crow Claw carrying her ever closer to the final goal line.

Then, she felt the presence of her deceased grandfather, Eagle Hunter. He had been a person who could attract the favor of spirits but could never demonstrate enough power to be revered among the tribe as a shaman or medicine man. Nevertheless, Eagle Hunter had taught her some things he knew.

"You can bring the spirit of the wind or the speed of passing clouds inside of you," he once told her. "Feel them here," he said, as he ran the palm of his hand in gentle circles around his chest and solar plexus. "Feel them," he repeated, "call out to them," he said, "and they will hear you. Bring them within you to feel their lightness and motion."

Paniya looked to the sky, to a small cloud above her that seemed to be moving with her, like it knew her. Her pace had become rhythmic, in tune with the beating of her own heart and she became one with the steady, pulsing flow of air moving gently in and out of her lungs until her body began to feel new energy. She called out to the wisp of cloud vapor and she brought it into her chest and abdomen. *Bring me your lightness and the swiftness that takes you so rapidly cross the sky.* And she felt herself becoming one with the cloud.

She moved then in synch with all the rhythms of her own body and the lightness of a cloud. Without weight or burden she began to speed across the field, her feet barely touching the ground to a sudden howling of the crowd. She held onto the feeling inside her. She caught up to Crow Claw and ran beside her with ease.

Paniya watched over her shoulder while Crow Claw gradually fell behind, wheezing, panting, fighting for breath, pounding her powerful legs even harder and pushing herself ever faster beyond all reasonable limits of speed until Crow Claw collapsed somewhere just before the finish line. Paniya sailed between the goal posts, her eyes on the sky above her and the magic of the cloud inside of her.

Amidst a roar of celebration, the women of her camp raced onto the field to embrace her. She noticed that Two Bears had kept up to her as she raced across the entire field. He watched her finish from the sidelines with a wide grin of approval across his face.

CHAPTER 12

It was Paniya's sixteenth summer. It had been a winter of much snow and spring came late. As usual she passed the winter at the fort working for Hardisty and she looked forward more than ever to joining the encampment of her mother's people for the summer. It had been the most terrible year of her life. Over a year ago her father had left with the annual trek of the voyageurs and had not returned. It was also more awkward for her mother now, living in the fortress; she said she felt greater acceptance by her own people and living in a teepee with her brother and his wife. Sky Woman said she longed for a teepee of her own.

But Paniya was grateful for the promise of springtime. She was using the moon house now and she had been honored by her people with a ritual called the *Berry Fast*. She was denied solid food during this time and ate soup brought to her by her mother and other women of the camp. When she came forth from the moon house there was a great feast in her name. But life quickly returned to the chores and celebrations of summer.

Paniya was with her mother scraping hair from the hide of a doe for tanning. "Two Bears has made it known that he wants you for his second wife," said Sky Woman.

Paniya was silent a long moment. "I know," she said, "he is always watching me. I have long dreaded when the time came for conversations about a husband. I like being single and free," she said, "not tied to either a man from the fort or a man from the village. I would have to give up one or the other and it's not what I want."

Paniya stopped and gathered up hair from the doe that was piling up on the ground. She placed the furry remains into a leather pouch for a pillow later and began scraping again.

"The fort life is easier and I could marry someone there," she continued, "but what if I really loved him? I would only be his country wife. When the time came he would leave me just like father left us to live on the other side of the ocean. I don't ever want to live with such sorrow again."

Paniya turned to face her mother; she had been feeling the worry for weeks now, pondering the dilemma of choosing a husband. "And a man from the Cree encampments is not what I want either. He would want me to give up the life I love to look after him. I don't want that. I like the fortress in winter working for Mr. and Mrs. Hardisty."

"But you must think of the future too," said Sky Woman. She worked energetically, holding the bone handled scraper with both hands now in a rhythm of downward strokes, tearing loose the thick coat of the deer as a fresh pile of brown hair began building on the ground. "You won't always be young," she said, "and soon I too will be too old to do the work to keep us alive. A man in our teepee would make life easier."

Paniya felt her body grow rigid and she stopped her labors for a moment. "I just see a different path for my future and I still prefer to be single. I want to learn the medicine in plants that you and Touches A Cloud can teach me. I want to be a medicine woman, to cure people. And I want to spend winters with Mr. and Mrs. Hardisty at the fort, practicing the numbers and the languages I am learning. That helps them and I get what I want in both worlds."

Paniya watched Sky Woman take a wooden bowl and mix together the fat and brains from the deer into a thick paste. Together they began rubbing the mixture onto the scraped rawhide.

"There is something that worries me even more though," Sky Woman finally responded as she stopped her work and turned to face Paniya.

"You know the power of the supernatural world as much as anyone and the powerful shamans that summon the spirits, some of them evil. I see Night Walker watching you. I know what he wants. He is far too old for you and would never be a good husband for you or a provider for us. But we all know what will happen if you turn him down. There will suddenly be accidents, starvation and disease strike our teepee. Because he has that power."

Sky Woman was silent for a long moment. She looked away and appeared to be studying the distant tree line when she turned back to Paniya and she had the expression of someone struck with a great idea.

"Maybe Two Bears is perfect for you," she said coyly and turned back to preparing the hide again with much renewed energy.

"How is he perfect for me?"

"Two Bears has one wife already and she does all his work around the camp and moving. She is strong and still quite young with many years left. She likes the work of beading, tanning and cooking for him. Maybe you have to talk to him, bargain with him to get what you want."

Paniya stopped rubbing down the hide and turned to face her mother. "Bargain for what?"

"To have a man share our teepee, to feed and protect us when we get older."

"But he will want me to give up the life I want, the single life."

"I know what he wants from you. I can tell by how he looks at you; it is what any man would want from you. And he wants children from a strong, young wife. Black Elk has not been able to give him children."

"I could not marry a man just for that. I would need to like him, to feel something more for him. I don't know yet if I could feel such things for Two Bears."

"If he is good to you, you would have the right feelings for him as time goes on. You shouldn't listen too much to what the white women of the fort say. They pretend what women do between the robes at night is something bad, something that should never be talked about. Our women talk about it all the time and we learn from each other. It is part of life. We even talk about it to men sometimes. Many white women believe it is evil, like something only the windigo would do. It makes me laugh! They all do it but let on like they don't enjoy it or it is evil. How foolish they can be sometimes.

"If they have no husband and are of child, they think they have to be ashamed. They have to hide their growing belly and even give their baby away.

"For us, a child is a gift of the great spirit. We never feel shame for our babies. And we can enjoy time at night on the buffalo robes with someone that is good to us and someone we like and develop feelings for."

Paniya and Sky Woman finished rubbing down the deer hide. They worked as a team because they had done the tanning many times before. Sky Woman unbound the hide from the willow frame and each held an edge as they carried it to a tripod erected above the fire. Paniya added three stout birch branches to the flames and Sky Woman placed a sprinkle of leaves and branches specially selected from green shrubs onto the flames to provide the right amount of heat and smoke to warm the paste impregnating the hide. Smoky vapors from the right leaves would complete the tanning and the color they wanted.

Sky Woman began, "Two Bears is a big strong man, a brave warrior and a great hunter. And quite good looking too. You might have to whisper softly in his ear at night to slow him down. Men always go too fast. You must teach him what feels good to you. Teach him what you want. Most men are eager to please their wives. I think you will find that married life is not so bad."

"But would he let me live at the fort in the winter and work for Mr. Hardisty?"

"Why not? Let him buy some things at the fort on your accounts. Two Bears would like that; he likes the things he can trade for at the fort. He still has another wife when he needs her.

"Tell him what you want," emphasized Sky Woman. "That you will only be his second wife if you can practice as a Medicine Woman. And you want to spend winters at the fort when he is away all the time hunting anyway. If you don't like what he says, ignore him and walk away. If he agrees, we all get something, and when we are old he will provide for us. He is a good hunter. And there would be worse things for a woman than sleeping between the robes with Two Bears."

***

Two Bears rode into the camp, tall and erect on his appaloosa stallion leading a bay mare behind. He rode directly to the teepee of Sky Woman and offered the mare to her in exchange for Paniya as his second wife. Sky Woman accepted the tether of the pony.

"But you need to talk to Paniya. I will only accept the mare if she agrees to sleep through the dawn with you."

With grunts and nods Two Bears left. Paniya was sewing beads onto a dress on a sunny hillside beside the teepee and overheard her mother speaking with Two Bears. She set down her work and watched him striding towards her. Two Bears was truly a magnificent figure. His body was oiled and his hair in long braids hung over his powerful shoulders.

He asked Paniya if he could come to her camp with his first wife and if she would be his second wife.

After a long moment Paniya responded. "I will be your second wife," she said, not trying to mask some reluctance, "and do some of the things required of a wife. But I must be free to practice as a medicine woman and to live and work in the fortress during winter months while you are out hunting. I would be willing to share my income with you, providing goods from the fortress. But above all else I need you to provide for my mother who is getting older and has no one suitable to share her teepee."

Two Bears seemed to have already anticipated what she would want in return for sharing her teepee at night. Again, he grunted his approval. "I will give you the freedom you want and your mother will be well cared for. We will share the sleeping robes of the teepee some nights."

"Okay," said Paniya. "My mother has accepted the mare."

Two Bears left and returned later. He brought his wife on a pony behind him and three dogs saddled with their belongings.

Paniya found the teepee was plenty large enough for all of them and all were used to the ways of living together inside. Initially, they talked very little and avoided watching each other. Paniya found she could easily share space with Black Elk who seemed to be a peaceful and quiet woman motivated to do the bidding of Two Bears and the endless chores that were needed to maintain a camp.

Paniya knew she must establish from the very beginning the arrangement Two Bears had agreed upon and she spent much of the day with her mother and two other women of the village. Two Bears stayed around camp that day. Paniya told him she would be gone to gather plants for healing. He said nothing and did not look up from notching his arrows with feathers and grinding the shafts straight between fitted stones. As she walked away she heard him stop his work and she felt him watching her.

That evening they returned and Paniya found ways to help Black Elk prepare food; she collected water, gathered wood and attended to camp chores. Black Elk mostly ignored her and Paniya was never sure if she was liked by Black Elk or not. Sky Woman worked in various ways with the plants they had selected, separating roots from stems and leaves, preparing them to be used or stored as medicine and healing poultices or wrappings for wounds. All of them spent the first day going about their business and no one spoke.

Paniya felt her apprehension growing as night time approached and she knew the teepee would soon be quiet inside, the flaps would be closed and the bottom edges brought down where fresh air came through during the day.

She did not know what to expect from Two Bears. In the last dim light, she watched him undress. She felt a strange excitement, followed by more apprehension and even moments of fear. Two Bears was a magnificent man and his body reflected the remaining daylight.

She was also deeply afraid. Her heart began pounding as much from fear as the excitement that he managed to stir inside of her. For a fleeting moment she thought of the men he had slain in war. His reputation was widely known for fearless and violent victories in battle. She wondered if he had ever raped the women he conquered or pillaged the vanquished encampments of the Sarcee, Blackfoot or, on one occasion, victory over a Sioux camp far to the south.

To Paniya's surprise he completely ignored her. He crawled under the covers of his older wife and Paniya turned her back to give them whatever privacy they might desire. She lay her arm against the cool covering of the teepee and tried to think of what she would do tomorrow. Maybe she would go with the medicine women again to a faraway favourite spot where they would collect plants for food and badly needed medicine. That would help solidify her bargain with Two Bears. She was not a camp wife but a woman insisting on having her own freedom within the confines of the relationship with him.

She could not escape the sounds inside the tent, especially the moaning of Black Elk. Paniya gained a clear impression the other wife was immensely satisfied with Two Bears as a partner between the robes. It also occurred to her that maybe there was an embellishment, a message in the sounds of apparent ecstasy from Black Elk emphasizing what Paniya was missing out on. But mostly Paniya was relieved. She had at least postponed whatever might be in store for her from Two Bears.

She woke just as a faint morning light was coming into the top of the teepee. Two Bears was standing over her, his massive erect body before her as he roughly pulled her robes away. She pushed him back. It was not what she wanted and she told him, "no, not like this, not yet, I need to know you better first." He ignored her and proceeded anyway, forcibly pulling up her night shirt and coming inside her creating immense pain. She shouted out for him to stop, but he continued until he had satisfied himself.

He rolled off her and moved back under the robes of his other wife. Paniya lay awake for the rest of the night, feeling shame and disappointment. She had longed for something far more satisfying and tender from Two Bears.

She began to fear Two Bears was not someone she was likely to develop affection for. He was handsome and strong, an attraction she had felt for a long time. She had been willing to wait for him to learn the tenderness she longed for. But Two Bears seemed to mistake affection for aggression and as time went on it was obvious he was completely oblivious to her overtures. His domestic relations seemed to be only an extension of the only other life he understood: that of a warrior, subduing fighters of the Blackfoot confederacy with lance and spear.

At least he showed much deference to Sky Woman. Occasionally he would move around the fire to provide her a place where there was less smoke to inhale. Sometimes he would see to it that she could go first to the spit of meat over the fire where she would claim the choicest portions. And always he was a good provider, bringing home an abundance of game and hides prime for the women to tan and prepare: tunics, moccasins, bags and dresses that would please them. Sky Woman was happy with him as a man in camp, providing everything she needed to sustain a good livelihood. She hoped in time Paniya could grow fond of him.

But when Paniya was alone with Two Bears and Black Elk, when Sky Woman was away gathering medicine, Two Bears was simply the alpha male demanding the best portions and greater share of boiled meat, wild parsnip or charred root portions for himself.

At such times he expected subservience from her and the greater share of everything when there was any kind of shortage, like it was all he understood. And he continued to be a warrior between the robes at night, not a lover. After weeks of trying to tame the raw instincts of Two Bears, Paniya told him, "You should spend the nights with your other wife. From the sounds of her, she wants to be with you more than I do."

It was rare that Two Bears would even talk to her, but this time he stopped to stare down at her: "I look after your mother, I bring home food for you both and the finest fur to keep you warm. All summer I keep you safe from the treachery of the Blackfoot and Sarcee who would harm you or take you away to be a slave in a strange land."

He climbed in beside her, his hard, erect body seeking to penetrate her and she offered no resistance. Maybe from habit by now, but never from desire. It had been many weeks sharing her nighttime robes with Two Bears and there had not been a union of spirit. And there would be no children. She would not allow his seed to grow inside of her.

She followed her mind now, far away from her body and the suffocating weight of Two Bears. She drifted through the vent opening of her teepee and high into a night sky speckled with the lights of a million campfires. She searched among them until she found the campfire of her grandparents, White Raven and Eagle Hunter, who had left this earth years before. She only needed to follow what was in her heart to find them glowing in the light of their fire more beautiful than she had ever remembered; their dark braids shone and their skin was brown and beautiful. They were young again and in love, enjoying the never-ending vistas of a vast, living universe.

She hid nearby in the darkness and listened to their talk. "Two Bears is not right for Paniya," they said. Then they felt her presence and noticed her shadow nearby and called her to join their campfire.

Shyly, she came forth and they embraced her with all the love she remembered from them. She stood in the glow of their firelight and they spoke to her.

"Two Bears is cruel to you," they told her, "his way has never been the way of our people who have tenderness with their wives on the night time robes. What he does to you hurts us too. You must show him you have power.

"Tell him about a vision that we will share with you. We see in the future when Two Bears is hunting. It is a time when all the animals escape from him and he catches nothing. He is sitting by his fire with much disappointment. Then with the morning light he goes out to check his snares and finds a single rabbit caught.

"He bends down to take the rabbit from his snare. A lynx drops from a tree branch above him, a lynx that wanted the rabbit for itself. In a great fit of ferocity and snarling, it bites and claws Two Bears viciously all over his head, his neck and down his back. Then, before he can pull his knife or draw his bow, the lynx springs back into the bush and disappears. Tell him his injuries will be severe and he will have much infection and pain.

"This will happen soon. Tell him so that he sees the supernatural power you have and that you can see and even decide his future. Tell him he is clawed by the lynx because of his cruel indifference to you at nighttime. He will see that you have power of the spirit world and he will fear you and no longer bully and hurt you. You and Sky Woman will be free to live with him on your own terms."

Paniya drew away from her grandparent's fire, through the stars and back to her teepee. She lay again between her robes. Two Bears was done with her body and was snoring loudly beside Black Elk.

CHAPTER 13

The men of the Northwest Mounted Police were graciously provided for by Factor Hardisty. Each of us were given quarters in a long row of housing within the fortress walls with bunks and a fireplace in each room. Stephen and I were given a room together. The officers were assigned their own quarters.

It was the greatest comfort we had known in a very long time. No doubt, the Hudson's Bay Factor had long awaited the arrival of law and order in a lawless, isolated land with much tribal descension.

That evening Hardisty invited every man for dinner in the Factor's expansive dining hall. A Catholic priest said grace and we sat down to a grand feast that included fresh buffalo tongue, venison, roast wild goose and prairie chicken. All along the lengthy tables were dishes of beaver tail, roast duck, boiled buffalo hump and an assortment of vegetables from the fortress gardens. Dessert was a small bowl of assorted berries in a light cream.

One of the servers was a Metis lady called Paniya, probably in her early twenties and I could not keep my eyes off her. I didn't know if it was just such a long time since I had seen the female form or if she was the most beautiful woman I had ever seen.

She must have noticed me staring at her and she smiled and asked, "Can I get you anything else, constable, maybe coffee?"

"Please, just call me James," I said and smiled at her. She was even more striking up close.

"Okay," she said. "We were instructed to call each of you 'constable,' but it will be *James* after this."

I was tongue tied and could not think of another thing to say; I just smiled at her until she was off to continue her duties at another table.

After dinner, we relaxed in our chairs as the Chief Factor provided some background regarding our new home for the next several months.

"Welcome to Fort Edmonton," he began, looking around at the long rows of seated constables, all of us in clean scarlet tunics and blue striped trousers that we had managed to keep in storage for such occasions.

"In 1861 our Fortress was given world-wide attention," Hardisty continued with a strong measure of pride in his voice and demeanor. "We were featured in a British Travel Series, *The Illustrated Record of Voyages, Travels, and Adventures in All Parts of the Globe*. The journal presented engravings of the Wailing Wall, a pillar from the Temple of Solomon, The Enchanted Lakes of the Philippines, and a view of the palisades of Fort Edmonton, the most isolated fortress in the world."

Hardisty smiled a crooked smile and looked out over his audience. "And now a historic moment at Fort Edmonton," he continued, "law and order has come to the northwest of our great dominion."

We all had a glass of some opaque liquid that tasted remotely like mildly fermented dandelion wine for a toast. Liquor was not typically available at the fort because of the example expected to be set for the indigenous people but it was not an unknown commodity either, as Stephen would quickly figure out.

Hardisty lifted his glass, "To the arrival of the Northwest Mounted Police at our great northern fortress."

We all toasted and drank down the bitter sweet beverage.

"I am grateful for your presence. Enjoy your rooms gentlemen. Feel free to make yourselves comfortable in our expansive courtyard and dining halls. I hope you enjoy your time at Fort Edmonton."

Jarvis commenced a round of applause for our gracious host, and then we all scraped back our chairs and went our separate ways. We were provided a couple of days to simply relax in the courtyard, our rooms, or around the fort to rest and regain our health. Our only duty for two days would be care of our horses and oxen.

I could not be more pleased that Marks and Leslie, the ringleaders of the former militia group, were now gone and I felt a lot less under attack; however, it was not uncommon to catch a malicious glance from Jake Lynch, Billy Lillico or Gerome Carlisle. So far, I had been successful in ignoring them. Freddy seemed to be spending more time than ever with the former militia men but I suspected that when he became thirsty he would seek out Stephen; it was their usual pattern, and they seemed always able to escape somewhere to share their stashes of liquor unnoticed by officers.

Stephen and I walked out of the dining area and along the palisade wall leading to the inner court. Some of the high wall was recently rebuilt and still smelling of freshly hewn pine. I ran my hand along the bark-textured guardrail leading to the open air of the inner space.

It was a most impressive fortress. It was warm and sunny in the courtyard and I stopped a moment to look around and savored the sweet smell of cured tobacco sheaths hanging high up along the factory walls and the musky smell of wolf and beaver pelts drying in the sun. We passed the trading house and the agitated voices of Cree traders inside and the deliberate sounds of Cree interpreters trying to calm them. Trading was obviously serious business.

The area around the inner court was expansive, boasting a blacksmith's forge, a windmill for grinding wheat or corn, an internal water well, and a carpenter's shop in addition to all of the accommodations for both single and married families: dining halls, stables, and the Factor's grand house which covered most of the length of one side of the fortress.

We took a chair in the courtyard. Pierre and Julien were in conversation with two of the Metis who lived at the fort. They obviously knew each other and were having a good time with occasional glances at us. I heard reference to *Shit-For-Brains* a few times and howls of laughter from the men. I was pretty sure Pierre was relating my exploits with the oxen and I had no doubt the story would be thoroughly enjoyed by the Metis men.

Then, Pierre waved Stephen and me over to join them. I expect the group could already tell that we were outcasts among the constables and I knew they were big hearted men who would take in anyone who enjoyed their fire, their stories and their songs, which I certainly did.

Pierre introduced us to the two Metis, Gabriel and Malcolm. They both had a story for us and their own way of orienting Stephen and me to our new life at the Edmonton fortress.

"Constables," Malcolm began, "there are many languages around the fort: Cree, French, Gaelic, English, Blackfoot and even more. One word of caution. With the Cree when you say, *'my pig'* it means *'I am a pig.'*"

Malcolm took a long drag of smoke through his clay stem pipe, blew the smoke in a cloud above his head and continued. "Our first missionary here was never warned. He ran around looking for his pig and questioning everyone giving a description of 'my pig' to the howls of delight from the Cree camped below the fort." Malcolm roared with laughter at his own story and we all joined in like a contagion.

"Speaking of the dogs, constables," Gabriel inserted, "The fort has between twenty-five and a hundred fifty people living here depending on the season, not counting hundreds of Indians camped below every now and then. You will notice that most of the time there are more dogs than people at Fort Edmonton and they will drive you crazy until you get used to them." Gabriel held up his hand to show he wasn't finished his story as he ripped off a chunk of dry jerky, chewed it back and swallowed from a flask of water.

He continued. "In winter, they have great value, pulling sleds with supplies to far off destinations and hauling our game in. But in summer, all they do is make love, war, steal everything in sight and harmonize all night under the moon, keeping you awake. You have to get used to them. They are just being dogs!"

Malcolm was hired to hunt game for the fort. He cut into the conversation, "James," he said, "today I spotted a herd of buffalo grazing on the flats a couple of miles downstream from here. Would you like to come with me in the morning?

I will show you the Indian way of hunting buffalo, but there can only be two of us."

"Of course," I responded, "I would love it, and it is my day off."

"Meet me by the canoes below the fort around nine o'clock and I will teach you something new."

In the morning, I waited by the canoes with my carbine in hand until almost ten o'clock when Malcolm showed up carrying a long flowing wolf hide intact with head, eyes and flopping legs. A buffalo calf hide was similarly endowed.

"We must hurry in case they decide to move on," said Malcolm. We both paddled hard until we approached a meadow about two miles below the fort where we unloaded and Malcolm signalled me to follow him. He crouched low and trotted to the top of a hillock below which was a herd of maybe seventy buffalo grazing.

Malcolm whispered his instruction. "You pull the wolf hide over you, like this." He showed me how to robe myself. "I wear the buffalo calf. Follow me and when I signal, you jump on me like a wolf on a buffalo calf and then just follow my lead."

We crept over the hill on hands and knees in our costumes and I followed Malcolm to within a few hundred feet of the buffalo who continued to graze. Malcolm poked an arm out and waved for me to jump on top of him. I climbed all over him like I was eating him alive and he began the most hideous bawling and wailing as the herd suddenly turned toward us, their heads high, snorting loudly, bounding back and forth, their eyes wild and then they charged.

The entire herd came down upon us, easily within range of our rifles, but Malcolm continued his pathetic wailing with such authenticity that I was sure the entire herd of pounding hooves and flashing horns would grind us into the dirt. At the last moment Malcolm leaped up, rifle in hand, firing into the herd, as did I. We brought down a dozen buffalo before the herd managed to whirl in a cloud of dust and clods of flying meadow grass, racing away from us.

Malcolm grinned and tossed off the last of his calf hide. "You can handle that carbine pretty good," he said through a wide grin.

"Yeah, but I almost filled my pants first," I responded, "couldn't you get them any closer?"

Malcolm tilted his head back, white teeth gleaming and howled with laughter. It was a good day's hunting.

CHAPTER 14

Sam Steele awoke at dawn, looked around at his new quarters and threw a block of firewood into the fireplace. He lay back down but could not sleep. Jarvis had given him much responsibility for the success of the northern force, a responsibility that Sam took to heart. And Sam had his own vision that he reinforced with his command at every opportunity. The constabulary must enforce the law with courage and an even hand. Justice must apply equally to the whites and the Indians who were not used to the laws of the dominion.

Sam got up again. The mercury on a thermometer outside his door recorded twenty-three below. The courtyard in front of his window was piled with six inches of fresh snow. It was not quite five am. He could already smell cooking stoves roasting venison and bannock frying in lard. Soon it would be time to drill the men below the fort, but first he would see Hardisty who was notoriously among the first to arise in the morning. It had been a long time since he had known such comfort but the challenges ahead were daunting and pressing. He dressed and walked through the morning darkness towards Hardisty's office where candlelight was already glowing in his window. The Big House of Hardisty was three stories high. The Factor did business on the main floor where he could look out over the courtyard.

He quickly ushered Sam inside. Hardisty's desk was piled high with documents and writing paper behind a deep inkwell with an assortment of quill and metal nib pens attached. His working quarters were large and opulent compared to most frontier fortresses that Sam had encountered. A lit fireplace of quarried stone stood high on an inside wall and a flint lock rifle hung over the polished mantle. Four wooden, high backed chairs with bevelled arm rests and cushioned seats were arranged around the table where Hardisty worked. There was no doubting that the Hudson's Bay Company continued to be profitable even after relinquishing much of the northwest to the Dominion.

Hardisty pulled out a chair for Sam. Then he summoned a pretty Metis woman whom he called Paniya to bring tea. She set out two china cups and a teapot from a small cabinet in Hardisty's office and left.

"I like your place, Richard," Sam said, looking around.

Hardisty laughed. "Well, I guess I am the benefactor of a previous Chief Factor, John Rowand. You may have heard of him. He had expensive tastes but he also made the company very profitable.

"I must say, Sam, I deeply admire your fortitude. It must be a most daunting task, bringing law to such a raw and vast northwest."

"That's where I need your help, Richard. You know this land and the tribes that live here better than anyone. How do you think they will respond to police presence?"

"I belief that most of the Cree, Stony and Blackfoot confederacy will welcome your peaceful intervention; although, that is yet to be decided," Hardisty replied. "Historically they have fought brutal wars, murdering each other even just outside our walls."

Paniya returned with a boiling kettle, filled the teapot, placed ground tea leaves inside, stirred quickly and poured two cups. She offered sugar and cream. Hardisty thanked her. She smiled and left.

Richard continued, "The defiant whisky traders, most of them from south of the boundary line but some from eastern destinations, continue to bring in wagonloads of whisky and they make huge profits. They know their trade is illegal and they probably understand the devastating effect it has on the tribes but they don't care."

Hardisty blew into his tea cup, sampled it, and set his cup back down. "When confronted they arrogantly respond that, 'we know all about your laws but who is going to stop us?' And they more or less peddle their rot-gut openly. One thing leaves little doubt: whisky is the cause of most of the trouble with the local tribes."

Settling back in his chair, Hardisty continued. "The tribal leaders clearly see the problem, but even they have little influence over the young warrior bands who become increasingly reckless with alcohol and in a frenzy to settle old scores. Bad blood has existed between some of the tribes for decades, maybe even centuries. With the whisky trade, much of the old animosity has come to the forefront with murdering, revenge, and open warfare."

He sighed and looked out his window for a long moment. "The death of so many young men coupled with so much sheer drunkenness is putting the economies and wellbeing of the Indian communities at risk of survival. They aren't used to what Europeans have brought here; they haven't had a history with alcohol and no chance to become accustomed to the Whiteman's 'fire water' and its effects."

Sam drew in a long breath. "Going after the whisky trade must be a first priority then. Do you know where these traders operate from?"

"One of my hunters was recently near Buffalo Lake where a congregation of Indians and Metis occasionally inhabit cabins in the Metis settlement there. They like to hunt, but many of them like to party even more when the opportunity allows. The understanding of my hunter was that a whisky outfit was on their way. I expect they would have arrived by now."

Sam thanked Hardisty and left. Freezing cold or not, Steele wasted no time. He immediately selected seven men whom he thought had demonstrated competence, skill, marksmanship or loyalty during the time he led the contingency. After drill, he called out their names: James McGinn, Billy Lillico, Willie Savine, Ervin Milner, Freddy Baker, Doug Lynch and Stephen Woodward.

The Metis employees prepared a dog team and sled for the supplies that Steele thought necessary to take. He chose not to bring tents or stoves that would slow progress in spite of a temperature of twenty-three below and getting colder. Seven hardy mustangs were saddled up for the trip; they were now well broken in and able to stand freezing temperatures much better than the thoroughbreds.

The men dressed for the weather in their buffalo great coats, bear hide fur caps and buffalo hide mittens. Beneath the buffalo fur coats, open in a V shape starting from the navel, they still exhibited their scarlet tunics buttoned tight across their necks. They wore blue striped woolen pants of the Northwest constabulary.

Steele headed south with the small force of mounties towards Buffalo Lake. It was two days travel. He set up camp an hour before dark allowing the mustangs time to settle in with oats and shelter beneath a stand of pine. The men shovelled out a section of snow down to the ground leaving a high ridge to reflect heat from the campfire. Firewood was gathered and they lit a high blaze before laying buffalo hides down around the fire. They roasted buffalo hump, ate bread and drank tea before settling into their buffalo robes around the fire. The dogs slept at their feet and volunteers stoked and kept the fire burning all night. All of them woke appearing well rested. It had been a comfortable night in spite of the cold.

It was late afternoon when Steele and the constabulary arrived on the wind-swept shores of Buffalo Lake with scores of log cabins scattered among the trees along the lake. Only a few had smoke curling above the chimneys. Steele retrieved a brass scope from his saddle bags and surveyed the cabins and adjacent area. He sent McGinn and Woodward to investigate a wagon partially hidden among stands of aspen half a mile from the clusters of buildings. The wagons appeared to have hogshead barrels stacked inside.

"Full of whisky," McGinn reported upon his return, "and piles of empty wooden barrels stacked in the bush."

Steele led the men closer to a cluster of cabins that showed the most chimney smoke. They were met with the sounds of laughter and lively fiddle music. Steele moved to the cabin where foot stomps pounding on plank floors was the loudest. Cigar smoke and howls of laughter rolled out the open door.

Steele split up the men. Baker, Lynch and Milner were sent off to the cabins to inquire about the owners of the wagons and question the inhabitants regarding newcomers to the settlement. Lillico and Savine were left to guard the horses.

Steele chose McGinn and Woodward to flank him. Sam walked through the door and the fiddle music stopped and the dancers seemed to freeze in stride.

"I want the owners of those wagons and horses tethered in the bush to step forth. You are under arrest."

No one came forth.

Freddy Baker showed up. "May I have a word, sir."

Steele looked out across the group of partiers. "No one leaves here until I say," commanded Steele with authority. "McGinn, Woodward, make sure no one leaves." Then he turned to the group inside, about twenty of them men and eight or nine women. "Any person tries to leave they are disobeying an officer and will be shot."

Steele stepped outside with Freddy. "What did you find out, Baker?"

"I have the owners of the wagons, sir. One of the cabins has four older Metis women inside and they are scared to death. The partiers get drunk and assault them. They told me the main trader is a bulky man in a green checkered woolen jacket with a thick head and his name is Coffman, she thinks Bill Coffman. His partner is Arnold Schultz. The other two, one of the women thinks, are hired helpers and they are called Pony Deal and Scruff."

Steele went back in. "Okay, I want Coffman, now!" Nobody moved. There was one man in the room who fit the description; he wore a green checkered shirt and his thick neck and head were more or less continuous. McGinn and

Woodward kept their revolvers levelled at the group. Steele approached slowly without looking at Coffman. Then, he put one hand on the man's arm and another on the back of his collar, hauling him through the open door and pushing him face first into the snow bank. "McGinn," he commanded, "keep your service revolver on the back of this guy's neck."

Steele went back in. "Okay, now it's Schultz." A slim man with pointed nose and sweaty bare chest from partying hard came forth. "Take it easy," he said, "I'm Schultz."

"Bring Deal and Scruff with you or I'll pull them out one at a time."

Schultz nodded towards two men who were already moving for the door. "Scruff, Deal, come." The two men walked in a wide berth around Sam Steele and moved outside under the watchful eye and levelled revolver of Freddy Baker.

"Everybody else go back to your cabins," Steele commanded.

The group quickly dissipated and the constables marched the four whisky traders back to the wagons. The traders had three more wagons parked nearby, each filled with buffalo hides, firearms and ammunition. Eight horses were tethered in the bush. Steele sent Lillico to the dog sled for an axe.

He turned to Coffman, "take the axe and spill every drop of whisky from the hogsheads. Then split the empties while you're at it."

Coffman took the axe, started towards the barrels then swung the axe hard at Sam's head. Steele could have shot and killed him but he ducked and then laid Coffman out cold with a single punch. Sam took the axe and turned to Schultz.

"Your turn, spill the whisky." The trader was still sweaty and bare chested in the freezing cold.

"Then split the empty barrels. It'll warm you up," Steele added.

The police confiscated 125 buffalo robes, four Henry rifles and four Colt revolvers. Three of the wagons and six of the horses were seized.

By now Coffman was aroused and sitting on a tree stump. "Hope your pockets are full as your fine is one hundred dollars each for you and Schultz and twenty each for Deal and Scruff here. Otherwise, you all are cuffed and chained and it's a long walk back to Fort Edmonton."

Schultz rooted around in the wagons with Stephen's revolver trained on the back of his neck. He eventually came up with the cash and counted it into Steele's hand.

Sam Steele recounted the money, then he directed them, "head back where you came from. Hang around and you will spend Christmas vacation in the guard house. Tell your friends that you got off lucky compared to what they'll get if they show up here." Sam motioned towards the horses and wagons. "You'll have one wagon and two horses. Go get your coat on Schultz. I want you out of my sight before dark."

***

Sam had barely arrived back at the fort when Hardisty summoned him to come to the Factor's quarters. He met Sam at the door with a wide grin. "The view from my window tells me you found the devils and cleaned them out. Congratulations." Hardisty moved away from his desk and offered Sam a seat. They settled into chairs on either side of the fireplace.

"We caught them by surprise which made everything a lot easier," Sam reported. He described how they discovered the identity of the traders, arrested them, destroyed their whisky stashes and confiscated everything of value connecting to their trade and levied a stiff fine.

"Well done," Hardisty responded, "Now I have new intelligence that I think will interest the police." He leaned back in his chair and clasped his hands behind his head studying Sam. "Some time ago, before your arrival we had trouble with a rascal whose name is Tahakooch," Hardisty began. "He is a Cree who often camped near the fort with his brothers. He is a well-known murderer, robber and general troublemaker."

"Two Sarcee showed up to trade at the fort," Hardisty continued. "Tahakooch pretended to befriend them, invited them to his teepee for the night. The next day the Sarcee needed to travel back to their tribe, a two-day trip. It was getting evening but the Indians often travel at night as much as during the day," Hardisty explained. He stoked the embers in the fireplace and threw on more wood.

"Tahakooch told them they would need provisions from the fort for their trip home. The man on watch at the gate had been in the bastion as they approached. He could see that Tahakooch had a rifle concealed under his coat. He knocked at the fort door and the attendant let all three inside. The Sarcee bought pemmican, blankets and ammunition." Hardisty reached for a box of cigars and offered one to Sam, which he declined.

"Then our attendant watched from the bastion as they left the fort and continued across the meadows below. On the far side, Tahakooch fell behind them and then fired into the two Sarcee with a double barrel gun. One fell dead, the other was wounded and made a run for it with Tahakooch right behind him."

Hardisty lit up his cigar and continued. "The attendant witnessed a most brutal knife fight, the wounded Sarcee trying to defend himself and fight back, but he was no match for Tahakooch who ran him through with a knife five or six times. Then he took all the Sarcee's purchases from the fort, proceeded to go through the rest of their stuff, took what he wanted, including their horses. He came back to his brother's teepee. They loaded up, left the area and have not been seen again, until yesterday. One of our Metis workers reported seeing him.

"Where?" asked Sam, "and how long ago?"

"Well," responded Hardisty, "just this morning. Gabriel had been collecting firewood from a mature stand of birch about five miles out. It was hard work and he left his coat with his supplies on the dog sled. When he returned his coat was gone and most of his supplies. He followed the robber's tracks to the top of a high hill where he could look across a stretch of frozen marshland and spotted Tahakooch on the pinto mustang that he rides. And it isn't hard to identify Tahakootch. He always rides a certain way, maybe a habit, but unique to him, always sitting turned half sideways where he can watch behind him as much as in front. That's how he always rides."

"What time?" asked Sam.

"Gabriel told me all this about an hour ago and it was probably an hour ride back to the fort from where he last saw Tahakooch, so late this morning."

"Thanks," said Sam getting up. "Still enough daylight to go after him. I would like Gabriel to come with us."

"I'll get him," said Hardisty.

The seven Mounties were putting away horses after the trip from Buffalo Lake. The dogs were still in harness chewing on a ration of frozen white fish.

Sam met the men at the stables. "I want McGinn and Baker. Saddle fresh mounts and come with me."

Gabriel took control of the dog sled. Steele, McGinn and Baker followed. They set out for the birch stands and Gabriel led them to the high knoll where he had last seen Tahakooch heading east across the frozen muskeg.

Sam Steele followed the tracks of Tahakooch to the top of a frozen watercourse and a Cree encampment of four teepees nestled among a grove of pine below. Two moose were gutted and hung in the trees. Four dogs were feeding nearby. There was not a sound from the encampment. Most likely everyone was inside out of the freezing cold.

"Probably two families," replied Gabriel. "Moose hunting for a few days, then moving on."

Gabriel pointed out Tahakooch's pinto gelding tethered with three other horses.

"I'm going in and I want Gabriel to come with me as interpreter.

"McGinn, Baker, you stay here near the horses. If Tahakooch makes a run for his horse or on foot, bring him down but not with sidearms unless your life is threatened. I mean use a physical restraint, catch him and bring him down, use your handcuffs. He most likely carries a knife, possibly a rifle, so be cautious, shoot only if you have to but I prefer to bring him in without injury."

Sam and Gabriel approached the largest teepee with much smoke exiting the draft. The dogs were occupied, snarling at each other and pulling apart the entrails of the moose and had no time for Sam or Gabriel. Sam pulled open the tent flap and stood back. Four men were sitting around inside, keeping warm by the fire.

Sam began, "I come in peace for just one man. We are the police, bringing the laws of the great white mother to the north."

Gabriel interpreted.

"I am only here for Tahakooch, who has broken the law and he must come with me. He will be treated fairly." Sam had not drawn a revolver or pointed a rife, although his sidearm was easily accessible. There was something about the power and authority that Sam Steele had when he spoke that men listened and Sam knew it. It was obvious who Tahakooch was; all the men looked towards him. He was a lean man with a large crooked nose, pocked face and one blind eye.

They all watched Sam for several moments. No one spoke or moved. Then Tahakooch rose slowly, bent down to exit the tent and stood outside. His cold gaze looked Sam over, head to foot. Sam told him to turn and face the tent. Gabriel passed the word in Cree. The warrior turned slowly. Sam put handcuffs on him and they walked back to the horses and dog team. Baker gave up his mount to the prisoner. Steele took the halter shank of the prisoner's horse. Baker rode with Gabriel on the dog sled and McGinn followed behind the prisoner with his firearm ready if needed.

Sam Steele had completed the arrest of Tahakooch. They returned to the fort before dark. Sam would have the prisoner escorted tomorrow by two constables to Fort Walsh for trial.

CHAPTER 15

Stephen and I were given time to rest the next day. Our only chores including participation in the morning drill and routine chores caring for the horses and oxen. It was a pleasant day. The temperature had risen suddenly and there were the welcoming sounds of melting snow dripping off the fortress walls and roofs of trading buildings.

Outside, the south fortress wall was lined with wooden benches and a few narrow tables where many of the men were soaking up the sun and socializing. Several of the militia men were arm wrestling at one of the tables and Carlisle seemed to be the top dog and no doubt feeling cocky having pinned most of his comrades. Stephen, Malcolm, Julien and I were sitting further down.

Gerome was the biggest man among them, about my height and probably several pounds heavier. I could feel his eyes on me. Finally, he called out amid a mixture of grins and glares from his comrades. "Hey, McGinn, tough guy, come over and try the champ."

"No thanks, Carlisle," I responded, "no desire to spoil a nice day."

I knew there was heavy sarcasm in my voice which was more or less what I intended. And that, apparently, didn't go down well with Gerome.

"What's the matter," he said, "I'm not defenseless enough for you, like Tom when you wanted to leave him for the wolves." I stared at him. He was triggering me in a way that I didn't really want to be triggered.

"Fuck em," said Malcolm. "Let them have their sport. Who cares." I turned slowly back to my group and tried to ignore Carlisle.

"Or maybe you'd rather sneak up on me and shoot me in the back like you did Spider. Some hunting trip eh?"

It was suddenly more than I could bear. I walked over to him. He swung around in his chair to face me. I sat across from him. "Want to settle it with a little arm wrestle do you Gerome?" I asked.

"Sure," he said, "for starters."

I had no doubt he would bring me down in an arm wrestle and I wasn't about to play his game. He sat there, his arm cocked on the table, flexing his bicep with a smug grin, waiting for me.

I should have ignored his bluster but I was seething inside and had already resolved to knock the smirk off his face. I swung with everything I had and connected with the side of his chin as his head snapped back and his jaw twisted and cracked and his cheek stretched above his rows of yellow and missing teeth. The back of his chair split open landing him on his back in the wet snow.

Men scattered from the table and to Carlisle's credit he found his feet and came at me with both fists flying. I heard Lynch calling out for him to knock the piss out of me and the next I knew we were both on the ground with him on top of me first and then me on top when Jarvis came around the corner, grabbed me by the back of my collar and pulled me off.

"Can't keep yourself out of trouble can you, McGinn?" He completely ignored Gerome, who sat back down on his chair as if he was the most innocent son of a bitch that ever lived while I was catching the full wrath of Jarvis.

"Piss on you," I finally responded, "what about this smart aleck cocksucker piping off and starting the whole thing."

Jarvis grabbed my shoulders and spun me around. "You need a couple days under lock to cool down." He looked like he was pleased to finally catch me on something. All his smoldering grudges from our many conflicts along the trail had obviously been fomenting. He pressed me towards an unused storage building that was apparently doubling as a guard house. He pushed me inside and barred the door. There was no heat. "I'll send someone over with a blanket," he called from outside.

It was a dark and hungry couple of days and the temperature dropped to freezing cold. I don't know how long I huddled inside my blanket wondering if they would find me frozen stiff when they decided to let me out. Jarvis came the next day to unbar the door with a lecture and warning.

"You have shown yourself to be a good enough police officer, McGinn, but make no mistake, keep up your attitude and you'll get to know the inside of this place very well."

I said nothing and gave him a cold stare. I expect he knew it wasn't the last he would have to deal with me. The irony was, I believed that none of it had been my fault.

The cold spell stayed and over the next several days the temperature dropped so low that Sam Steele had to suspend drill to prevent frost bite affecting the men. One thing I had learned about Edmonton: the weather was as unpredictable as Jarvis's moods. Our only duties for the next few days was attending to the livestock.

After chores one morning, Stephen and I walked across the courtyard past a huge fur press and into the trade stores for a look around. An air tight stove kept the place warm and we huddled by the heater for a moment. Cree traders were negotiating in a back room accessed from outside the fort. They were not yet allowed into the store. They presented their fur through a window into the main trading area.

Paniya was with the clerks and trader in the trade room, interpreting. It was the first I had seen her for several days and I felt my chest already beginning to pound. I was surprised that I still reacted to her the same way and I could not take my eyes off of her until Stephen poked me in the ribs.

"I think she has a Cree husband," he said. "I'm told he hunts during the winter."

"I laughed, "so why you telling me?"

"Yeah, I wonder why," he said, a cynical smile crossing his face. "haven't you had enough trouble already: Jarvis, the militia men?"

Paniya finished interpreting for the trader. The Cree man was allowed into the trade store to select his merchandise. His credit was apparently good and a clerk provided the goods he wanted and recorded them in a ledger.

"I have to check on one of the horses," Stephen said, opening the door and letting in a blast of cold.

Paniya turned from the trade counter.

"Hi James," she said with a warm smile. "See, you get a personal greeting. You're not just *constable* anymore," she laughed.

I was dumb struck again and not sure I could think of a thing to say. I smiled at her. Then, I managed to say, "you wear a lot of hats around here," then I wished I could have thought of something a lot more elegant or romantic.

"Fort Edmonton is a large, complicated place," she said. "You don't know half the things I can do." She laughed and her teeth were beautiful and her smile always got to the pit of my stomach in a way that I couldn't really describe. I was struck with the realization she was flirting with me and I couldn't think of a damn thing to say to her.

"I heard that you've been busy the last two days," she said. "I am so glad you sent the whisky traders away. They cause more trouble for our people than anything else. And then catching Tahakooch. I never trusted him and we all feel a lot safer now."

"Thanks," I responded.

"But you know, James, you do need to keep yourself out of trouble with your boss. I wouldn't want to see you sent away so soon, I'm barely getting to know you!"

"I promise I'll stay out of trouble from now on. It's my resolution for the up-coming new year, to start 1875 off on a brand-new footing."

"Well, I hope you stick to the promise, I have enjoyed you being here. And you know, James, when it warms up I will show you around the fort and all the things I can do here."

"I would love that," I said, "and I know I'll be impressed."

She laughed. "Well, I have to run," she said. "And I hope to see you at the Christmas party."

"This is the first I knew about it," I responded. "And I'm really looking forward to a tour of the fortress as well," I said.

She smiled at me over her shoulder as she opened the door and then moved quickly out into the cold.

The next morning after drill Sam Steele informed us of the annual Christmas party at the fort. Every single one of the men agreed to give up a month's pay to finance the party. Jarvis wanted to invite guests from the fort and settlements for miles around as a critical opportunity for the police to introduce themselves. I did not catch a glimpse of Paniya again for several days. Christmas rolled around and I was looking forward to seeing her.

On Christmas day a grand feast was laid out in a large room that was initially intended to be a reception area for the leaders of the tribes that came to the fort; the room was decorated to impress the indigenous chiefs. I too was impressed to find such decor in a vast and isolated fortress. Center pieces of gilded scrolls covered the ceiling and the wallboards were painted liberally with bright gaudy colors of red, yellow and green. The area was warmed with two stone fireplaces and mantles decorated in a Christmas style with pine boughs, dried rose hips and ribbons. Paniya was not there. Maybe she would be serving.

Lengthy tables were prepared in simple magnificence: long boards of polished birch construction and colorful china unique for a frontier fortress, graced the dining tables at Fort Edmonton. Everyone found a seat as servers brought in great platters of food: buffalo hump, called *boss ribs* by the locals, white fish browned in buffalo marrow, dishes of dried moose nose called mouffle. More favorite dishes were piled on the polished plank table until it was full. Servers brought in sliced beaver tails, roasted wild goose and hind quarters of buffalo. Two servers on either end of a long metal platter brought in a steaming boiled buffalo calf taken by C- section, a tender delicacy and preserved in the icehouse for the Christmas festivity. Vegetables included roasted potatoes, parsnips and beets. Plum puddings and mince pies were served for dessert.

One of the largest storerooms in the fortress was decorated for a dance following the feast. The room was embellished at either end with huge fireplaces fueled with long sections of birch logs that kept a constant heat. Main doors opened onto the courtyard to cool the place down if it became too heated up. The dance hall slowly filled up. There was an assortment of humanity from more different backgrounds than I had ever imagined could show in the same place at the same time. A half-dozen different languages were bounced about and very little of it was English.

Leaders of the local tribes, mainly Cree chiefs of some distinction, showed up in their buckskin apparel, a few of them with feathers in their hair and some had white or red paint across their faces. The Metis guests glittered with ornamental dress and bright colors while the voyageurs turned out in wide colorful sashes, and high leather leggings. Slowly, one side of the room filled up with the women and girls taking a seat on benches on the opposite side of the men. Everyone waited as the fiddlers scraped and tuned their instruments.

Only then did I see Paniya. She came in alone and sat at the very end of the row of women, closest to the door as the place was nearly full. She was absolutely stunning with her shiny black hair braided and pinned around the back of her head. She wore a green fitted brocade jacket with long sleeves that buttoned down the front with a full skirt and high beaded moccasins. I knew I was staring at her. She looked across the room and smiled at me, a smile that started my chest pounding. I smiled back, but I felt a bit foolish because I realized I had been staring at her.

Then the fiddlers set off with lively music: The Red River Jig, the Eight Hand Reel, Lord MacDonald's Reel and many more favorites. But when the first cord struck, men leaped from their seats, practically in unison with tunes flying off fiddle strings as fast as the fiddlers could shuffle their bows. There was a rush across the room to pick a partner. I started late but pushed to the head of the pack, afraid that someone would ask Paniya onto the floor before I had a chance. I was the first to her and she looked relieved as I took her hand and asked her onto the floor.

"My, James, you are fast!" she laughed. "And I prayed that you had not been sent out on the trail of a killer or band of whisky traders on Christmas day."

"I didn't see you at dinner either," I replied, "and was afraid something had happened to you."

"I was cooking in the kitchen, just another one of my hats, as you would say."

I stood with her in the middle of the floor. Suddenly I didn't know what to do, I was never at a dance like this one before.

"Well James," she said patiently, "what would you like to do now?"

I looked around at all the dancers. Most of them stood separate but facing each other, each bounding, shuffling or swinging to their own beat of the music.

"We can dance the Indian way or the Whiteman way," Paniya said. "I can do either. In the dances of the Cree we face each other, occasionally catch hands and move to our own beat. Or we can dance the Whiteman way where we hold each other and move together to the music. When it comes to dancing, I prefer the Whiteman way," she smiled.

"That's a very safe choice," I responded. "If I stick to what I know, I won't be bounding all over you."

"That would be interesting," she laughed.

I took Paniya in my arms and held her close as we began a lively waltz, carving our own way in circles around the expansive dance hall and she followed me every step of the way. By midnight we took a break.

"It's a warm night, Paniya," I said. "Remember the tour you promised me when the weather warms?"

She took my hand and led me out through the palisade walls across a clearing to the edge of the forest. It was a beautiful warm night and she took me where the snow had been cleared away for workers chopping wood and we sat down on a long chopping bench.

The wilderness was about as dark as it could possibly get. But high above, the sky was ablaze with the most dazzling array of stars and northern lights that were more brilliant than any I ever had occasion to observe. They waved in bands of blue and violet across the entire zenith of the heavens from north to south with a ball of red in the center like a misty sun sending out rays that turned from red to blue to deep orange.

Paniya moved close to me and held my hand. "Aren't they beautiful," she said. "Do you know what they are?"

"Nobody knows for sure," I said, "Maybe the residue of a comet that has crossed the sky."

"Oh James," she said. "White people know so little." She smiled. "The lights are so incredible. They are the spirits of our ancestors. People that loved us so much and have now gone. I think they're here just for you and me, sending love and beauty across the heavens just for us.

"And they are so sensitive," she said looking up at me, her dark eyes deep and serious. "Let me tell you what happened once." She moved closer to me squeezing my hand on her lap.

"One night a grandfather was with his grandson, camped out, trapping muskrats, and the lights came. 'Never whistle at them,' the grandfather said, 'because it is an insult to the beautiful low whispering sound they send out to the people of the earth.'

"The grandson was arrogant and full of his own ego. He stood up, tilting his face and whistled loudly into the night sky. The lights waltzed suddenly towards them and hovered overhead. A red light opened up straight above them, hissing and rattling like a snake with a gaping mouth and fiery red fangs. The grandfather folded up on the ground like a fetus in the snow. From a leather pouch he lit a braid of sweet grass with matches and smudged a drum from his bag. He waved the drum in circles through the smoke and then began beating the drum in a soft rhythm to appease the insulted ancestors.

"They waved gently and slowly they moved back into the sky. A year later the arrogant grandson was dead. It is a true story."

"I shall only revere them, now more than ever," I said.

We walked on a long path outside the palisade of the fortress and I asked her about her life here.

"Well, I only spend winters in the fort. I have no children and I have a husband," she said, "but my heart has never been with him. He has two wives and he has always provided well for both of us and for my aging mother as well with his trapping and hunting, which he is very good at. All are afraid of him except me. I have some power over him."

Paniya stopped and gazed up at me, her beautiful eyes looking deep into mine. "I have stayed with him because there was no other that I wanted to be with and he keeps my mother well cared for, which is the most important thing to me. And I am faithful to him, more or less," she laughed, "but I cannot say we really live as man and wife."

She took my hand and we began walking again. "His other wife is a good person and she gives me freedom to do most everything I want and I get along well with her. She has no children either, and she seems to like the camp life whereas I like my work at the fort in winter and learning from the medicine women in the summer village.

We walked back through the fortress walls and into the dance hall where I held her close to me and could feel the warmth of her and the gentle curves of her body as we waltzed the night away. With the first signs of morning lighting up the eastern sky I walked her back to her room in the Big House.

"I hope to see you again soon," I said.

"Oh James, it was such a lovely time. I want so badly to see you again too."

Then she stood on her tiptoes gave me a warm kiss on my lips and turned to open the heavy door. She looked deep into my eyes for a long moment, squeezed my arm and walked inside.

CHAPTER 16

The next day after drill, I found my Metis friends talking outside on wooden benches enjoying another burst of warm winter weather and the slowly melting snow. I joined them and took part in their story telling. It was a place to catch up on outside news or anything new going on in Fort Edmonton society.

Gradually the men went about their day's business and it was only Malcolm and I, so I asked him about Paniya.

"Oh, you be careful about that one," he said. "She is a wonderful girl, loved and admired by all of us. And there is not a man among us who would not give his back teeth to share her wigwam. But she is married to Two Bears, he is a fierce warrior and a great hunter who can also be a trouble maker."

Malcolm's eyes became wild. "He is not one to mess with and he is feared even by the men in his own village. He is not encouraged to come to the fort but he comes anyway and most of the time nobody can really stop him. His wife works here and she speaks all the languages: Cree, English, Gaelic, some pretty good French, and she has picked up a lot of the Blackfoot tongue from listening around the trading room. She can interpret languages for any of the groups and she is of immense value to the Factor. She is as smart as she is beautiful."

Atonement to a Greater God

Malcolm filled his pipe with tobacco and lit up with a sulphur match, blew a cloud of smoke above his head and continued. "Two Bears likes the money she brings in and he spends it as fast as she makes it on supplies from the fort, ammunition, tobacco, anything else that catches his eye. But mainly he shows up here to spy on her and I warn you, don't cross Two Bears, he is very jealous. He would kill you in an instant if he thought you were interested."

***

The days passed quickly. Sam Steele never neglected to remind us that we were still a police force. Every morning at bugle call we were on the field below the fort for drills before 5:30 am, even in thirty below weather. He increased the number of drills and inspections as our official duties had diminished considerably.

One day as drill was just finishing, Hardisty came down from the Big House to speak to Sam while the rest of us were still gathered around our drill instructor. Hardisty's mouth was a thin line and he spoke quickly to Sam.

"Kiskawasis, the wife killer, arrived at the fort early this morning with furs to exchange. He has been away hunting and trapping since last fall and left here before you arrived," Hardisty explained. "He is most likely unaware that the mounted police are stationed here. Old habits seem hard to break and he is accustomed to strutting around the fort like a bantam rooster. No one wanted to confront him." Hardisty sighed.

"Where is he right now?" asked Sam.

"He started a fire on the flats below the fort waiting for the trading room to open."

"People here have witnessed his crimes?" asked Sam.

"Oh yes," said Hardisty. "Several of the staff witnessed the whole thing. It was a brutal murder and not the first that Kiskawasis is known for. His wife had been running to the fort screaming and pleading for her life. He overcame her, threw her down to the ground in a most barbaric manner, then beat and stabbed her to death and left her on the ground. He left immediately on his horse and this is the first we have seen him since."

Sam Steele turned to us. "I want James McGinn and Willie Savine." Steele always seemed to be on my side no matter how much trouble I had been in with Jarvis. "Bring only your side arms," he instructed me and Willie, "and keep them holstered unless you need them."

At the top of the hill, we watched Kiskawasis roasting meat over a lone campfire with his horse tethered nearby. "Stay here," instructed Sam. "Do not interfere unless something happens to me. Then it will be up to the two of you to complete the arrest."

We watched as Sam approached the campfire. Kiskawasis stood up, studying Sam closely, then the Cree extracted a wide bone handled knife from a leather pouch tied across his waist. He stood with his feet wide apart and his knife raised towards Sam, ready for a fight. Sam continued to walk casually toward him without drawing a weapon and the Cree crouched, his knife in hand and began circling towards Sam.

"Kiskawasis?" asked Sam rather casually.

The man straightened, then nodded ever so slightly at Sam, maybe surprised to hear his name. In an instant Sam brought his high leather boot straight up, kicking the knife from Kiskawasis's hand and sending it in a high looping arc through the air; he then tackled Kiskawasis, like a linebacker in a game of football, bringing him down hard into the snow. He struggled furiously as Sam pinned him on his stomach and handcuffed him. The arrest was complete.

Kiskawasis was escorted to Winnipeg the next day to stand trial for murder.

***

Two days later day a gathering of twenty or more Cree camped below the fort began a steady beating of tom-toms, lighting great circles of fires, and voicing a steady chant to the rhythm of the pounding drums.

A Cree messenger arrived at the fort. He relayed that the great Cree leader, Meechin, wished to speak to the chiefs of the white mother and to smoke the pipe of peace. Sam and Jarvis went down to meet them and many of us were instructed to come too, without firearms or horses to demonstrate our peaceful welcome and gestures of good will. Jarvis brought gifts of calico, tea and ammunition.

Most of the gathering were older men decorated with feathers and dressed in handsome doeskin apparel replete with beads and dyed porcupine quills. The Indians assembled in a circle outside their teepees. Jarvis and Steele approached Meechin and offered gifts. Meechin invited them to sit with him. The rest of us formed an outer circle.

Meechin wore a resplendent bonnet of red and white eagle feathers and carried a long stem pipe decorated with buckskin fringes, fragments of elk ivory and shells. He spoke English amazingly well.

He began, "Talk of the many things done since the white Queen's soldiers arrived has travelled far among all the tribes in every direction from here," he said, as he moved his arm through a wide arc in the air. "Some of the tribes are our friends and some of them have been our enemies for a long time.

"We all watched when the first white men brought their wagons loaded down with bad whisky. Only our young men welcomed them and we knew the trouble that would follow but young people have their own minds," he said, his voice dipping with resignation, "and nothing will stop them." When he spoke again his voice was strong. "We hear that some of the worst whisky traders have been caught and the rest are running like rabbits before the wolf pack. Everything the Red Coats have done is good," said Meechin to the assembled groups. "And the tribes respect their even-handed work, their bravery and fairness.

"The great mother's chief did not disappoint us when he arrested the worst among us, like Tahakooch and Kiskawasis, trouble makers that got slowly worse with the flow of whisky that brought so much murder and drunkenness to our encampments. Since you came, we have started to live in peace with our traditional enemy, the Blackfoot. We both come to the fort at the same time now, to trade without fear of each other, something that we didn't do before.

"Now we invite the Queen Mother's chiefs to smoke with us, to celebrate a great peace with our white brothers."

Meechin sat down to light the pipe. Then he stood and chanted words that I didn't understand as he drew in the smoke and let it out again. When the pipe was warmed up and releasing much smoke on its own, he waved the pipe with long streams of smoke to the four points of the compass, then towards the sky and down to the ground as he continued a low chant with much reverence. Then with great dignity and grace he took a seat on the ground and passed the pipe to Jarvis who smoked and passed it to Steele, each of them drew on the pipe with expressions of quiet contemplation and released small clouds of smoke towards the center of the gathering.

Jarvis stood and spoke to the assembly of Cree. He explained that the Indians tribes need never fear the police who will only enforce punishment on individuals who break the law. Never will they inflict war on entire encampments of men, women and children as white settlers have done south of the Medicine Line.

In time, Sam Steele talked with all the great chieftains that came to Fort Edmonton: Blackfoot, Cree, Stony and Sarcee. Many smoked with Sam and all seemed to agree with the Cree chief, Meechin.

***

Our official duties were considerably reduced compared to our first weeks at the northern fortress. Occasionally there were arrests made usually theft of property by whites, Indians, or Metis alike.

But Steele never ceased to keep the force ready and strong. We began drills, training and equestrian riding skills twice a day along with inspection of our uniforms, kits and regular chores to maintain the animals. We were also expected to pull our weight on the home front and there was no end to the work needed to maintain the fort.

We assisted the fort employees, sawing out blocks of ice from the North Saskatchewan with crosscut saws and dropping the ice into a man-made reservoir covered with a log structure to keep the sun, the rain and the dogs out. The fort workers referred to it as the ice house. By fall the structure contained over 30,000 white fish, 500 butchered buffalo and other game for preservation. We hauled and filled in water between the cracks of the ice allowing it to freeze before covering everything over with straw.

We cut down and brought in firewood by dog teams. Daily, we loaded dog sleds with 150-pound sacks of pemmican manufactured at Fort Edmonton for Metis drivers to take to far northern, smaller Hudson's Bay trading posts. The winter went by quickly and to my great disappointment I rarely caught a glimpse of Paniya.

Before spring, Jarvis received word to build our new barracks twenty-five miles east on the south bank of the North Saskatchewan River near Sturgeon Creek. I would have to leave Fort Edmonton and went looking for Paniya but I was told she had already left for the spring and summer, as was her annual pattern. Her husband came to get her to live in the Cree encampment miles from the fortress. She would not return until fall.

I was enormously saddened and I moped around for several days feeling the deepest despondency and regret that I had not tried to find her sooner. But being busy helped to keep my mind off of her. Work on the new barracks kept us all going from early morning until night and I had little time to think of anything else. Much of the work we did ourselves: cutting shingles, raising walls and putting on a roof until we completed the living quarters, stables and a guard house at our new Fort Saskatchewan barracks. Summer came fast and it was as hot and dry as the previous summer had been cold and wet. We completed the transition to our new quarters.

***

It was early in the morning and I was one of the first up in the new barracks. Water detail was my responsibility. With the drought, the gardens needed plenty of it to say nothing of the kitchen and baths. I harnessed one of the stabled horses, hooked him to a buggy with four wooden water barrels and a pail on board. As I started through the gates an officer called over to me, "No one is supposed to leave until Jarvis approves." He was struggling with the sliding irons that kept the gates open, apparently preparing for further word. I ignored him and rode through as he wrestled with the iron bars of the gates.

I headed past the barracks on my water haul. One of the mule skinners was already outside and getting his wagon ready for a transport haul. He stopped, turned towards me and held up his hand. I ignored him. A keener, I decided, reinforcing some arbitrary rule concerning closure of the gate. Probably somebody was in trouble, likely smuggling in liquor after hours and I hoped it wasn't Stephen. I tongue clucked my horse into a trot past him and down a compact trail towards the river and a watering hole over a mile further down.

I had barely travelled a quarter of the distance when I heard a rider galloping rapidly towards me and I moved as far over as I could to let him by; he was obviously in great haste. The rider hauled back on the reins bringing his mare to a sudden stop in a cloud of dust beside me.

It was the mule skinner. He passed me a note without saying a word. Then he spun his mount around quickly and spurred him back towards the fort. I took the paper and called back thanking him. He waved a bottle of whisky at me before slipping it into his pocket and heading back to his supply wagon.

I unfolded the message. It appeared to be written with charcoal:

I'm under guard for murder. Go now! Stephen.

My heart pounding, I skimmed the note again. Stephen likely bribed the driver with whisky from one of his stashes to bring me the note. I looked around as the urgency became ever more apparent and a sinking feeling came over me. Stephen was in terrible trouble. It could only be the business with my old professor, Trelawney. Almost a mile of trail existed ahead of me to the watering site. I drove ahead briefly, then stopped to listen. The air was silent without a breath of wind. I could hear only birds in the trees and then the sound of a carpenter pounding nails inside the fort.

I pondered if I should unhook the wagon, mount the horse and light out. Or should I leave my mount and make my way back through the trees and attempt to free Stephen from the guard house. I was momentarily paralyzed with indecision when shouting began back at the fort, followed by the sound of horse's hooves pounding hard on the trail towards me.

I laid the whip on my horse sending him racing towards the river. I tied the reins onto the front rail of the buggy and let him run free. The horse and wagon rounded a bend on the trail and I bailed beside a thicket of undergrowth and rolled as far as I could. I rushed forward and then crouched as two riders came around the bend, Jake Lynch and Billy Lillico, their horses racing hard after the wagon. I felt for my pistol, which was still intact on my belt. Then I ran for my life.

There was no time to help Stephen. I stopped for a quick breath, took a bearing of the sun and headed northwest, keeping a rapid pace through the trees, panic gripping my stomach.

I encountered a small dry creek and followed it. I listened for anyone coming after me but the bush was quiet. I followed the watercourse far into the wilderness until it swung back to the east. I abandoned the creek and continued as rapidly as I was able to through the increasingly dense brush, stepping as lightly as I could to avoid sounds that might alert my pursuers and I kept a bearing to the northwest.

Thoughts of capture and a murder trial took over my mind. Nothing terrified me more than the thought of being the subject of a public execution. I thought about Stephen. By now he might well be on his way to Toronto under heavy guard to face trial and quite possibly hanging or firing squad. How naive we had been expecting to burn down a cottage simply to destroy exam papers and thinking nothing more would come of it. There had been no mount tied outside the cottage or other evidence that Trelawney was inside that day. The cheating was now obviously in the open and a motive for murder. I pushed myself harder.

The thick undercover slowly changed and I moved into open poplar and occasional dark expanses of pine and spruce. By now I knew I was about as hopelessly lost as anyone could be. I remembered as a child playing with Stephen in wooded areas along Lake Ontario. We became lost but eventually found the lake shore and followed it home. I was not familiar with any of the terrain in this vast northwest. How I wished that Stephen were with me now to share the fear and desperation.

I did not stop again for a long time, simply charging ahead driven by fear. I kept up a pace all through the day until the sun set and darkness closed in. After all these months on the frontier, facing the most extreme exposure to weather and life-threatening perils, capture and execution for the death of Trelawney had never stopped being my worst nightmare.

Briefly, I stopped to gather my thoughts. There were some decent trackers in the force but they would not be able to find signs of my trail in the darkness. I also knew they would not easily discontinue their efforts to apprehend me. By now they would clearly have determined my direction as consistently moving northwest through the wilderness and their best effort would be to continue on that trajectory in search of me in spite of the dark.

With darkness, I could make out the big dipper and the north star. I changed my course to travel northeast to evade their likely path and I maintained a steady pace into the brush as the unrelenting unease continued to grip my stomach and drive me forward. There were likely several more officers spread out in the dark, hopefully still travelling northwest and trying to stay within calling distance of each other. One thing I did not underestimate: their determination to capture me dead or alive; they were a proud force and already diminished by two of their own indicted for murder.

I realized that the darkness would provide my best opportunity to make distance between them and me. I pushed into the dense underbrush feeling the sting of branches across my face and my trousers ripping on the underbrush and low branches. Thorns ripped at my sleeves, shredding them. But I could not stop. I was becoming thirsty and there had been no source of water since I left. Pure adrenaline kept me moving forward. I thought of doubling back in the dark and finding the North Saskatchewan for water but that would be the most obvious to them and where they would patrol and were probably already posting sentries watching for me.

There was some light from a half moon now above the trees giving me an opportunity to dodge around obstacles and set a course for short stretches and increase the amount of distance covered. Once again, I moved into a forest cover with mature stands of spruce and balsam with less underbrush; it was easier going and I was able to accelerate my pace through the sparse trees.

I was grateful for the many hours I spent on the rowing team, the track team and the wrestling team as I whiled away my time at Trinity. Hard work on the force had kept up my stamina. I maintained a dogged pace throughout the night, stopping occasionally when I encountered a clearing in the forest or a barren side hill to listen and search behind me in the dim light of the moon for any sign of my pursuers. I rested my breath momentarily, retrieved a bearing on the North Star and maintained my northeast direction.

Worst now was the thirst that was beginning to affect my energy and stamina, only the coolness of the night helped. I checked every low area or swale for signs of water but the drought had left nothing behind. I knew I had made good progress. My stops continued to be brief, reminding myself never to underestimate the tenacity of the officers, especially since some of them, like Jarvis, already hated my guts which would motivate them to endure the greatest strain to capture me. My hope was to run into water soon as my thirst was gradually becoming unbearable.

I struggled to my feet after a brief stop and found the Great Bear constellation once more in a dark sky that told me I was still maintaining my direction. My legs were gradually becoming numb, my energy was dissipating and my thirst becoming intolerable. A dome of light in the eastern sky was the first sign of morning. I had made it through the first night, the most critical time, without capture. I had covered much distance.

With the rising sun came the condensation of dew on the leaves and grass. I stopped, grasped clumps of grass to suck the moisture from then. But soon the scant dew evaporated into a rising hot sun. The sky was clear. There would be unbearably heat in a few hours. I listened to the stillness of the morning for any sounds of my pursuers and detected nothing. But still I knew they would not turn back until every possibility of my capture was extinguished. I trudged on. Much of the terrain now was rolling with downward travel relieving the aching in my legs and the steep upper slopes quickly draining me.

The sun became bright and the morning coolness dissolved quickly into the blistering sun and I pressed onward through the bush. Moments of dizziness were affecting me now and the constant burning thirst only intensified. My body was no longer producing sweat and every creek I encountered was dry. On barren south facing hillsides the dry grass crackled beneath my feet and grasshoppers had spawned by the millions. There was no water.

CHAPTER 17

Jarvis woke to pounding on his door. He checked his watch: 4:30am. He opened the door for Constable Savine who was on night guard. He was accompanied by a young stranger who identified himself as Allen Saunders, a messenger sent on behalf of the Ontario Police Service. He handed Jarvis a sealed envelope.

"It's a warrant served on two of your constables, McGinn and Woodward, for murder," said Saunders.

Jarvis opened the sealed envelope. Inside was the warrant under the seal of the *Honorable William Henry Draper, Chief Justice of Ontario,* for the arrest of *James McGinn* and *Stephen Woodward*, and an order to escort the suspects to Toronto for trial.

"Can you supply me with details," responded Jarvis. "Who did they murder and when?"

"Well," replied Saunders, "My duty is just to deliver the warrant. What I'm told is that the men were Trinity medical students about to be expelled for cheating on examinations. Apparently, they thought no one but their professor knew about the cheating so they trapped him in his country cottage and burnt him alive."

The messenger studied Jarvis for a long moment. "People are saying that they joined the Northwest Mounted Police as a way to escape from Toronto and justice."

Jarvis sat back down on his bed, his head in his hands for a long moment, then stood up abruptly, paced to his window and looked out across the courtyard. He slammed his open hand against the door and then turned towards Savine and the messenger.

"The smug little son of a bitch," he said. "A trouble maker from the beginning. And I could have discharged the little bastard for insubordination many times." Then he turned to Willie Savine. "Where are McGinn and Woodward bunked?"

"The third door down, sir, in the men's quarters."

Jarvis instructed Savine: "Find the attendant and have him prepare to secure the gates. Find Saunders a room to rest overnight and show him the constable's kitchen if he's hungry."

Jarvis pounded on the third door of the men's quarters. A sleepy Woodward let him in.

"Where is McGinn?"

"Gone for water, I believe, sir."

Jarvis passed him the warrant.

"What is it, sir?" asked Stephen.

"A warrant for your arrest, for murder," Jarvis told a stunned Woodward.

"Murder!" responded Stephen, "who?"

"I think you know, a professor in Toronto, Dr. Trelawney. You will be escorted back for trial. You have five minutes to get dressed and grab your essentials."

Jarvis stood near the door skimming over the warrant for McGinn as Stephen got ready. Then Jarvis placed him in handcuffs and brought him outside. A Metis mule skinner was already outside the gates gearing up for a long haul to

Fort MacLeod. Jarvis stopped to question him. "Have you seen anyone outside the fort this morning?"

"Just the water haul man, I'm the first one up, sir, like always. My day starts in the middle of the night when almost everybody else is still sleeping."

He gave permission for the mule skinner to continue with his duties. Then Jarvis turned his attention to the gate keeper instructing him to finish securing the gates and maintaining his post, ensuring no one enters or leaves the fortress until further notice. The Inspector then led Stephen to the guardhouse which still smelled of fresh cut timber. He put Stephen inside and turned the lock.

"The first prisoner," he said, "and I never thought it would be one of our own."

Bill Lillico and Doug Lynch came out of their quarters dressed for morning drill.

"Lynch, and Lillico, you're needed here," called Jarvis.

"McGinn is making his morning water haul," he explained, "and gone to the river. I have a warrant for his arrest. Murder, in an eastern jurisdiction. Bring him back to me. Put him in cuffs, he's a prisoner."

Lillico and Lynch asked no questions speaking only to each other and apparently excited to go after McGinn as they raced to the stables, disappeared for a few minutes, came out on saddled mounts. The attendant let them out and they charged down a dusty path to the river.

Jarvis waited for their return. He paced in front of the fort, then returned to his desk in the officer's quarters and penned a response for Saunders to take to the honorable Judge:

Honorable William Henry Draper, Chief Justice:

I am in receipt of your warrant for the arrest of constables, James McGinn and Stephen Woodward for murder. The Northwest Mounted Police acknowledge and promptly respond to your request. You will find, in custody, McGinn and Woodward, escorted for trial by two of our fine officers.

Your faithful Servant,
W.D. Jarvis
Inspector,
Northwest Mounted Police

Jarvis waited until just before noon when Lynch and Lillico tethered their mounts to a hitching rail outside the window of Jarvis' quarters. The Commissioner moved promptly outside to meet them. "Where's McGinn?"

"We don't have good news, sir," began Lynch looking anxious and pulling his pillbox hat off his sweaty head and holding it in both hands.

"He must have known, sir. When we got close, he flogged the hell out of his horse sending him speeding down the trail and sending up a cloud of dust we couldn't see through. We raced after the buggy until the horse eventually stopped several miles down. McGinn was not on board, sir, and obviously bailed somewhere."

"That was not all, sir," Lillico cut in. "The horse had tried turning around in the bush to come home and got tangled and speared itself through the stomach with the dead branch of a tree. We had to free it up, got the branch out and let it come back to the stable on its own. We pursued the suspect."

"It was a goddam horse! Was that horse wanted for murder? No, but McGinn is a goddam killer at large. My instructions were you bring him back. Now I have to tell a high nose eastern police force that the Northwest boys can't even bring in one of their own."

"Sir, we did have luck finding where he parted from the wagon, the bush all knocked down and his trail busting through the tangles of deadfall heading northwest," responded Lynch. "We followed him to a dried-out creek a mile or so in where we lost his track in the grass along a bare ridge."

"Alright men, I'll send you back out with Leville. He is one of the few guides we have left here. We'll see if he is worth his salt."

***

Jarvis instructed the gate attendant to bring food and water to Woodward until such time as they escorted him to North Dakota and a train ride east. He torn up his letter to the Chief Justice and penned a new one:

Honorable William Henry Draper, Chief Justice:

I am sending the prisoner, Stephen Woodward, under escort, at your request. James McGinn, also indicted, is currently on assignment far to the north of the Edmonton fortress. He will be arrested immediately upon his return and escorted to your jurisdiction to face charges as you requested.

Your Faithful Servant,
W.R. Jarvis
Inspector
Northwest Mounted Police.

Jarvis briefed Sam Steele and the other officers concerning the warrants for McGinn and Woodward. Then he paced the grounds outside the fort until night fall waiting for the two constables and the tracker, Leville, to bring in McGinn. Finally, he heard the approach of horses as three men came into view and dismounted before Jarvis.

"Where is the prisoner?"

"We found his trail, sir, it wasn't easy, but we found some sign." Leville began, nervously tugging on his shirt bottom.

"We established his trail about three or four miles out where we found his cap in dense underbrush. We knew we were close. He had been running consistently northwest as if by compass point.

"The ground is baked, sir, from the drought. There were no boot marks to track him. But whenever we lost sign of him we kept on course to the northwest and eventually found more evidence of his trail: disturbed grass, broken limbs. Then, several hours out we found sure sign of him, blue and white threads from police trousers torn from the leg of his pants in tangles of willow and wild rose thorns. We knew we were on his trail again.

Leville, pulled his bag of tobacco out as if to smoke, then changed his mind and shoved the pouch back into his shirt pocket. He looked nervously at Lynch before starting again.

"Then the bastard hit an open stretch and we were beat. Elk had been grazing, tromping the ground down for miles along the grassy slopes. There was no way to track him. Still, we combed the countryside for miles to the northwest, the three of us fanning out, looking for any sign whatsoever but there was nothing."

Leville took out his tobacco again, patted his pants pockets, feeling for his pipe and looking at the other constables for some support.

"It was impossible to track him through the trampled grass after a herd of elk moved through," Lynch explained. "We took separate routes and circled for miles along the edges of the slopes, looking for where he might have gone back into the bush, but it was dark. We lost all sign of him," said Lynch.

"You three couldn't find a goddam hobbled mule in a cross-rail corral!" exploded Jarvis. "If I've learned one thing in the last twelve months it's that we have the sorriest trackers in the northwest." Jarvis turned away from the men.

He paced back and forth to settle himself down. Finally, he responded, "I want Potts up here." He began speculating on all he had heard about Jerry Potts. "They tell me that Potts can find anybody, anywhere." Jarvis said. "The man is a goddamn spirit. I had a man in E division say he walked ten miles with Potts in a whiteout blizzard once, and the man came out exactly at the settlement. I want Potts on the trail of this little son-of-a-bitch, McGinn."

Jarvis turned to study the three men. "Do you see what this does to the reputation of the Northwest Mounted Police? One of our own, a murderer, and we can't even catch him," said Jarvis. He looked towards the expansive wilderness beyond the barracks. "I want him found or I want his body found dead in the bush and brought back. At daylight I'm sending south for Potts to come fix this."

"To find Jerry Potts and bring him back here will take weeks, sir," responded Lynch, "even a rider with fresh mounts."

"I don't care how long it takes!" exploded Jarvis, "And I am sending you, Lynch, to get him. I'm moving Stephen Woodward out tomorrow."

Jarvis left the men and located Saunders, provided him the correspondence for the esteemed judge and sent him on his way. Jarvis walked back to the guard house, unlocked the door of Stephen Woodward's cell, entered, and re-locked the door behind him, passing the key to an attendant. Stephen sat on the edge of his wooden framed bed, on a straw mattress. The bed took up half of his cell with barren walls of crosscut logs on all sides, except for a thick plank door and a small window with bars looking into a barren hallway. Stephen had touched none of the food delivered to him.

"Tell me about the murder in Toronto," demanded Jarvis.

"There was no murder."

"You knew a Professor Trelawney?

"There was no murder," repeated Stephen.

"Where did McGinn go?"

"To get water from the river."

"After that?"

"I have no idea."

"You and him had a plan just in case, didn't you? Tell me where he was headed and it will be a lot easier for you."

Stephen sat back on the bed, his head resting against the wall, looking at Jarvis without expression or comment.

"You got a message to him, didn't you? Probably slipped something to the mule skinner, who's well on his way to the southern fort by now."

Stephen stared at the ceiling.

"You'll think on this for a while which might prompt your memory. Otherwise, you'll be escorted in chains to

Toronto. McGinn will go as soon as we catch him." Jarvis turned back to the window and summoned the guard.

"That's if you catch him," Stephen finally responded.

Jarvis turned back to Stephen. "You locked a man in his cottage and burnt him alive. You deserve to have your neck stretched from a pole alongside McGinn."

CHAPTER 18

I altered my direction, deliberately seeking out lower areas that might provide water and relief to my dehydrating body while still continuing generally northeast with the sun hovered above my right shoulder and gradually moving behind me. Soon night gathered around me and more than ever I felt in the pit of my stomach the ominous threats of the thick darkness and the loneliness of a vast, expansive northwest wilderness.

The terrible thirst affected me more than anything else. I pressed on into the second night struggling now with a much denser undergrowth of dogwood and thick poplar. I had lost a sense of time, estimating that it had been at least two days and two nights since I slept. Fatigue was starting to numb my brain and my body was on fire with thirst. My throat became parched until I could feel the swelling and could no longer bring forth an audible sound. Dawn came and went and I pushed on doggedly through another blistering day.

My mind was often leaving me now. Frequently I forgot where I was, instinctively knowing I must press on. The sun was angling through the trees and the landscape simply a mosaic of shadows and light before me and I, a blind man staggering to stay on my feet until I pushed into a tangle of willow, stumbled and fell to the ground where I lost consciousness.

When I awoke the sun was already high in the sky and beating down once again upon me with unrelenting fury. The dryness inside me was unbearable and my pounding head felt like it was split with an axe. For a length of time I could not decipher where I was. Thinking surely my mother or a servant would see my helplessness and drag me home to safety. Then I remembered the chase, the wilderness and the incredible thirst. I knew what dehydration would bring: confusion, delusions and insufferable pain. I thought I heard the coursing of water, I looked around and there was only dry earth and a tangle of willow. Terrible hallucinations of water came and went.

During moments of lucidity I pondered all the worst facing me. Death in a gallows, the terror of being lost and alone and succumbing to dehydration. Still I hoped somehow to revive myself and carry on, to find water.

I drifted in and out of consciousness, waking up only to find my body burning for water. Then came the devil's delusions of a flowing stream, torturing me, singing its song of a sodden paradise. I lost consciousness again, got up like in a dream and moved into the sound of water, bathed in a pool and drank from a flowing stream. I revelled in the coolness. I forced the water past my swollen lips into my constricted throat. I submerged my pounding head into the cool water and stood up again to drink without end.

Gradually a real world began to materialize around me. The water seeped from a hillside spring into a willow bog, forming pools that flowed away in a lively, bubbling stream. I lay back in the water. The sun had set once again below the trees and night closed in around me. I slept, my bed a bubbling stream and my pillow a matt of soaking moss and water reeds.

I woke as the morning sun cast long rays of light though the willows. I climbed out of the pool in my soaked clothing. I hung my ammunition belt up to dry, not knowing if the cartridges would ever be able to fire. I wiped my pistol down with the bottom of my tattered shirt and hung it in the crutch of a tree to dry. I stripped my clothes and strung them along a branch on the sunny side of the creek. Finally, I sat back naked on the shallow bank and let the sun bathe my wrinkled, water-soaked body.

For a long moment, I pondered divine acts of providence. It was true that I had sought out the lowest areas in the hope of finding water but still, I suddenly felt the greatest gratitude, like an arm had guided me here in my moment of unbearable stress and my ability to function severely compromised. I had never been a good person. Yet something beyond me seemed to care about me, a wretched little person lost in a desolate wilderness. I had never believed in all the religious talk of the churchgoers and the so called great, pious men of the community but I took a moment now with my head in my hands and relayed my gratitude to the divine.

Then, how quickly I came back to my real existence. I found fleeting relief in my own brief thoughts: how could they ever find me now, a speck of humanity in a vastness that stretched to the very top of the earth? Surely, they would huddle together with their maps and compasses and assess the odds; maybe deciding to allow their fugitive to succumb on his own to a death by exposure. Nevertheless, I could not underestimate the resolve of leaders like Inspector Jarvis or Sam Steele.

I stood naked in the rapidly warming morning sun and took stock of my surroundings. The pools around me were part of the headwaters of a stream that collected outflows from the seeping springs. The basin also collected run off from a semi-circle of hills just beyond.

The pools before me contained several sporadic willow clumps below which were acres of grass covered meadows that were subject to more frequent flooding from the headwaters.

Flies had already begun to stir with the morning sun. A hawk circled high in the sky above me on rising waves of summer heat. I decided I must stay here, at least temporarily, as this was surely the only reliable source of water for miles around.

I took a moment to assess the condition of my clothing. My boots were in good condition in spite of the distance I had travelled but one leg of my trousers was ripped almost completely free just below the top of my high riding boots. The cloth would be a hindrance so I tore it loose and hung the resulting material on a willow spike beside me.

Now my urgent concern was safety from my pursuers, at least to the extent that I could protect myself at all. Above me, a quarter of a mile distant was a barren side hill with a section of tall grass, most likely the site of another spring outlet. Above the spring was a grove of balsam poplar that reached a great height, most likely a result of abundant moisture from the spring and a south facing exposure.

I walked up hill to the outflowing spring and the balsam grove just beyond. I managed to climb the tallest tree until I could survey the countryside. I was on the highest point of land for a very great distance, with smaller rolling hills moving away from me towards the horizon. I was struck once again by the immeasurable vastness of the northwest and the eerie loneliness that continued to grow inside of me.

However, there was also some consolation with the realization that this spot was an invaluable lookout, making it possible for me to survey the land for miles in all directions, including the terrain I had just traversed where the police, if still pursuing me, were most likely to appear. I moved back towards the pools which I had marked with the blue cloth and white stripes of my torn trouser leg. This would be my new home.

I took inventory of everything I had available to me including under garments and the clothes I wore. I had my hunting knife and leather scabbard. In the deep pocket of my jacket was a section of thin rope that I had attached to the pail handle when extracting water from the river on my water haul. Also, inside an inner pocket was my billfold, with all my pay for several months. I was struck with the irony: the bills were of absolutely no use to me and I could not even think of any purpose for them, except that they might fuel a fire if I was able to start one. Nevertheless, I separated the dripping wet bills and gingerly placed them out to dry.

I pulled a small box of matches from my pant pocket that were almost certainly ruined with the sulphur ends near completely dissolved. I spread them out on a mat of grass to dry in the hottest sun. I had my pistol belt with my hand revolver and thirty rounds of ammunition that might well be ruined after laying for hours in the pool of water. I had lost my cap somewhere in the chase.

It was critical that I test my ammunition to see if the prolonged period under water had ruined the cartridges. I was reluctant to attempt firing a shot in case the cartridges were functioning and the discharge sound would carry a great distance, alerting anyone that might be pursuing me. Above the willow clusters on higher ground, sparse stands of balsam poplar had grown, died and left dead fall. Some had rotten, hollowed centers. I retrieved my revolver and selected two cartridges that I placed into the cylinder. With my knife, I enlarged the rotted center of the deadfall until I could extend my arm far inside, holding my pistol and using the log as a silencer, muffling the report of the fired cartridge. To my great disappointment the cartridge did not discharge. I tried the second cartridge which did not fire either. I realized more than ever my vulnerability and restricted ability to get food or protect myself.

I walked back to the meadows below me, to assess my surroundings for a place to create shelter from weather and predators. With my hunting knife, I dug a few inches into the soil, hoping there might be moist clay underneath that could be useful in preparing some kind of shelter, maybe an adobe. But the soil beneath was dry organic dirt that quickly crumbled.

Eventually, I selected an area partway between the pools and my lookout where I discovered a small stand of mature spruce with extended canopies and very little under brush. I selected the largest tree and commenced building a shelter that took me two full days. With my knife, I cut small spruce branches for a place to lie down. From the meadow, I selected long sections of the tall grass, cut them loose above the roots with my knife and carried several armloads of the pliable material to soften the spruce branches that made up my bed. The long boughs above me created a partial shelter from the rain. I reinforced those boughs with another layer of spruce branches that I arranged perpendicular to the attached branches until I had a substantial roof over my bed.

Water plants with wide leaves floated in abundance along the shallow edges of the pools. I selected dozens of them and spiked their stems through the modified spruce canopy over my bed, arranged the leaves in rows starting from the outside and working to the inside overlapping them in a way that would shed rain. Then I covered the leaves with another layer of spruce boughs to keep them from blowing off. I secured the entire canopy with criss-crossing rope, that I then knotted onto the trunks of adjacent trees.

My completed living area was then high enough to sit upright and well sheltered from sun and rain. I lay on my bed and found it comfortable. My location provided a view of the water pools below. I felt a moment of elation having created a decent shelter. Now I faced perhaps my biggest challenge. I had long since stopped feeling hungry as my body sustained me with fat reserves; however, I knew I must find food soon to survive. I also longed for a fire to keep me warm, to cook any food I might secure, to repel predators and perhaps more than anything else, to help relieve my loneliness during the long evenings and the darkness of night.

The matches from my soaked pocket had now dried thoroughly in the hot sun. I took several hands full of dry meadow grass and compacted them beneath a pile of dry twigs. I selected a match that appeared to have the most sulphur head attached and drew it quickly across the striker plate of the box. The sulphur head crumpled and peeled away. I tried several more matches and none would strike. I threw the box of matches into the bush in disgust and disappointment.

The day was hot. I drank from the pools and climbed to my shelter and lay down on my bed. A sense of frustration and helplessness had been building inside of me. I fell asleep and woke as the sun sank below the horizon covering the land in twilight.

I rose up and stared out across the dark meadow knowing that I would no longer be able to sleep. The evening was quiet except for a chorus of frogs that had begun croaking in the pools, and then went suddenly silent. Something was below me and I focussed on forms of the landscape until my eyes adjusted to the darkness. I didn't know if the movement was real or if my tired and undernourished brain was deceiving me. Slowly I could make out the dark shape of a buck moving slowly onto the meadow. He stopped, raised his head, checking the air for scent. Then he stood remarkably still for several minutes.

My heart pounded with the sudden realization that the springs were a magnet for predators and prey alike seeking relief from the drought. The buck walked to the edge of the pool, lowered his head and drank. I reached for my hunting knife, crouched low and crept rapidly towards him. I was twenty paces from him before realizing the sheer folly of my endeavors. He raised his head suddenly, looked at me, whirled and bound into the darkness.

The next day I became obsessed with finding a way to bring down the abundant game that came for water in the late evenings and nighttime. The pools would also attract predators: grizzly, wolves and black bear. Cougar and wolverine were occasionally sighted in the northwest and known to be aggressive. I needed protection from them all.

I selected a long straight trunk of willow tree, cut it free with my hunting knife and peeled off the branches until I had a straight shaft of about ten feet. The rope that I used to secure my roof had a length of about ten inches hanging from the final knot. I cut it loose and carved two deep, circular notches on the end of the willow, a spearhead where I embedded the rope and bound my knife securely onto the shaft. I spent the afternoon practicing my aim on a rotting stump until I could drive my knife deep into my target at twenty paces. The victory was small but it solaced my mind and I felt optimistic that finally I could secure food.

The next evening, I took cover in a clump of willow near the pools that provided a space for me to stand with room to navigate my spear and I waited for game to come for water. Darkness settled in all around me and nervousness crept into my stomach reminding me that predators would also come to the springs. The entire first night I huddled among the willows, fearful and yet hopeful as I contemplated what might show up for water.

After considerable time, my legs became cramped and my arms began to ache from maintaining a ready grip my spear. I hunched over and shuffled to a new location behind willow cover where I watched vigilantly for several more hours, noting every cracking sound in the forest and the slightest movement of underbrush, but no game showed up. At the first sign of dawn I gave up the hunt. I was deeply disheartened and wondered if there were any prospects before me at all, except that of eventually perishing from starvation. I spent the day sleeping.

My body was clearly becoming emaciated from lack of food. The tops of my hip bones extended upwards and I had to adjust my belt length to keep my trousers on. The next evening, I selected a different location. Animals that used the pools regularly would surely recognize any difference at all in the shapes or shadows of the willows where I hid in ambush. I felt some renewed optimism. I decided to lay flat in the long grass adjacent to the pools. Besides, laying prone in the grass might mitigate the exhaustion I experienced in my arms and legs the previous night. The deer had come in from the west so I positioned myself in that direction.

With the gathering darkness, I took a position where the tall grass was slightly thinner and I could see through it. I watched the pools closely. The sunlight slowly dissipated and the night was still and a slight breeze blew in from the south creating waves in the grass. Rapidly, it had become too dark to see more than a few yards in front of me. Still I continued to lay in wait, hoping for some easy game to come within my reach.

A monstrous shadow suddenly loomed across me covering my restricted field of view. I sprang to my feet, more out of terror than anything else. A large moose with a vast spread of antlers was upon me. He abruptly wheeled and lunged away as I launched my weapon. The spear careened wildly striking the animal broadside on his hind end sending him pounding for cover.

I was greatly disheartened and to make matters worse, my knife dislodged from the shaft of my spear and I spent much of the next day searching until I found it buried several inches in the ground. My hopes of feeding myself were diminishing rapidly. I decided to take a walk down the stream with hopes of discovering fish that may have swam upstream from some larger connecting watercourse below.

I followed the stream for a mile with no trace of anything that might feed me. I caught a bull frog, smashed his head and stripped the slimy meat from his back legs which I swallowed and threw the remaining carcass away. I continued along the watercourse that began spreading out with stagnant pools forming adjacent to the main stream. In one pool was a swarm of minnows about an inch long. I selected a willow and cut it down at the first branch leaving a Y shaped end with a length of handle about four feet long. I undressed and peeled off my underwear, modifying the drawstring and shaped the garment to form a pouch. I tied the cloth onto the Y portion of the stick. I scooped up a dozen minnow in a single swipe and hauled them onto shore.

I selected the minnows one at a time and let each slip down my throat. Initially I felt a wave of nausea but I remained determined to keep the life-saving protein inside my body. I endured the temptation to throw up as I made my way back to the shelter. However, the nausea did not subside but became steadily more overwhelming. It had been a long time since I had eaten anything. Eventually the sickness grew until I succumbed to nausea and vomited the raw fish and meat of the toad. My insides ached. Deeply discouraged, I crawled onto my bed and fell asleep.

The following morning, I decided to start a more intense search for berries. It was a time of year when fruit should be appearing on the bushes but because of the drought I had not encountered anything. However, I took up my spear for protection and commenced to walk a margin of land between the forest and the meadows along a south facing slope where I hoped to discover fruit bearing trees. Eventually I came upon saskatoon and chokecherry bushes where the shrubs grew in some abundance but the fruit was scant and shrivelled from the drought. Nevertheless, I spent the entire afternoon and into the evening collecting what I could. I ate the berries as I went along but most likely I had barely picked off the equivalent of a couple handfuls; however, the berries would provide not just food but badly needed vitamins and nutrients critical to my survival. I was able to keep the berries down and I felt some energy from ingesting them.

Birds were plentiful at the pools where they came for water. I decided to try my luck at capturing some with the net I had devised to scoop out the minnows. Time and again I lunged at the small creatures with my improvised net only to learn how incredibly quick they were. I realized that if they could elude hawks, owls and ground predators I was unlikely to be any more fortunate. Evening came down and I fell asleep early as my energy was drained.

At sunrise, I struck out along the meadows and back into the brush with my spear in hand hunting for smaller game or less reactive bush fowl that relied on camouflage for protection. I followed the circle of hills that surrounded me and was soon attracted to crows gathering in flocks over a section of the tree line where they were descending in and out of the bush. Their incessant cawing drew me easily to their location in a small hollow. From above the knoll I saw that they were clustered thick onto the body of a dead moose. The flock vanished in a noisy black cloud as I approached.

The moose had likely been dead for a couple of days. Two arrow shafts extended from the back of the dead animal. The beast was extremely thin and his entire flank was covered in running pockets of puss that flowed down his back legs. It was apparent that the animal had been wounded with the arrows a considerable time ago but was able to survive and travel a great distance eluding the native hunters before giving in to the infection. I braced my foot against the carcass of the animal and extracted the arrows. Instinctively, I knew they could be of some use to me. The uncooked meat of the animal would surely be toxic given the extensive infection. I could think of no further use for the carcass.

At my campsite, I examined the craftsmanship of the arrows which were straight and smooth as if fashioned by some Toronto machinist on a lathe. I was struck by the remarkable symmetry of the flint arrowheads that were sharper than my knife: an incredible work of art as well as military precision. It was easy to envision how the arrows penetrated their full shaft into the dense muscle of the moose.

Fascinated by the workmanship, I struck the hard points together in a glancing motion and to my amazement they created a spark. My excitement grew as I articulated their potential usefulness.

I collected two clumps of dry grass, separated them slightly, holding one flint stone on the bottom segment while striking the second flint across the first. After several strikes, I could produce a spark but not sufficient to ignite the dry grass. I selected one of the undischarged cartridges and carved into the base of the lead tip to extract some powder but the matting inside would not release the granules.

I picked up a large striking stone, lay the cartridge on a second rock embedded in the ground and pounded the brass base until it flattened out extending the edges and releasing a trickle of powder. I rubbed the black substance between my fingers. The material clumped together and was clearly wet. I extracted about a thimble full, scattered it onto a broad leaf and placed the leaf in direct hot sunlight.

I left the damp substance to dry until it flowed evenly off the tips of my fingers. Then I sprinkled the material onto a mat of dry grass, struck the flints over it and a blue flame shot through the gun power and the grass ignited into a soft yellow flame. I piled on more grass, twigs and pieces of dry branches until I had a blazing fire. I stepped away, hooting, leaping, howling and dancing with pure unadulterated joy. I kept the fire burning all night and I simply relished the heat and the leaping flames that seemed to relieve my loneliness. I savored this time and the sheer happiness of my fire in spite of the trials that I knew still lay before me.

CHAPTER 19

The next morning, I decided to trek back to the moose. With fire and a thorough charring, I might be able to cook and eat portions of the animal's meat that were not as badly infected as the hind quarters were. However, I had just commenced my hike into the forest when I had the good fortune to encounter a porcupine that is every lost hunter's joy. The animal is easy to take down with a club and the meat is tender and sustaining. I immediately killed it and dragged the porcupine back to my camp where I eviscerated him, being careful to avoid the quills. I extracted the hind quarters and embedded the meat directly into the coals of my fire, which I fed occasionally with a supply of dry wood.

The remaining meat from the porcupine I staked into the cold water from the spring; I expected the water to keep the remaining staple fresh for several days. I was confident I could start a fire again if this one burnt out and I kept an additional stock of dry grass under the canopy of my shelter for just such occasions.

I badly needed a receptacle for water and I experimented with several options. I found a large deadfall birch tree with a rotted-out core and fully intact cylinder of bark. I cut a two-foot length and fashioned a bottom onto the cylinder with a circular portion that I cut from the remaining birch bark with my knife. While waiting for my porky to roast, I chiselled out a quantity of spruce gum that was abundant on the trees around me. I spread the material onto a large flat stone and placed it on the edge of my fire until it softened from the heat and I pressed the resin into the seam at the bottom of my receptacle. It dried quickly into a large, leak-proof container and I retrieved a bucket of water.

The aroma of roasting meat was the most tantalizing thing I had ever known. The roast was now fully charred on the outside, juicy and thoroughly cooked on the inside. I was determined this time to eat slowly, a small strip at a time using a quantity of water with each bite to avoid nausea. Over a period of hours, I indulged the entire hind quarters of the tender meat, drank the cool water and enjoyed the greatest feast of my life.

I slept well and rose at first light. I decided to return to the moose carcass with two goals in mind: to extract what might be an edible portion of meat now that I had a fire to prepare it and to skin out a section of the hide for clothing and protection from the cold. When I got to the carcass the smell of decaying flesh was most unpleasant but I commenced cutting into the dead animal when the most surprising thing caught my eye. Not twenty yards away laying among the poplar and staring at me with fearful eyes was a moose calf, perhaps three months old. I approached the small creature and realized it was too weak to stand. I suddenly felt the greatest sympathy for the orphaned animal. Perhaps she reminded me of my own loneliness and the perils and struggle for survival in a hopeless world.

I decided to experiment. I cut into the udder of the dead mother. The milk was a blob of curds and thin liquid. I bathed my hands in the liquid and approached the orphan. At first, she was fearful and reluctant and swung her head away from me. I approached ever more cautiously, reaching out to her. At about four-foot distance she turned and stretched forth her long snout to sniff gingerly at my hands. I moved closer and she began licking the substance from my skin. I sat with her for the longest time, returning occasionally to retrieve what I could of the curds and fluid of the mother's udder. She licked my hands and even further up my bare arms to retrieve what she could of the milk.

I postponed my goals for the moose carcass, swept the orphan into my arms and carried her back to my camp. I laid her beside my shelter and took my receptacle to retrieve water. I selected some of the soft stemmed water plants beside the pools, crushed them into a slurry of mulch between two rocks and mixed the milky fibrous material thoroughly into the water. The orphan calf stretched her neck towards the bucket, sniffed vigorously and then drank until the vessel was drained. I returned to the spring and prepared the same formula of crushed water plants and water. She drank half the amount and turned away, obviously satiated.

A few minutes later she stood as the water and nutrition were obviously taking effect. She sniffed at her new surroundings then jumped playfully around before returning to sniff my hands. I was delighted with my new companion. I felt bonded to the small creature and I think she felt a bond with me. I loved her playful jumping, reminiscent of any joyful child and I decided to name her Bonny.

The next morning Bonny was sniffing around the pools, nibbling at the water plants and drinking the water. I let her be, to go where ever she chose. I would never be able to take her down for food. I would rather perish myself. I realized for the first time how much the wilderness had changed me.

Perhaps the first time I had ever placed another living thing above my own selfish need.

Suddenly something came back to me that I thought I had long since forgotten. I remember the day I ended up in Louis Packett's cabin when he took me in from the cold, and something he told me: *facing death and surviving will change you in ways you never thought possible.* That, out of the mouth of Loonie Louie whom no one ever took seriously. For the first time, I thought long and hard about Louie and the incredibly wise and courageous man that existed behind his wild eyes and violent head spins. I fell asleep thinking about Louie and I didn't sleep well.

I awoke as the sun was rising. Bonny had been laying in the grass just outside my shelter. She went down to the springs and I watched her sink her long snout below the surface of the pools, coming up with dripping water plants; she tilted her head back, bouncing the plants gently and letting the long stocks slip down her throat. Finally, she returned, bunted me playfully and then tried to suckle my rear end. I had to shove her gently away which launched her into a round of playful romping, bucking and circling back to nudge me.

I gave her a scratch behind her long ears and she seemed to relish my touch. But I had work to do so I shoved her gently away. Every day I needed to secure enough food for my own survival. I decided to experiment with the crushed water plants: if they provided nourishment for Bonny perhaps they would do the same for me. I selected a few of the more tender looking ones, beat them into a pulp between rocks, and scooped part of the mess into my mouth. They were bitter and fibrous and frankly I didn't see how Bonny could stand them but I swallowed some down anyway. There might be nutrients in them that would help sustain me.

After only two days Bonny was already beginning to show some meat on her bones; however, I was about as skinny as I could get. Nightly, I heard game coming into the spring but I had become discouraged with the effectiveness of my homemade spear. I desperately needed my revolver and cartridges and I thought of attempting to retrieve power from the shells, drying and replacing it, but I knew the sheer folly. I could not seal the damaged brass shell again which would not properly repel the lead. I had witnessed men with hands blown off from firing just such damaged cartridges. But I decided to try once more. I had left my ammunition belt in the most direct sunlight I could find. I selected a bullet from the belt, placed it in my revolver and used the same hollow log for a silencer. The result was once again disappointing. My only hope was to continue exposing the cartridge belt to the hot sun: since moisture got in somehow maybe eventually it would evaporate out.

I returned to the pool of minnows far down the stream. With my modified net, I scooped out a dozen or so of the small fishes and captured four large toads from adjacent stagnant pools. Returning to my fire, I extracted what viscera I could from the minnows, cleaned the toads and roasted their fleshy hind legs along with the minnows. I cooked the meat thoroughly, then separated edible portions from the bones and ingested the protein slowly managing to keep it all down. I also had a few pounds of the porcupine left that I ate sparingly and the cool water was successful in keeping the meat reasonably fresh.

I decided to return once again to the moose carcass, possibly salvage some of the animal's flesh for food but also to skin out a portion of the hide that might eventually be useful against the cold. Bonny followed me into the bush. When I arrived, the carcass was gone. For a moment, I thought I had made a wrong turn or perhaps my direction was confused. I scoured the ground until I found the exact location where the carcass had been laying and was now crawling with a mass of maggots. The dead animal had been dragged away leaving a clear path that I followed out of curiosity at first, but slowly fear and apprehension grew inside of me. I took a firm grip on my spear and crept slowly forth.

The carcass had been pulled into a low-lying area where the remains had been partially buried in leaves and dirt. I moved closer. In the disturbed dirt was the fresh imprint of a massive grizzly. I looked quickly around. Bonny had stopped at the top of the knoll. Long hair stood high on the top of her hump as she stared into the forest beside me.

From the edge of my sight, a clump of willow moved and then the entire bush flattened with crashing and busting of branches as an enraged grizzly came over top. I tossed my spear with all my strength and lost track of where it landed. The grizzly was on top of me in a flash of reddish fur. His enraged muzzle, gleaming wet gums and massive yellow fangs tore into my shoulder and I heard bone crunching. He shook me violently, his massive head churning wildly side to side; I believed my neck would surely break and pains shot through my upper body. The beast then tossed me high into the air as if I had no weight at all. I landed on the ground where he pinned me under massive claws. Blood and saliva trailed from his teeth that he buried again and again deep into my shoulder, my groin, and my side, shaking me relentlessly with every new vice-like grip of his jaws.

Then, the animal whirled and lunged for Bonny. The last I saw of her, she was bounding towards the trees, her neck far outstretched, her long ears laid back and her thin legs pounding hard against the leaf-littered ground as she disappeared into the bush. The enraged predator charged after her with a terrifying guttural moan.

I lost consciousness for a brief moment before climbing to my feet and stumbling forward on a wave of terror towards my shelter with barely a glance behind me at the empty forest. I arrived, threw dry grass and brush onto the coals of my fire, hoping the high blaze would deter the beast. I looked around for the grizzly or any sign of Bonny and saw none. My body was shaking and numb. I took off the tattered clothing that stuck to my skin in patches of drying blood and chunks of torn flesh. Gradually revealing my severely damaged body.

My arm brought me the most terrible pain when I tried to move it. I sensed my shoulder was broken, or worst, dislodged from its socket. The bear had sunk his teeth deep into my side and my groin. The worst bleeding was from a crushed femoral artery high in my leg that spurted a stream of blood when I brought my trousers down. I cinched my belt tightly around my groin until the bleeding stopped. I lay back on my bed of boughs and lost consciousness.

I came to and managed to stand beside my fire and search the tree line for any sign of Bonny. Then I listened for her but there was only silence. Life-threatening infection was now my worry. I needed water but I was terrified of leaving my fire, fearing the enraged beast was stalking me.

Finally, I summoned my courage and left with the birch bark receptacle for water; but I had no way of boiling the water to disinfect my wounds. The best I could do was retrieve the torn pant leg I had previously removed and hung in the willows. I soaked the soiled cloth and heated it over my fire until steam was coming from the material. I began cleansing my wounds with it. Only my right arm was functioning and I managed to tolerated the immense pain as I wiped down the seeping gashes in my flesh. Nighttime closed in and I used a reserve pile of wood and branches to maintain my fire.

I lay awake long into the night, tossing wood onto my fire and keeping a high blaze. Near morning I fell into a deep sleep. My fire burned down and the grizzly came to the edge of the firelight. Standing high on his back legs, he stared through at me, his eyes glowing red. Then he dropped down, circling at the edge of the fire, wheeling back and forth, waiting only for my rapidly diminishing flames to die out. I remained completely still, defenseless and unable to move. I had no gun, knife or weapon to defend myself.

I woke with a start, my heart pounding and then a flood of relief that I had been dreaming. I feared going back to sleep knowing the beast would come again. Finally, I fell into a deep coma like rest, waking to the sun high in the sky and feeling as if I had not slept at all. I sat up and listened to the quiet. I looked around for Bonny. She had not returned.

Cautiously, I moved out of my shelter and down to the spring watching vigilantly for any sign of the bear returning to finish me off. I hoped that predators had not discovered the remaining porcupine meat in the spring. To my relief the remaining carcass was undisturbed.

I extracted about a pound of the flesh, using the sharp edge of the arrowhead before spiking the remaining carcass back under the water with a willow fork. I gathered what firewood I could find with the compromised use of my arm.

I roasted and ate the meat. Then I examined my wounds and felt most disheartened; the deepest lesions, including a wide margin around them, were turning scarlet with infection. I soaked and boiled my washing cloth and bearing the immense pain as best I could, I cleaned the mangled flesh. Afterward I fell exhausted onto my bed and into deep sleep.

I woke up in the middle of the night. My body was shaking with chills and my face hot with fever. I drifted in and out of sleep. I dreamed the wilderness was a terrible living thing, drawing closer, smelling the stench of my rotting flesh, savored the scent and moving in slowly to finish me.

I dug into the piles of dry grass on my bed bringing it over me; I was as much seeking a place to hide from a killer as a cover for warmth.

I awoke. The night was black and I could not see beyond the top of my canopy. My body was on fire. Faintly, I could hear the running stream. Then a wolf howled far away and another one answered closer and his howl became a human voice taunting me, that my time was near. I lost consciousness again.

Now the creek sound was different. Something was splashing through, bumping rocks that collided on the bottom, wading towards me, then coming over me, kneeling and staring into my eyes. Trelawney's face hovered over me, his skin raw and ravaged with the wounds of fire. He turned and shuffled away walking stiff as a dead man walks.

I followed him. He entered a cottage and closed the door behind him as the building erupted into an inferno of flame.

He was in the window, his face a mask of horror and his eyes locked on mine.

I awoke with a start, my heart pounding and I could smell the kerosene I used that day to light the fire and I could hear the rattling of Diamond's harness as he shook his coat to expel the sweat. I watched a trajectory of the matches I threw and a blue flame that fizzled; and then the orange flames that leaped high against the side of the cabin. I caught the pungent smell of Diamond's singed manes and then Trelawney's face peered again from the window beyond a curtain of fire. It was what I chose not to see that day that came back to me. What was real? My own face was on fire with fever.

I fell into a tormented sleep and woke before morning. I looked at the dark canopy of boughs over my head and the charred remains from my fire. I ran my hands over my burning skin. I knew my time was near.

Now my father was speaking to me. *Very bad news,* he said, *Professor Trelawney has passed.* Then he looked down at me as I straightened on a garden bench in the courtyard. *Do try to make this work, James. The penalty for murder is still execution,* he said, *even in the new confederation, sometimes firing squad, sometimes hanging. I doubt they will find you for a long time if you remain on the frontier.* He walked away and it was the last I saw of him.

I fell asleep again and Louis Packet was there. *When your finger on the trigger is numb with cold you can't hit shit,* he said. I sat on a chair glad I could escape the cold and enjoy the warmth of his fire and the comfort of his cabin. *It's a strange thing waiting the last while to die,* he said. *Things flow back to you.*

He moved on his creaking chair, his head twirled to focus his eyes and he swayed to keep his balance. Then he watched me closely. *Maybe someday you will feel it,* he said. *Things you locked away coming back fresh and vivid when you wait the end. And the flashes you have while waiting never stop coming back either.* He was just Looney Louie, hardly a real person at all. And me, only grateful for the tea.

***

I had been unconscious for a long period; whether hours or days, I didn't know. But someone was near me. They held my head and touched a receptacle to my lips. My body burned with thirst. I tried to move, to open my eyes but there was not an ounce of strength anywhere inside me. It took everything I had to swallow and not choke as the bitter fluid trickled slowly into my throat. I fell back and slept again.

It was nighttime when I woke. There was a fire nearby and Paniya sat beside the fire, more beautiful than ever. Something else was different and I felt across my body. A heavy paste was drying on the wounds of my chest and shoulder. The same substance had also been applied to the wounds on my side and pressed there under a cloth. My trousers had been taken off and retrieved again. The thick paste had been applied to the wounds of my groin and held in place with a cloth and a string encircling my thigh to hold the substance tight against my infection.

I closed my eyes and slept. I woke once again to an early sun that barely touched the darkest shadows of the meadows and willow groves. Paniya stood near the embers of a dying fire, her lovely face towards the first light and her chin high. She chanted a high, waffling song more beautiful than anything I had ever known, a sound that resonated with the morning twilight and with everything that had ever existed and deep inside my soul. I knew the song was for me; the chanting of love to a spirit greater than either of us, a great spirit of healing that heard her song.

When I woke again the sun was high in the sky. Paniya was standing over the fire, stirring a steaming broth in a metal pot on the coals. "Welcome back to life," she said with a smile. "I wasn't sure if you'd make it." I held out my hand to her. She squeezed my fingers tight and then turned to stir the broth.

I remembered the bitter drink and the song that she had chanted into the early morning light; her medicine had brought life back inside my dying body. With great effort and immense pain in my shoulder, I managed to sit up on the edge of my bed.

She came to me with a wooden ladle of liquid from her kettle. She blew into the hot broth, touched it to her lips and then offered it to me. "Drink this," she said, "it will help you."

I drank it down. "What's in it?" I asked.

"Rabbit," she said, "wild turnip, onion and a few other things." She gave the pot a gentle stir.

"I thought wild onion was poisonous."

"Well you have to know what you're doing," she laughed, "and no, I'm not trying to poison you, you're in enough trouble already," she smiled.

"There are rabbits around here?" I asked.

"Oh yes, they are quite numerous," she said. "Their trails are all through the willows and they come for water too," she added. "And very easy to snare." She held up a circle of sinew. "Anybody could catch one."

It was the first humorous thing I had heard in days. I couldn't even see them in the willows. I thought about what it might have been like trying to spear one. Surely it would have been entertainment if nothing else.

Between my bed and Paniya's fire, she had spread out plants, a virtual pharmacy like nothing I had ever seen before. I recognized only a few: cattail roots and stems, lichens and mushrooms, clover heads and a pile of crushed white yarrow, some still on a section of wood where the stems and flowers had been beaten into a pulp and, I suspect, applied to my wounds.

"I owe you so much Paniya," I said, "and I think my wounds are healing, including the ones on my groin."

She smiled. "I covered my eyes," she laughed. "And I wondered if you knew how lucky you had actually been."

"Well, you'll only get modesty from me," I said. "Just glad to be alive and apparently intact." I added.

I attempted to stand up from my bed but the pain in my shoulder became unbearable, I moaned out loud, held onto my arm and sat back down.

"Let me look at that," she said. She commenced to move my arm half way up at my side, rotating it back and forth, in spite of my howls of pain.

Finally, she stopped. "I'm not going to help you if you are going to be a baby," she said, turning away with hands on her hips.

I had expected more sympathy. "Okay, I'm sorry," I said, "go ahead and twist the arm."

"I already know what's wrong," she said with a slight lift of her chin. "The shoulder has come away from its socket. It needs to go back in soon or it will never go back."

"Do you know how to do that?" I asked.

"I've seen it done," she said, "but you need to lay down on your back, relax the arm and not fight me or I can't help you."

"I'll try." I lay back down and she took my outstretched arm and tugged on it until I slid off my bed in a torrent of moans.

She walked away from me, I think she was frustrated. "You need to brace yourself proper, or it won't go back."

With her help, I moved down on my bed where I could brace my legs against an adjacent tree. But my legs were without strength and my knees could not resist the force when Paniya pulled my dislocated arm. The pain was overwhelming and the shoulder badly separated and extremely stubborn.

Paniya put her arms under my shoulders and helped to straightened me back on the bed in spite of my moaning. I was embarrassed at what a burden I had become and I mumbled an apology but her mind was somewhere else.

She lay on her back perpendicular to me on the ground and placed her bare feet against my bandaged side. Paniya was slight and barely chest high on me but she was lithe and strong. She gripped my arm firmly with both her hands and pulled it between her bent knees and across her chest. Unrelenting, without mercy, I felt the incredible intensity of her strength as she straightening her trembling legs, against my side, stretching my arm beyond any normal limits across the length of her body until my shoulder and chest muscles began to spasm and convulse as if ready to tear apart, then she released my arm and it collapsed with a great clunking sound back into its socket. I howled with pain and relief. It was perhaps the greatest moment of pain remission in my entire life.

CHAPTER 20

Jarvis appointed Constable Reid, the youngest man on the force, to accompany Stephen back for trial. He provided Reid a sealed envelope with the note he had re-written for the judge.

The days passed slowly for Jarvis as he awaited the arrival of Potts. He sent men back out on the trail of McGinn but with no luck. Finally, he decided to simply wait for Jerry Potts.

The heat and drought increased. Dark clouds that rose above the horizon simply drifted easterly overhead, without rain. Jarvis assigned two new men to do the water haul, twice a day now, to keep the gardens from wilting. Life carried on as usual at the barracks, completing the many details of erecting a new complex for the Northwest Mounted Police. Eventually Lynch arrived from the southern barracks but without Jerry Potts.

Doug Lynch met Jarvis in his office. "Potts says he is not coming, sir." Lynch reported.

"Why the hell not?" asked Jarvis.

"He said it was too far to come to chase a scared rabbit through the bush." Lynch shuffled his feet as he continued to stand before Jarvis. "But he says he can tell you exactly how to catch your fugitive."

"How? What did he say?"

"Here's more or less the message from Potts: There has been a severe drought, he told me, the worst he has seen since he was a boy. He says there is no water in the bush and a man on the run will not last four days without water. He says there are three places to find McGinn."

"Go ahead," said Jarvis impatiently.

"First, Potts says, the fugitive could double back to find the North Saskatchewan for water. You should patrol the river.

"Or, Potts says, three to four days of running, once he shifts his direction to the lower lands of the northeast, he will find water that never dries up. The Indians call it Medicine Springs. And, Potts says, there is a third place: locate the howls of the coyotes at night. They will be feeding on his remains.

"But Potts says there is one man who knows the area to the northeast like he knows the inside of his teepee. His name is Two Bears. In summer, he will be camped with the Cree about ten miles northeast of Fort Edmonton along the river. He will bring you to the Medicine Springs in three days. And, Potts says, that is where you will find your man."

Jarvis dismissed Lynch. He found Leville and questioned him about Two Bears.

"Yes, I have heard all the talk about him," said Leville. He will be camped in one of several summer camps of the Cree. It will take some time but I can find his camp. That will be the easy part. Finding the man will be harder. I'm told that Two Bears hunts more than most, even in the summer. If I do find him, he may or may not come depending on his mood which I'm told is either neutral or foul."

"Tell him I'll make it worth his while," responded Jarvis.

Jarvis left Leville to his own devices. If Leville couldn't find the Cree summer camp by himself, he need only stock up on tobacco and many of the local Cree would tell him exactly where to find the camp of Two Bears.

Four days passed without hearing from Leville. Jarvis began to wonder if his guide was off on another wild goose chase.

The sixth day Jarvis had been overseeing Sam Steele drill the men when Leville emerged from the edge of the wilderness and across the drill field jogging to keep up behind Two Bears. The Cree man was tall and muscular. Leville was as fit as any of the guides but remained two strides behind, struggling to keep up with the Indian. They approached Jarvis and Leville introduced Two Bears.

Jarvis reached out to shake the hand of the Cree warrior who ignored him.

"He wants to know what is so important that you drag him away from his hunting," interpreted Leville.

Jarvis explained the situation with McGinn and the message he had received from Potts. "I want you to find him," Jarvis said. "I will make it worth your while."

"He wants to know how much you will give him," Leville said.

"I will give him tobacco, tea, sugar, copper pots, maybe a knife, all that."

"Two Bears says he wants a long barrel rifle, ammunition for a year, a bone handled knife, and six sheaths of tobacco that he will hang in the sun beside his own teepee."

"Tell him he wants way too much. That is more than my men receive in a year for wages."

"Two Bears says he will take nothing less. Otherwise you find your own constable. He says you waste his time. Right now, he is after the fattened bear and her cubs, cubs that roast tender and juicy over the coals of his fire and pleases his appetite. The mother is round and waddles when she walks from feeding on wild berries. She gives him fat that greases his hair, his arrows and his cooking fire."

Jarvis looked sternly into Two Bears eyes for a long moment and then turned away. "That is goddamn robbery," Jarvis said to Leville, "but don't tell him I said that yet.

"Okay," said Jarvis. "Tell him he will get what he wants but nothing until he brings the prisoner back, dead or alive."

"Two Bears says he wants the rifle, knife and ammunition now, and all the tobacco he needs to make the trip. He will take the rest of the tobacco when he returns with the white man, dead or alive."

Jarvis commenced pacing back and forth with increasing agitation. He finally answered, "I have no choice. Tell him I will give him everything he wants, the rifle, knife, ammunition and tobacco; but he must show honor or he will get no future deals from me."

"Two Bears says he is an honorable man."

CHAPTER 21

Paniya slept beside her fire. The intense heat during the day had dried out the landscape and small game came with regular frequency to the springs for water. Paniya had no difficulty catching enough game to feed us. A favorite for me was the wild grouse she called *partridge* that she would catch in her snare and roast over the fire. The meat was white, tender and delicious.

Occasionally she left for several hours returning with plants I had never seen before and applied her potent poultices to my wounds. She convinced me to consume a variety of foul-tasting potions that she said would heal me if I had any desire to get better.

In a few days, the inflammation began to disappear and my wounds began closing with new tissue. I could move my injured arm over my head with very little pain and I regained most of my strength. I was able to gather wood now and collect water in birch bark containers. Everyday Paniya cleaned my wounds with a bath of some herbal concoction and applied the healing paste.

In the next few days she showed me how to skin and preserve the rabbit hides by scraping the hide clean of any attached tissue, roughing up the surface with a stone scraper and vigorously impregnating the rawhide with the animal's brains and fat before warming it over the fire. She showed me how to fillet a fish she had caught downstream of the springs.

She cut the fish into thin, boneless strips, exposed them to the smoke of our fire and dried them in the sun to preserve the meat. She was teaching me to survive on my own if I ever had to.

One evening came a gentle rainfall and the low rumble of thunder in the distance, Paniya moved her deerskin bedding underneath my canopy beside me for shelter.

"Oh James," she said, "I always fear the lightning and thunder more than anything else. To me it sounds so angry and I don't understand the spirit that gives it such a voice."

I felt the greatest longing and affection for her and I craved for her to lay on my bed with me but I was resigned to let her decide with complete freewill whatever she wanted to do with me. I hoped she felt safer from the thunder and lightning by being closer to me.

We were both up early the next morning. The shower didn't last but the dry land soaked up the rainfall and the meadows below us broke out into the most beautiful wild flowers: clusters of bluebell, tiger lily, paint brushes and orchids that brought bees buzzing back and forth past our camp adding a slight fragrance of nectar and warm honey to the air. Along the edges of the spring fed pools, yellow marsh flowers bloomed and the pond lilies became favorite landing sites for the frolicking dragon flies with their iridescent wings of purple and blue.

For the first time, with Paniya near me, I felt a level of comfort and peace that I had not known for a long time. I let the days go past now, allowing my wounds time to heal.

With the drought, mosquitos had been scarce but since the rain they began humming about again until Paniya applied a smattering of leaves across the fire that kept them at bay.

The air was often filled with campfire roasting rabbit, porcupine and a mallard that Paniya had captured with a light netting she carried in a leather bag. On cooler evenings, our campfire was warm and she and I sat together. Sometimes she taught me conversation in Cree. She told me stories about growing up with one leg in each of two cultures: tribal life among the Cree with her mother; and life inside the fort at Edmonton when her father was still a voyageur and her mother lived with him in the fortress.

The next morning Paniya and I decided to walk further down the outlet stream past where I had caught the minnows in search of larger fish. She carried a length of fishnet she had woven on her own.

The morning was bright and warm with small flocks of yellow warblers that burst out of the willow trees in a cloud of yellow feathers when we approached the pools. The birds had nested in the willows and now the young birds were flying on their own. We walked above the pools through pockets of red and pink clover and fireweed that was growing in abundance just above our campsite.

Paniya held her hand against my chest to stop me. She bent to examine an overturned log with scrambling masses of ants, centipedes and other insects still moving about in the rotted debris of the disturbed log.

"Bear, likely grizzly," she said. Then she pointed out a huge track in the soft earth beneath the deadfall. "The claws are straight, not curved like the black bear. A grizzly is not far away." She frowned and her face became pinched and worried. "Normally they give a wide berth to a campsite like ours where they smell humans. Something is wrong with this bear," she said, "he shouldn't be this close to us."

I looked around feeling vulnerable.

"Let's stay in camp today," she said. "These animals are territorial and stay out of each other's way except in breeding season when they find each other to mate and the males fight. This time of the year they hunt over a great distance and this bear should be far away by tomorrow."

I didn't need much convincing. Besides I liked being around the campfire with her and there were always chores to be done.

We returned and I didn't take long reigniting the fire. I was still on edge and suffering much anxiety at the thought of a grizzly so close. Was he the same one I had encountered or had another bear taken over his territory? I thought of Bonny. I had seen no sign of her and I feared the worst.

Earlier, Paniya had found the burrow of a groundhog on the bank of a stream below the pools. She had set a snare for the creature before we had left for fishing. We circled past the snare on our way back. She had caught the groundhog, enriching our meat supply which was preserving well under the spring waters.

Back at camp I had begun repairing the canopy above my bed and Paniya had moved to the far edge of our campsite to eviscerate and clean the groundhog. Then I heard the most terrible screams from her.

I recognized the red grizzly who was now upon her, pinning her with his massive claws and coveting the groundhog carcass. I grabbed the arrow that I saw as my only weapon, then thought of my revolver and the cartridges that I had not checked for several days. I ran towards her, still gripping the arrow and feeding cartridges into the revolver. A few feet from the beast I fired my revolver three times into the animal but none of the cartridges discharged.

The bear was still on top of her. In my mind's eye, I saw a tin type of a bullfighter I once knew who had thrust his spear into the hump of a charging bull piercing its heart. I dropped the revolver and sprang onto the back of the grizzly driving the arrow to its hilt into the grizzly's bristling hump.

The animal twisted wildly lunging to find me with his teeth and sending me through the air. He rushed me, a froth of blood spilling behind him until he stood on his hind legs before me. For a moment, my life stood still. Flashing before me, a child I was beating on the playground, hitting him, bloodying his nose long after he was helpless on the ground and the teacher telling me, *you are an evil little boy James McGinn and someday you will pay.* I thought of Spider Marks, the blood flowing from his throat as I watched him die on the ground beside me, fear coming into his eyes.

The bear hovered over me, the frothy blood blowing forth through his nostrils; then he began weaving violently back and forth, snarling and shaking its head, his muzzle and fangs now running streams of bright blood as I waited for him to finish me. Then the beast careened backwards, falling onto the remaining arrow shaft and thrashing wildly in the grass before laying still.

Paniya was hysterical in my arms. I held her tight against me. Finally, both of us exhausted and mentally worn out sat together in the grass, holding onto each other and crying. When we could stand up I checked Paniya all over.

She had a long scratch down one arm but was otherwise unscathed. We were lucky to be alive. I pondered a feeling of providence that guided my arm on the arrow that penetrated the heart of the grizzly. Why was I spared? The beast was as needy as I was.

Paniya stood now, pale and shaking and still trying to collect herself in the aftermath of the attack. "He seemed more interested in the groundhog than in me," she said.

We examined the beast and found him in very poor shape, thin and emaciated. I ran my hand over his abdomen and extracted a broken portion of a spear handle, the one I threw at him the day he attacked. My knife was still attached and yellow exudate rolled out of his stomach cavity when I extracted my knife. I looked into the face of that bear, his eyes vacuous and his gums still pressed back in a snarl.

I no longer felt fear or anger or satisfaction. Suddenly, I felt only empathy for the great beast. Like me, he was struggling to find food, to stay alive, to endure the enormous pain of my broken spear inside his abdomen. Did he feel the sheer hopelessness that I had known before Paniya found me? Life was a struggle for all of us. Maybe it should have been me that fed the bear.

"This bear was starving and very ill," Paniya said, "and drawn by the smell of the groundhog. I should have been more careful."

I put my arm across her shoulders and she moved her arm around my waist, drawing me close to her and we walked together back to camp. I feared that her scratches would become infected and asked where to find the paste she had used on my wounds. I gently applied the medicine on the long wounds down her arm and tenderly wrapped them with a cloth from her bag. I attended to the fire and she came again to me, holding me close to her and her body still trembling. We lay down on her deerskin robe. I held her tight and spoke softly to her, telling her that she was now safe now, that I would stay with her, that her wounds would soon heal.

Our fire burnt to embers and an evening sky gathered around us. I wanted to live forever in this moment with Paniya close beside me. I felt only her warmth and her gentle breathing against me. I stroked her long beautiful hair and her black shining eyes locked onto mine. I kissed her pretty mouth and with every breath I inhaled her beautiful spirit deep inside of me where I wanted to nurture and protect her and take her with me always. She removed her clothing and mine and we joined as one. I wanted to be with her like this for all of eternity and prayed that tomorrow would never come.

I woke only once with Paniya, her warm, brown skin still against mine. The moonless sky was ablaze with stars in long fingers that waved endlessly across the universe. We slept through the dawn and far into the morning light.

We woke again to a bright sun in the meadows. Panyia started the fire and I walked back to the bear. I cut into him to extract his liver for the nutrient it could provide. Then I would skin him for his ragged coat and practice the tanning that Paniya had shown me. I discovered the arrow had penetrated the aortic artery attached to his heart and filled his chest with blood.

Often, I had wondered about the fate of Bonny who might have lost her life that day while mine was saved. I missed her immensely and prayed that she had survived the attack and was able to survive on her own somewhere in the wilderness obviously able to feed on her own the succulent swamp reeds and tender twigs.

That evening we lay on Paniya's robe under the starlight far into the night without starting a fire. Finally, she asked me something we had both been avoiding. "What brought you away back here to these springs, James? Only the Indians know of them. Something else is wrong," she said. "I felt it since the beginning and hoped you would tell me."

I had lived in dread of the time when Paniya would ask why I had come here. And I knew when the time came I would only tell her the truth of my past and why I was running. We sat up together on her robe and late into the night I described all that had happened to me: that Stephen and I had been medical students, we cheated on examinations and burnt down the cottage of the professor to destroy evidence of our cheating. We didn't know that the professor was inside and he burnt alive. We joined the Northwest Mounted Police force to get out of Toronto. There was now a warrant on me for murder. Jarvis and the police came after me. I ran, Stephen was arrested.

Paniya listened through my entire story and remained quiet for several minutes afterwards. She stood up for a moment, looked down at me and then sat back down beside me. "That was reckless and foolish, James. But it was not murder. Would you have killed him to avoid being caught or expelled?"

"No, I would never have harmed Dr. Trelawney, I liked him."

"I don't know the Whiteman's law but the Cree would judge you by what was in your heart. Maybe you are running for nothing."

More than anything, I wanted to articulate what was different for me now and explain it to Paniya. Since the day I ran from the fortress into a wilderness that was so terrifying and unfamiliar, something had changed inside of me. I should have died from dehydration. Before Paniya came I was wracked with pain and burning up with fever. I heard voices from the howling wolves that my time was near.

Finally, I knew what I had to tell her. "Staring into the face of death and then given my life back has changed me," I said. "I knew with certainty that I would die after the grizzly mangled my body and the infection was killing me. And something *did* die inside me, but something else was born.

"That morning, in the early twilight, facing my final hours, I heard your song of healing and I knew it was for me and it was so beautiful and was heard by a spirit greater than anything I had ever known. It was a song so powerful that it brought my spirit back inside me and healed the infection that was killing me. My life is different now and I am different; I feel all the pain and suffering I have caused, my selfishness and sarcasm and all the violence. I feel the sheer horror of professor Trelawney burning alive. I am different now. I feel reverence for life, and I feel the tenderness."

I lay back on the robe with Paniya and she held me close to her until I could feel her trembling and then her silent tears bathed my skin and I cried with her because we both knew our worst fears had finally come.

"I'm going to lose you, James, just like I lost my father so long ago. We both know you must go back," she said, "to tell the truth and let the great spirit decide what should happen to you. Only he will know and only then will you be free."

CHAPTER 22

Before the first morning light, I left Paniya sleeping and climbed to the highest point of land in the hills above the second set of springs as I frequently did. There, with the first sun I looked out across the landscape for anyone pursuing me. I had become familiar with the curve of the landscape, the blue line of distant hills, every open meadow, muskeg, marshland and swale.

Several miles distant I recognized a great gathering of crows erupting above the trees then circling like a small dark swirling cloud. This early, crows should still be roosting in the treetops. Something had disturbed them.

I climbed to the top of a balsam on the edge of the hillside for a better look. Between me and the crows was a long stretch of grass on a south facing slope. Anyone approaching would need to cross the open space to get to me. I waited. The cloud of spiralling crows began to settle again. I decided that perhaps something else had disturbed them, a moose or bear, perhaps an animal or hunter moving in a different direction entirely. I waited perhaps an hour and the sun was moving above the trees casting a shadow over the wilderness below. I was looking southeast into the rising light making it hard for me see. I was preparing to leave, to collect firewood on the way back. Paniya would most likely be roasting meat for our breakfast, maybe adding the peelings from rosehips boiled into a thick jelly with berries, petals and tender root of stalks from the pond to go with the meat. I was getting hungry.

I turned for a final survey of the landscape below and was preparing to skinny down the balsam when something caught my eye emerging from the forest and moving onto the open grassy slope in the distance. My chest began to pump with fear. Then I felt sudden relief as I clearly recognized the outline of a native hunter in leather leggings carrying a rifle, apparently tracking game. I would have nothing to fear from him.

Then two scarlet clad men emerged from the bush behind him. By their posture, gait and relative height, I began to recognized them, Lillico and Lynch, two police that would just as soon bring me in dead as alive. The man with them was likely an Indian guide hired by the police. He was a huge man. Lynch was almost as tall as me and the guide was head and shoulders taller than Lynch and he moved quickly across the open slope. I did not recognize him. At the rapid pace they travelled, I estimated they could be at the springs in less than an hour. I quickly returned to camp.

Paniya watched me coming down the slope towards her, her smile turning slowly to an expression of concern as she witnessed the apprehension in me.

"Two constables with a third person, an Indian guide is my guess coming for me," I told her. "I recognize the two police: Doug Lynch and Bill Lillico. They both hate me. I have no idea about the guide, a very tall man, much taller than the other two. They're less than an hour out." She stared at me a long moment, then peered towards the hills behind me and back again.

"I've been expecting them," she said. "And the tall Indian, he's sometimes a guide that knows this area better than anyone else. Most certainly he is Two Bears."

"You have to go back to the fortress where you will be safe," I told her. "I will take whatever comes along. I can travel north to the Athabasca River. There's a fort up there, Fort Assiniboine, I can try to find it. Or I'll wait here for them and take my chances. But I will never be their captive. Lynch and Lillico don't plan to bring me in alive. I will deal with that. You must go back."

Paniya looked into my eyes for a long moment and raised her chin. "I am not going without you James; I'm not leaving you here like this. If you are heading north, then so am I. And we will both starve or freeze to death because Fort Assiniboine has long been abandoned. Richard told me. Besides, your plan would never work. Two Bears would eventually find you. That I know for sure. He already knows what options you have. He finds everything he sets his mind to, like a fox eventually gets the gopher that tries to hide."

"It will be even worse for you if Two Bears finds us together," I said. "You go. I'll stay here and face him."

"James, you have to let me worry about Two Bears. I want you to trust me, I know this land and I know these people and you have to let me try to help you. Let me take you back to Fort Edmonton," she said. "No one needs to know you're there," she continued. "From Fort Edmonton I can help you escape. Your constables are twenty miles away from there at Fort Saskatchewan. I have a canoe that belonged to my father and a sack of pemmican, 150 pounds, that will easily sustain you. But you must go back, James, to face the

Whiteman justice, to tell the truth, only if you face what you have done will you ever be free."

Paniya moved close to me and squeezed me tight against her and I held her like I would never let her go. But the realization came, the sheer folly of ever being able to be with her. Finally, she let go, stood on her tiptoes and looked over my shoulder with great apprehension. "We must hurry and gather our belongings," she said. "It is still a long walk to Fort Edmonton."

She began collecting her things and placing them in a leather carrying pouch. She rolled up her robe and secured it with sinew. I retrieved my few belongings and hoisted Paniya's packs across my back as we started out along the pools and into the bush. I followed Paniya and she smiled over her shoulder at me. "In my mother's camp it was always the women who had to bear the weight of travel and follow behind."

"Well, in this Whiteman's world you're the guide and I am the pack mule. Things change in a crisis." I was glad I could still joke with Paniya in spite of the tragedy affecting us and it was music for me to hear her laughter. She continued at a rapid pace and I kept up with her as she followed a small stream from the pools and then headed south into the noon day sun.

We kept up a pace all day and far into the night when we stopped, ate some of the food Paniya had packed and drank water from a water pouch she carried. So far, there was no evidence that anyone was following us but that was hard to ascertain given the thick wilderness we had been travelling through. It was quickly becoming too dark to travel further in the dense bush and both of us needed rest. We found a large overhang of spruce boughs and spread out the robe for a few hours' sleep. We didn't risk starting a fire because we needed only each other for warmth.

Then Paniya turned to face me. "I will tell you what needs to be done once we get to the fort because there will be very little time." She sat up on the robe. "My canoe is stored under a lean-to in the bush near the river. You have to stay by the canoe where no one will see you. I'll bring you some provisions and ammunition."

Paniya lay back down beside me and looked into the night sky. She sighed and told me about her father. "He made that voyage every spring in a boat piled high with furs for sale in cities across the ocean. In the evenings before he left he told me stories about the journey he would be taking. As a little girl I followed him every mile in my day dreams and in my night dreams too, and I reminisced his stories and I saw everything that he saw.

"I always waved good bye to him when he started his journey on the river below the fort, just as you will. He paddled at the back of the boat, just in front of the steersman who was always Maurice, a tiny little man and my father could always wave good bye to me over his head.

"But first, he and other voyageurs would push the boat away from shore and then jump in. My father's moccasins, tied down with two feet of thongs, were dripping mud and always soaking wet when he jumped in the boat. The men paddled with the current and once they got started, the boat went very fast. Like my father, the voyageurs were strong and hardened with work; by the time they rounded the first bend their boat was moving as fast as a slowly galloping horse."

I took her hand and she spread her fingers open and I clasped them tight between mine as she moved closer and continued describing what I must do.

"My father said that the river took them four long days of paddling to Lake Winnipeg. Then he always went east across the lake to find another river that led to the ocean ports and the ships. But my father said that if he had gone south across Lake Winnipeg, paddling for about four more days, he would have found a river at the end flowing south cross the boundary near Fargo. I'm told that is where the railway runs now."

She turned to look at me. "He said he always wanted to go there for a look around. He had never seen the prairie, the herds of antelope or the miles of buffalo grazing on the great open plains. As far as I know he never went. But that is how you can go back, James, to catch the train." She smiled. "I just know this stuff," she added, "it sticks with me."

CHAPTER 23

Jarvis woke to knocking on his door. He swung his feet onto the floor and hollered, 'doors open,' as Lillico and Lynch stepped gingerly inside.

"You got him?" asked Jarvis.

"I'm sorry sir, we don't have him yet, but all is not lost either, sir."

"Where the hell is he then?"

"Two Bears took us to the Medicine Springs," said Lynch. "He had no trouble finding it. But remember sir, it has been many weeks since his disappearance."

"Don't patronize me!" bellowed Jarvis, "I know goddamn well how long it has been. Did you find any trace of the little son of a bitch or not? Just give me the whole goddamn story."

"We found where he had been holed up at the Medicine Springs," Lynch continued. "He'd likely been there for a very long time. He made a shelter, killed a bear somehow and had been thriving on a whole variety of small game, birds, even fish.

"Something about McGinn's living arrangements didn't set right for Two Bears." Lynch turned to Lillico. "Wouldn't you say, Billy, something seemed to infuriate Two Bears about the set up?"

"He was seeing red, furious," said Lillico. "Anybody could see it. Especially when he found sign somebody had been living there with McGinn. Two Bears kept babbling in Cree, maybe trying to tell us something, maybe just pretending the motions of telling us something, without wanting to tell us a damned thing. But he was mad about something, sure as hell," said Lillico."

"When he wanted to communicate to us," interjected Lynch, "he had no trouble getting his meaning across. He was going after the fugitive alone and told us to go back to the fort. We insisted we had to come, to make a legal arrest. Nobody can keep up with Two Bears in the bush. It's sheer impossible. We tried for a while but he left us miles behind. Finally, we headed south to the river and followed it back here."

"Before taking off, Two Bears said: tell the white chief I'll be back with his constable, maybe alive, maybe dead," said Lillico. "And he said to have the rest of his tobacco ready for him when he gets here."

"Well, that's one hell of a showing by the Northwest Mounted Police trying to arrest a man," said Jarvis, "Even if the man is their own little bastard and a cold-blooded killer. Now we'll just have to see what Two Bears brings back with him."

CHAPTER 24

Paniya and I awoke at the first light of a gray morning. We decided to take time with a small fire and food before commencing the long and gruelling trek through some of the densest wilderness we had yet encountered towards the fortress. Paniya had gone for water from a stream nearby. I started a fire. I had an eerie sense that something was behind me. There was not a sound or a shadow that alerted me.

I turned quickly to face the largest warrior I had ever seen and I knew immediately that he was not a friendly visitor but someone with the most malicious intent. He had a long barrel rifle strapped across his back with much ammunition in belts strung across his shoulders and torso. He wielded a wide, bone handled knife and before I could move to protect myself, he brought me down hard to the ground with the sheer force of his massive body and incredible strength.

He pinned me on my back and for several moments he simply stared into my face, studying my features, maybe to remember me or to gain a sense of the person he was about to dispatch with his knife now firmly against my throat. I was completely at his mercy. He mumbled a string of words foreign to me. I barely had time to think about my fate when I heard strong words from Paniya.

He stopped immediately to look up at her. She spoke in Cree and her tone was scolding and sharp. Now my greatest fear was for her and I struggled desperately again trying to push aside the knife and remove his weight from me, but I was a child in a struggle against a grown man. He held me down with one huge hand around my throat but relinquished the knife and spoke to Paniya.

For several minutes they argued back and forth until he slowly released his grip on me, extracted my revolver from my holster and threw it into the bush. Then he got up and faced Paniya. I stood beside her as they argued in a language I did not understand. I had never seen Paniya as determined. She spoke sharply, then looked to the sky raising her palm upward, then moving her same palms toward the chest of Two Bears without touching him.

He simply stared at her for a long moment, his features expressionless. Maybe resigned to something words could not explain. Gradually he turned, staring at me with hatred in his eyes. He backed into the forest, replaced his knife into the back of a leather thong around his waist. He continued backing away, glancing behind himself occasionally, sweeping branches aside with his hand until finally he disappearing into the thick bush.

She watched him disappear. Then she turned to me and held me close to her as she felt across my neck and throat for wounds. She kissed me on the lips. "Oh James, I dreaded that this day would come. I knew how jealous he would be if he saw us together and I never wanted him to hurt you like this."

I knew I had just taken a beating and Paniya had saved my life yet again. "Well," I said, "that man of yours is strong as an ox and a lot more dangerous! What did you say to him?"

"Strong, yes, but he is simply a brute. Beyond fighting, killing, hunting and putting fear into everyone, he has the sensitivity of an ox.

"You must be careful, James. He quit because I made him quit. If he can quietly stalk you without me knowing, he will surely kill you and that puts the worst fear in me."

"How did you stop him?"

"That's a long story that might be hard for you to understand because you don't know the ways of my people that are very different from what white people believe."

For several moments I continued to stand there beside her. I could not stop watching where Two Bears had disappeared, hoping he wouldn't have a change of mind. Paniya remained calm. She obviously saw my apprehension and took my hand. "Come sit with me," she said. "I don't think he will come back as long as I'm here." We sat back down on the robes. She began to tell me about her past with Two Bears.

"The greatest power that my people know and respect comes from the supernatural," she said, "spirits that only some people have an alliance with. At times in my life I have been gifted by them but only when I live with my people. Spirits do not come into the white world in the same way."

She put her arm around my waist and moved closer to me. "Let me tell you what happened once." She looked up at me with her beautiful dark eyes and continued. "Two Bears often bullied me and a vision came to me one night from my grandparents. They told me that Two Bears would be hunting and a lynx would be hiding along the branch of a tree, its eye on a struggling rabbit that became entangled in Two Bears snare. He bent down on hands and knees to take the rabbit. The hungry lynx, furious at being robbed, dropped onto Two Bear's back, snarling and sinking his teeth deep into his neck and raking his back with its claws. Before Two Bears could find his knife or draw his bow the lynx escaped into the bush.

"I told him of my vision many days before he left for the hunt. He ridiculed me. 'How would a woman have such powers?' he asked. He added that 'Two Bears fears nothing and never the vision of a woman.' He laughed at me.

"Soon after, it happened just the way I described to him. He returned from hunting with deep wounds from the lynx.

Paniya looked up at me her eyes serious, searching my face for understanding.

I nodded. I knew the truth of what she was telling me. Since our encounter at the Medicine Springs I understood the power of her beautiful spirit.

She continued. "His injuries were badly infected and he was sick with fever and unable to hunt or lead his warriors against the Blackfoot for several days. I made the right preparations for him and he soon healed. Now he sees me as a medicine woman, even if he says nothing, I know he fears my power. I warned him today that there are totems far mightier than the claws of a lynx and if he harms you more powerful spirits than ever before will bring their wrath upon him."

***

On the early afternoon of the fourth day we saw the towers of the fortress at Edmonton come into view over the treeline. We moved along the shore until Paniya stopped.

"My canoe is in the trees near here," she said as she stepped off the gravel shoreline and walked into the bush. I set the pack down and followed her to a place maybe two hundred yards from shore where she had turned her canoe over inside a grove of overhanging spruce. She had inserted a wooden prop beneath to allow air to circulate under the craft. Then she had covered the canoe with more spruce bows for camouflage and further protection from the rain and snow.

I helped her pull away the boughs and bring the canoe out where we examined it. The canoe was still in very good shape. "I have used it occasionally over the last years," she told me, "and always repaired any leaks or damage with tar from the fort. Once I had Kelly, one of the carpenters, replace some damaged ribs. It should take you back where you need to go." I pulled the canoe down to the water and Paniya left to get supplies for my journey.

She soon returned with a paddle and two sacks of supplies which I loaded in the canoe. I took her into my arms and held her tight and kissed her pretty lips and felt her warm tears flowing down her face and across my skin. Finally, she pushed me gently away, "James you have to go now," she said. I held tight to her hands looking deep into her dark eyes and I could not let go. Finally, I looked beyond her to the fortress above which felt more like a home to me now than any place I had ever been before. Could I ever return? I didn't know. Slowly I realized that the longer I stayed the more likely she was to be seen and placed in jeopardy for assisting the escape of a murderer.

It was already late afternoon when I finally pushed the canoe into open water of the North Saskatchewan and paddled briskly with the current and the prevailing breeze. But I found little solace in rendering my escape but instead a tremendous weight was placed on me knowing that Paniya may be lost to me forever. I turned to find her standing on the edge of the water still watching me.

I waved back to her and she at me. It was a memory that would forever haunt me. The slender beauty of Paniya, her silhouette against the dark moving water. More than anything I felt the great sorrow inside of her that captured the space between us as vivid and alive as the magic of her touch and I knew that something of Paniya's great spirit would follow me on my journey.

Throughout the evening I paddled. A bright moon rose above the forest, casting shadows through the trees like a thousand living things moving about in the wilderness until I discovered that they were not mere shadows. A line of six wolves followed along the shore in the wake of my canoe, their faces grinning and their tongues wagging as if being with me brought them great joy.

I was fascinated by them, even slowing my canoe to let them catch up to me and make eye contact. I revelled in their presence, their gleaming eyes, without malice, following me. The pack helped to relieve the sorrow inside of me and they stayed near my canoe for miles, sometimes bounding ahead of me along the shore, then dropping back beside me or sometimes falling behind as they took time to sniff out something that attracted their attention or investigated something of interest in the trees. Then they rushed back to accompany me. Eventually, they left the shore line and were swallowed up by the blackness of the wilderness.

I badly needed to rest my arms. I had grown unused to the hard work of paddling and finally I pulled up onto the shore to camp for the night. I selected a place to sleep among a light stand of poplar, above a small embankment of the river where a narrow stream of clear water emptied into the North Saskatchewan River. The bubbling sound of a stream always helped to soothe my mind and bring sleep. It was a perfect over-night location.

At dawn I awoke and started a fire to warm my ration of pemmican when a powerful unease came over me again, like something was watching me. High above the tree tops were small entrails of smoke that moved higher creating a grey funnel against the morning sky.

Something else caught my eye and I turned to find Two Bears approaching me through the open poplar, covering me with his rifle and his mouth forming a twisted grin, relishing the sudden fear that must have shown on my face and the paralysis that took over my body at the sight of him.

He must have followed me throughout the night, most likely watching my canoe pass by as he progressed west towards the fortress or Cree encampment. Then he found my camp and made the decision to dispatch me in the clear light of day.

He stopped on the lip of the churning creek a few yards away, his rifle still trained on me. I watched him scanning my campsite considering my full situation. My carbine was on the other side of my fire and out of reach. I wore no holster bearing a side arm or hunting knife.

I felt his intense jealousy and hatred. He knew Paniya had been with me and by now he surely knew her feelings for me. I was becoming more certain that his bitterness would prompt him to disqualify a quick death in favor of watching me succumb to his great personal power, enduring prolonged suffering and a tormented death.

He slowly lowered his gun and extracted a knife secured around his waist. I had no defense whatsoever, nor did either of us have any doubt that he could physically bring me down with ease, whether I decided to run or not, and render whatever death he chose to deliver with his knife or his bare hands. He would lift my scalp, and probably while I was still alive. My last thoughts were of Paniya suffering the rest of her days with an inhuman brute.

Then, I caught only a glimpse of them streaking forth as one, their heads lowered and hair bristling high along their spines, their canines flashing white as they attacked with a ferocity unlike anything I had ever seen before. Two Bears had barely turned to see them when the pack as one brought him down, a mass of unrelenting fiendish fury. They had moved quietly below the embankment of the stream bed without being detected by either of us.

I ran to collect my carbine and then I rushed towards my open fire, fearing I might be next. But they had finished the job on Two Bears, ripping him to shreds and seemed completely uninterested in me or even the remains of the Cree warrior. They turned slowly, all six moving in single file back below the stream embankment and out of sight.

Paniya had grown up in two worlds and now I knew the sheer power of her Cree world. It could have been nothing other than the great spirit of Paniya that willed the wolves to follow and protect me. I looked around as if to see her among the trees or hear her voice in the bubbling stream but there was only wilderness, the river and the shredded corpse of Two Bears.

I sat by my fire for the longest time, trying to calm my nerves and my mind unable to stop the scenes running through my brain of the wolves tearing him apart. I pondered all the ways that Two Bears might have rendered his jealous rage upon me, eventually killing me. I realized again how much the past months had moulded and changed me in a manner that filled me not only with wonder, but also with distress and much regret.

No longer could I tolerate the violence, death and murder that had been my life, violence that had once left me so unaffected. Now the images would come to me in my night dreams and in the daytime; images of Trelawney's death mask of scarred tissue, the massacred Crow warriors, and the frontier messengers relating the details of murders that took place at the fortress: people mutilated, scalped and a woman de-robed in front of the fort, stabbed and murdered as she screamed and begged for her life.

At times I felt the stickiness of Spider Mark's blood on my hands, a feeling that would not wash away even with the most rigorous scrubbing of soap and water. Sometimes there were daytime flashes that took over my consciousness of a mangled Tom Leslie laying on the prairie helpless, waiting for the wolves to devour him. I thought of Stephen and Freddy, both beaten unconscious, bloody and swollen from merciless poundings by Leslie and Marks. And now it would be images of a mangled Two Bears. I was heart sick of violence, murder and death.

Finally, I pressed myself to abandoned the site and paddle away from the grisly scene, still trying to clear my mind of the images of Two Bears. I paddled for several hours before finding a grove of spruce close to the water and the sound of the current, a peaceful place to make camp and try to clear my mind.

CHAPTER 25

I watched my fire burn down to a pile of glowing embers and still I sat staring into the red, flickering coals. I felt a great loneliness that only grew deeper. Finally, I retrieved the buffalo robe I had for sleeping and rolled it out on the ground. I lay on my back far into the night, thinking of the many hours I spent with Paniya beside me; the most wonderful times of my life. I watched an oval moon inch its way across the dome of a dark sky. I recalled thinking I should re-start my fire to keep predators away but I could not pull away from the fatigue that was finally catching up to me and I fell into a deep sleep.

A dream came to me of being a child at home in my bedroom with all the opulence afforded me by my successful father. I felt the security of the strong walls of home and the warmth of my loving mother. In my dream I followed the night time rituals of childhood, my mother putting away a storybook that she had been reading to me and then cleaning me up for bed. I felt the wet sticky sensations down my arm as my mother lathered and bathed me with thick soap as she told me, *James, I don't know how you get so filthy.* Suddenly I pulled away from the dream, I was not in my bed on the estate of my parents but in the middle of a dark wilderness. And the wet sticky on my arm was not my mother bathing me.

I jumped up as something bounded away from me crashing into the bush and then returning stretching her long snout towards me, and commencing to lick my arm once again. It was Bonny. I felt the greatest relief at seeing her. I ran my hand along her sleek out-stretched neck and scratched behind her long ears before moving my arms around the base of her neck with the greatest warmth and affection I had ever known for any animal. I scratched under her chin and down the underside of her neck and spoke softly to her telling her my great joy at finding her alive.

She turned again to lick my arm whether for the salt on my skin or out of affection for me I did not know or care. I continued to speak softly to her and she nudged my chest. I ran my hands along her smooth back and sides. Her fur was sleek and a layer of fat had formed under her skin and I could not stop the tears that came into my eyes knowing she was alive and thriving.

She had escaped the life-threatening terror of a grizzly. Maybe my knife inside the bear's abdomen had slowed it down enough to allow Bonny's escape. She obviously had the great instinct to leave the territory of the bear far behind and find the river which would supply her with water and the many oxbow stretches filled with reeds and marsh grasses to sustain her.

I simply stood beside her for the longest time, stroking her sleek body and scratching under her long neck until finally she lay down at the foot of the buffalo robe. I placed a small amount of wood on my fire and went back to sleep. I awoke at dawn and Bonny was gone. I never saw her again.

***

The morning was warm with a clear sky and I put in a long day of leisurely paddling. I found a campsite on an open stretch of grass by the river where I could start a fire and sleep under the stars. I made myself as comfortable as I could on my buffalo robe but still did not fall asleep until almost dawn when I finally surrendered to the weariness and slept long into the morning.

I no longer felt the urgency that had plagued my life for so many weeks. Paniya had packed a small pouch of coffee into the bag she provided for my journey. I decided to make coffee which I had not enjoyed for a very long time. I build a small bonfire and went to the river beside my canoe to fill a brass pot with water. I was filling the pot when I noticed something floating past me in the current, a small object, the size of a matchstick. It caught an eddy near shore where it swirled slowly before catching the current again and continuing downstream. I quickly grabbed a paddle and raced after it until I could reach my oar out into the stream and directed the object back where I could retrieve it.

As I suspected from the first glimpse, it was a matchstick. The charred end was still mostly attached to the wooden stem. I was certain that an object as small as a match would only stay above the surface for a few hours before becoming water logged and sinking. In addition, I squeezed the charred end between my fingers and it still blackened my fingertips. The match had not been in the water that long. Someone was on the river behind me and not far back. Perhaps someone lighting a pipe or some other form of tobacco, dropping the spent match in the water before preparing camp. Or, like me, getting water for morning coffee before leaving camp.

I began to fear that someone was following me. I pulled my canoe far up on shore, camouflaged it in a grove of aspen and dogwood before wiping down the abundant tracks I had created in the mud with my foot prints and the imprint of the canoe. I extinguished my fire and waited for about two hours and no one passed on the river. Still the match was a troubling mystery. The fort was two full days travel behind me. If someone working at the fort had tossed the match into the water it would have sunk long before now. Most certainly the charred portion would have completely dissolved after only a few hours in the water.

I decided once again to re-enter my canoe and commence paddling for my remote destination. Nevertheless, I remained vigilant. I loaded my belongings while keeping the canoe undercover in the bush and once loaded, I pulled the whole thing rapidly to shore, surveyed the river behind me, jumped in and paddled hard to create some distance. I kept up the paddling for about five hours. Still distressed by the discarded match, I decided the best way to ease my mind was to camp early and watch for anyone on the river behind me.

I pulled my canoe far above the shore where I found the beginning of a small oxbow of stagnant water, an ancient section of the river no longer joining the main stream. I moved my canoe along the oxbow and hid it under a dense overhang of willow.

I used branches again, as best as I could, to wipe down my tracks in the mud of the shore. Then I followed back down the river and climbed a high barren knoll on a side hill above the current where I could get a full view from shore to shore for at least a half mile stretch of the river before it bent to the south and out of view. I set out my bedding, a ration of pemmican, my side arm, ammunition, and a flask of drinking water and watched the river flowing past below me.

It was hot and I took off my tattered jacket to cool down and give my body some sunlight. I realized how completely compromised my clothing had become after so many weeks of running. My pant legs were barely streams of thread now, that hung down over my scratched and scarred legs. My undershirt was thin and a mass of sweat stains in spite of repeated washing in the pools. Fortunately, my boots were worn but still holding together. I was certain my appearance now was similar to any beggar that I might have encountered on the streets of Toronto.

I watched the river flow by and began to trace scenarios in my mind of what might have happened. Could someone at the fort, maybe Hardisty himself, have seen me heading out in the canoe and sent word to Jarvis. A fast messenger on horseback could have gotten the message to Jarvis in a few hours. Canoe travel to Fort Edmonton from Fort Saskatchewan would be another six or seven hours. Someone could conceivably be only a half day travel behind me.

Ducks landed and took off again from the river. A beaver swam upstream carrying green branches of willow in his mouth for a winter reserve. He dove beside his lodge with the branches that emerged again inside a tangle of green willows that were likely secured in the mud below.

A coyote sniffed along the shore by the beaver's lodge then retreated into the bush. The river flowed past me without providing anything further of interest and I dozed on the hillside. I jerked awake after a few minutes, fearing that I could have missed anyone who might be following me. Then I began to wonder if I was simply succumbing to paranoia, that my imagination had made the spent match out to be something that it wasn't. Maybe a Cree hunter hunting along the shore had cast it off.

Evening was settling in and the river to the west of me was reflecting a silver glare, the eastern portion remained well-lit and every nuance of the river terrain was now burnt into my brain. I was dozing again and must have been almost asleep when fresh movement on the river brought me back. Three red jackets in a long canoe rounded the bend of the river all hunkered over their oars, paddling hard in hot pursuit of their man.

I watched them draw closer until I made out the third man at the back of the canoe behind Lynch and Lillico; it was Gerome Carlisle. He no doubt volunteered for the mission out of hatred for me and Jarvis no doubt granted him permission knowing that if anyone was motivated to find me it would be Gerome. Besides, he was a brute who would argue that he could paddle faster than any two other men. It would be the right argument for Jarvis.

All three kept close to shore where the current was swifter around the bend and the most likely place for anyone paddling a canoe to travel. They were studying the embankment for any sign of where I might have landed and I watched them pass by below me. In spite of my best efforts to cover my tracks, Lynch pointed to the disturbance where I had come on shore. They pulled over, got out, checked their carbines and hand revolvers and strolled around the area where I had been only a few hours previously.

They combed through the long grass looking for any further sign of me or hints suggestive of my activity. They stood together talking. Carlisle lit up his pipe and tossed the match into the river. After a short conversation they walked back towards the shoreline, I think they were satisfied my canoe was not there, that I must have moved on. I was immensely grateful for the extra time I took to bring my canoe into the back-water and hide it among the thick overhang of willow.

They walked to their canoe and I moved down the slope towards them until I could make out part of their conversation.

"Maybe the son-of-a-bitch came on shore to take a shit." said Lillico. "There's no canoe or we would have found it by now."

"We can make up the lost time," commented Lynch. "There should be a few hours paddling yet before dark."

They stowed their sidearms in the canoe to free their arms for the work ahead. Gerome untied the canoe and all had their backs to me preparing to get on-board and shove off. I pulled my revolver and advanced to within a few feet of them. "You boys looking for someone?" I asked.

All three stood frozen beside the canoe then turned slowly towards me looking like they saw a ghost.

"I bet you were ready to shoot me down like a dog, weren't you?" I said.

Gerome was the first to speak. "You're wanted for murder, McGinn," he said. "You're under arrest."

I laughed. "Well aren't you just in a fine position to make an arrest," I said. "In fact, what an opportune moment. I could use a few more supplies and a change of clothes. I might even let you go with your lives if you cooperate."

"You're an evil bastard, McGinn," said Lynch. "We saw your campsite back down the trail. You killed Two Bears and left him for the wolves to rip apart, like you wanted for Tom."

I held my revolver high, sighting it along a line toward all three. I wanted them to be scared as hell so they would cooperate. I had no appetite for hurting any of them and certainly did not want to risk having to kill one of them. I regretted even having to kill a grizzly bear that was starving like me.

Nor did I have any interest in becoming their captive. I felt their hatred even as I stood near them and I knew the abuse they would surely inflict upon me as their prisoner. I was certain they would find a reason to kill me and relate to Jarvis that I tried to escape or some other lie in order to render their own justice. My best hope was to scare the hell out of them so they would give me what I needed.

"Me evil, Lynch?" I said, "You have no idea how evil I can be. I burnt a man alive once just to watch his face through the window begging me to let him out," I lied. "And your friend Spider Marks, he snuck up and tried to kill me just before I gut shot him, sending shit from his insides spraying across the trees. I left him to die a slow death, and I could hear him wailing and moaning and begging me to help him as I walked away." I made up the lies as I went along and I could tell they were getting scared as hell.

"And my greatest regret, not getting to watch Tom Leslie's face when the wolves came for him just like I watched the wolves feast on Two Bears. None of that will be as much fun as what I have in mind for you three if you don't cooperate." I watched Carlisle go pale and the other two were frozen stiff just watching me.

"But there is honor in me when I'm treated properly," I said. "You could even go free but first I need a change of clothing. As you can see my uniform is a bit tattered. Skinny out of those pants Carlisle, you're close to my size."

He looked at me blankly then he squeezed out a timid, "fuck you McGinn." I fired my first shot between his open legs, missing his balls by a few inches as he scrambled out of his pants faster than I ever saw a man undress in my life. "And undershorts, too," I added.

"Now I need your shirt, serge, pants and under clothes, Lynch." He peeled them all off. "Lillico, all I need from you is your pants and unders. I don't need another serge. You get to keep yours. It won't fit me anyway. And you can thank your lucky stars that I'm in a benevolent mood today, letting you all keep your boots. Lillico, you can toss that hunting knife under your coat onto the ground."

I got them to move away from their canoe. I cleaned out their belongings, left them some food, kept a rifle, some of their ammunition and tossed the remaining firearms into the middle of the river. I set their canoe adrift in the North Saskatchewan.

"Now come with me." I waved them ahead of me to retrieve my canoe from the oxbow. I sighted the rifle onto their shiny backsides and had them haul my canoe back to the river for me.

Then, I got them to load my few belongings into the canoe. "Now run like hell!" I demanded. I commenced firing all around them as they took off bare-assed for the bush faster than a naked bat out of hell. I took to my canoe and paddled away rapidly. I looked back to find them standing on the shore staring after me. I was relieved by knowing that I had not injured any of them, except their pride, of which they were overly endowed to begin with. I had left them enough food to survive. In a few days they would make it back to Fort Edmonton fully intact, albeit in the raw.

CHAPTER 26

Willie Savine was on gate duty when a messenger arrived from Fort Edmonton on a sweaty mount still frothing at the mouth. The messenger said his name was Pillsworth from the Fort Edmonton Factor's headquarters and announced that he needed to see Jarvis immediately.

Willie brought him to Jarvis who ushered the man inside and requested the nature of his visit.

"It's about your fugitive, sir, James McGinn."

"He's in custody at the fort?"

"I'm sorry sir, no such good luck. I'm told he escaped, sir. Your men, Lynch, Lillico and Carlisle, wish to know if they should begin anew to track him by canoe from the Edmonton fort."

Jarvis was silent for a long moment, bracing himself for what he knew would not be good news. "Fill me in on the details of his escape."

"Well sir, your constables had paddled all through the previous night and were quite exhausted. They watched for places where the fugitive might have camped and were still assuming the killer had to be several hours ahead of them with no reason to think otherwise. After nearly two days of paddling they went ashore to rest and McGinn appeared out of nowhere, sir, getting the drop on them, taking their supplies and leaving again."

"They had their firearms. Why didn't they continue to pursue him?"

"Well, they had no clothes sir, no ammunition or firearms and he released their canoe into the river.

Jarvis sat down, stared at the wall a long moment before holding his head in his hands. Finally, he looked up at the messenger. "When did Lynch, Lillico and Carlisle get back to Fort Edmonton?"

"Just this morning sir. Badly worn and exhausted."

"Clearly McGinn is headed to Fort York, following the trek of your voyageurs each summer," said Jarvis. "He wants a ship back to where ever he came from, maybe Ireland. This means he has six or seven days head start on anyone coming after him." Jarvis stopped to calculate for a few moments.

"We won't catch him on the river. Whether or not a messenger with fresh mounts travelling back on Carlton and making the connection from there to York can make it in time to arrest him is anybody's guess. I frankly doubt it and we have no jurisdiction outside the Dominion."

"What message should I provide to the Factor and your men, sir?"

"I'll have somebody get my constables some clothing to send back with you. Pass them my orders to come back here. Tell them we have work to do." Then Jarvis added, mostly to himself. "How unfortunate, the wily little bastard could have been a good policeman."

CHAPTER 27

After ten days of paddling, my canoe broke onto the expansive waters of Lake Winnipeg. There was no other shore as far as I could see and for a moment I wondered if, somehow, I had encountered the ocean but the water was fresh to the taste.

I set up camp on the west shore of the lake and suddenly I felt the urgency of my decision, thoughts that had ruminated in my mind for several days. This was my last opportunity to decide my future. I could continue east across Lake Winnipeg, finding an outflow to the sea where eventually I would encounter sea ports on Hudson's Bay and ships that would take me across the ocean to England. Or, I could continue south across the lake, taking the most southern outflowing river until I intersected the railway line to Fargo and from there eventually back to the place where I was born. I would turn myself in to the Toronto police and let them decide my fate.

I found myself once again looking east far across the endless blue waters of Lake Winnipeg towards the ocean that lie beyond. I could make a new life in England or Ireland, my ancestral home. There would most certainly be relatives there that would have known of my grandfather, Murdock McGinn, from the County of Cork.

Such thoughts took over my mind as I prepared a fire and feasted on pemmican and boiled a pot of coffee. I thought of Paniya, when she asked me about Trelawney, *Would you intentionally kill him?* I told her I actually liked Trelawney and I would never have purposefully killed him. She said, *I don't know the Whiteman's law but the Cree would judge you by what was in your heart. Maybe you are running from nothing.* But then, she hardly knew the stilted laws of the Whiteman's world where innocent men were often hung.

I could make that journey of many thousands of miles across the ocean but it would not leave behind the memories of what I had done or resolve the turmoil inside of me. I thought of what Paniya had told me: *We both know you must go back, James, to tell the truth and let the great spirit decide what should happen. Only he will let you be free.*

My fire burned out and I lay back down on the buffalo robe. I slept better than I had in many days and woke knowing I would make my own case in Toronto and leave the rest to fate whatever the ultimate consequence. I felt the greatest longing for Paniya. Facing up to my past was my only chance of ever seeing her again. I got up at sunrise, loaded my canoe and took a bearing to the south.

I lost track of the days, simply paddling towards the sun at its noon peak until the lake narrowed and I found a river running south. In time, I crossed under a railway bridge that I knew would lead to Fargo. I pulled my canoe into tall reeds among the elaborate footings of the bridge and followed the train tracks into town and a railway station that had once been the center of a rodeo grounds where a fledging Northwest Mounted Police turned the place into a stampede. I remembered the sheer delight of the local townspeople watching us. Already a year had past.

I dug through my trouser pockets to retrieve my bill fold with my money badly stained from soaking in the Medicine

Springs. I purchased a newspaper and then went quickly to the wicket as the train was shooting jets of steam through a whistle, a call for boarding to St. Paul and beyond. The conductor counted out my fare and sent me inside. I found a seat by myself, sat back and opened the newspaper. The headlines read: *Sioux Mutilations Fuel Cavalry Campaign.*

The article went on to report: *For many months, the Sioux have been agitated by white settlers going onto their sacred Black Hills in search of gold. The savages have begun marauding the nearby settlements and settlers have been murdered. General Custer and the Seventh Cavalry are vowing to punish the Sioux for their treacherous indiscretions.*

I had heard about the Union's treaty with the Sioux who were given their sacred Black Hills. I thought the Sioux had a point but I knew the reputation of the cavalry. Once they organized a campaign, no Sioux man, woman or child would be spared their wrath. I turned back to my newspaper:

The Sioux are not satisfied with extracting revenge on local settlers. Most recently, an inexperienced Canadian Police Officer escorting a prisoner for trial apparently became lost on the prairie. They missed Fargo by fifty miles and ended up in Sioux country. Both were scalped, mutilated and their bodies left on the prairie to be discovered by our men of the 7th U.S. Calvary.

Realization struck me like a sledge hammer. The prisoner would surely be none other than Stephen. I sat stunned in my seat for several minutes barely able to breath before laying the paper aside. I had convinced Stephen to join the Northwest Mounted Police. The irony sickened my stomach. Stephen was the one most reluctant to leave Toronto and I the one pushing him, thinking I was saving us from execution.

Now Stephen was murdered and I was returning to Toronto, the city he never wanted to leave. I was returning to face the consequences of Trelawney's death which I am now certain would have been Stephen's first choice had I not pushed him to run from all the trouble with the dead professor.

I could not help ponder Stephen's final hours. Was his death fast or slow? I could not imagine that a war party of enraged Sioux would have any interest in a quick or painless death. Maybe the only consolation was that he might be spared a public execution which was the horror that I faced. Now, more than ever, I was determined to find out what fate would have been in store for Stephen had we not decided to run.

***

I slept through most of the two-day journey from Fargo to Chicago waking only when the train stopped to take on coal and water and a change of locomotives in St. Paul. There I strolled about the town, bought some food, and retraced the footsteps I had taken with Stephen over a year ago. I reminisced our old conversations, Stephen telling me about *Old Pigs Eye* and how the city had its roots in whisky. I had to smile at my fond memories of him and I missed him terribly.

I got back on the train and fell asleep almost immediately. I woke to the slow clanging of steel and the locomotive puffing its way into the Chicago station. I disembarked and made my way to a livery close by and with the last of my water stained money I purchased a horse, saddle, bridle and halter from *Ben's Stables* and commenced the last leg of my journey home.

Atonement to a Greater God

It was early morning when I found the McGinn estate more or less as I had left it. The dozen or more fine bred horses that once roamed over the grassy meadows inside a white painted fence were gone. Except, to my great joy, Diamond and a favorite mare of his that grazed together in a remote corner of the pasture. I walked through the abandoned barnyard and into a hay shed where I collected a bucket of oats from a barrel, fed my mount and turned him loose into the pasture. I walked back through the barn where I found Jesse, the attendant, sound asleep in his cubby.

He sat up slowly, wiped the sleep away and blinked at me. "My God James, welcome home!" he said as he quickly swung his legs out of bed. He was pleased to see me and provided an explanation for the state of things as I found them.

"I am so sorry to give the news, James, but your father passed with a major heart attack about a month ago." Jesse got down from his bunk, pulling on his pants and shoes. "If it is any consolation," he continued, "your father lived a full and productive life right to the end. He died right here, mounting his horse for a ride into Toronto where he represented his riding for so many years."

I was stunned at the loss. The news of losing him gripped my insides like a frozen hand. He had been a hard man in so many ways and a severe disciplinarian and I had to admit that we were never close as father and son but he had always been there when I needed him most. He was a high strung, ambitious man just like his father. Neither one of them had reached their sixtieth birthday. I had often wondered how long he could last given his many bouts of volatility. But it was sad news for me although not totally unexpected.

"Your mother was quite despondent when your father died and always dreaded living alone. She had no idea if or when you might return. So, she returned to Ireland to be with your grandmother who was in poor health and wished to live out her remaining years in the land of her roots which she fondly remembered."

"Your mother tried to contact you when your father died," Jesse said, "but she couldn't find any record of you on the frontier or with the Northwest Mounted Police. When you came home she wanted me to tell you to look in the safe. She said everything was in there and the combination was hidden in your favorite old hiding place."

"Thanks for all you've done, Jesse," I told him. "I want to be alone on the estate for a few days. Why don't you take some time off, visit the old fishing holes that always drew you."

I found the house almost as it was when I left. I was drawn upstairs to my old room and found that my mother had cleaned it. Most of my old clothes still hung in the closet. I stripped off my uniform and donned clean clothes. I had filled out since my college days but my pants buttoned up well enough on the front and a pair of my old suspenders took up any slack. My shirt and jacket were tighter but not uncomfortable. My parents' room was the same except my mother's closets were bare. My father's things were untouched. His dressers were still filled with his socks, under garments and garters. Tuxedos, jackets, vests and pants still hung on iron hangers. It was now my wardrobe. His clothes would be the proper length but far too baggy and not much use to me.

His study was the same except the perennial clutter of papers on his desk were cleared off. The shelf above his desk was still lined with things precious to his heart: an encased shamrock, signed family pictures of grateful constituents, a tintype of him with my mother and me as a small boy. And most prominent, a bust of Sir John MacDonald whom my father revered.

The safe was where it had always been, but I could not remember what was supposed to be my *favorite hiding place*. I thought maybe she meant in the hay loft where I would hide from Stephen and other kids when we played. I propped a ladder against the stable and climbed into the loft. I could not even imagine where the combination number might be written there. I looked for a number scrawled in pencil on a roof rafter or the bare floor or a piece of paper nailed on a wall somewhere. But there was nothing. I began to fear that I would never find the combination at all and decided to sleep on it.

I awoke in the night remembering where we used to hide sketches of nude woman that Stephen brought to my house and we used to ogle over them. Later I hid love notes in there that a girl in junior high used to pass to me. Surely my mother never knew of that hiding place.

In the morning I climbed into the attic of the house and checked where the chimney met with a rafter on the roof leaving a concealed crack below the shingles. I felt behind and pulled out the nude sketches and all the love notes and an extra piece of paper fluttered to the floor. The combination was written on it in pencil. I didn't think anyone but Stephen and I knew.

The combination opened the safe and inside was a stack of money in high denominations, a deed to the property and a note from my mother.

Dearest James: I pray this note finds you safe. As you will know by now, your father passed suddenly from a massive heart attack. I have gone to attend to your sickly grandmother overseas. The estate is now yours.
   Forever in my thoughts,
   Your loving mother
   Gwen McGinn

I left the house and walked across the pasture into the woods and the river that flowed through my estate and eventually drained into Lake Ontario. I had spent much time here as a kid with Stephen, swimming, having water fights, chopping down trees and building forts where we fought off the imaginary Indians. Sometimes we were fugitives, evading capture by lynching mobs. Always, we were the bad guys defying the highest authorities of the land and nobody messed with us.

The irony of my boyhood dreams were not lost on me now. I wandered through the bush until I discovered the uprights of our play fortress, splayed at various angles from decay and the fallen posts now growing over with moss. Inside I found a stone circle where we built our fires and boiled water for tea in a brass pot that still hung on a branch near-by.

Under layers of musty smelling and decaying grass, I kicked up the rusted remains of an old dismantled rifle, a candle holder, a brown corroded pocket knife, empty soda bottles, the decaying fork of a wooden slingshot, rotted fragments of underwear and more stockpiles of rock ammunition depots than I could count.

Atonement to a Greater God

Here we massacred everything that moved: squirrels, garter snakes, mice, chipmunks, rats, crows, whisky jacks and sparrows. But these woods were no longer my woods. I moved away from this place of my childhood following the stream deeper into the bush until I was near the boundary of my estate with Stephen's. I could make out through the trees the endless waters of Lake Ontario. Here I collected wood and built my fire. I lay back in the tall grass until evening came and a time that was right for me.

I watched the stars ignite and I felt the living forest come alive with a spirit that I had come to know, a spirit far greater than anything from my childhood, a spirit that possessed the grass beneath me, the murmuring stream, ghostly silhouettes of rock embankments, the tall pine, crowded underbrush, waters of the lake and every tiny living creature that dwelt among the cracks and reeds.

I could have gone down on my knees and prayed but I rose instead to stand beside my fire, to summon a power greater than anything I had ever known. My eyes to the stars I chanted the song that Paniya had sung for me. The chanting took a life of its own inside of me and everything that existed in the universe; it was my song to a great and powerful spirit that knew my flawed soul and once before had given my life back to me.

I asked the Great Spirit to rescue Stephen, a decent soul that I had tarnished with my callous wantonness and savage misdeeds. I asked the Great Kisemanito to know my heart now, to see my intentions, to walk with me and give me whatever justice I deserved in the days to come so that my spirit might finally be free of the evil that I had done.

CHAPTER 28

I had much to do before turning myself in to the Toronto constabulary. I brought Diamond and a buggy down to St. James Cemetery with a spade and a wide blade hoe. First, I located my father's grave that was still piled high with fresh dirt and a monument with his name and as well as his birth and death dates and an epitaph: "loving husband, father and member of parliament." His funeral had obviously been well attended with countless wreaths, some still surprisingly fresh and a number of simple crosses and crucifixes. I stayed with him several minutes and tried only to remember the good times we had growing up.

Then I sought out the gravesite of Louis Packett. It had been five years since I attended his burial and that area of the cemetery was now grown over with countless unmarked graves. I found a simple metal marker, likely provided for the cemetery's own records where Louis's plot was sunken and covered with nettle and crabgrass. I retrieved the shovel and hoe from my buggy and spent an afternoon chopping away the long grass, filling in the depression and levelling it over. I rode to City Hall and inquired as to stone carvers who might prepare a grave stone for a great war veteran and was referred to William Hull whom I was told was expensive but did the finest work. The following day I located Hull and commissioned him to prepare a stone with the following epitaph:

Louis Packett
War Hero of 1812
Died May 1870

Hull placed angels on the upper corners and flint lock rifles on the lower corners of Louie's stone. I moved some dirt around at the head of Louis's grave with my spade and leveled the ground necessary for a stone slab foundation. Hull and I dropped the heavy slab from his buckboard and skidded it into place with his team of horses. Then, with horses and rope, we erected his heavy tombstone on the slab at the head of Louie's grave and secured it in place.

Hull left and I remained with Louie reminiscing our times together. *Loonie Louie*, my friends and I had called him for his unfocused eyes, his head spins and the strange way he walked, swinging one arm for balance. He had taken me in from the cold the day I was hunting in the woods along Lake Ontario and I only enjoyed his company for his tea. Now I remembered a sensitive man who endured the pain of his handicaps and the mockery of all those *who didn't know a damned thing*, as Louie described it. I felt the deepest shame for how I had treated him. I remembered our final conversation: *Facing certain death and surviving will change you in ways you never thought possible.* Those were the last words I remembered Louie saying to me.

I left the cemetery and made my way to a livery. I paid the attendant and left instruction for him to take good care of Diamond, to feed and water him and return him to the McGinn Estate. I walked along a dusty street towards the old town market and St. Andrew's Hall which housed the Toronto Police Station where I would turn myself in on charges of murder.

***

A burly policeman sat behind a desk reading reports with his feet up on his desk when I came in. He looked nothing like the youthful, lean and hardened Northwest Mounted Policemen I had left far behind. The sign on his desk said *Detective Murphy*. Murphy was fortyish and pudgy with a handlebar moustache. He was the first Ontario policeman I had seen for a while. Their uniforms had changed. His high, helmet style hat with a dark maple leaf engraved on the front was on a hanger beside him. He wore blue serge with an abundance of brass buttons all the way up to where a ridge of soft fat hung over his collar. I stood before him and introduced myself. "I'm James McGinn, wanted on charges of murder."

"You're McGinn, fugitive from the Northwest Police?" he said. Then something like a jolt of electricity seemed to snap his jaw shut, his feet hit the floor and he bounced off his chair like someone poked his arse with a stick. "Damn rights you're him," he said. "You're the exact description." Then he called out, "Everett, Clarke, get in here," as he came around the desk and put one pudgy hand on my shoulder while holding the other hand onto the handle of the revolver still in his holster.

"Relax," I said, "I came to turn myself in."

"You're under arrest for murder," he said as he pulled a pair of cuffs out from the back of his belt and ordered me to turn around.

The other two constables charged in, stopped and looked me over. "God damn! I'd say it's him, alright," said the short one. "What do you think Everett?"

"Sure's hell." Everett answered.

I got the clear impression they knew all about me from their investigations after the fire that killed Professor Trelawney and the evidence they pieced together. Then, word of my escape from the grasp of the Northwest Mounted Police. News such as that always travelled faster than a wild fire with gossip moving from trader to trader, fortress to fortress and settlement to settlement. At least I had no difficulty convincing them of who I was.

Everett and Clarke took charge of me. They didn't seem satisfied with just handcuffs. They took my jacket and boots and placed me in ankle cuffs with a chain between them. They escorted me onto the street and down a few doors to the courthouse where a Judge Brewer took an affidavit from me and I swore that I was James McGinn. I was maintained under arrest to await trial.

A horse drawn omnibus with bars instead of windows and four other prisoners escorted me to the Toronto jail where I would await trial. The jail was located on the Don River and I had ridden past it many times as a boy with my father who never missed an opportunity to tell my mother and me that the jail was dubbed The *Don Gaol* and it was much more than a detention center. It was an execution center. The scaffolding was still visible where townspeople flocked in by the hundreds to witness condemned men struggling against their chains as rope nooses tightened around their necks and wooden platforms dropped beneath their feet. State sanctioned murder.

I tried not to remember the explanations of my father as he slowed his horse and buggy to show us the Don Gaol and the scaffolding. "Not a pretty sight," he had said, "watching an execution. I attended several so as to ensure loved ones in my riding that justice had been duly rendered."

The place always depressed me and I never expected to be an inmate of the Don Gaol. I was escorted by Everett and Clarke through iron doors into the east wing where prison guards took custody of me.

After three days, I was placed back in irons and escorted through the front doors to the same black omnibus with barred windows on all sides pulled by a different team of blue roan draft horses. I was transported along with two other prisoners one of whom sat on the bench beside me, a slight-built boy likely no more than ten or eleven years old looking around defiantly with criss-crossing chains that shackled him and probably weighed as much as he did.

He was terribly unsettled, shuffling along the bench, peering from window to window with each turn in the road banging his chains against the floor with every movement until a warning from the guard that he would be strapped down with leather and flogged upon arrival if he didn't stop. The boy quit moving, called the guard a "turd pushing cocksucker," and then became quiet but commenced to stare with hardened hatred into the face of the guard who tried to ignore him.

The prisoner across from me was a grizzled old man with sunken face and a white stubble of beard. He hung his head the whole way staring at the floor, swaying with every movement of the carriage oblivious to the disturbances of the boy. The old man's gnarled, arthritic hands were folded on his lap and his wrists handcuffed together. I felt a heaviness in the pit of my stomach. I didn't know what awaited any of us.

Through the window I followed familiar landmarks along Queens Street until the row of buildings opened into a grass and tree covered entrance in front of the three-story limestone and gothic structures of Osgoode Hall. The omnibus pulled off the cobbled street and moved down a dirt trail towards the back of the building where we were escorted inside and separated.

Two guards took me through a long echoing stone corridor where I was placed inside a waiting cell and my leg irons removed. The guards left and slammed the iron door that locked behind them. It was dark inside and smelled like stale piss. I had no idea how long I waited or what would happen to me next until the guards came again and brought me down an adjacent corridor through a side door and into a packed court room.

The room was already prepared for trial, my trial. They moved me towards the prisoner's cage until the bailiff approached and asked who was representing me. I said I was representing myself. The bailiff spoke to the guards and I was taken through a small swinging gate behind the prisoner's dock to a wooden bench which I was told was the defense table. One guard remained standing at the wall near the end of my table. Across a narrow isle was the prosecution table, already filled with lawyers in robes and their assistants.

I sat alone facing the judge's bench, an elaborate carved chestnut half wall elevated a few feet above the floor. Over the judge's chair hung a chandelier beneath a high dome that extended far above the ceiling. Behind him was a full-length oil painting of a stern and vindictive appearing Queen Victoria.

The back of the courtroom was filled to capacity, most of them sitting among grim-faced reporters with pad and pencil in hand. Obviously, most were curious citizens who had caught word of my arrest and trial for murder. My story no doubt captured space in all the newspapers. I searched the faces behind me and recognized no one.

The back doors were closed and locked by a guard and the place became suddenly quiet. A bailiff announced, "All rise, The Superior Court of Ontario is now in session, Judge Jeffry Spragge presiding."

The judge, in his black robes ascended a short set of stairs to sit behind his lofty bench where he took a moment to straighten his robe and then looked over a sheet of paper on the desk in front of him. He tilted his head back, turned his gaze to peer at me through a thin pair of spectacles that rode high on the crook of his hawkish nose. His bushy eyebrows lifted across his forehead. He cleared his throat and looked out over the rest of his courtroom before he slammed his gavel and turned to the bailiff. "Call the case," he said.

"In the matter of Her Majesty the Queen verses James McGinn. Counsel shall state their appearance for the record of this court."

There was silence. The judge looked at me. "Mr. McGinn, who is representing you?"

"I'm representing myself."

His face puffed up red and he demanded, "you will approach the lectern to address this court and address this magistrate with the respect demanded in my courtroom."

I approached the lectern before the bar. "I am representing myself, sir."

"May I remind you, Mr. McGinn that you are on trial for murder. You still choose to represent yourself?"

"Yes, sir, to tell the truth of the matter no matter what."

He glared at me a very long time before responding. "Very well, the prosecution will state their appearance. Mr. Donnelly, proceed."

Donnelly spread his papers across the lectern, took a breath and commenced. "Your honour, no more heinous and sadistic crime have I prosecuted in the name of our great queen than that which I am about to present today. My duty as prosecutor in this opening statement is to acquaint you with evidence of her majesty in right of the Dominion of Canada, to demonstrate the facts of the case and to submit to your honour the truth beyond any reasonable doubt."

The prosecutor shuffled through a stack of papers on the lectern and began again.

"Your honour, during the late afternoon on the eighth of June, 1874 in the year of our Lord, Mr. James McGinn, accompanied by Mr. Stephen Woodward, now deceased, strategized, prepared and executed a plan to murder Professor Lucius Trelawney. The motive of Mr. McGinn was to salvage his education as a medical student at Trinity college where he faced a disgraceful expulsion."

Donnelly glanced up at the judge, cleared his throat and continued his discourse.

"Earlier that day, Professor Trelawney had a meeting with the father of the accused, Milton McGinn, now deceased. The senior McGinn was told that James was suspected of cheating on final examinations and the penalty was permanent expulsion from the medical college. The senior Mr. McGinn was advised that a final determination was to be made after all examination papers were corrected and to determine who else might be implicated in the cheating. McGinn confronted his son that evening and relayed the cheating accusations.

Affidavits filed by the Dean of Medicine, Dr. E.J. Toerper have record of these conversations and events.

"The accused then recruited the assistance of one Stephen Woodward. Together they made their way to Professor Trelawney's summer cottage where it was known that Trelawney corrected examination papers."

Donnelly took a drink of water from a glass on the lectern and looked out over the courtroom. He turned back, glanced at me in a most threatening manner, turned back to the judge and continued.

"The accused, James McGinn and his friend, Stephen Woodward, loaded fuel onto a buckboard pulled by a well-known Standardbred mount known locally as *Diamond*. They proceeded to the cottage and targeting the doorway and window of the cottage, the only window large enough to provide an escape route for Professor Trelawney. Both the front doorway and the window described were targeted by the accused as they were the only possible escape routes for the professor inside. The two commenced to soak down both areas with lamp fuel, ignited the cottage into a ball of flames and left the scene by horse and buggy."

At that point, Donnelly pointed a long finger at me.

"The accused, Mr. James McGinn, sitting in that chair before us did willingly and with planning and forethought murder in a most cold-blooded and heinous manner the good professor, Lucius Trelawney, medical professor at Trinity College. When called upon by the honorable magistrate we will provide testimony and witnesses to prove these matters beyond a reasonable doubt." Donnelly stepped down and took a seat.

"Mr. McGinn, your appearance for the record," said the judge.

I had never felt more vulnerable or lost for words. Prior to now, I simply had faith that the truth would be my greatest ally; I would simply relate what happened and that reasonable people would see my intentions. I stood before the judge.

"Sir, I had no intention to kill Professor Trelawney. My only intention was to destroy the examination papers which were the only evidence of my cheating on the final exams, I concede to that. Stephen was able to pick the locks on the cottage and we took the exam key and studied the answers. I didn't know Trelawney was inside when we burned the cottage. We set fire only to destroy papers. There was no horse outside or anything else to suggest Trelawney or any other person was inside."

Donnelly stood before the judge. "I reserve the right to cross examine Mr. McGinn," he said.

"Granted," was the judge's response.

I took an oath to tell the truth and entered the witness box.

"Mr. McGinn," began Donnelly, "when did you learn of the death of Professor Trelawney?"

"The next evening. My father came home and informed me that Professor Trelawney had passed. That he died inside his cottage when it burned down."

"That was the first you knew he had passed."

"Yes."

"Then you joined up with the Northwest Mounted Police to escape the consequence."

"That is true."

"No more questions," said Donnelly.

I stepped down from the witness box and returned to the defence table. Donnelly continued to call witnesses. The next being the Dean of Medicine at Trinity, Dr. Ernest Toerper. The Dean testified under oath that Professor Trelawney had informed him of the details concerning cheating by James McGinn and possibly others on examinations. He had also spoke with James McGinn's father, Milton McGinn, briefly the following morning.

Next, Donnelly examined Mr. Barney Carl, a local horse breeder and a witness who stated he was familiar with Diamond, a standardbred racing horse that he used to own prior to selling the animal to the McGinn estate. Furthermore, he testified that he had previously met the accused, James McGinn, and he pointed me out in the courtroom. Carl reported that he was certain the driver of the carriage drawn by Diamond was the accused.

I had no need to question any of these witnesses. I only wanted to get at the truth and there was no disputing their testimony.

Donnelly then called Police Detective Marvin Murphy to the witness box where he identified himself, took an oath from the court clerk and sat down.

"Explain for the court your investigation on the morning of June 9th, 1874."

"Well sir, a report was received of a fire at the Trelawney cottage the previous night and I went out to investigate."

"What did you find."

"The front of the cottage was burnt down and I was able to gain some insights about the fire."

"What did your investigation reveal."

"There were fresh buggy tracks that pulled in close to the house, maybe ten feet away. Lamp fuel was spilt in the grass beside the tracks of the buggy. I knew it was lamp fuel by the smell. The most severe fire damage was on the front door and front window where the fire obviously started. I could tell because the building was still damp from a rain shower the previous morning. It was clear that where the fire was most intense was where it was drenched with fuel, the front door and front window."

"Were there other places on the building where escape would have been possible if someone were inside."

"I'd have to say no from what I could determine."

"What else did you find, detective?"

"Well, there was a trail round the back of the house that led to a small stable behind a thicket of pine, maybe a hundred yards from the building and not visible from the cottage. A bay gelding was housed in the stable and from the manure piled up behind I would guess it had been there more than a few hours, likely a day or two."

"Did you recognize the horse?"

"Course I couldn't be sure, he wasn't the only bay gelding around but I knew Professor Trelawney somewhat and it looked a lot like the gelding he rode sometimes and the saddle that was hanging up beside the horse had LT burnt into the leather on the back of the cantle. Likely for Lucius Trelawney."

"What was your next course of action, detective."

"Well, the whole thing was starting to smell fishy, meaning what the hell was going on with a house burnt down and a horse still in the stable for that long a time. Anyway, there were many scenarios that could explain it but I decided I better call the coroner's office to investigate just to be on the safe side."

The detective's testimony knocked the wind out of me. I never knew there was a stable. And my best argument was that there was no buggy, horse or other means of transportation beside the building giving me any indication that someone might be inside.

"Do you wish to cross examine the witness, Mr. McGinn?" asked the judge.

I knew I should say something but was not even thinking straight at that moment. I got up and wandered to the lectern and got another scolding from the judge.

"I expect an answer when I ask a question," he said.

"Of course I have a question," I answered. Then I decided I should watch my protocol but I was beginning to feel everything was stacked against me. I managed to add, "sir." The judge scowled at me and after a long hard stare he told me, "proceed."

"I didn't know there was a stable or a horse," I said. Then I realized it had to be a question. "Could you see the stable from the cottage?" I asked.

"I already said it wasn't visible," answered the detective.

I sat down to another long scowl from the judge. "You aren't impressing me with your attitude or your cross examinations, Mr. McGinn. I suggest you show some decency and respect. This is a court of law." Then he asked Donnelly if he had any more witnesses.

"Yes, your honor, I wish to call Dr. Benjamin White, District Coroner, to take the stand.

Dr. White," Donnelly said commencing his examination of the coroner. "Please relate the events that prompted your involvement in this case."

"On June 9, 1874, I was contacted by Detective Murphy to investigate a fire at the Trelawney summer property," said the coroner.

"What did you find at the cottage," asked Donnelly.

"There was a charred body inside."

"Were you able to identify the body?"

"During autopsy I took dental impressions and assessed the dental work that subsequently matched the dental records of Dr. Lucius Trelawney."

"And the cause of death?"

"Smoke inhalation and severe burn trauma."

"And Dr. White, when you first located the body inside the house, describe for the court the exact condition, location and position of the body."

"Fragments of undergarments and what appeared to be melted portions of linen, possibly a night shirt, remained on the charred body. Dr. Trelawney's feet would have been bare prior to his body burning as there was no identifiable ash, char or fragments of material that would suggest he was wearing any type of footwear."

"And the exact location of the body, Dr. White?"

"There were the charred remains of a high bench or cupboard running the length of the room below the main living room window, the only window in the cottage. The full ventral portion of the charred body was prone on the upright remains of the cupboard. The right hand was still grasping a charred section of window sill and the other hand was bent around a brass window opener which appeared to be once part of the right window sill. His face and portion of upper body were encased in molten glass from the window."

"So, in layman terms, Dr. White, in his last moments of life, the good professor's stomach was against a narrow cupboard below the window. His left hand grasping the window sill and his right hand apparently trying to pry loose the window with a brass latch still locked into his hand. His face was pressed against the glass just before or just after he succumbed to heat, smoke and flames of the fire."

"That is correct. My theory is Dr. Trelawney was unable to break the thick glass with his hands or fists and there were no suitable tools found nearby, as evidenced by adjacent ashes devoid of any such suitable implement. The brass crank either came loose as he attempted to open the window or he wrested it loose in order to break the glass."

"In any event, Dr. White, clearly the professor labored before the window, to orchestrate an escape or perhaps attempting to summons help from outside."

"I cannot preclude either possibility."

"No more questions, your honor."

"Do you wish to cross examine the witness, Mr. McGinn?"

I was totally unprepared for the sheer horror of the coroner's testimony. The images were reminiscent of my own worst nightmares and the flashbacks that tormented me when I was on fire with my own fever and facing my own mortality before Paniya rescued me.

"No sir," I responded. "I have no questions."

"We will commence tomorrow morning at eight o'clock. Since there are no more witnesses, I will call for final arguments before I make my decision. The judge banged his gavel. "Court adjourned," he called out.

The court room crowd burst into a roar of rancorous outcry. I looked over my shoulder. Trelawney's widow was dressed in black and weeping loudly. She was in the company of two men. One shouted out, "stretch the bastard's neck!" Another man answered from the open doorway of the courtroom. "Hanging, hell, cook the son of a bitch alive!"

I was ushered through a side door under heavy guard for transportation back to my prison cell. I felt a kind of panic rising inside of me and I contemplated escape. They had not replaced my leg irons, just the wrist cuffs. Only two guards were left to transport me in the omnibus with one other prisoner who was young, lean and strong-enough looking that I hoped could either assist me or at least remain neutral.

Once the angry crowd had been left behind and the guards were settled into the monotonous journey back to the Don Gaol, I could attempt to over-power them. Neither of them looked that formidable. I could acquire a firearm from one of them, release them out the door then confront the driver. He was an unarmed civilian employee as I remembered. I would demand he give up the reins and force him to jump clear. I could drive a team of horses as well as anyone and I knew the streets of Toronto perfectly well. I would make my way at full gallop leaving the downtown bustle and head for the eastern residential areas that I was familiar with, watch for some opportunity, bail out and run for my life.

But I knew the sheer folly of such a plan. And that was not why I came back to turn myself in. In my prison cell I pondered my future with more distress than ever before in light of the evidence of those prosecuting me.

Finally, I resolved that I would only speak the truth tomorrow and leave matters to a spirit greater than anything on earth. A spirit that allowed me to live once before. If it was time to pay back all that I had done or give my life for all the evil I had committed, I was ready. I would prepare my arguments as best I could, tell my truth in court and leave the rest to fate.

CHAPTER 29

Guards came to get me at first light. I was hand cuffed and escorted outside where there was a light drizzle of rain and the air was cold. They took me to an omnibus with four black horses, their heads drooping in the damp early morning darkness. Extra guards had been placed on the front, back and roof of the carriage, all of them heavily armed. I thought it was extra caution to prevent any escape attempt from a man who faced the gallows for murder. The escorting guards pressed me inside and took their place at the back and front of the carriage. The driver commanded his team forward to the rhythmic clopping of iron shoes against the cobbled street.

In the dim twilight of early morning we passed the scaffolding of the Gaol and commenced towards Queen Street. We approached Osgoode Hall where the grassy front grounds of the gothic building were packed with a mob who approached the prisoner carriage, trying to catch a glimpse of me inside and shouting their demands: *no mercy,* or *feed the gaol,* and, *lynch the son of a bitch.*

Now I knew why there were extra guards on top of the carriage. I watched their shadows below me on the dirt trail and grassy grounds as we proceeded towards the back entrance. They raised their firearms and shouted at the mob encircling us: "stand back or be shot!"

Under heavy guard I was brought through a side door into a packed courtroom. The noisy chamber became deathly silent when the judge entered the courtroom moments later and dropped his gavel to commence the proceedings. "I will hear the final arguments of the prosecution," he said.

Donnelly approached the lectern and quickly began his summation. "Your Honor, based on the evidence placed before this court, the prosecution will recount the events of June 8, 1874 when a most heinous crime was committed.

"On that evening, your honor, the accused along with his friend, Stephen Woodward, as identified by the witness, Mr. Barney Carl, who knew the accused, and by the accused's own admission, came to the cottage property of Dr. Trelawney, the victim, at about seven o'clock on a clear summer evening to commit, with foresight and malice, in the most hideous manner, the crime of murder."

Donnelly stopped his discourse to gaze a moment at the judge and then shuffled some papers on the lectern before starting again. "Let me remind the court of the testimony of Constable Murphy who related that there was a *well-worn* path to a stable adjacent to the cottage where a fresh mount was sheltered and would have been spotted by the defendant, clear evidence for any rational person that the cottage may well be occupied.

"Any reasonable person who was *not* out to commit murder would have made every effort to ensure no one was inside. I submit that the knowledge of Trelawney's horse being in the stable and likelihood that Trelawney was inside his cottage was precisely what the accused wanted: the perfect scenario for Mr. McGinn. The only man that knew about his cheating on examinations, reasoned McGinn, would soon be trapped inside his own blazing cottage and taken care of in a manner suiting the malicious and unconscionable objectives of the accused.

"Furthermore, let me remind the court of the testimony of Detective Murphy who said that the fire was started at the door and the window. Isn't that an amazing coincidence! The accused selected the door and the window precisely because they were the only possible escape routes for the professor. Would not a more reasonable action for someone with only the intent of burning the cottage select the west side of the building where a prevailing westerly breeze would have assisted the fire and a thorough burning of the entire cottage? Would not such a clean burn ensure that there was no possibility of the corrupt examination papers surviving the fire? But that was not the real objective of the accused who specifically chose to soak down with fuel and create an inferno at the only door and window where it would have been possible for the victim to escape."

Donnelly took a drink of water from a glass beside the lectern, shuffled more paper, allowed a long period of silence and a glance at the judge, before continuing his discourse.

"From the location of the body, as evidenced by the testimony of Dr. White, the Coroner, Dr. Trelawney's charred remains were found to be pressing against the window which would be the very window in full view of the accused. Even now, it takes very little effort to hear the cries of mercy, the window pounding, shrieks, the begging and pleading for his life. One can hear the desperate cries of Dr. Trelawney for the accused to help him, to commence extinguishing the flames, to help smash the window, to make every possible effort to free him. But the accused, James McGinn, in as cold-blooded manner as humanly possible, ignored the plight of the professor at the window and drove away leaving the good professor to a hellish fate: being burned alive in a horrible inferno of flame.

"And the motive of the accused: very simply, so that he may continue the good life of a student at Trinity, unaffected, undenounced and unaccountable for that most despicable action of any student: cheating on final examinations with mandatory expulsion. The best possible way of escaping detection, reasoned the accused, was to murder Professor Trelawney, whom Mr. McGinn believed was the only person able to initiate and ensure his dishonorable discharge from Trinity.

"Before I sum up, let me remind the court of a previous statement made under oath by the accused. The court records show Mr. McGinn's statement that he first knew of Dr. Trelawney death in the cottage when his father told him the next day. Clearly McGinn is a liar. He knew Dr. Trelawney was in the cottage when it burned down because he would have seen him through the window, begging for his life. Mr. McGinn is about to provide his last words in a summation to this court. Let me remind the court of an age-old premise in law: A man caught lying even once under oath is not believable on any subsequent testimony.

"The death penalty is the only just remedy for the heinous crimes of Mr. McGinn. The prosecution rests its case."

I approached the lectern before the judge knowing that I would be pleading for my life. I resolved only to tell the truth so that the evil in my life would be fairly judged and fairly rendered, whatever that might be. I had scratched out some notes that I might tell the court in my defense, hoping

I would not forget something critical, as this was my only chance.

"Your honor," I began, "I am here to tell only the truth and accept whatever fate is given me."

"Make your case," the judge said, and his tone was not friendly.

"Stephen and I were not familiar with Professor Trelawney's cottage. The times we had been there, we were always in a desperate hurry to pick the locks, find the answer key, and get out as quick as possible. From the evidence offered by Detective Murphy, the stable was not visible from the cottage but behind a thicket of pine. I did not know there was a stable nor did I know that Dr. Trelawney's horse was tethered there."

I continued. "Based on the coroner's testimony, he said the most likely apparel worn by the deceased when he died was possibly a light nightshirt. The evidence was that his feet were bare. I think the likely scenario is that Dr. Trelawney was sleeping when Stephen and I arrived. Thus, there were no sounds, sights or other evidence from inside the cottage that it might be occupied."

I made eye contact with the judge. At least he seemed to be paying attention. Then he wrote something down and I continued.

"The prosecution has argued that Stephen and I started the fire in the doorway and the window to block any escape routes of someone inside. That was not the case. Let me explain," I said. I looked at the judge again. He had a faraway look. I didn't know if he was paying attention or not. I had no choice but to keep going and I spoke louder to make my point.

"It had been raining earlier in the day, sir," I emphasized, "and the entire cottage was damp especially the west side where prevailing westerly winds, coupled with rainfall had soaked that side of the building. Contrary to the opinion of the prosecution, we chose the door and the window sill as both were inset, as doors and windows typically are. Thus, they were dryer than the rest of the building and the only place we could get our lamp fuel to ignite the cottage."

The judge looked at me. His expression seemed completely blank.

"I do not recall seeing Trelawney's face in the window at the time we set the fire. I have only seen an image of him in my nightmares. And I never knew what was real. I have told only the truth. We had never intended to hurt Professor Trelawney, only to destroy the examination papers that we knew would be inside. I have nothing further to say."

The judge pounded his gavel. "I have heard final summations from the prosecutor and the defendant. We will reconvene in an hour when I have had time to consider the evidence and render my verdict. Court is dismissed."

I was brought back to a cell, handcuffed and shackled. It was the longest hour of my life. Even through the thick walls of Osgoode Hall I could hear the hysterical wailings of mob violence and calls for me to hang. To keep my sanity, I thought back to all the times I had spent with Paniya. The Christmas party at Fort Edmonton, our walks around the fortress and our times together at the Medicine Springs. I thought of a great spirit that Paniya had summoned to save my life. I wondered how she would ever learn of my fate.

The guards returned, each holding onto one of my arms, maintaining me in cuffs and chains and guiding me back down the corridor through the side door and directly into the prisoner's dock with my back to the crowded gallery. The judge came in from his chambers, climbed to his chair behind the bench, slammed the gavel and called the court to order. The room hushed.

"The prisoner will rise and face the bench." The judge glanced at me as I stood and then he looked back at a sheet of paper in front of him on his desk. He was silent for a long moment before looking out across his crowded courtroom and then he began.

"After a detailed review of all the evidence before me and the testimony of witnesses and arguments of prosecution and defense, the court finds the actions of Mr. James McGinn to be callous, irresponsible and destructive. His careless actions have resulted in the death of Professor Lucius Trelawney.

"But after careful consideration I find the evidence does not rise to the burden of proof required for a conviction of murder. It is the belief of this court that the testimony of the accused was truthful. It was never the plan or intention of Mr. McGinn to physically harm Professor Trelawney in spite of an abundance of tepid evidence to the contrary. Nevertheless, the behaviors of the accused have cost a man his life. Careless and mindful only of his own gain, the accused made no effort to ensure the cottage was unoccupied. Such a mindless transgression cannot and will not go unpunished under the laws of the Canadian Dominion. I find the accused, James McGinn, guilty of the lesser crime of manslaughter. I sentence you, James McGinn, to seven years in prison with hard labor and no option for early parole."

CHAPTER 30

The first golden rays of sunshine chased the darkness from a ring of hills surrounding the Medicine Springs. The wild rose was in full bloom creating a swath of pink and red that separated the pin cherry shrubs from the greening meadows. A robin had already begun her song from the highest tip of an evergreen while fledgling warblers in flashes of orange and yellow began fleeing their nests among the willows to explore a brave new world of clear pools and groves of poplar. A stag, sleek and tanned with the color of early summer, raised his head to capture the scent of the meadow, then he drank a long drink from the springs before moving, unhurried, back under the forest cover.

Paniya continued to sleep where she always slept when she came to the Springs. She had prepared fresh boughs over the old beneath the canopy of spruce, just as James had left it. He had been gone almost two years now. She came here often because this was where the most vivid dreams often came to her. There had been no news, but she listened carefully to the spirits, trying to learn something of his fate. Sometimes he came to her in clear pictures, sometimes symbols that told a story. She had seen a carriage come and go, James inside the thick black lines that covered him. The white man's prison.

She slept and a dream came to her with a feeling that quenched her longing. She dreamed of being with James once again at the Christmas Ball and of looking down at his high riding boots as she danced with him to the strains of fiddle music, her own beaded moccasins moving between his feet while he held her and they moved in a rhythm that was beyond time or the world they lived in.

Then a vision of hope came to her when she slept. She saw his high riding boots beside her beaded moccasins on the ground. She felt the greatest exhilaration at such a vision and the hope that it offered. Then in a flash, only his riding boots remained prone on the grassy earth. Her dream world came to an end. The visions came no more.

CHAPTER 31

Kingston prison was a hell hole carved in stone. I spent my nights in a stone cell two feet wide, six feet long and eight feet high. A two-foot thick slab of stone separated me from inmates over me, under me and to the left and right. The prison was entombed in a fifteen-foot high wall of stone and I labored hours in a workshop quarrying stone for new prisons or maintaining the old. No one was allowed to talk, laugh, wink or nod. The faces of guards and inmates alike became carved in stone as were their hearts.

Every morning from my cell I endured the screams of inmates down a long corridor, some as young as eight years old, flogged for talking, laughing, whistling, stealing or spitting.

But fortune is a play in contrasts. In time I considered myself a most lucky man. Fifteen of us in a prison population of twelve hundred got to work in the stables with horses, feeding, cleaning and exercising the animals. The manure of the equine population was sweet and wholesome compared to the sweat, gas, excrement and vomit from unhealthy men slaving at stifling temperatures in close quarters encased in stone with the barest ventilation holes covered over with iron bars.

Fortune came to me once again during my incarceration. A new movement swept through the Dominion for prison reforms with one overriding premise: educate the inmates, give them more religion. A library and chapel were built inside Kingston. I asked for books and received them: Botany, Human Physiology, Human Anatomy and Pathology, Pharmacy, Neurology, Dermatology, Cardiology, Paediatrics and more.

A new warden heard of my medical school background and interest. He came one day and assigned me to assist the prison surgeon who was vastly overworked. It saved the prison the expenditure of hiring a medical assistant. I was instructed to make rounds with the surgeon which I was more than pleased to do.

I soon gained immense satisfaction in healing men through my learning and the instruction of the prison doctor who was a competent man, a good teacher and he became interested in my development as a surgeon. Under his instruction I became skilled with a scalpel and mastered the healing properties of countless medicines, potions and tinctures that restored the health of many I served in the inmate population.

I thought of Stephen who once said to me, *all I ever wanted was to be a doctor and heal people.* In my mind I had scorned him. How narrow his life I thought as I continued to be swept up in the excitement at Trinity College: sports, clubs and night life. Now I was beginning to understand Stephen in a way I never could before.

Slowly I gained favor with the new warden through the work I was doing and I suspected the prison surgeon had spoken positively about my proficiency with scalpel and knowledge of treatments. I had no difficulty getting the latest books from Trinity and other medical facilities in Ontario. By the end of my incarceration, I was prepared to challenge any examinations at Trinity Medical School on all aspects of their curriculum if I chose to do so.

CHAPTER 32

June 10, 1882. It seemed like a lifetime had come and gone while I awaited this day. It was warm outside when the prison doors of Kingston were opened to me and I walked outside alone, a free man. No one came to greet me. I had been provided with the clothes I wore the day they arrested me, seven years ago. I was paid two dollars per month for my entire time in Kingston. It was enough to get started.

I purchased a mount from a nearby livery and made my way to the McGinn estate. The land and buildings appeared to be in good repair and a herd of cattle were grazing on the pastureland where Diamond and the other horses were once kept. I made my way to the house. The door was unlocked and I went inside. Jesse was there, by himself, preparing a meal of roast beef and potatoes.

"James!" he exclaimed as I walked inside and he seemed genuinely pleased to see me. "Welcome home, I've been expecting you." he said.

"I didn't know," I said, "I thought the entire world had passed by without anyone knowing what ever happened to me."

"Well, that wasn't the case for a long time," Jesse told me, "In the summer of 75' the newspapers had nothing else to talk about. Every page was something to do with the murder trial of James McGinn, son of our great member of

Parliament and cabinet minister for Sir John A. MacDonald." He looked me over for a long moment and took a deep breath.

"It tears me apart to tell you this, James, but we all thought you would hang. It was a terrible time for us and I kept your mother informed of everything by letters whenever news came out in the paper. Professor Trelawney was very popular at Trinity and, in fact throughout the city. People desperately wanted somebody to pay for his death."

"Thanks Jesse, for keeping mother informed. I also expected I could be facing the gallows."

"She was so greatly relieved when we sent her the news of the manslaughter charge. That was when she wrote to me making the offer for me to stay and manage your estate."

"At this point I just want it all behind me," I said.

Jesse invited me to partake in the meal he had prepared and I willingly agreed. Jesse had always been a good cook and it had been a very long time since I had eaten anything that was not the texture and taste of animal by-products or boiled grains of various kinds.

"It still all belongs to you, James," he said, "and I can move back to the cubby if you want. Your mother has been most generous and accommodating to me."

"You were a loyal and able hand Jesse and we appreciated the work you did."

"Have you heard from your mother?" he asked.

"No," I said. "Where I've been we weren't allowed to get mail or send any. I knew very little about the outside world except what prisoners managed to pick up and pass along and that wasn't much since no one was supposed to talk. But I'll write to her now."

Jesse served up roast beef fresh out of the oven, sliced thin with gravy. He shared his mashed potatoes with me and a fresh loaf of home-made bread. It was the best I had eaten for longer than I could remember.

"Your mother has kept up the taxes on the estate all these years and she told me that what I produced on the farm would be mine in lieu of wages. She sold a few acres on the east end and otherwise the estate is the same. She made it clear she would not sell the property until you came home and you could decide what to do with it. I was more than pleased with that agreement." Jesse sat down and started shovelling back his mashed potatoes with gravy.

"She set me up in the very beginning with a herd of five cows and a bull," he said, "and I have grown the herd and produced bushels of produce from the gardens and the haylands ever since. I've managed very well and paid any bills that came along and the cost of improvements or repairs that were needed on the estate along the way.

"So, it's yours now James and I just hope to stay in your employ. I'm not young anymore and this is the only home I've ever known."

"Let's keep the arrangement you made with mother, Jesse. And no matter what, this will be your home for as long as you want. I'll sell off another chunk of land on the east side again if needed to pay taxes. The McGinn estate is very large and the extra land will hardly be noticed."

Jesse set a section of rhubarb and saskatoon pie before me that he had baked himself. I lit into it with my fork and had never tasted anything better. I cleaned up another piece and set my plate aside.

"I need to go away again, Jesse," I told him, "to the territories of the Northwest. I don't know for how long, or if there is anything left for me there. But it's the only way I'm going to find peace of mind or know what my future holds."

I slept in my old bed upstairs where nothing had changed, the sheets were stiff and smelled dusty, but the bed was as comfortable as it always had been. I left the master bedroom to Jesse.

In the morning I checked the safe. Everything was there as I had left it, the note from my mother, the property deed and a bundle of money. I took five hundred dollars. I would give a hundred to Jesse to replace Diamond and the mare who had both died during my absence and maybe even a new buggy. I had no doubt that Jesse could stretch a dollar.

CHAPTER 33

The world of 1882 was much different than the world of 1875. I made my way to the Hudson Bay Steamship Lines in downtown Toronto. For decades they had steamship transportation throughout the great lakes, mainly serving the American ports. I inquired about any kind of passenger transport, either inland or water, that might access the territories of the northwest.

A wispy little man sat behind the wicket wearing a long bill cap with a strap behind his head. He wore a pair of gold rimmed spectacles that perched on his thin nose like a bird's beak. I asked if there was any transportation to the northwest, Fort Edmonton, or were people still using the Carlton Trail from Fort Garry.

"Where you been for the last five years, son?" the little man cackled. His wicket looked like a pretty lonely place and the little guy seemed bored.

"Jail," I responded with a wide grin and he cackled again, thinking I was pulling his leg.

"Well, son, if you read the papers you'd know about the *Lily* and the *Northcote*. But since you was in jail all this time," he grinned, "I'll lay it out for you. Now, you'll have to start out on a new section of the CPR that will take you to Winnipeg the end of the line. From there you catch the *Lily* and the *Northcote* into the heart of the Northwest. Now, the *Northcote* is a real beauty. She's made her way up the North

Saskatchewan all the way to Fort Edmonton three times now to work out all her kinks and she had a few.

"Our *Lily* has made the trip successful too but she's just a little thing." He smiled with some apparent affection for the *Lily*.

"We drydocked the *Northcote* last winter though," he continued, "bored out the steam cylinders and put some real bulk onto those big old pistons plunging back and forth inside her. Now the *Northcote* has got real power to handle the bounce in any of them rapids and high currents on the North Saskatchewan. She'll be making regular trips now into the northwest."

The little man pulled out a long ledger with schedules written in a most tidy ink pen. He flipped through and scrutinized the pages, his eyes skimming up and down. Then he looked at me. "If you want to get all the way through to Fort Edmonton we're sailing there in ten days, July first, and we expect to make shore at Fort Edmonton before the end of the month. I can sell you a cabin ticket for 69 dollars. You can buy meals and even drinks on board or bring your own."

He looked down at his ledger. "If you just want a place on the deck for 39 dollars I can sell you that too."

Then he spoke in a confidential way as if I was his best friend. "It's a heck of a lot more comfortable in a cabin if you can afford one though. It's a long month just sitting around and sleeping on deck." He tipped back his long bill and wiped his forehead and settled his cap back down again. "I heard rumors floating around now that the new captain is an old Mississippi Riverboat man; he says a beauty like the *Northcote* could take Fort Edmonton in eighteen days. That *would* be something," he said, his eyes lighting up in apparent wonder. "I can sell you tickets for the Lily and the Northcote from here."

"Thanks," I said, "sell me everything I need for Fort Edmonton, and I'll take the cabin."

I wandered around in the downtown core of Toronto. So much had changed. I bought a few things I would need: a coat, blankets, soap and shaving blades to take back with me into the hinterlands of the frontier. There were novelty items I had never really found in a hardware store before. I bought a spool of fishing line and some interesting hooks wrapped in colored feathers that the clerk called *flies*. "Good for catching grayling," he told me. I bought a few, purchased ammunition for my carbine and an interesting device called a *jackknife* on the hardware shelves. I once had a pocket knife but this was rather a new invention since my world of 1875. It was an ivory handle with two spring loaded knives folded inside along with a spoon, tiny saw and an awl. It was one dollar so I purchased it and dropped it into my pocket. I also purchased a canvas bag with draw string to put my belongings in and I was ready to travel back into the dominion's Northwest.

***

The CPR rail to Winnipeg was a freighter geared to moving heavy steel and supplies for completing their rail line west across the dominion. There were two passenger cars crowded with railway workers and I managed to get a seat. The journey took four days and I slept and ate out of my bag of provisions most of the way. In Winnipeg I caught the *Lily* to Grand Rapids. The settlement had only a few scattered buildings and I was astounded at the number of passengers waiting for inland travel. Only seven years ago the Canadian interior was of little interest to anyone but fur traders, a few merchants and the occasional adventurer.

The *Lily* docked a few hundred yards from a gleaming white passenger steamship, the *Northcote,* anchored on a wide delta in the shade of tall spruce where the dark current of the Saskatchewan River flowed far out into Lake Winnipeg. The wicket clerk hadn't told me any lies. The *Northcote* was a beautiful, modern, two decker steamship and a contrast to the cramped rail car and the small steamer that had taken me thus far.

A long line-up was already waiting for boarding across a gangway onto the *Northcote* under the hot July sun. I followed the lineup to a seaman checking tickets and bellowing at passengers to, "keep moving, shove back" and "make room." He quickly checked my ticket and pointed towards a corridor on my right. "Your number 43," he said and turned back to the lineup streaming on board.

My room was small but seemed comfortable enough with a bed and night stand. I had a small window looking out on a line of spruce beside where the ship was docked. I came back on deck and joined a curious crowd watching a busy crew working to untie the thick rope that secured the steamer to a wooden dock. Slowly the *Northcote* eased away from shore where a pilot in the wheelhouse allowed her to catch the current as he guided her far out onto the lake.

Then the engines of the steamer fired up under clouds of black smoke that rolled into the sky. She moved under her own power now and circled far out on the calm waters of Lake Winnipeg where she lined up on the tumultuous rapids of the Saskatchewan River. At full throttle, the ship slowly gained speed as black smoke now trailed in a line over our heads. The *Northcote* charged ahead until her hull hit the high out-flow of the river, her engines pounded and gradually she overcame the rapid current of the river and moved up-stream maintaining a good speed.

We made it around the first bend and straightened out down the center of the watercourse with a steady hum of the engines as the crowd moved away. Many wandered inside where they could buy liquor or a meal if they wanted. I stood at the railing where a hypnotic stream of shoreline and balsam poplar trees moved past me until finally I decided to go inside for a drink.

I took a chair alone at a table near the door and watched the groups of people that formed around the various tables. I was surprised that so many seemed to know each other. But there were two very distinct groups. I was an outsider which seemed to be my way in life and I cannot say I was completely uncomfortable with it.

One group crowded around four large tables with men that seemed to be of Metis origins but somehow different than most of the Metis I had gotten to know so well in the northern fortress. They were family men, many of them older, maybe farmers from the more southerly settlements of the Dominion. The other group were much younger men, burly, bearded guys that seemed to be a hardy bunch, maybe from farm families as well. Quite a few were accompanied by their wives and many brought their children. But most disconcerting was the apparent tension between the two groups. It was clear they were talking about each other with furtive glances across the empty spaces that separated them. I was never too comfortable with all the chatter of crowds anyway and I went back to my room.

I stretched out on the cot and took a botany book from my pack. I had an interest in learning something about the plants of the northwest that had always fascinated Paniya. I remembered her dark eyes skimming the terrain with much interest in the plant life. She would often get excited at finding something she rarely came across and then she busied herself with a metal spoon, digging up roots, then carefully selecting leaves, excising specific sections of stalks or cutting out pieces of root that suited her, all for her pharmacy of diverse plants.

Her familiarity with plants and their healing qualities always fascinated me and never more than now with all the medical training I had acquired. Surprisingly, few of my medical books referenced any knowledge of the healing power of the plants that obviously had such salient properties. From my botany books, I recognized a few plants that always excited Paniya, ginseng being one.

Eventually the hum and vibration of the ship put me to sleep. I don't know how long I slept but it was dark outside and I was once again wide awake so I came out on deck.

Some had gone back to their rooms. Many were sleeping on floor mats on the deck with a few watchmen along the railing of the steamer. I recognized one of them as someone who supervised the men as they untethered and launched the steamer. I went over to him, smiled and introduced myself. He said he was Raphael Beaumont.

I asked him about the steamship. He had worked for the Hudson Bay Company most of his life, working his way up from a deckhand to the first mate responsible for most operations on the passenger liner. He was more than willing to chat it up and tell me all about the Northcote and the Northwest.

"She's tailor made for the fast rivers of the northwest," he said, "outfitted with a steel hull and capacity to carry 75 passengers and 100,000 pounds of cargo while only taking fourteen inches of draft." He seemed as proud of the *Northcote* as the clerk that sold me my ticket.

I asked about the many passengers on board. For a moment he looked at me puzzled, like I had lived my life here-to-fore under a rock. He asked where I was from and I told him I had been a medical student, now practising.

"Well," he said, "to answer your question, there's a land rush going on is the best way I can explain it. Pieces of the northwest are surveyed now and reports have come out that rich farmland is to be had. And everything is more valuable since the Northwest Mounted Police have settled things down with the whisky traders and tensions between the tribes. The police did a real job up there of bringing law and order. Now different factions are land hungry, looking to acquire a piece of the action."

"Fort Edmonton, has it changed much?" I asked.

"The fort is still doing business with the Indians like they always have, although it has slowed. There is no longer the demand for beaver hats in Europe but still a demand for fur. There has been negotiation with the tribes for treaties and some resolved but the tribes pretty much live off the land as they always have.

"But I think there is going to be some real change and much trouble," he said, with a side long glance at me. "I don't like how the Canadian government is treating the Indians and neither do many of them, especially the Metis."

"I guess I am out of touch," I said. "What kind of trouble?"

"I spent last winter in the Red River Settlement," he said, looking me over, like wondering how I could be so naive. "Maybe by now you have heard of Gabriel Dumont?"

I shook my head.

"Well, he's an old friend of mine," said Raphael, "he's a great old trapper and a warrior from away back but also a natural leader which is how I got to know him. He sees what is going on and he's letting people know it. Many Metis and the tribal nations never knew that they legally owned the whole northwest." He stopped for a moment to look suspiciously at a group of men just coming on deck. Then he turned back to me.

Raphael continued. "Legal title was given to the Indians and Metis long ago and it's still the law of the land. The English king, George the Third, proclaimed the land belonged to the Indians and title could only be extinguished through proper negotiation. The king called it his *proclamation of 1763*. But the Dominion wants to take the whole northwest and give the Indians and Metis practically nothing and now that the buffalo are almost annihilated and the people hungry, they are not in a position to bargain.

"MacDonald is a shrewd one," he continued. "He wants all the original people that had this land for thousands of years to settle for a few trade goods each year and farm implements. It's robbery. The government says they can all be farmers," Beaumont said, shaking his head. "MacDonald doesn't know these people. Now there is Riel, Louis Riel, he repeated the name, looking me over like I should know of him. I probably looked blank. Then he continued. "He is a strong leader of the Metis and he means business. Rebellion if necessary."

"But none of that's my worry," he said. Raphael looked me over head to toe. "Want to know about my worry?" he asked with a wild look in his eye.

Before I could answer, he told me. "Right on board this ship are Metis from the Red River settlements. Most are going to Metis communities of the northwest to spread the word of Dumont and Riel, calling for governing rights for the rightful owners, the Indian and Metis. He looks to protect their lands and demand that other settlers wait. Some have family in the northern settlements and many come with their wives to renew old ties and inform everybody of the aspirations of Dumont and Riel."

Raphael stopped for a moment, lifted his cap and ran his hand through his greying hair. "Also, on board this steamer are the English," he said. "Many come with their families to settle on the surveyed land. But the two don't mix, you see? Some come to settle and others to halt settlement, looks like trouble, eh?" he said. I think he already saw how naïve and out of touch I was. "Don't you agree?" he added.

I nodded. "Could get bad, I suppose," but I really knew very little that had been going on in the country for the last seven years.

Raphael continued. "And I'm responsible if there's trouble on board the steamer." He turned away for a long moment, sizing up more groups that had just come on deck. Then he looked back at me. "The captain, he's an American who understands none of this. I tell him my worry and he says, 'Raphael, you look after it. America already had their civil war.' So, I'm on my own," he said.

***

Atonement to a Greater God

I slept late and came back on deck close to noon. Raphael was pacing the deck. I went over to greet him.

He looked at me for a long moment and then he responded, "James, I'm worried. Some of the young Metis heading for Duck Lake have been drinking all night. Now they are saying to the English settlers, 'take the next steamer back to where you come from if you know what is good for you'. They say Riel will have a provisional government soon. Settlers who don't wait for that, well, Riel will burn them out. I doubt they even represent Riel. They are just radicals, but dangerous. Now the settlers are ganging together as well."

It was close enough to lunchtime and I went in for a meal. Inside the dinner hall it was becoming rancorous. The lunch staff had simply left their posts and there was much drinking. I took a seat, opened a book I had been reading and minded my own business. Nobody bothered me. But they were getting louder.

"It's MacDonald and the Canadian Dominion that opened the settlements, not Riel!" said a burly white settler with bushy beard, sending his comments towards the Metis in a loud voice.

"You think so?" responded someone from another table. "It's time you knew that Riel will be taking over and setting up his own government for the real people of the west." He was a middle-aged Metis man of some obvious esteem among his group.

"Fuck Riel, and your Dumont too," the bearded settler called out, knocking his chair over as he stood up and bristled with rage.

Someone from a table of young Metis threw a bottle at him, barely missing the settler's head and smashing a deck window behind him. The burly man and four more settlers rushed the table of young Metis and soon tables were falling and breaking as fists and boots were flying.

Someone fired a bottle that shattered a long glass mirror above the bar and immediately there was a general melee of fighting that spilled out across the deck. Several men had unsheathed knives and were now into deadly knife fighting. Two burly wrestlers broke through the railing and into the river below.

I moved out of the way. Raphael and another mate came running.

"They are tearing my ship apart!" he shouted.

"Tell them there is a fire," I said, "or do you have fire hoses to turn on them?"

Raphael's mother didn't raise a fool. His eyes lit up at my idea and he disappeared in a flash down a stairway to the lower level. Soon black smoke was seeping up from the cooking fires below deck. He had put something inside the hot stoves, maybe raw cabbage, that raised a terrible stench as the smoke rolled up between the cracks of the floor boards. Raphael was beside me with a mega phone.

"Fire! Fire!" he shouted out, "The lower deck is on fire!"

Men stopped fighting and separated from each other to stare at Raphael, then at the smoke now drifting across the deck in thick gray sheets. Some sheathed their knives and all looked around for an escape.

"We are hauling up on shore and everybody out!" shouted Raphael.

Through a layer of smoke, the gangway was lowered into the river thirty feet from shore. Some carried their children and all were pushing through waist high water towards the gravelly shoreline.

When everyone was off, Raphael stood on the railing with his revolver in hand. "There was no fire," he said. "We are hundreds of miles from settlement, shelter or food. Most of you have left everything on board. And this is grizzly country. I say good luck. If any of you make it to Edmonton you can collect your belongings at the fort."

A half dozen men howled like banshees and rushed the gangway. Raphael remained cool and commenced firing his revolver into the water in front of them until they backed off."

He turned and began instructing his crew to raise the gangway while keeping his pistol loaded and aimed at the wild crowd milling and howling on shore.

"Please, let us back on! Don't let our children perish," one woman called out. The crowd began to quiet down.

"Okay, shall I let the women and children back on?" He shouted across the crowd. There was a chorus of women pleading – "Yes! Yes! Let us back on!"

"Okay, I'll let the women and children back on. But if I let your men back on do you promise to make them behave until Duck Lake or Fort Ellice or Fort Edmonton where they can all get off and kill each other if they choose?"

There was a roar of women standing up to their knees in water closest to the steamer, some holding their babies in the air and all were shouting, "We promise, let our men back on!"

"Men, you will behave? Or would you rather fight it out right there in the bush and then walk home."

The men hung their heads walking back and forth on shore.

"Those who want back on hold up your arm. The others better get moving if you want to find shelter before winter." A few raised their arm, most raised a hand and all raised at least a couple of fingers.

"Ok then," was all Raphael said. He ordered the stink and smoke in the kitchen stoves be extinguished. Then he lowered the gangway and slowly the passengers filed back on board most of the men looking down at their soaking wet boots.

At Raphael's request, I kept busy for the rest of the day setting broken noses, preparing ice bags for concussions, treating sprains and stitching up knife lacerations. All the passengers kept the peace, even the single men who were constantly under the cold and vigilant stare of women from both sides. The young men shuffled forward, their eyes on the floor whenever they passed near the women.

Trouble was avoided and most ate their meals in silence and went about their business quietly. The *Northcote* broke a record, from Grand Rapids to Edmonton in just eighteen days.

CHAPTER 34

It was July 18, high noon, and steaming hot on the deck of the *Northcote,* still pushing steadily forward through the rapid current of the North Saskatchewan River. The captain was up in the wheelhouse now with the pilot and Raphael was vigilantly watching from the front deck. We came around a sharp bend in the river and the towering palisade walls of Fort Edmonton materialized out of the wilderness before our eyes.

Beaumont signalled to the captain and the pilot cut one engine and we slowed down under a ceiling of rolling black smoke and hissing steam. The steamship was barely overcoming the strength of the current as she sidled towards a long docking platform below the fortress, an embellishment that had not existed seven years prior. We had been advised that we might reach Edmonton today if all went well and everyone was prepared, carrying their bags, with bedding cinched together in bundles on the shoulders of the men.

Families with children lined up first and the gangway was lowered onto the docking platform and secured with heavy rope. There were some definite changes to Fort Edmonton. A few merchant buildings and even a substantial hotel now existed outside the fortress walls. The crowds all progressed toward the mercantile, the hotel and an area where white canvas shelters had been set up between the three or four merchant establishments.

I separated from the crowd and progressed on a long upward slope towards the fort, past a scattering of native teepees on the river flats below. Near the fortress I looked up to the bastion where an attendant was watching. I signalled for him to let me in. The attendant, who I did not recognize, met me at the gate. There I told him I used to work here and he motioned me inside. I looked across the open courtyard hoping to see Malcolm smoking his clay pipe and blowing rings into the air, or Gabriel in the midst of a group, his head back laughing or simply mesmerizing everyone with his stories. But I recognized no one.

I identified myself to the attendant as James McGinn formerly of the Northwest Mounted Police, once stationed here. I requested to speak with the Factor and was pleased to find that Richard Hardisty was still the man in charge. The attendant told me to make myself at home in the courtyard and he would see if Mr. Hardisty was available.

The inner court had barely changed at all and I felt the warmest sense of nostalgia. I inhaled the sweet smell of the great sheathes of tobacco hanging at the top of the wall in the sun and the smell of hides curing. I passed the entrance to the great dining hall where I had first met Paniya. I could still see her in my mind like an ancient portrait of the most profound beauty lost in time. She had smiled and called me *constable* and I said my name was *James*. She said that she was supposed to call us *constable* but after that I would be *James* to her.

I couldn't keep the smile off my face as I walked past the trading room and the familiar voices of the Cree men bargaining inside: it was where I had heard Paniya speak so fluently in all the languages, interpreting for the traders. I recalled her beautiful face turning to smile at me as I walked in and she said: *Oh, hi James, see you get a personal greeting now, not just constable anymore.* I was grinning like a Halloween pumpkin when the attendant came up beside me. "Mr. Hardisty will see you now," he said.

Hardisty had a few more grey hairs but he, like the courtyard, had hardly changed. I introduced myself in case he had forgotten me. I'm James McGinn. I was on duty as a police officer before I went back for crimes in Toronto," I said. "Now I've done my time and I'm a free man."

A smile of recognition crossed his face. "Yes, I remember you well, James. The last I heard you had gone to Toronto to turn yourself in rather than use the local constabulary. I suppose that was a wise choice." Hardisty motioned for me to come in and he pulled out a chair for me.

"I remember that you were a good officer, James," he continued, "and I greatly respected your involvement in driving out the whisky traders and making some key arrests. Welcome back, and what can I do for you today?"

I had many questions and Paniya was first and foremost on my mind but I decided to talk to him a while first, to see what had changed in the northwest. "Well," I said, "I just wanted to catch up on changes since I left here seven years ago."

"Much has changed," he said, "and I think we are only seeing the beginning of it. Land around our fortress has been surveyed and as you can probably see a few commercial places have already been built along the river. I expect a town will soon spring up here and more agriculture. So far it is remarkable that business is much the same: fur trade with the indigenous peoples and most tribes living pretty much as they always have in spite of some treaties signed.

"And the Northwest Mounted Police, any changes?"

"Some," he said. "Major Steele was promoted just after you left. He is now Inspector Steele, immensely respected, serving many posts in the west and most recently put in charge for safe completion of the Canadian Pacific Railway across the Dominion."

"And Jarvis," I asked.

"Well," said Hardisty, not trying very hard to hide a smile of satisfaction. "He and French had a major blow out, and Jarvis left soon after. That happened a few years ago. Jarvis was replaced by a good man though, Inspector Antrobus, who seems to understand our needs here at Fort Edmonton a lot better than Jarvis ever did."

I added my own smile of satisfaction. I had a hunch Hardisty remembered full well my conflicts with Jarvis and I suspect he had a few of his own. I took a deep breath before asking about Paniya. I felt my chest start to pound out of fear that I had simply been gone too long.

"I need to inquire about Paniya," I added. I couldn't think of what else to say. Maybe I didn't need to.

Hardisty grinned. "She was very fond of you back then James, but of course none of that is, or was ever, any of my business." He stopped, reached for a bowl of hard candy and offered me one which I declined. He unwrapped something cherry red, put it in his mouth and wallowed it around a while, starring out his window and back at me, like he was judging me and I wondered if there was more he wanted to tell me.

Finally, he answered. "She is still around though; she comes here in the winter our busiest time for the fur trade. She is invaluable to me and she could probably run the place without me," he said with a booming laugh. "But most of the year she lives with the Cree.

"I never ask about her personal life though," Hardisty continued, "who she shares a teepee with or any of that. I do know she is quite respected as a medicine woman among her own people. Her routine in the middle of summer is finding medicine, often visiting the Medicine Springs to collect plants. I suppose if you wanted to see her that's where you would start."

I thanked Hardisty for seeing me. Then I purchased trade goods from the fort to sustain me on my journey back to the Medicine Springs. I hoped I could still find my way. With a bedding roll, supplies and ammunition, I commenced following along the North Saskatchewan River towards the northeast for over two days of walking. The third night I camped beside the river and re-filled my canteens. I took a bearing on the North Star; I would keep generally to the northeast, looking for the long row of blue hills that formed a horseshoe shape containing the pools and an out-flow of the Medicine Springs in the middle.

The following night I set up camp on a high grassy knoll where elk and mule deer had been grazing in abundance. I started my fire at the edge of a long ridge with a creek flowing far below me. In the distance I could see the start of a long range of hills that would eventually circle back, encompassing the springs.

There had been an early morning shower that woke me and I pulled up camp and took another bearing on the hills. Once inside the thick bush they would no longer be visible to me. But I only needed to travel towards the sun at mid-morning to eventually encounter the hills. By late morning the tree cover had dispersed along a southeast facing ridge with scattered aspen cover and grassy clearings. I had found the edge of the range of hills and now I only needed to follow along the inside slope to my destination.

By early afternoon I was encountering willow covered bog areas just below the slope of the hills. I began to recognize the terrain and I was getting close. Over the tops of the low-lying willow I could make out a high balsam peak, the highest point around which I realized instantly was the lookout I once used above my campsite. I took a bearing toward the high peak and walked about an hour until I broke out into a vast open stretch of high grasses with clusters of purple vetch, tiger lilies and golden rod that grew across the meadows of the Medicine Springs.

Now I could see the grove of spruce where I had once made my bed. Initially, I felt a stab of disappointment, hoping by now to see campfire smoke, maybe drying racks for plants, fowl, fish or other evidence of Paniya staying there but there were no such signs. When I found my old campsite, however, I was once again filled with hope. Someone was camping there. My old bed of boughs had been stripped off and fresh new tips of spruce and fresh grasses from the meadow were arranged under a buffalo robe. But then there was a second sleeping area just beyond the first, tucked under the low sweeping boughs of spruce.

The second was less than an arm-length from the first and likewise covered in fresh boughs, grass and buffalo robes. Food supplies hung with hemp in the boughs of the trees away from the bears. The campfire was cold but the ashes fresh with no evidence they had been dampened by the early morning shower.

Then I heard her voice, a voice that had been so familiar to me, a sound so precious that I had almost forgotten and my heart pounded remembering and feeling her so close to me once again. Then I realized that she was not alone. I felt immensely awkward. What did I expect, I wondered, it has been such a long time. The realization came quickly: my life had been on hold all this time, stuck in an unchanging prison world but that would not be the case for Paniya who would be in the prime of her life and living it fully as a beautiful young woman.

I stood quietly in the shadows of the grove of spruce. The tears started in my eyes and I blinked them back. I could see her now and she was more beautiful than I had ever remembered; I had been used to seeing her mostly around the fortress, dressed in European fashion like the rest of the women. She now wore a deerskin dress beautifully tapered around the curves of her small, pretty body. Her shiny black hair flowed around her face and her shoulders.

Something stopped me from running forth to meet her. Then the voice of a child answered her. I realized she had her own family now. I had made a terrible mistake and should not have come. After all this time my presence would surely do nothing more than upset her. Too much time had passed. It was far too late for Paniya and me.

I moved slowly back into the shadows and quietly turned towards the ring of hills. I felt the greatest emptiness and could no longer see my way ahead. I stopped to rub away the fogginess in my eyes and leaned against a dead fallen poplar to clear my vision. I would start again. Go back to my estate. I could write my exams and practice medicine.

Then, I was certain I heard Paniya say my name although I could no longer see her through the trees. But I did not mistake the sound of my own name: maybe she had seen me. Maybe she had called out to me. I moved quietly back through the trees until I could see her again. She was talking to her child but she seemed oblivious to my presence. I simply watched them for the longest time. Finally, I decided I had come a long way. I must at least have the courage to come forth and let her know of all that had happened to me. The child walked back to the edge of the trees where he was picking berries from a pin cherry bush. She began talking to him again when I walked out of the shadows towards her.

She had bent down to pull something up from the earth when she must have heard the sound of me approaching. Suddenly she stood up straight and watched me and for a moment she appeared frightened. Then I saw recognition dawn on her face, still she looked away from me towards the child and back again. "James?" she asked, with something approaching incredulity in her voice.

I stopped a few feet away as she stood staring at me. Then she looked into my eyes. "It has been a very long time, James. Do I still know you?"

"Seven years," I said. "Can we talk, or would you rather I leave? I can see you have a life of your own and family and I would never interfere with that or distress you in any way."

"No," she responded, "don't leave. I want you to meet someone."

The child had started back from the edge of the forest, then stood still watching us. "James," she said to the boy, "come over here for a few minutes."

The child approached us. "I want you to meet your father." She smiled again and then looked at me. "James Eagle Hunter McGinn, this is your father, also James McGinn."

The child looked up at me and he seemed pleased. He was a most handsome little boy. I beamed at him and suddenly felt more joy than I had known for a very long time. I squatted down before him and smiled and held out my hand and said, "I'm immensely pleased to meet you, James." I could feel him looking me all over. Finally, he shook my hand weakly, then he shyly stood back and watched me. He had his mother's beautiful dark eyes and shiny black hair with my fair complexion. He appeared to be tall for his age, he would be six, not yet seven years old.

I suddenly remembered a tintype picture of me at that age, one that my mother kept on her bed stand; I was dressed in long pants staring at the cloth draped camera's eye. I remembered the occasion well. It could have been a photo of little James.

"He will need some time," Paniya said to me. "But I hope you will stay with us and we can talk and get to know each other again."

"Nothing would make me happier," I said.

***

Paniya put little James to bed early and we talked beside the firelight far into the night and I asked her about little James.

"He is so much like both of us," she said. "It was May and I was living in the Cree camp when he was born. There were the usual rituals of my people, a feast, and those with power to know the spirits and speak of the child's nature came with visions and names for him. They described what they saw; he is a child who will have much power and he will be able to summon the spirits and he will be a great shaman.

"They had names for him from their visions and I appreciated the things they had done but I already knew what his name would be. I wanted to use the traditions of my father and his father, I would name him according to family names passed down. When I first looked upon my newborn and saw his bright and loving face I saw only you, James, so he is named after you and my grandfather, Eagle Hunter."

"I cannot even describe what an honor that is for me," I told her. "Can I spend time with him and become his friend?"

"That would make me so happy," she said and she turned to smile up at me.

"What does he like?" I asked.

Paniya was quiet for a long moment. "Mostly, he is like any other little boy. He loves to explore his world, to play with other kids." She dropped a branch in the fire and then began gently stirring the red coals in front of her with a long stick, like she was contemplating something. "He is so smart, James, already I see how he studies things in nature all around him. And he loves to learn about the plants and healing and he finds plants I am looking for and sometimes I don't even know how he knows what I am seeking, like he reads me or like he reads the plants. He is a special boy."

"I studied botany in prison," I said, "and learned what our science has to say about plants which I don't think is very much, just a description of each plant, sketches, and how to classify them. Maybe it is something I can share with little James."

"He would love that, he takes so much interest in Hardisty's books when we spend our winters in the fortress, just like I did as a little girl," she said.

We sat a long time just staring into the fire. One thing I knew more than anything else, there would never be anyone else for me and finally I spoke to her about it. "I never forgot you Paniya," I said, "you are buried deep in my heart. I want to be with you."

She sighed a long sigh and looked up at me again with the deepest sincerity. "I need time James. We have been apart too long. There have been some others but no one I ever really wanted. So, I lived my life for my people. I am there for them and they respect me as a medicine woman and I have some powers, I know that.

"I've learned the healing plants from my mother and grandmother since I was small. My time now goes to little James and to them. And I have never felt more confused about you and I. Since you left so long ago I have had daytime visions and night time dreams. I ask the spirits about you and about our future together and the visions are confusing for me. I need time James and little James needs time too."

"Yes," I said, "and I never want him to see me as someone who is taking you away from him."

"But please stay with us James, at least for a while, to become acquainted again."

Evening had set in and I laid out my blankets away from Paniya and little James and slept under the starts. I felt contentment in spite of Paniya's confusion, just seeing her again and knowing that we shared little James. I allowed myself to imagine the beginnings of my own family but then I had to remind myself I was only dreaming. Seven years was a long time and much had happened in the world beyond the rock walls of Kingston penitentiary.

CHAPTER 35

The next morning I woke up early. Paniya and little James were still sleeping. Quietly I walked into a willow grove and selected a long, straight, supple branch and cut it free with my jack knife. I brought it back to the campfire, dropped some dry wood on the coals and blew into the ashes until the fire started.

Then I sat down on the improvised bench where Paniya and I had spent the prior evening. I began fashioning the long branch into a fishing pole, pealing away excess bark and small branches and paring back some of the stem. Little James was now sitting up on his bed watching me. I continued to fashion the willow pole where he could see me. Finally, I summoned him to come over and I would show him the knife. He came shyly over to me, but then looked upon my work with great interest and grinned at me as I folded and unfolded the blade and opened the small saw to cut off a knotted branch.

"Ever see one of these before?" I asked, then I opened up all the rest of the tools in the jack knife. I was reassured that the implements would lock in place for safety. I showed him the spoon; I improvised on the awl and used both tools to dig out the long root of a plant beside us. I asked if he wanted to skin off some bark with the blade. His eyes were shining and he nodded. He was right handed so I helped him hold the pole with his left hand securing the long end under his arm, holding the knife in his right hand and pressing downward with his blade on the short end and skinning off a long layer of bark.

He set the bark strips aside and I learned later that he used the inner layer of the bark for medicine. When he was done pealing the long willow stem, I notched the end of the pole where I would later employ fishing line, while he watched me.

When I was finished, I said, "I already have a knife," and I showed him the hunting knife on my sheath. "You can have the jack knife if your mom says it is okay." I showed him how to fold all the implements back into the handle and press the safety notch to ensure nothing opened until he wanted to use them. His eyes shone with wonder. Obviously, he had seen nothing like it.

Would you like to have it?"

He grinned and nodded.

"Well, show your mom and if she says it is okay, then you can keep it for your own."

He took the jack knife and raced towards Paniya who was now sitting up watching us. I saw her look it over carefully while he showed her all the implements, how to open and close them and the safety latch. Then she looked over at me and smiled. He grinned at me too, then raced back to me. I let him pare down his own willow stick and sharpen it into a spear.

I remembered that earlier I had found crow feathers by my bed, wondered at their symmetry and I still had them. I asked little James if we should attach them to the spear and he said, "okay." I tied them loosely together with fishing line, notched the end of the spear and tied them a few inches back. He looked at my work and grinned again. Quite possibly a pretty amateur effort on my part but I passed it over to him and he commenced spearing every log and stump in sight to his delight and mine.

Paniya roasted two partridge breasts over the fire and served the meat to both of us on a tin plate with some charred roots that were very tasty and a mush of some sort that could have used a bit of salt. But the food was wholesome and I thanked her. Afterwards James commenced playing with his spear as Paniya and I talked. "I think he likes you," she said.

"Well, that's mutual," I responded. "Maybe all three of us can track down plants today. It's a budding interest of mine and I have my books with sketches."

"I think it will be fun and I think James will like it too. I retrieved a book from my pack. It was *John Macoun's, 1862, Catalogue of Plants of the Western Dominion.*

"Can I show you the sketches first?" I asked Paniya. "If James is interested I think he will come over."

She smiled and slid close to me on the bench. "He loves books. It isn't *if* he will come, but how soon he'll get here," she laughed.

We flipped open the pages and little James crowded in between us for a look. I opened to a sketch of *Western Dock,* a plant I had never seen before though it apparently grows in the north west.

"I know that one," he said.

"Can you find it?" I asked.

"Sure," he responded, "want me to show you?"

I looked at Paniya. She shrugged. "You lead the way," she told little James and he bounded forth across the meadows, then waited for us to catch up before he led us further across the grassy plain and moved into the forest towards an open slope several hundred yards up hill. There was a single plant of *western dock* growing on the hillside.

"What does the book say?" he asked.

I flipped open the sketch. "Well, Macoun just gives it a funny name, he calls it, *Rumex Occidentalis.*"

"What else does it say? asked little James.

I read the description, "It grows two feet high, has long pointed leaves that alternate on the stem, flowers with six pedals...."

"That's all?" he inquired. "It doesn't say that when you mash the leaves and put it on old people with pain in their bones it helps them, or it heal sores in their mouth?"

"I'm afraid it doesn't mention any of that," I said.

"It's not a very good book," he replied after several thoughtful moments.

Paniya and I had a good laugh. We spent the afternoon looking at sketches and finding plants. I learned more about the healing properties of plants than was ever taught to me at Trinity.

We walked back towards camp in the late afternoon.

"I never showed him the *Western Dock*," she said, "and I would never let him go into the forest like that all by himself. He always amazes me, he knows so much. And I don't know anyone that taught him that."

***

I slept later than usual but Paniya and little James were already up. Paniya was starting a fire and James was catching insects and letting them go.

"I should lay out my nets today," she said. "We could use some more fish."

I opened my pack and showed her the fishing line and artificial flies I had purchased in Toronto and little James was beside us now, his eyes shining in wonder over the colored feathers of the fish hooks.

"I would like to try my luck for fish in the pools downstream. Would you and James like to come with me?"

She looked at James. "Why don't you take James," she said, "I have much work to do here with all the plants I have - getting them ready to take back."

"Would you like to come with me James?" I asked.

He nodded. From my recollection it was a long hike past all the small streams that eventually joined together from the Medicine pools for a major flow and a place where trout would likely migrate up from the lakes and rivers below. We walked far down the stream and I knew it would be a difficult trek for him. "Would you like to ride on my shoulders for a while," I asked.

He looked up at my shoulders and finally he nodded that he would. I carried him down stream until I found a rapid current that descended into a quiet pool. I saw the ripples of trout striking the surface. We stopped and he stood beside me as I prepared the pole and the spool in my hand and I hefted the line several times back and forth over my shoulders before releasing a feathered fly far out into the stream.

Then I let him hold the fishing pole. I showed him how to allow the feathered bait to drift with the current until it dropped into the quiet pool below. Immediately he received a strike and I helped him haul in a healthy grayling. Then I helped him cast the fly again into the stream and soon we pulled out seven more grayling.

He carried the largest fish on a string and I carried the rest and we headed back for camp. Soon I knew he was tiring of the walk. I asked him if he would like a ride again and he said "sure," so I lifted him onto my shoulders and we made our way back along the streams and eventually to our campsite.

Paniya had seen us coming and she came to meet us. She held my hand as we walked back across the open flats until I set down little James by the fire. She hugged him and asked if he liked the trip and he vehemently nodded and his eyes shone as he began telling her of our adventure and our great catch of grayling.

"Why don't you let me make supper," I said, "and you spend time with James?"

"Are you sure?" she asked.

"I'm sure," I said, "I think James missed his mom and would like the time. Besides," I joked, "I'm probably a much better cook than you think."

I filleted the grayling just as Paniya had once shown me, before extracting a pan from my pack and frying the grayling in deer fat that Paniya had left by the fire. I had bought a few potatoes and parsnips from the gardens at the fort and threw them in my satchel before leaving. Now I boiled them in a brass pot and added some salt from my pack. By my own estimation it was a pretty good meal and little James ate it all down with a gusto.

Paniya put James to bed and then joined me by the fire.

"James loved spending time with you," she said, "and it makes me immensely happy too. I was so hoping that you two would be friends." She sat close to me on the bench and I felt the joy from her once again.

"Oh, James," she said, "I don't think you have any idea how much I missed you and I'm so happy to have you back. I was afraid that the time away would change you. That you would be someone different. But it hasn't." She looked up at me and then kissed me on the lips and then she sat back.

"You asked if we could be together. It's what I want more than anything in the world, but I could not tell you that until I knew it would be okay for little James. I needed to know you would not leave me, like my father left his country wife. Now I know that you came back just for me. There was no other reason." She was quiet for a long moment, looking deep into my eyes she finally asked. "Would you share a teepee with me and little James and my mother?"

"I want it more than anything," I said. "But will your mother agree."

"I know she will," Paniya laughed. "She has been pestering me since you left that we need a man to share our teepee, to help us with all the work and hunting."

"But I am a white man."

"Oh James," she laughed, "you have already forgotten that she once married a white man. My father was a Celtic Scotsman, almost like you." Anyway, you can ask her but I already know what she will say."

I laid out my bedding beside the fire and Paniya lay beside me and we slept through the dawn together and awoke to a darkening sky and the low rumble of thunder in the distance.

She checked on little James who was still sleeping and returned to lay beside me.

"I don't like the thunder," she said. "It scares me. Sometimes it reminds me of Two Bears in a jealous rage. I never liked it or the lightening since I was a small girl. It feels like an angry or jealous spirit that I could never understand. Tonight we can sleep under the spruce boughs, like we did before and she smiled. And it is safer there from the summer storms. Then I think we should go back and you can get to know my mother too."

***

The Cree encampment was much closer to the Medicine Springs this year and we made the trek in two days. Little James enjoyed riding on my shoulders and he swatting at branches and insects as we went along.

I had only seen Sky Woman once before when she came to the fortress with Paniya, the winter before I left. I was surprised that she had not aged well and was losing her eyesight. However, she recognized me and smiled. "I don't see very well anymore," she said, "but I recognized your voice."

Paniya stood beside me and little James squeezed in between. "I want James to share our space with us," she told Sky Woman. "I love him very much," she said, "and he and little James are best friends."

"I want more than anything else to be part of this family," I said, "but I want you to be okay if I come here."

Sky Woman looked at me and smiled. "I'm not used to men asking me if they can move in. I am sure Paniya already told you that I would be okay if it was someone she liked. We only met once but Paniya has talked about you so much I feel I know you well."

I wanted to prove my worth and I spent several days collecting firewood. When the first good hunting day came, with a strong breeze blowing to dampen sound and dissipate our scent in the bush, I collected my carbine and asked Paniya and little James to come with me. We hunted the open meadows along Whitemud Creek where I bagged a young buck and carried it back to camp with me and butchered the animal. The meat was tender and delicious. Paniya smoked and dried much of the hind quarters for winter. And Sky Woman was very happy with me.

There was much summer left and we spent the long days together taking walks with little James, collecting plants, digging up roots and enjoying laying on the warm summer slopes watching the sky while little James played.

We walked back to camp after a long day of exploring as towering thunderheads rolled high in the eastern sky and we went inside to escape the impending weather.

"I think we could have quite a few days of rain," Paniya said. "We need to prepare to be inside for a while."

Sky Woman slept on her robes while Paniya went for water and I helped little James collect extra firewood. I chopped the dry deadfall into chunks and little James began stacking the pieces when torrents of rain suddenly began pounding us and I had never before heard the deafening roar of thunder crashing all around us at the same moment that blinding lightening flashed across the encampment.

I was suddenly afraid for Paniya. Holding tight to little James, I raced for the stream where she went to collect water and we found her collapsed at the edge of the water. The clothing on her back was singed with tendrils of smoke. I felt for her pulse and there was none. I blew breath into her lungs and pushed hard against her heart to restore life inside her. She opened her eyes and looked up at me and grasped the hand of little James. "Take care of him," she said, and then I knew beyond any doubt that she was gone from us forever.

Little James held her head and squeezed his arms around her neck and called out for her to come back and I held her hand as the torrents of rain pounded us. We stayed with her as the storm subsided and the darkness of the evening came down and little James knew as well as I that she would never come back to us.

Finally, he laid her head back down and he came to me, his small arms around my neck. I felt his tiny heart pounding against mine. At that moment he was not a young man destined for greatness but a little boy grieving the terrible loss of his mother. I held him tight to me and we cried together.

***

For four days the people of the camp grieved in their own way with rituals as old as time. People came from encampments all around, many who had known her well from double ball, and the many games of summer. In the beginning it was a solemn gathering. Gifts were brought and laid beside her for the long journey of her spirit to the afterlife. People of all ages and groups spoke of her, telling stories and reminiscing times with her and ways they knew her, stories of her prowess in the games, her speed on foot and her healing talent as a medicine woman. There was dancing, chants and laughter as all of us were celebrating her wonderful life.

Sky Woman and I took turns being with little James when he slept, his head on Sky Woman's lap or mine. We kept him warm with a robe during the nights when it cooled off. We all participated in dances and songs. Little James would awaken and watch intently, then he joined the dances and chanted with us and listened to the stories about Paniya's life. He told his own story to the group. "I was with her once," he said, "we watched from outside Red Hawk's teepee. We saw it shaking and we could feel all the great spirits coming." Then little James told everyone how she was once looking for snakeroot in the forest and he helped her find it.

Finally, we placed her body high on a platform in the tops of a poplar grove with a view to the stars. We would celebrate again next summer, in the same place, to connect with her spirit beyond once again.

People were exhausted. The gathering had lasted four days with very little sleep for anyone. Sky Woman said, "I need to go back to the teepee for rest."

Little James looked from Sky Woman to me. "Can we still do the fortress after summer is gone," he asked.

"I don't see why not," I said, "I've learned a lot about medicine in the last few years and they need healers there too. Should be lots of work for us to do."

"The white man's medicine?" he asked.

"Yes," I answered.

"And I know Cree medicine," he said, looking up at me.

"I think we'll be a great team then," I told him.

"But we still need more of the white flowers for treating skin sores," little James said. "And we can use ginseng root now to help our old people because when I slept between you and Sky Woman I saw them in a dream. I know their five leaves like arrow points and two red berries and I know where to find them."

"Why don't we go right now and collect them."

He smiled up at me and then pointed towards a bare hillside far beyond the last teepee.

"They are up there," he said, "where the trees are thinner."

We fell in lock-step across the encampment on our quest to find them. We both knew there would be much to do before the winter snows came.

AUTHOR'S NOTE

Although the novel follows the route of the first and second wave of Northwest Mounted Police bringing law to the frontiers of the Canadian Dominion; and

although many of the challenges of the police force depicted in the novel were actually encountered; and

although the setting for frontier fortresses are congruent with actual sites and infrastructures depicted in the novel; and although certain characters in this work are historical figures, and certain events portrayed did take place, this is a work of fiction; and

although there are many depictions of indigenous cultures throughout, the writer does not propose to be an expert on First Nation peoples. Nor is the novel intended to be an historical treatise or documentary but merely an effort to portray the author's research and countless conversations with First Nations people to gain a sincere and respectful understanding for the creation of this fictional work.

AUTHOR BIOGRAPHY

Dan Martin is a semi-retired psychotherapist living in Edmonton, Alberta.

Throughout his writings when Dan describes wilderness settings or wild animal habitats, they are places he has known and terrain he has explored. Dan grew up in a family of guides and outfitters in Northern Alberta and is a former licensed game guide. He worked several years as a field officer with Alberta Forestry, Lands and Wildlife before completing three degrees with concentration in psychology and clinical social work.

Dan's writings often feature complex characters in malevolent as well as nurturing roles. Characters are frequently a projection of personalities Dan has known during many years as a psychotherapist, counselling male offenders, children who are victims of abuse, psychopathic personalities, as well as ordinary people dealing with oppression or life adjustment problems.

Dan's previously publications can be viewed at www.danmartinbooks.com

Made in the USA
Middletown, DE
07 July 2019